D1321885

LAURIE R. KING lives in northern California. Her background includes such diverse interests as Old Testament theology and construction work, and she has been writing crime fiction since 1987. The winner of the Edgar, the Nero, the Macavity and the John Creasey awards, she is the author of highly praised stand-alone suspense novels and a contemporary mystery series, as well as the Mary Russell/Sherlock Holmes series.

By Laurie R. King

The Beekeeper's Apprentice
A Monstrous Regiment of Women
A Letter of Mary
The Moor
O Jerusalem
Justice Hall
The Game
Locked Rooms
The Language of Bees
The God of the Hive
Pirate King
Beekeeping for Beginners
(a novella)
Garment of Shadows

-◆-

Touchstone
The Bones of Paris

THE MOOR

LAURIE R. KING

Allison & Busby Limited
12 Fitzroy Mews
London W1T 6DW
www.allisonandbusby.com

First published in 1998.
This paperback edition published by Allison & Busby in 2014.

Published by arrangement with Bantam Books,
an imprint of The Random House Publishing Group,
a division of Random House, Inc., New York, NY, USA.
All rights reserved.

A CIP catalogue record for this book is available from
the British Library.

10 9 8 7 6 5 4 3 2

ISBN 978-0-7490-1515-2

Typeset in 10.5/15 pt Adobe Garamond Pro by
Allison & Busby Ltd.

The paper used for this Allison & Busby publication
has been produced from trees that have been legally sourced
from well-managed and credibly certified forests.

Printed and bound by
CPI Group (UK) Ltd, Croydon, CR0 4YY

For Ruth Cavin,
editor extraordinaire,
with undying thanks and affection.
A blessing on you and your house

EDITOR'S PREFACE

THIS IS THE FOURTH manuscript to be recovered from a trunk full of whatnot that was dropped on my doorstep some years ago. The various odds and ends clothing, a pipe, bits of string, a few rocks, some old books, and one valuable necklace might have been taken for some eccentric's grab bag or (but for the necklace) a clearing-out of attic rubbish intended for the dump, except that at the bottom lay the manuscripts.

I thought that they had been sent to me because the author was dead, and for some unknown reason chose to send me the memorabilia of her past. However, since the publication of the first Mary Russell book, I have received a handful of communications as ill assorted as the original contents of the trunk, and I have begun to suspect that the author herself is behind them.

It should be noted that in the course of her story, Ms Russell tends to combine the actual names of people and places with other names that are unknown. Some of these thinly disguise true identities; others are impenetrable. Similarly, she seems to have taken some pains to conceal actual sites on the moor while at the same time referring to others, by name or description, that are easily identifiable.

A walker on Dartmoor, therefore, will not find Baskerville Hall in the area given, and the characteristics of the Okemont River do not correspond precisely with those in the manuscript. I can only assume she did it deliberately, for her own purposes.

The chapter headings are taken from several of Sabine Baring-Gould's books, with the sources cited at each.

CHAPTER ONE

When I obtained a holiday from my books, I mounted my pony
and made for the moor.

— A BOOK OF DARTMOOR

THE TELEGRAM IN MY hand read:

> RUSSELL NEED YOU IN DEVONSHIRE. IF FREE TAKE EARLIEST TRAIN
> CORYTON. IF NOT FREE COME ANYWAY. BRING COMPASS.
> HOLMES

To say I was irritated would be an understatement. We had only
just pulled ourselves from the mire of a difficult and emotionally
draining case and now, less than a month later, with my mind
firmly turned to the work awaiting me in this, my spiritual home,
Oxford, my husband and long-time partner Sherlock Holmes
proposed with this peremptory telegram to haul me away into his
world once more. With an effort, I gave my landlady's housemaid
a smile, told her there was no reply (Holmes had neglected to send
the address for a response – no accident on his part), and shut the
door. I refused to speculate on why he wanted me, what purpose
a compass would serve, or indeed what he was doing in Devon
at all, since when last I had heard he was setting off to look into
an interesting little case of burglary from an impregnable vault in

Berlin. I squelched all impulse to curiosity, and returned to my desk.

Two hours later the girl interrupted my reading again, with another flimsy envelope. This one read:

ALSO SIX INCH MAPS EXETER TAVISTOCK OKEHAMPTON,
CLOSE YOUR BOOKS. LEAVE NOW.
HOLMES

Damn the man, he knew me far too well.

I found my heavy brass pocket compass in the back of a drawer. It had never been quite the same since being first cracked and then drenched in an aqueduct beneath Jerusalem some four years before, but it was an old friend and it seemed still to work reasonably well. I dropped it into a similarly well-travelled rucksack, packed on top of it a variety of clothing to cover the spectrum of possibilities that lay between arctic expedition and tiara-topped dinner with royalty (neither of which, admittedly, were beyond Holmes' reach), added the book on Judaism in mediaeval Spain that I had been reading, and went out to buy the requested stack of highly detailed six-inch-to-the-mile Ordnance Survey maps of the south-western portion of England.

At Coryton, in Devon, many hours later, I found the station deserted and dusk fast closing in. I stood there with my rucksack over my shoulder, boots on feet, and hair in cap, listening to the train chuff away towards the next minuscule stop. An elderly married couple had also got off here, climbed laboriously into the sagging farm cart that awaited them, and been driven away. I was alone. It was raining. It was cold.

There was a certain inevitability to the situation, I reflected, and dropped my rucksack to the ground to remove my gloves, my waterproof, and a warmer hat. Straightening up, I happened to turn slightly and noticed a small, light-coloured square tacked up to the post by which I had walked. Had I not turned, or had it been half an hour darker, I should have missed it entirely.

Russell it said on the front. Unfolded, it proved to be a torn-off scrap of paper on which I could just make out the words, in Holmes' writing:

> *Lew House is two miles north.*
> *Do you know the words to 'Onward Christian Soldiers'*
> *or 'Widdecombe Fair'?*
> *– H.*

I dug back into the rucksack, this time for a torch. When I had confirmed that the words did indeed say what I had thought, I tucked the note away, excavated clear to the bottom of the rucksack for the compass to check which branch of the track fading into the murk was pointing north, and set out.

I hadn't the faintest idea what he meant by that note. I had heard the two songs, one a thumping hymn and the other one of those overly precious folk songs, but I did not know their words other than one song's decidedly ominous (to a Jew) introductory image of Christian soldiers marching behind their 'cross of Jesus' and the other's endless and drearily jolly chorus of 'Uncle Tom Cobbley and all'. In the first place, when I took my infidel self into a Christian church it was not usually of the sort wherein such hymns were standard fare, and as for the second, well, thus far none of my friends had succumbed to the artsy allure of sandals, folk songs, and Morris dancing. I had not seen Holmes in nearly three weeks, and it did occur to me that perhaps in the interval my husband had lost his mind.

Two miles is no distance at all on a smooth road on a sunny morning, but in the wet and moonless dark in which I soon found myself, picking my way down a slick, rutted track, following the course of a small river which I could not see, but could hear, smell, and occasionally step in, two miles was a fair trek. And there was something else as well: I felt as if I were being followed, or watched. I am not normally of a nervous disposition, and when I have such feelings I tend to assume that they have some basis in reality, but I could hear nothing more solid than the rain and the wind, and when I stopped there were no echoing splashes of feet behind me. It was simply a sense of Presence in the night; I pushed on, trying to ignore it.

I stayed to the left when the track divided, and was grateful to find, when time came to cross the stream, that a bridge had been erected across it. Not that wading through the water would have made me much wetter, and admittedly it would have cleared my lower extremities of half a hundred weight of mud, but the bridge as a solid reminder of Civilisation in the form of county councils I found encouraging.

Having crossed the stream, I now left its burble behind me, exchanging the hiss of rain on water for the thicker noises of rain on mud and vegetation, and I was just telling myself that it couldn't be more than another half mile when I heard a faint thread of sound. Another hundred yards and I could hear it above the suck and plop of my boots; fifty more and I was on top of it.

It was a violin, playing a sweet, plaintive melody, light and slow and shot through with a profound and permanent sadness. I had never, to my knowledge, heard the tune before, although it had the bone-deep familiarity possessed by all things that are very old. I did, however, know the hands that wielded the bow.

'Holmes?' I said into the dark.

He finished the verse, drawing out the long final note, before he allowed the instrument to fall silent.

'Hello, Russell. You took your time.'

'Holmes, I hope there is a good reason for this.'

He did not answer, but I heard the familiar sounds of violin and bow being put into a case. The latches snapped, followed by the vigorous rustle of a waterproof being donned. I turned on the torch in time to see Holmes stepping out of the small shelter of a roofed gate set into a stonewall. He paused, looking thoughtfully at the tell-tale inundation of mud up my right side to the elbow, the result of a misstep into a pothole.

'Why did you not use the torch, coming up the road?' he asked.

'I, er . . .' I was embarrassed. 'I thought there was someone following me. I didn't want to give him the advantage of a torchlight.'

'Following you?' he said sharply, half turning to squint down the road.

'Watching me. That back-of-the-neck feeling.'

I saw his face clearly by the light of the torch. 'Ah yes. Watching you. That'll be the moor.'

'The Moor?' I said in astonishment. I knew where I was, of course, but for an instant the book I had been reading on the train was closer to mind than my sense of geography, and I was confronted by the brief mental image of a dark-skinned scimitar-bearing Saracen lurking along a Devonshire country lane.

'Dartmoor. It's just there.' He nodded over his shoulder. 'It rises up in a great wall, four or five miles away, and although you can't see it from here, it casts a definite presence over the surrounding countryside. You'll meet it tomorrow. Come,' he said, turning up the road. 'Let us take to the warm and dry.'

I left the torch on now. It played across the hedgerow on one side and a stone wall on the other, illuminating for a moment a French road sign (some soldier's wartime souvenir, no doubt), giving us a brief glimpse of headstones in a churchyard just before we turned off into a smaller drive. A thick layer of rotting leaves from the row of half-bare elms and copper beeches over our heads gave way to a cultivated garden – looking more neglected than even the season and the rain would explain, but nonetheless clearly intended to be a garden – and finally one corner of a two-storey stone house, the small pieced panes of its tall windows reflecting the torch's beam. The near corner was dark, but farther along, some of the windows glowed behind curtains, and the light from a covered porch spilt its welcome out across the weedy drive and onto a round fountain. We ducked inside the small space, and had begun to divest ourselves of the wettest of our outer garments when the door opened in front of us.

In the first instant I thought it was a butler standing there, the sort of lugubrious aged retainer a manor house of this size would have, as seedy and tired as the house itself, and as faithful and long-serving. It was his face, however, more than the old-fashioned clerical collar and high-buttoned frock coat he wore, that straightened my spine. Stooped with age he might be, but this was no servant.

The tall old man leant on his two walking sticks and took his time looking me over through the wire spectacles he wore. He examined the tendrils of escaped hair that straggled wetly down my face, the slime of mud up my clothing, the muck-encrusted boot I held in my hand, and the sodden stocking on the foot from which I had just removed the boot. Eventually he shifted his gaze to that of my lawfully wedded husband.

'We have been waiting for *this* person?' he asked.

Holmes turned to look at me, and his long mouth twitched – minutely, but enough. Had it not been that going back into the night would have meant a close flirtation with pneumonia, I should immediately have laced my boot back on and left those two sardonic males to their own company. Instead, I let the boot drop to the stone floor, sending small clots of mud slopping about the porch (some of which, I was pleased to see, ended up on Holmes' trouser leg), and bent to my rucksack. It was more or less dry, as I had been wearing it underneath the waterproof (a procedure which made me resemble a hunchback and left the coat gaping open in the front, but at least guaranteed that I should have a dry change of clothing when I reached my destination). I snatched at the buckles with half-frozen fingers, jerked out the fat bundle of cloth-mounted, large-scale maps, and threw it in the direction of Holmes. He caught it.

'The maps you asked for,' I said coldly. 'When is the next train out of Coryton?'

Holmes had the grace to look discomfited, if briefly, but the old man in the doorway simply continued to look as if he were smelling something considerably more unpleasant than sodden wool. Neither of them answered me, but Holmes' next words were in a voice that verged on gentle, tantamount to an apology.

'Come, Russell. There's a fire and hot soup. You'll take your death out here.'

Somewhat mollified, I removed my other boot, picked up my rucksack, and followed him into the house, stepping past the cleric, who shut the door behind us. When I was inside and facing the man, Holmes made his tardy introductions.

'Gould, may I present my partner and, er, wife, Mary Russell. Russell, this is the Reverend Sabine Baring-Gould.'

One would think, I reflected as I shook the old man's large hand, that with two and a half years of marriage behind him the idea of having a wife would come more easily, at least to his tongue. However, I had to admit that we both normally referred to the other as partner rather than spouse, and the form of our married life was in truth more that of two individuals than that of a bound couple. Aside, of course, from certain activities rendered legal by a bit of paper.

The Reverend Sabine Baring-Gould made the minimum polite

response and suggested that Holmes show me upstairs. I wondered if I was to be allowed back down afterwards, or if I ought to say goodbye to him now. Holmes caught up a candlestick and lit its taper from a lamp on the table, and I followed him out of the warmth, through a dark-panelled passageway (my stockings squelching on the thin patches in the carpeting), and up what by the wavering light appeared a very nicely proportioned staircase lined with eighteenth-century faces.

'Holmes,' I hissed. 'Who on earth is that old goat? And when are you going to tell me what you dragged me down here for?'

'That "old goat" is the Reverend Sabine Baring-Gould, squire of Lew Trenchard, antiquarian, self-educated expert in half a dozen fields, and author of more books than any other man listed in the British Museum. Hymnist, collector of country music—'

A small light went on in my mind. '"Onward Christian Soldiers"? "Widdecombe Fair"?'

'He wrote the one and collected the other. Rural parson,' he continued, 'novelist, theologian' – Yes, I thought, I had heard of him somewhere, connected with dusty tomes of archaic ideas – 'amateur architect, amateur archaeologist, amateur of many things. He is one of the foremost living experts on the history and life of Dartmoor. He is a client with a case. He is also,' he added, 'a friend.'

While we were talking I had followed the candle up the stairway with its requisite portraits of dim and disapproving ancestors and through a small gallery with a magnificent plaster ceiling, but at this final statement I stopped dead. Fortunately, he did not go much farther, but opened a door and stepped into a room. After a moment, I followed, and found him turning up the lights in a nice-sized bedroom with rose-strewn paper on the walls (peeling up slightly at the seams) and a once-good, rose-strewn carpet on the floor. I put the rucksack on a chair that looked as if it had seen worse usage and sat gingerly on the edge of the room's soft, high bed.

'Holmes,' I said. 'I don't know that I've ever heard you describe anyone other than Watson as a friend.'

'No?' He bent to set a match to the careful arrangement of sticks and logs that had been laid in the fire place. There was a large radiator in the room, but like all the others we had passed, it stood sullen and cold in its corner. 'Well, it is true. I do not have many.'

'How do you know him?'

'Oh, I've known Baring-Gould for a long time. I used him on the Baskerville case, of course. I needed a local informant into the life of the natives and his was the name that turned up, a man who knew everything and went everywhere. We correspond on occasion, he came to see me in Baker Street two or three times, and once in Sussex.'

I couldn't see how this sparse contact qualified the man for friendship, but I didn't press him.

'I shouldn't imagine he "goes everywhere" now.'

'No. Time is catching up with him.'

'How old is he?'

'Nearly ninety, I believe. Five years ago you'd have thought him a hearty seventy. Now there are days when he does not get out of bed.'

I studied him closely, hearing a trace of sorrow beneath his matter-of-fact words. Totally unexpected and, having met the object of this affection, quite inexplicable.

'You said he had a case for us?'

'He will review the facts after we've eaten. There's a bath next door, although I don't know that I would recommend it; there seems to be no hot water at the moment.'

CHAPTER TWO

There existed formerly a belief on Dartmoor that it was hunted
over at night in storm by a black sportsman, with black
fire-breathing hounds, called 'Wish Hounds.'
They could be heard in full cry, and occasionally the blast
of the hunter's horn on stormy nights.

— A BOOK OF THE WEST: DEVON

HOLMES LEFT, AND I hurriedly bundled my wet, muddy clothes
into a heap, scrubbed with limited success at my face and arms
in the frigid water of the corner basin, and pinned my hair into a
tight, damp knot. I hesitated briefly before deciding on the woollen
frock – perhaps I had better not test the old man's sensibilities by
continuing to appear in trousers. Ninety-year-old men probably
didn't believe that women had legs above the ankle.

The frou-frou of women's clothing takes longer to don than
simple trousers, but I did my best and in a few minutes carried the
candlestick back out into the gallery under that intriguing ceiling,
which had struck me as not quite right somehow. I allowed myself
to be distracted by the paintings (some of them very bad) and the
bric-a-brac (some of it belonging in a museum), and stood for a long
moment in front of a startling African-style wood carving that formed
part of a door surround leading to one of the bedrooms. The proud,

dark, nude female torso looked more like a fertility shrine than the decoration to a Victorian bedroom; I know it would have given me pause to have passed that lady each time I was going to my bed.

I continued my slow perusal, meeting a few Baring-Goulds whose faces were more interesting than their artists' techniques, and then made my way down the handsome stairs again in pursuit of the voices. When I came within earshot, Baring-Gould was speaking, sounding sternly critical.

'—only two miles, for pity's sake. I've done it in sleet at the age of fifty, and she can't be more than twenty-five.'

'I believe you'll find she has more than ample stamina,' Holmes replied easily. 'That was irritation you saw, not exhaustion.'

'But still, to fling the maps in your face in that manner—'

'As I remember, you yourself had a very quick temper, even when you were considerably older than Russell.'

There was a pause, and then Baring-Gould began to chuckle. 'You're right there, Holmes. Do you remember the time that fool of an innkeeper outside of Tavistock tried to throw us out?'

'I remember feeling grateful you weren't wearing your collar.'

'Good heavens, yes. I'd have been dubbed the Brawling Parson forevermore. But the look on the man's face when you—'

Although I was certain that the reason Holmes had distracted his companion into this bout of masculine reminiscences was that he had heard my approach, I nevertheless counted slowly to thirty so as to allow the changed topic to establish itself before opening the door.

The stone fireplace was giving off more smoke than warmth, and the dank air was thick and cold. The long refectory table had been laid with three lonely places, with Baring-Gould in the middle with his back to the fire, and Holmes across from him. I came forward and sat in the chair to Holmes' right. Our host made a brief obeisance to manners by raising his backside a fraction of an inch from the seat of the chair as I sat down, then he reached forward and removed the lid from the tureen of promised soup. No steam came out. By the time he had pronounced a grace and served us, the soup had cooled even more, and to top it off, when I tasted the tepid mixture, it was obvious that it had been made a day or several before.

Still, I ate it, and the fish course and the stewed rabbit that came after. The rabbit was bland and chewy, as was the custard that followed.

There was very little conversation during the meal, which suited me. I was pleased, too, at the lack of toothless slurping noises that old people so often succumb to when their hearing goes. If one discounted the actual food, it was a pleasant enough, if quiet, meal, and I was looking forward to an early entrance into the feather-bed and thick eiderdown I had felt on the bed upstairs.

This was not to be. Baring-Gould folded his table napkin and climbed stiffly to his feet, gathering his sticks from the side of his chair.

'We will take coffee in the sitting room. That fire seems to be drawing better than this one. Probably a nest in the chimney.'

As we obediently trooped – slowly – behind him, I had the leisure to study his back. I realised that he was smaller than I had thought, probably barely an inch taller than my five feet eleven inches even when he was young. Now, stooped over his canes, he was considerably shorter than Holmes, but despite his obvious infirmity, his frame still gave the impression of strength, and he had eaten the tasteless food with the appetite of a young man.

He led us through to the adjoining room, which was indeed both warmer and less smoky. The curtains were drawn against the night, and the steady slap of rain against the window-panes underscored the physical comfort of the room. If the company inside the cosy room made my feminist hackles rise, well, I was always free to slog back to the train tomorrow.

'I must apologise for the non-functional state of my radiators,'

Baring-Gould said over his shoulder to me. 'They are normally quite efficient – I had them installed when my wife's rheumatism became bad – but yesterday we awoke to discover that the boiler gave no heat, and I am afraid the only person competent to quell the demons is my temporarily absent housekeeper. Like its master, my house is becoming tired.' I reassured my host that I was quite comfortable, and, although I did not think he believed me, he allowed my reassurances to stand.

When we reached the sitting room, Baring-Gould made for a well-worn armchair and addressed himself to Holmes. 'I received a gift today that I think might interest you. That small jug on the sideboard. Metheglin. Ever tasted it?' While he spoke, he propped his sticks against the side of an armchair and lowered himself into it, then reached to the side of the fireplace and picked up a meerschaum pipe with a stem nearly a yard long, which he proceeded to fill.

'Not in some time,' said Holmes. I looked at him sharply, but his face showed none of the humorous resignation I thought I had heard in his voice.

'A powerful substance – I would suggest a small dose if you're not accustomed to it. Distilled from heather honey. This batch is seven years old – I should warn you, never drink it if it's less than three. Yes, I'll have a drop. It helps to keep out the cold,' he said, in answer to Holmes' gesture. I took my husband's unintentional hint and demurred, reassuring my host that coffee would be sufficient to warm me. While they discussed the merits of the contents of their glasses, I examined my surroundings.

The room was panelled in oak and had a decorative plaster roof similar to that in the gallery upstairs. Up to head height the panelling was simple oak, but above that the wood was carved in ornate arches framing dimly seen, painted figures that marched around the entire room, all of them, as far as I could tell, posturing ladies in billowing draperies. I took up a lamp from the table and held it to the figure there, a woman with dogs held straining against their leads: *Persuasio* it said in a caption above her. Above the fire I found portraits of *Gloria* and next to her, *Laetitia*; between all the figures alternated the phrases *Gold bydeth ever bright* and what was, very roughly, the French equivalent, *Toujours sans tache*.

'The one over there might be of interest to you,' Baring-Gould suggested, and tipped his head at the inner wall.

'*Gaudium Vitae*?' I asked doubtfully, looking at the figure in her gold tunic, its gold ties blowing dramatically behind her and a massive gold chalice held nonchalantly in slim fingertips at the end of an outstretched arm.

'I think he means the next one,' Holmes said.

In the panel to the left was a woman clothed in orange garments flecked with a design of black splotches that looked alarmingly like huge ants. She had wings sprouting from her temples, and her right hand pointed at a flying white bird that might have been a dove, although it looked more like a goose. At her feet a small white pug-faced dog, tail erect, had its nose to the ground, snuffling busily. Above the wings the caption read, *Investigatio*. I turned to look at Baring-Gould, suspecting a breath of humour, but he was no longer paying attention to anything but his yard-long pipe. I ran the lamplight over a few more: *Valor* (this figure was a man, wearing a short tunic), *Harmonia* with a cello, *Vigilantia*, *Ars*, *Scientia* – a room of virtues.

'Daisy painted them. My daughter Margaret,' he explained.

'Really? What was here before?' There must have been something, as the upper portion of wall was obviously designed for decorations. I wondered what Elizabethan treasure had been lost in this slightly clumsy restoration.

'Nothing. They are new. Not new, of course, but the walls were built since I came here, to my design.'

I examined the walls more closely. They did look considerably fresher than the seventeenth century.

'Local craftsmen, my pattern based on a house nearby, my daughter's painting – I restored an Elizabethan house out of a small and frankly decrepit base.'

'The ceilings too?'

'Nearly everything. I am particularly proud of the fireplace in the hall. It belongs to the reign of Elizabeth, without a doubt.'

The idea of a heavily restored and adapted original explained the very slightly odd feel to the gallery ceiling upstairs – far too ornate for a country house, and much too new and strong for the age of its design.

'The ceilings are very beautiful,' I said. 'Does your daughter still live here with you?'

'No. Most of my children have scattered, making their way as far afield as Sarawak, where one of my sons is with the white rajah. Although one of my daughters lives just up the road in Dunsland, and my eldest son and his American wife have lived in this house for the last few years. I think they thought me too feeble to be alone.' His glare dared me to argue. 'At present they are in America, where Marion's mother is ill. I admit, I am enjoying my respite from the American regime.'

'How many children have you?'

'I had fifteen. Thirteen still living. Twelve,' he corrected himself, without elaboration.

His response brought me up short – not the numbers, which were common enough, so much as the vivid contrast it evoked, of this solitary house with its silent rooms compared to the vital place it must have been, a busy household, throbbing with life, ringing with footsteps and voices and movement. I put the lamp back on the sideboard and took up the chair Holmes had pulled over to the fire for me. I accepted coffee, declined brandy, and waited with little patience while pipes were got going. Finally, Baring-Gould cleared his throat and began to speak, in the manner of a carefully thought out speech.

'My family has lived on this land since 1626. My name combines two families: the Crusader John Gold, or Gould, who in 1220 was granted an estate in Somerset for his part in the siege of Damietta, and that of the Baring family, whom you may know from their interests in banking. My grandfather brought the two names together at the end of the eighteenth century when he, a Baring, inherited Lew. After my birth we lived a few miles north of here, in Bratton Clovelly, but my father, who was an Indian Army officer invalided home, did not like living in one place for long, so when I was three years old he packed us and the family silver into a carriage and left for Europe. My entire childhood was spent moving from one city to another, pausing only long enough for the post to catch us up. My father was very fond of Dickens,' he explained. 'When his stories came out, I used occasionally to wish it might be a long one, so that we might be tied down for a longer period while we waited for the instalments to reach us. Although I will admit that *Nicholas Nickleby* was a mixed blessing, as it found us in winter, in Cologne, living in tents.

'Still, it was an interesting childhood, and I scraped together enough education to enable me to hold my own at Clare in Cambridge. I took holy orders in 1864, and spent the next years doing parish work in Yorkshire and East Mersea.

'My father was the eldest son. His younger brother, as was the custom, had taken holy orders, and was the rector here at Lew Trenchard. It wasn't until he died in 1881 that I could come and take up the post, as squire as well as parson, for which I had been preparing myself.

'You see, when I was fifteen years old I came here, and my roots found their proper soil. I had known the moor before, of course, but on that visit I saw it, saw this house and the church, with the eyes of a young adult, and I knew what my future life was to be: I would restore the church, restore this house, and restore the spiritual life of my parish.

'It has taken me forty years, but I like to think that I have succeeded in two of those endeavours, and perhaps made inroads into the third.

'What I had not envisioned, at that tender age, was the extent to which Dartmoor would lay its hands on me, heart and mind and body. It is a singular place, wild and harsh in its beauty, but with air so clear and pure one can taste it, so filled with goodness that illness has no hold there, and ailing young men are cured of their infirmities. It is odd, but although no part of it falls within the bounds of my parish, nonetheless I feel a responsibility that goes beyond legal boundaries.' He stopped and leant forward, looking first at Holmes and then, for a longer time, at me, to see if we understood, and indeed, there was no mistaking the man's passion for the moor. He eased himself back, not entirely satisfied but trusting to some degree in our goodwill. He shut his eyes for a moment, rallying his strength following the long speech, then opened them again with a sharp, accusing glance worthy of Holmes himself.

'There is something wrong on the moor,' he said bluntly. 'I want you to discover what it is, and stop it.'

I looked sideways at Holmes, in time to see his automatic twitch of impatience slide into an expression of quiet amusement.

'Details, Gould,' he murmured. The old man scowled at him, and then, to my surprise, there was a brief twinkle in the back of his keen eyes before he dropped his gaze to the fire, assembling his thoughts.

'You remember the problem we had with Stapleton and the hound? Perhaps I should explain,' he interrupted himself, recalling my presence, and proceeded to retell the story known to most of the English-speaking world, and probably most of the non-English-speaking world as well.

'Some thirty years ago a young Canadian inherited a title and its manor up on the edge of the moor. The previous holder, old Sir Charles, had died of apparently natural causes (he had a bad heart) but under odd circumstances, circumstances that gave rise to a lot of rumours concerning an old family curse that involved a spectral black dog.'

'The Hound of the Baskervilles.'

'Yes, that's it, although the family name is not actually Baskerville. As I remember, Baskerville was the driver your friend Doyle used when he came up here, was it not?' he asked Holmes.

'I believe so,' said Holmes drily, although *friend* was not the word I might have chosen to describe his relationship with Dr Watson's literary agent and collaborator. Baring-Gould went on.

'The moor is poor ground agriculturally, but rich in songs and stories and haunts aplenty: the jacky-twoad with his glowing head and the long-legged Old Stripe, the church grims and bahrghests that creep over the moor, seeking out the lone traveller, the troublesome pixies that lead one astray, and the dogs: the solitary black animals with glowing eyes or the pack of coal-black, fire-breathing hounds leading the dark huntsman and his silent mount. Of course, any student of folklore could tell you of a hundred sources of devil dogs, with or without glowing eyes. Heavens, I could fill a volume on spectral hounds alone – the dark huntsman, the Pad-foot, the wisht-hounds. In fact, in my youth I came across a particularly interesting Icelandic variation—'

'Perhaps another time, Gould,' Holmes suggested firmly.

'What? Oh yes. The family curse of the Baskervilles. At any rate, old Sir Charles died, young Sir Henry came, and the mysterious happenings escalated. Holmes came out here to look things over, and he soon discovered that one of the Baskerville neighbours on the moor was an illegitimate descendant who had his eye on inheriting, and made use of the ghost stories, frightening the old man to death and attempting to harass the young baronet into a fatal accident. Stapleton was his name, a real throwback to the wicked seventeenth-century Baskerville who was the original source of the curse, for his maltreatment of a young girl. Stapleton even resembled the painting of old Baskerville, didn't he, Holmes? In fact, I meant to send you a chapter of my *Old Country Life* where I discuss inherited characteristics and atavistic traits.'

'You did.'

'Did I? Oh good.'

'So what has the Stapleton case to do with Dartmoor now?' Holmes prodded.

'I do not know except—' He dropped his voice, as if someone, or, something, might be listening at the window. 'They tell me the Hound has been seen again, running free on the moor.'

I cannot deny that the old man's words brought a finger of primitive ice down my spine. A loose dog chasing sheep is a problem, but hardly reason for superstitious fears. However, the night, my fatigue, and the stark fact that this apparently sensible and undeniably intelligent old man was himself frightened, all came together to walk a goose over my grave. I shivered.

Fortunately, Holmes did not notice, because the words also had an effect on the man who had uttered them. He slumped into his chair, suddenly grey and exhausted, his eyes closed, his purplish lips slack. I stood in alarm, fearing he had suffered an attack of some kind, but Holmes went briskly out of the door, returning in a minute with the cheerful, rather stupid-looking woman who had brought our dinner. She laid a strong hand on Baring-Gould's arm, and he opened his eyes and smiled weakly.

'I'll be fine in a moment, Mrs Moore. Too much excitement.'

'On top of everything else, the cold and the worry an' all. Mrs Elliott will never forgive me if I let you take ill. Best you go to bed now, Rector. I've laid a nice fire in your room, and tomorrow Mrs

Elliott will be back and the heat'll be on.' He began to protest, but she already had him on his feet and moving towards the door.

'Time enough tomorrow, Gould,' Holmes called. We followed the sounds as the woman half-carried her easily bullied charge upstairs to his bed. A far-off door closed, and Holmes dropped back into his chair and took up his pipe.

'Twenty years ago that man could walk me into the ground,' he said.

I took some split logs from the basket and tossed them onto the fire before returning to my own chair. 'So I came all the way here to help you look for a dog,' I said flatly.

'Don't be obtuse, Russell,' he snapped. 'I thought you of all people would see past the infirmities.'

'To what? A superstitious old parson? A busybody who thinks the world is his parish – or rather, his manor?'

Holmes suddenly took his pipe out of his mouth, and said in pure East-End Cockney, ''E didn't 'alf ruffle yer feathers, didn'e, missus?'

After a minute, reluctantly, I grinned back at him. 'Very well, I admit I was peeved to begin with, and he didn't exactly endear himself.'

'He never has been much of one for the politic untruth, and you did appear very bedraggled.'

'I promise I'll behave myself when I meet him again. But only if you tell me why you brought me down here.'

'Because I needed you.'

Of all the clever, manipulative answers I had been braced to meet, I had not expected one of such complete simplicity. His transparent honesty made me deeply suspicious, but the real possibility that he was telling the unadorned truth swept the feet out from under my resolve to stand firm against him. My suspicions and thoughts chased each other around for a while, until eventually I simply burst out laughing.

'All right, Holmes, you win. I'm here. What do you want me to do?'

He rose and went to the sideboard to replenish his glass (not, I noticed, from the small stoneware jug that held the metheglin) and returned with a glass in his other hand as well, which he placed on the table next to my chair before moving over to stand in front of the fire. He took a deep draught from his drink, put it down on the floor beside his foot (as there was no mantelpiece), and took up his pipe. I sank down into the arms of the chair, growing more apprehensive by the minute: All of this delay meant either that he was trying to decide how best to get around the defences that I thought I had already let down, or that he was uncertain in his own mind about how to proceed. Either way, it was not a good sign.

He succeeded in getting his pipe to draw cleanly, retrieved his glass, and settled down in his chair, stretching his long legs towards the fire. Another slow draught half emptied the glass, and with his chin on his chest and his pipe in his hand, he looked into the fresh flames and began to speak.

'As Gould intimated, Dartmoor is a most peculiar place,' he began. 'Physically it comprises a high, wide bowl of granite, some three hundred and fifty square miles covered with a thin, peaty soil and scattered with outcrops of stone. It functions as a huge sponge, the peat storing its rain all winter to feed the Teign, the Dart, the Tavy, and all the other streams and rivers that are born here. The floor of the moor is a thousand feet above the surrounding Devonshire countryside, from which it rises abruptly. It is a thing apart, a place unconnected with the rest of the world, and it is not inappropriate that a very harsh prison was set in its midst. Indeed, to many, Dartmoor is synonymous with the prison, although that facility is but a bump on the broad face of the moor.'

'I have seen the Yorkshire moors,' I said.

'Then you've a very rough idea of the ground here, but not of Dartmoor's special character. It is much more of a *hortus conclusus*, although this walled garden is no warm and fruitful paradise, but a rocky place of gorse and bracken. As Gould said, it does not generously part with its wealth. It is a land of great strength – men have broken their health and their fortunes trying to beat it down and shape it to their ends, but the moor wins out in the end. The men who chose to build a prison here set great value on breaking the spirits of the men they were guarding. The moor will not be farmed, nor made to grow any but the simplest crops. Tin miners have been the only men to draw much money from the place, and even they had to work hard for it. On a basic level, however, it has provided spare sustenance to its inhabitants for thousands of years: One finds mediaeval stone crosses mingling with Neolithic ruins and early Victorian engine houses.

'Most of the moor is a chase or forest, which as I'm sure you know does not necessarily mean trees, and here most emphatically does not. In this sense, a forest denotes a wild reserve for the crown to hunt, although I imagine the Prince of Wales must find the game somewhat limited on the moor itself, unless he is fond of rabbits. Much of it is a common, grazed by the adjoining parishes with fees collected at a yearly gathering up of the animals, called the 'drift'. Other parts of it are privately held, with an interesting legal right of a holder's survivors to claim an additional eight acres upon the death of each subsequent holder. These 'new-takes' at one time ate into the duchy's holdings, but are not often claimed now, because the traditional moor men are dying off, and their sons are moving to the cities. Do you know, when I was here thirty years ago it was not impossible to find a child of the moor who had never seen a coin of the realm? Now—' He gave out a brief cough of laughter. 'The other day in the Saracen's Head pub, right out in the middle of the moor, one of the natives was singing an Al Jolson song.'

'You've been up on the moor, then? Recently?' I asked.

'I travelled across it from Exeter, yes.'

A hike like that might account for his heavier use of brandy than normal, I thought, as well as his position in front of the hottest part of the fire. He went on before I could ask after his rheumatism.

'The people of the moor are what one might expect: hard as granite, with low expectations of what life has to give, often nearly illiterate but with a superb verbal memory and possessed of the occasional flare of poetry and imagination. They are, in fact, like the tors they live among, those odd piles of fantastically weathered granite that grace the tops of a number of hills: rock hard, well worn and decidedly quirky.'

'A description which could also apply to our host,' I murmured, and took a sip of the surprisingly good and undoubtedly old brandy in my glass.

'Indeed. He may not have been born on the moor itself, but it is in him now. It is not paternalism speaking in him – or not only paternalism. He is truly and deeply concerned about the stirs and currents abroad on the moor. I wouldn't be surprised if he can feel them from here.'

'So you agree there's something wrong up there?' I heard the last two words come out of my mouth with a definite emphasis, and thought with irritation that this habit of referring to a deserted bit of landscape as if it were another planet seemed to be contagious.

'There's certainly something stirring, though truth to tell I cannot read the currents well enough to see if it be for ill or not. I will say I received a faint impression that the moor was readying itself for a convulsion of some sort, though whether an eruption or a sudden flowering I couldn't say.'

He stopped abruptly and looked askance at the empty glass balanced on the arm of his chair, and I had to agree, it was very unusual to hear him wax quite so poetic. He picked up the glass and put it firmly away from him onto the nearby table, then settled back with his pipe, not meeting my eyes.

'As with any isolated setting, the moor seethes with stories of the supernatural. Unsophisticated minds are apt to see corpse lights or 'jacky-twoads' where the scientist would see swamp gas, and long and lonely nights encourage the mind to wander down paths poorly illuminated by the light of reason. The people firmly believe in ghostly dogs and wraiths of the dying, in omen-bearing ravens and standing stones that walk in the dark of the moon. And pixies – the pixies, or pygsies, are everywhere, waiting to lead the unsuspecting traveller astray. The author of a respectable guidebook, published just a few years ago, recommends that the lost walker turn his coat out so as to avoid being "pygsie-led" – and he's only half joking.'

'What does Baring-Gould make of all that? He's an educated man, after all.'

'Gould?' Holmes laughed. 'He's the most gullible of the lot, full of the most awful balderdash. He'll tell you how a neighbour's horse panicked one night at the precise spot where a man would be killed some hours later, how another man carried on a conversation with his wife who was dying ten miles away, how – Revelations, visitations, spooks, you name it – he's worse than Conan Doyle, with his fairies and his spiritualism.'

All this made the purported friendship sound less and less likely. Sherlock Holmes was not one to suffer fools even under coercion, yet he was apparently here under his own free will, and without resentment. There was undoubtedly something in the situation that I had thus far failed to grasp.

'I was here for some weeks during the Stapleton case,' he was saying, 'and since then once or twice for shorter periods of time, so I have a basic working knowledge of the moor dweller and his sense of the universe. The stories he tells are a rich mixture that range from the humorous to the macabre. They may be violent and occasionally, shall I say, earthy, but they are rarely brutal and have thus far appeared free of those terrors of the urban dweller, the two-legged monster and the plagues of foreign diseases.

'This time it is different. In two days, nursing my beer in the corners of three moorland public houses, the stories I heard could as easily have come from Whitechapel or Limehouse. Oh, there are the standard stories too, the everyday fare of the moor dwellers, although the recent preoccupation with ghostly carriages and spectral dogs that has Gould worried does, I agree, seem unusually vivid and worth investigating. Still, they are a far way from the other stories I heard, which were along the lines of a dark man with a razor-sharp blade sacrificing a ram on top of a tor and drinking its blood, and a young girl found ravished and dismembered, and an old woman drowned in a stream.'

'Have these things happened?' I asked sharply.

'They have not.'

'None of them?'

'As far as I can discover, they are not even patched-together exaggerations of actual incidents. They seem to be rumours made up of whole cloth.'

I could think of no proper response, but as I took another swallow from my glass, I was aware for the first time of a feeling of uneasiness.

'Yes,' I said. 'I see.'

'Except,' he added, 'for one.'

'Ah.'

'Ah indeed. The death of Josiah Gorton is both undeniable and mysterious. It happened three weeks ago, just after I left for Berlin. Gould's letter took a week to find me, and by the time I got here the trail was both cold and confused.'

'A common enough state of affairs for your cases,' I commented.

'True, but regrettable nonetheless. Josiah Gorton was a tin miner – although that may be a deceptive description. Tin seeker might be more accurate, one of a breed who wanders the moor, putting their noses into every rivulet and valley, poring over every stone pile in hopes of discovering small nuggets of tin that the more energetic miners of the past left behind. He spent his days fossicking through the deep-cut stream-beds and his nights in caves or shelters or the barns of farmers.

'I met Gorton once, in fact, many years ago, and thought him a harmless enough character even then. He affected the dress of a gipsy, with a red kerchief around his throat, although when I met him he looked more like a pirate, with dark, oiled locks and a heavy frock coat too large for him. He was a colourful figure, proud of his freedom, and he had a goodly store of traditional songs tucked into the back of his head, which he would happily bring forth for the cost of a pint or a meal. He was a last relic of the old moor 'songmen', although his voice was giving way, and with more than three pints under his belt he tended to forget the words to some of the longer ballads. Still, he was tolerated with affection by the innkeepers and farmers, as a part of the scenery, and in particular by Gould, for whom Gorton had a special significance.

'You need to understand that with all the work he has done in a wide variety of fields, Gould regards his greatest achievement in life to have been the collecting of West Country songs and melodies, a task begun more than thirty years ago and only reluctantly dropped when he became too old to take to the moor for days at a time. Josiah Gorton was one of his more important songmen. I suppose it could be said, by those of a psychologically analytical bent, that Gorton represents to Gould the fate of the moor, overcome by progress and forgotten in the shiny, shallow attractions of modernity.' Holmes' fastidious expression served to make it clear that he was merely acknowledging the possible explanation given by another discipline. He continued, 'Whatever the explanation, there is no doubt that Gould is deeply troubled not only by the fact of Gorton's death, but by the manner it came about.

'On the night of Saturday, the fifteenth of September, Gorton was seen walking north past Watern Tor. You did study those maps you brought down, I presume?'

'Not studied, no. I glanced at a couple of them.'

'You didn't?' He sounded amazed and more than a bit disapproving. 'What on earth were you doing all that time on the train?'

'Reading,' I said evenly. I actually had deliberately buried myself in the most arcane piece of theological history I could lay my hands upon, as a protest and counterbalance to the forces pulling me to Devonshire. In retrospect, it seemed a bit childish, but I bristled when Holmes gave me that look of his.

'Reading,' he repeated in a flat voice. 'Wasting your time, Russell, with theological speculation and airy-fairy philosophising when there is work to be done.'

'The work is yours, Holmes, not mine – I only agreed to bring you the maps. And the speculation of Jewish philosophers is as empirical as any of your conclusions.'

His only reply was a scornful examination of his pipe-bowl.

'Admit it, Holmes,' I pressed. 'The only reason you so denigrate Talmudic studies is sheer envy over the fact that others perfected the art of deductive reasoning centuries before you were even born.'

He did not deign to answer, which meant that the point was irrefutably mine, so I drove home my advantage: 'And besides that, Holmes, what I was reading does actually have some bearing on this case – or at least on its setting. Were you aware that in the seventeenth century Moorish raiders came as far as the coasts of

Devon and Cornwall, taking slaves? Why, Baring-Gould might have relatives in Spain today.'

He did not admit defeat, but merely applied another match to his pipe and resumed the previous topic. 'You must study the maps at the earliest opportunity. Watern Tor, since you do not know, is in a remote area in the northern portion of the moor. Gorton was seen there, heading west, on a Saturday evening, yet on the following Monday morning, thirty-six hours later, he was found miles away in the opposite direction, passed out in a drunken stupor in a rain-swollen leat on the southern reaches. He had a great lump on the back of his head and bog weeds in his hair, although there are no bogs in the part of the moor where he was found. He died a few hours later of his injuries and a fever, muttering all the while about his long, silent ride in Lady Howard's carriage. He also said,' Holmes added in the driest of voices, 'that Lady Howard had a huge black dog.'

'Huh,' I grunted. 'And did the dog have glowing eyes?'

'Gorton neglected to say, and he was in no condition to respond to questions. There was one further and quite singular piece of testimony, however.'

I eyed him warily, mistrusting the sudden jauntiness of his manner. 'Oh yes?'

'Yes. The farmer who found Gorton, and the farmer's strapping son who helped carry the old miner to the house and fetched a doctor, both swear that in the soft ground beside the body, there were clear marks pressed firmly into the earth.' I was hit by a cold jolt of apprehension. 'The two men have become fixtures in the Saracen's Head, telling and retelling the story of how they found Gorton's body surrounded by—'

'No! Oh no, Holmes, please.' I put up my hand to stop his words, unable to bear what I could hear coming, a thundering evocation of one of the most extravagant phrases Conan Doyle ever employed.

'Please, please don't tell me that on the ground beside the body, Mr Holmes, there were the footprints of a gigantic hound.'

He removed his pipe from his mouth and stared at me. 'What on earth are you talking about, Russell? I admit that I occasionally indulge in a touch of the dramatic, but surely you can't believe me as melodramatic as that.'

I drew a relieved breath and settled back in my chair. 'No, I suppose not. Forgive me, Holmes. Do continue.'

'No,' he continued, putting the stem of his pipe back into place. 'I do not believe it would be possible to distinguish a hound's spoor from that of an ordinary dog – not without a stretch of ground showing the animal's loping stride. These were simply a confusion of prints.'

'Do you mean to tell me . . .' I began slowly.

'Yes, Russell. There on the ground beside the body of Josiah Gorton were found' – he paused to hold out his pipe and gaze in at the bowl, which seemed to me to be drawing just fine, before finishing the phrase – 'the footprints of a very large dog.'

I dropped my head into my hands and left it there for a long time while my husband sucked in quiet satisfaction at his pipe.

'Holmes,' I said.

'Yes, Russell.'

'I am going to bed.'

'A capital idea,' he replied.

And so we did.

CHAPTER THREE

Oh! these architects! how I detest them for the mischief they have
done. I should like to cut off their hands.

— FURTHER REMINISCENCES

Iᴛ ʀᴀɪɴᴇᴅ ᴀʟʟ ᴛʜᴀᴛ night, a quiet, steady rhythm that soothed
me into a sleep so sound that, although I woke briefly in the
early morning to the click and murmur of hot water pushing its way
through cold radiator pipes, I went back to sleep, and did not wake
fully until nearly eight o'clock. Finding to my satisfaction that the
dawn noises had not been an hallucination, I bathed and dressed
– in trousers, despite my host's sensibilities – and put up my hair,
before making my way downstairs.

At the foot of the stairs I paused and listened. The old house was
content in its restored warmth but utterly silent; I could not even
hear the rain. I took the opportunity to explore the various rooms
we had bypassed the night before, finding, among other things, an
airy, light-blue-and-white ballroom of wedding-cake splendour,
lacking only a cobwebbed dinner service and Miss Havisham to
complete the picture of merriment and life abruptly suspended by
the years. I did no more than stand inside the door, feeling no wish
to examine the intricate plasterwork more closely, and I could not
help wondering if Baring-Gould ever came into this room. I backed
out, closing the door silently.

Back in the hall, I paused to examine the fireplace carving that Baring-Gould had commended to me the night before. It depicted a hunt, a parade of hounds with their tails curled energetically over their backs, pursuing a fox, who had abandoned bits and pieces of the goose he had stolen and was now making for what looked like a pineapple. I puzzled over it for a while, and then went back towards the stairway and then into the dining room, where I discovered a pot of coffee bubbling gently into sludge over a warming flame, a mound of leathery eggs similarly kept warm, some cold toast, and three strips of flabby bacon. I poured a tiny amount of boiled coffee essence and a large amount of lovely yellow milk into a cup and walked over to the window.

Outside lay a small paved courtyard, deserted of life and leaves and with an arched walkway along the opposite side that looked like either a cloister or a row of almshouses. I went through a doorway and found the back stairway, and another doorway that opened into the kitchen, at the moment deserted although I could hear a woman's voice raised in harangue at a distance. I retreated, retracing my steps past the staircase to another door, and there I found host and husband in a large cluttered room lined with bookshelves and brightened by a number of tall windows that gathered in the light even on a grey day like this. The two of them were standing with their heads together and their elbows resting on top of a small, high, sloping writing table, across which had been draped an Ordnance Survey map.

My first impression on seeing the Reverend Sabine Baring-Gould by light of day was that schoolboys and sinners alike must have found him terrifying. Even now at the edges of his tenth decade, with his thin white hair brushed over a mottled scalp, his back bent, and his face carved into deep lines, he struck one as a powerful source of disapproval and judgement, searching out wearily the misdeeds that a long lifetime had proven to him must invariably lie before him. He was a man who had seen a great deal in his eighty-nine years, and approved of little of it.

Oddly, he was wearing two pairs of spectacles, one of them pushed up into his hair, the other on his nose. Seeing me at the door, he shoved the second pair up to join the first and straightened his back. He took in my trousers, and his face went even more sour.

'Good morning, Miss Russell. My friend here tells me that you prefer that peculiar form of address over the "Mrs" to which you are entitled.'

'Er, yes, I do. Thank you. Good morning, Mr Baring-Gould. Good morning, Holmes.'

'I see you found Mrs Elliott's breakfast,' Baring-Gould stated, seeing the cup I still held.

'I found it, yes.'

His old eyes beneath their remarkably rounded brows sharpened. 'Inedible?' he asked.

'It's all right,' I hastened to say. 'I often just take coffee in the morning.'

'Ask Mrs Elliott if you want something. I did tell her,' he said in an aside to Holmes. 'The only time the woman uses those chafing dishes is when there are twenty eggs to keep warm and a gallon of coffee. Was the coffee boiled away?' he shot at me.

'Almost, yes. I snuffed out the flame as I came through.'

'Never mind, she'll be making more shortly. When there are guests in the house she produces meals eighteen hours a day, and she'll be anxious to make up for the first impression you had of her household. Women are quite mad when it comes to hospitality.'

I bit down hard on my tongue, though truth to tell I wouldn't have known quite where to start. Holmes made a noise deep in his throat that was not quite a cough, and hastily returned to the map. I took a swallow of my coffee-flavoured milk and turned my back on the two men to peruse the books on the walls, stopping to remove one from time to time and glance into it.

'So, judging by this,' Holmes said, continuing the conversation that had broken off with my entrance, 'Josiah Gorton might readily have been brought from the place where he was last seen down to where he was found, without a soul seeing it.'

'Oh yes, easily, by anyone who knows the moor.'

'How intimate a knowledge would be required?'

'I should have thought a week or two of wandering might do it. That and a good map.'

'It's a great pity, Gould, that I could not come at the time. The body might have told many tales.'

The old man made no polite effort to excuse Holmes his preoccupation, although he admitted, 'I was not informed myself until after he had been prepared for burial. If you wish to speak with the women who laid his body out, I can give you their names.'

'I may do, later. Now tell me, where was this dog-and-carriage apparition seen? This is another reference to a local folktale, Russell,' he explained. I looked up from the encyclopaedia article on pineapples that I was reading. 'A particularly difficult local noblewoman—'

'Noble by marriage only,' inserted Baring-Gould.

'A woman who married a local lord,' Holmes corrected himself, 'lost him, along with three other husbands, under circumstances the local populace thought suspicious, with some justification. She was never officially accused and tried, but for her sins she is said to be condemned to riding in a coach made of the bones of her dead husbands, driven by a headless horseman and led by a black hound with a single eye in the centre of his forehead. The carriage drives at midnight from the ancestral house near Tavistock up to Okehampton castle for Lady Howard to pluck one blade of grass—'

'The hound plucks it,' Baring-Gould sternly corrected him.

'How could a hound pluck a blade of grass?' objected Holmes.

'I merely tell you what the story says.'

'But a hound—'

'Holmes,' I interrupted.

'Oh very well, the hound plucks the grass, and not until every blade is plucked – or bitten – can Lady Howard be free to take her rest. It's a popular story, with songs and such, that by the way probably gave Stapleton the idea for his personal variation on the so-called Baskerville Hound – which does not, in the legend, actually glow. It is said, I should mention, to be highly unlucky to be offered a ride in the coach, and certain death actually to enter in with Lady Howard.'

'So I should imagine,' I murmured.

'At any rate, Russell, the point is that Lady Howard and her hound have been seen on the moor.'

During Holmes' recitation, Baring-Gould, pausing occasionally to correct Holmes, had gone to a cupboard in the corner and returned with a very large, heavily worn, rolled-up map, which he now spread out across the worktable on top of the other. This one was of a smaller scale, the Ordnance Survey's one-inch map – although I saw, looking more closely at it, that it actually comprised portions of four or five adjoining maps, carefully trimmed and fastened together so as to encompass the entire moor and its surrounding towns. Corrections had been made in a number of places, roads crossed out and redrawn and the names of tors and hamlets rewritten: Laughter Tor had become Lough Tor, Haytor Rocks changed to Hey Tor, Crazywell Pool was corrected to Clakeywell. The writing was cramped and sloping, undoubtedly that of Baring-Gould.

Before Baring-Gould could begin, the door at the end of the room opened and a woman with iron-grey hair and an iron-hard face put her head inside.

'Pardon me, Rector,' she said, 'but you wanted me to tell you when the Harpers came in.'

'The Harpers? Oh yes. Would you feed them, Mrs Elliott, and get them settled in? I'll not be much longer here.'

The housekeeper nodded and began to draw back, then stopped and addressed Holmes. 'You're not tiring him, I trust,' she said, sounding threatening.

'We are trying not to do so,' Holmes said.

She studied her master for a minute, then withdrew.

'Another sign of the unrest on the moor,' Baring-Gould said with a sigh. 'Longtime residents, people with roots deep into the peat, pulling up and moving away. Like Josiah Gorton, Sally Harper's father was one of my songmen. I collected two ballads and three tunes from the man, oh, it must be nearly thirty years ago. He gave me an alternative verse to 'Green Broom', as I recall, as well as a sprightly tune, set with most unseemly words that I had to rewrite before it could be published. Sally was a blooming young thing then, and now she and her husband have had to sell off their farm up near Black Tor, a very old place with several generations of newtakes added to the original. Never had children, and although they have a bit of money from the farm sale, the house they have their eyes on near Milton Abbot isn't ready yet. I felt I ought to help out, and it'll only be for a few days. Hard to believe it was that many years ago. Where were we? Yes, Josiah Gorton.'

He bent closely over the fine lines of the map, squinting for a moment until he had his bearings, and his long, gnarled finger came down in the upper left quadrant of the map, tracing an uneven line down to the lower right.

'This is the most likely route for Gorton to have taken,' he said, which, I realised to my surprise, was for my sake, not that of Holmes, who had already been over the route. He then drew his hand back and put it down a short distance from where he had started. 'And here is the place Lady Howard's coach was seen, on the night Gorton disappeared.' This was, judging by the few roads and fewer dwellings, one of the most deserted areas of the entire moor, a place thick with the Gothic script map-makers use to indicate antiquities: hut circles, stone rows, stone avenues, tumuli and ancient trackways, as well as an ominous scattering of those grass-tuft symbols that indicate marshland. There were no orange roads for miles, or even the hollow lines of minor roads, only densely gathered contour lines, numerous streams, and the markings for 'rough pasture'. A howling wilderness indeed.

What was a *kistvaen*? I wondered, seeing the word on the map, but Holmes spoke before I could ask.

'Who on earth was out in that wasteland to see a spectral coach?' he demanded.

'It is not a wasteland, Holmes,' Baring-Gould corrected him sharply. 'Merely sparsely populated. A farmworker saw it. He was benighted on his way home from a wedding.'

'Why does that say "Artillery Range"?' I interrupted without thinking.

I felt two sets of disapproving male eyes boring into me, and did not look up from the map.

'Because,' said Baring-Gould, addressing me as if I were a regrettably slow child, 'the army uses it to practise with their guns. A fair portion of the moor is given over to them during the summer months, and is therefore off limits to the rambler and antiquarian. They do post the firing schedules at various places around the moor, and they are scrupulous about mounting the red warning flags, but it is really most inconvenient of them.'

I sympathised, but privately I could see why the army should want to make use of Dartmoor: There was probably less life to disturb in that hand's breadth of the map than on any other English

44

ground south of Hadrian's Wall. Even the map-makers seemed to have tired of the exercise before they penetrated to the middle, for most of the Gothic markings were along the edges. Or perhaps primitive man found the centre of the place too daunting even for him, I reflected. I suppressed a shiver.

'A farmworker on his way home from a celebration might not be considered the best of witnesses,' Holmes noted drily, returning to the subject at hand. 'How much had he drunk?'

'Quite a bit,' Baring-Gould had to admit.

Holmes' only comment was with his eyebrows, but that was enough. He bent to study the map for a moment, then turned to a familiar packet, selected a map, and spread it with a flourish over the top of Baring-Gould's marked-up old sheet. He then withdrew a fountain pen from his breast pocket.

'The sighting of the coach around the time Gorton was last seen was here, would you say?'

Baring-Gould patted around his pockets until he remembered where he had put his spectacles, and pulled down one of the two pairs on his head and adjusted them on his nose. He peered at the crisp new map briefly, then pointed to a spot on the left side of the moor. Holmes put a neat circle on the place indicated, and then moved the pen over until it hovered near a Gothic-lettered notice of 'hut circles'.

'Gorton was last seen here?'

Baring-Gould seized the pen from Holmes impatiently and automatically extended it out as if to dip into a well before he caught himself, shook the thing hesitantly, and then wrote a firm X a bare fraction of an inch from where Holmes had held the nib. He then moved his hand the width of the moor to place another X near the hamlet of Buckfastleigh.

'He was found here,' he said. 'And these are where the coach was seen. The first sighting, as near as I can find, was in the middle of July, somewhere in this area here. That I know only through hearsay, but on August the twenty-fourth, two people saw it, and I spoke with them both. The third time was the fifteenth of September; that was the farmworker.'

'And the dog?'

'What of the dog?'

It was now Holmes' turn for impatience. 'When was he seen, Gould? Only with the carriage, or has he also appeared by himself?'

Baring-Gould slapped down the pen, sending out a gout of ink that obliterated half the countryside between Bovey Tracey and Doddiscombesleigh. 'It is so irritating,' he declared querulously. 'One has the impression that a hundred people have seen both hound and coach, but all I can lay hands on is rumour. This is precisely why I need you, Holmes. I cannot go up and find the truth for myself. I know for certain that the couple who saw the coach in August specifically mentioned seeing the dog; does it matter if the hound was at times alone or invariably with the coach?'

'I do not know what matters until I have more data,' Holmes retorted. 'What certainly matters is ensuring that what information is available be both accurate and complete.'

'Well, I simply do not know.'

Holmes pulled out his handkerchief and began dabbing at the map in disapproval.

'Then we shall have to enquire,' he said heavily. 'And the farmer and his son who found Gorton's body? Their house is here?'

'Slightly below that.' Baring-Gould's finger touched briefly on a spot half an inch south of the X where Gorton had lain, and then suddenly he seemed to tense, and draw in a sharp breath. I looked quickly at his face, but what I had taken for a jolt of revelation was obviously something much more immediate and physical. The man was in pain.

Holmes' hand shot out, but stopped as Baring-Gould straightened his back slowly and shook his head briefly in self-disgust. He removed himself from the work-table and hobbled on his sticks over to an ancient armchair in front of the fire, lowering himself into it. He sat very still for a long moment, let out a pent-up breath, and went on. His voice was slightly constricted, but otherwise he showed no sign that anything untoward had taken place.

'The August sighting, as I said, was by a courting couple. The girl, when I had them brought here a week after, was still quite incoherent with terror, although I had the distinct impression that she might have been somewhat more sensible had her beau not been present. Still, she was rather stupid, and surprisingly high-strung, considering the peasant stock she comes from. The man was stolid and unimaginative, which makes me rather more willing to credit his story.'

'That story being?'

'They were seated on a stone wall that night (lying in the lee of the wall, more likely) when they heard a faint noise approaching, a rush and a jangle and a muffled beat of running hoofs. They peered over the wall in time to see it pass by: a faintly glowing carriage pulled by one or two horses invisible but for the gleam of moonlight off their harness trimmings, with a woman clearly visible inside. They heard the crack of a whip, and as the carriage was passing another dark shape appeared behind it. The shape turned and looked straight at them, and it whined. They were both clear that they had heard the whine. At that point in her story the girl broke down into hysterics, because when the beast turned to look at them, they could clearly see that it was possessed of a single eye, large and glowing, in the centre of its head. The driver of the carriage whistled, and the hound – or whatever it was – loped off, leaving the two lovers to collect what wits they might have, and their clothing, and race for the girl's cottage as if, as the saying goes, all the hounds of hell were after them.'

Baring-Gould allowed his eyes to close, and his mouth opened slightly. He was exhausted by his lengthy narrative, but Holmes continued to pore over the map, and I felt sure that if his old friend would benefit from a doctor's attention, Holmes would summon one. Not knowing quite what was called for, I thought I ought at least to comment on what the old man had so laboriously given us.

'I thought the hound was supposed to be leading the carriage, not following,' I said weakly.

Holmes replied, 'I don't think the displacement of the animal would negate the experience in the minds of the couple, Russell.'

I was surprised to see a tiny smile twitch at the corner of Baring-Gould's ancient blue lips, and then astonished when they opened and the old man began to sing, in a baritone that quavered a bit but was true enough, to give forth a tune that was simple, yet eerie.

My Lady hath a sable coach, with horses two and four,
My Lady hath a black bloodhound, that runneth on before.
My Lady's coach hath nodding plumes, the coachman hath no head,
My Lady is an ashen white, as one who is long dead.

He sat with his head resting on the back of the chair, a reminiscent smile softening his face. 'My old nurse Mary Bicknell used to sing that song to me when I was small.'

Personally, I thought that a woman who would sing something like that to a young child ought to be barred from her post, but I did not voice the idea. Baring-Gould, however, either read my thoughts or had a mind that ran in the same direction, because he opened one eye, looked straight at me and said, 'She did hasten to reassure me that Lady Howard was only on the road after midnight.'

'Which ensured that you would not venture out of your window at night,' I commented. He closed his eyes again, looking ever so faintly amused.

'Come, Russell,' said Holmes. 'We will see you this evening, Gould.' His only answer was one aged forefinger, tipped up from the arm of the chair in farewell.

It was still miserably wet outside, looking as if it intended to rain steadily for days, but I was not surprised when Holmes suggested that we go out.

'I neglected to bring monsoon gear with me, Holmes.'

'I'm sure the good Mrs Elliott could supply an adequate garment,' he said. 'Any house overseen by Gould is bound to have enough raiment for a small army.'

So it proved, although one might have wished for modern gum boots rather than the stiff gaiters made of oiled leather, grey with hastily scrubbed-off mildew. In fact, everything smelt as musty as a cavern. Still, aside from one or two places, the rain sheeted off us as we set off across the drive past the round fountain, which in daylight I could see featured the bronze figure of a goose-herd. I paused to look back at the house, this combination of white and grey stone, leaded windows, and slate, a family home both idiosyncratic and comfortable. My eye was caught by the stone carvings over the porch, with an indistinguishable coat of arms and the date 1620.

'Part of the house is original, anyway,' I noted.

Holmes followed my gaze. 'Original, yes, but not to Lew Trenchard. I believe the porch came from a family holding in Staverton, although that particular stone was once a sundial in Pridhamsleigh. Various other pieces came from Orchard, a house approximately five miles to the north of here.'

I laughed. 'Baring-Gould's Elizabethan house, composed of old pieces patched together, like the new ceiling upstairs.'

'The upstairs actually is old,' Holmes said, 'though Gould brought it here from a building in Exeter. It's the downstairs that's new.'

'Well, have you looked closely at the carving over the fireplace in the hall? It's quite nice, but the fox appears to be making for a pinery. The pineapple wasn't even introduced until the reign of Charles II, and wasn't cultivated until the early eighteenth century. I looked it up in his *Britannica*,' I added.

'True, although I believe the stone fireplace itself is considerably earlier than the carving surrounding it.' I gave up.

We set off through a low, weedy rose garden and by a gate into the long meadow stretching out towards the small river that had so plagued me the night before. The grass was ankle-deep and sodden, and we kept a close eye on our feet, lest we meet the sign of a cow's passing.

'Where did you go on the moor?' I asked after a bit. 'Not to where Lady Howard's coach was seen?'

'Actually, it was more or less the same area, although with a different goal. I was looking at the artillery ranges.'

I allowed quite a number of steps to pass before I finally asked, 'Are you going to tell me why you were looking at the artillery ranges?'

'Are you interested?'

'As I told you last night, I am here, Holmes,' I said heavily. 'I have not yet packed my bags and sloped off to Oxford.'

'I suppose that answers my question.'

'It damn well ought to.'

'Mycroft.'

He spoke the name as if that, too, were answer enough, and to some extent, it was. Mycroft Holmes (who was, I still had to remind myself, my brother-in-law) had been the instigator of many of Holmes' more, shall we say, official investigations. Mycroft worked for a governmental agency that it amused him to call the accounting office, although the accounts tallied (and occasionally settled) often had very little connection with pounds, shillings, and pence.

'The army this time?'

'A weapon they're testing. They wish to keep it secret and are not having much success.'

I stopped. 'Oh God. Doesn't the world have enough weapons? Have they learnt nothing from four years of war, millions dead, and whole countries brought to the edge of destruction?'

'They have learnt that the next war will be won by technology.'

'The next war.' The idea was physically revolting.

'There will be one, Russell. There always is.'

'I will not participate in an army spy-search. I absolutely refuse. I'd rather talk to drunken farm-hands about spectral coaches.'

'It is peripheral, Russell,' he said soothingly. 'I made the mistake of letting Mycroft know where I was going, and he asked me to do this while I was here. We are in Devon because of Gould's case, and any work for Mycroft is strictly secondary. Although I don't believe we need stoop to interviewing rural inebriates, particularly those who have had three weeks to build up a story.'

I wrenched my boots up from the muddy pasture and started walking again. We were mounting a rise, approaching a raw patch of ground with a few small trees trying weakly for a foothold. It seemed to be a wide oval depression in the earth, but that impression did not prepare me for what in a moment lay at our feet. I was so startled I took a step back from it.

It was a pit, an enormous water-filled crater with nearly vertical sides gouged straight into the green pasture barely a stone's throw from Baring-Gould's front door. A gush of water shot out from the bank on the far side and plummeted down into the lake, looking more like a furious storm drain than a debouching stream. A ramshackle boathouse, incongruously resembling a Swiss chalet, clung to the bank across from the waterfall.

'What on earth—?'

'Astonishing, isn't it?' Holmes was staring morosely at the water that lay a good forty feet below us. It was impossible to tell how deep the water was beneath that leaden surface, but it had a definite feeling of profundity. 'Gould's father had the brilliant idea of establishing a quarry here, as a source of income. You see the two ramps cut to haul it out? Nearly overgrown now. When Gould took over in the 1880s he diverted a stream to fill it. He claims it is pleasantly cool on a hot day, to paddle about in a boat.'

I looked at the gaping maw of the almost subterranean lake with distaste. 'It's monstrous. What could his father have been thinking of? Do you suppose Baring-Gould allowed his children down there?'

'Oh, indeed,' he said with a smile of what appeared to be reminiscence on his face. 'They were a rowdy lot, encouraged by their father. Even the girls. One of them nearly drowned during a race of leaky hip baths – Mary, I think it was.'

I could well believe that the sinister little lake might hold any number of drowned bodies. 'By the looks of the place, she was lucky not to have been swallowed up by one of Jules Verne's lurking sea monsters. May we go?'

We circled the foreboding pit cautiously and found on the other side a small house and a drive and eventually a road. I recognised the sheltered wall where Holmes had sat with his violin the night before, and we walked past it, past the churchyard, through the village and the wet, autumnal woods of Lew Trenchard and out into the surrounding countryside, not saying much, but working ourselves back into the rhythms of easy intimacy. My feet grew numb but my chest expanded, drawing in the rich air as my eyes rejoiced in the lush green landscape.

We stopped to take lunch at a small public house, where they gave us a rich leek soup and a thick wedge of game pie washed down with a lively dark beer. Rather to my surprise, Holmes asked after my academic work in Oxford. I told him what I had been doing, and over his post-prandial pipe he in turn brought me up to date on the progress of our previous case, the legal proceedings against the man whose arrest we had been instrumental in achieving the month before.

Nothing earth-shaking, but when we resumed our rain gear, we had resumed our sense of partnership as well.

Greatly content, we turned back to Lew Trenchard. The rain had let up slightly and the heavy clouds had lifted, so that when we came to the top of a small rise Holmes stopped and pointed out across the stone wall that bordered the road, over the small fields with their half-bare hedgerows, past a scattering of snug farm-houses with gently smoking chimneys, and beyond to where the ground rose and rose.

From here it looked like a huge wall, placed there to keep the gentle Devonshire countryside at bay. Green slopes around the base gave way to extrusions of dark rock, and the ridge, perhaps four miles away, seemed to tower over our heads.

'Dartmoor,' said Holmes unnecessarily.

'Good Lord,' I said. 'How high is it?'

'Perhaps twelve hundred feet or so higher than we are here. It appears more, does it not?'

'It looks like a fortress.'

'Over the centuries, it has effectively served as one. It has certainly kept the casual visitor away.'

'I can believe that,' I said emphatically. The moor loomed up, cold and fierce and daunting and uncomfortable, a geographical personality that seemed very aware of us, yet at the same time scornful of our timidity and weakness. In the distance, one of the hills dimly visible through the clouds was crowned with a shape that seemed too regular to be natural. It looked proud and tiny and out of place, as if trying to convince itself that the hill it rode on could not shrug it off if it wished.

'What is that building?' I asked Holmes.

He followed my gaze. 'Brentor Church. Dedicated in the fourteenth century, to Saint Michael, I believe.'

I smiled; of course it would be a church, and could only be to St Michael, the choice of missionaries the world around seeking to quell the local spirits by planting a mission on the site of the native holy places and giving it over to St Michael and all his Angels. Somehow, the valiant little outthrust of a building did not appear convinced of the conquest.

I looked back at the rising moor, and decided that I could not blame the Brentor Church; I myself did not relish the idea of breaching those walls and walking out onto the flat expanse of the moorland within, no more than I would have relished a swim in the quarry lake next to Lew House – and for similar reasons.

I became aware of Holmes, studying my face. I shot him a brief smile and pulled my coat more closely together over my chest. 'It looks cold,' I said, but he was not fooled.

'It is a place that encourages fanciful thoughts,' he said indulgently. However, I noticed that even he cast a quick glance at the presence on the horizon before we resumed our path to Lew House.

We arrived back in time for afternoon tea, which we took by ourselves, as Baring-Gould was resting. It was a superb reward for our day's wet outing, and I gathered that Mrs Elliott had taken advantage of the Harpers' presence to create a true Devonshire tea, the *pièce de résistance* of which was a plate piled high with hot, crumbly scones to rival Mrs Hudson's, a large bowl of thick, yellow clotted cream, and a second bowl containing deep-red strawberry jam. When we had finished, I hunted the cook down in her kitchen, where she stood watching while two elderly, time-worn moor dwellers methodically made their way through the plates of food before them, and I thanked her. She simply nodded, but she did so with a faint pinkness around her neck.

At dinner, Baring-Gould did appear, and afterwards regaled us with stories and songs of this, his native land. We went to bed early and slept well, and the next morning we set off for the moor.

CHAPTER FOUR

The interior consists of rolling upland. It has been likened
to a sea after a storm suddenly arrested and turned to
stone; but a still better resemblance, if not so
romantic, is that of a dust-sheet thrown
over the dining-room chairs.

— A BOOK OF DARTMOOR

A BRIEF HOUR'S TRAMP THROUGH wet woods brought us to the village of Lydford, nestled along a river at the very edge of the moor's rising slopes. There we succumbed to the temptations of the flesh and spent a glorious thirty minutes in front of an inn's blazing fireplace, drinking coffee and steaming our boots. When we shouldered our packs and pushed our way back out into the inhospitable day, it was with the clear sensation of leaving all civilisation behind.

The sensation quickly proved itself justified. Lydford was truly the final outpost of comfort and light, and the moor a grim place indeed. The ground rose and the trees and hedgerows fell away, and the ground rose some more, and all the world was grey and wet and closed-in and utterly still. We climbed nearly a thousand feet in the first two miles, but after that the ground began to level out before us.

It was, as Holmes had said, a huge bowl – or at any rate, what I could see of it seemed to be – a shallow, lumpy green bowl carved across by meandering dry-stone walls, dusted with dying vegetation and dead rocks, with many of its rises topped by weathered stones in bizarre shapes: Tors, the stones were called, and many of them had distinctive names given either by a fancied resemblance to their shapes (Hare, Fox, and Little Hound Tors) or by some reference lost in language (at least, to me) or in time (such as Lough, Ger, and Brat). There were nearly two hundred of the things, Holmes said, their fantastic shapes perched atop the rocky clitter around their disintegrating feet, and below that the low green turf, spongy with the water it held.

In a place where the hand of humankind had so little visible impact, where a person could walk for an hour and see neither person nor dwelling, it seemed only proper that the very stones had names.

We could see perhaps half a mile in any direction, but there was no sky, merely a cloud that brushed the tops of our hats, and the grey-green spongy turf beneath our boots merged imperceptibly into the light grey overhead, the dark grey of the stones that lay scattered about and the brown grey of the autumnal bracken fern. It was the sort of light that renders vision untrustworthy, where the eyes cannot accept the continual lack of stimulus and begin to invent faint wraiths and twisting shadows. Holmes' pixies, waiting to tease the unwary traveller into a mire, no longer seemed so ludicrous, and had it not been for Holmes, I might very well have heard the soft pad of the Baskerville Hound behind me and felt its warm breath on the back of my neck.

However, with Holmes beside me as a talisman, the spooks kept their distance, and what might have been a place of animosity and danger was rendered merely desolate to the point of being grim. I thought that Holmes' term *wasteland* was not inappropriate. *Godforsaken* might also be applied.

The morning stretched on, not without incident, although the time between incidents seemed to be very long indeed. Once, my dulled eyes were surprised to see one of the boulders we were passing turn and look at us – a Dartmoor pony, as shaggy as a winter sheep and only marginally taller. Its eyes peered out from behind its plastered-down forelock, watching us pass before it resumed its head-down stance of stolid endurance, hunkered up against the wind, belly and nose dripping steadily. Holmes said it was most likely a hybrid, crossed with Shetland ponies brought in during the war in an attempt to breed animals suited for the Welsh mines. This particular beast did not seem well pleased with its adopted home.

Once, we came across a weathered, lichen-covered stone cross, erected centuries before to mark the way for pilgrims, now proud in its solitude but starting to lean. One of its arms was missing and the other had been broken to a stump, and its feet were standing in a pool of water.

Once, we saw a fox, picking its delicate way through a sweep of bracken fern, and shortly after that we glimpsed a buzzard making disconsolate circles against the clouds. The high point of the morning was when a startled woodcock burst from beneath our boots and flew from us in terror. The excitement of that encounter, however, did not last long, and soon we were back in the melancholy embrace of the brooding moor.

Up a rise and down the other side, across a rivulet with sharply cut sides and a scurry of clear, peat-stained water in the bottom. Up again, avoiding a piece of granite the size of a bath-tub thrusting out of the rough grass. A meandering ridge on an approaching hill, resembling the work of some huge, prehistoric mole, became on closer examination an ancient stone wall nearly subsumed by the slow encroachment of the turf. A distant sweep of russet across a hillside, a scurf of furze and dying bracken fern, was cut by the dark of another ancient wall drawn along its side.

It was, I supposed, picturesque enough, given the limited palette of drab colours, but as a piece of Impressionist art it served to evoke only the disagreeable feelings of restlessness, melancholia, and a faint thread of menace.

After an hour or so Holmes attempted to smoke, but he could not get his pipe to stay lit. We trudged on, speech and camaraderie left behind us in Lydford, as stolid and enduring as the pony, placing one foot in front of the other on the sparse grass covering the deep, sodden peat beds that passed for soil.

By midday I was as grey and silent as anything else in that bleak place, edgy with an unidentifiable sense of waiting and aching for a spot of colour. Had I known, I might have worn a red pullover, but all my clothes were warm and masculine and dull, and there was no relief from the monotony until Holmes stopped and I walked straight into him. The shock of change nearly caused me to fall, but my irritation died the instant I saw what had caught his interest: a shelter.

It was a rough stone hut, used by shepherds, perhaps – short shepherds, we found, as once inside we both had to keep our heads well tucked down, but it had the better part of a roof, and even a cracked leather flap to cover most of the doorway. We had no fire other than the glowing bowl of Holmes' pipe, but at least our sandwiches remained dry as we ate them, and the now-tepid coffee in the flask that Mrs Elliott had given us seemed positively festive as it touched my chilled lips. The demons retreated out into the fog, and with their absence, humour crept back in.

'Well, Holmes,' I said, 'I can certainly see why a person would fall in love with Dartmoor.'

'It is said to be quite pleasant in the summer,' he said gloomily.

'By comparison, I'm sure it is. How much farther do we have?'

We did actually have a destination in this trackless waste. We had taken on the role of eyes and legs for Baring-Gould, but even Holmes, who had covered much of this same ground thirty years before, did not have the man's intimate knowledge of the place from which judgements could be drawn. The old man back in Lew Trenchard might instantly visualise the lie of the land at any given spot on the map, but his representatives needed to walk it first. Hence our expedition, and if the weather was not as we might wish, it did not appear that waiting for a clear day was a practical option. For all I knew this was a clear day, for Dartmoor.

Our trip was to be a large circle, putting up at a public house for the night halfway along. We were looking now for the place where the dead tin miner had last been seen, and after that would try to find the spot where in July a benighted farm-hand had been terrified by a ghostly coach and a dog with a glowing eye, and the other place, two miles away and a month further on, where the courting couple had been rudely interrupted by the same coach.

I finished my apple, Holmes knocked out his pipe and stowed it and we both settled our hats more firmly over our noses and ducked out of the leather doorway.

'Holmes,' I said, raising my collar and resuming the hunched-over walking position that was necessary in order to keep the rain off my spectacles. 'If Lady Howard stops her ghostly carriage to offer us a ride, I for one will accept. With pleasure.'

Josiah Gorton's last known path told us nothing whatsoever. Other than being one remote area among 350 square miles of remote countryside, there was nothing to distinguish it. According to Baring-Gould, the farm labourer who stopped to talk with Gorton lived over the hill and often travelled that way of a Saturday night, on his way to the inn where Gorton had spent the afternoon.

'Why, if he'd been snug inside all afternoon, did Gorton leave?' I asked. 'I'd have thought Saturday evening the high point of the week, particularly for someone accustomed to cadging drinks.'

'According to the publican when I was through here the other day, Gorton said he had business to attend to, unlikely as that might sound. No need to enquire further at the inn.' And so saying he turned, not in the direction of the inn, but towards the remote farm over the hill. Stifling a sigh, I followed.

It was a small farm-stead, mossy and pinched and cowering down into the hillside away from the elements.

'A place this size couldn't have more than one hired man.' Holmes observed, heading for the barn. There we found him, a young man with a head like a furry turnip, scratching the broad, flat expanse of it beneath his cap and pursing his lips as he stood staring down at a prostrate cow.

He glanced at us incuriously, as if we were oft-seen residents of the place rather than that rarity, the unexpected visitor, and then returned immediately to his perusal of the huge, heaving sides of the animal at his feet.

'I doan s'pose you knaw how ta turn a calf,' were his first words to us.

'Er, no,' Holmes admitted. 'Unless?' He turned to me, and the young man looked up in hope.

'No,' I said firmly. 'Sorry.'

His face fell back into its morose state. 'I can't do'n. I tried an' tried, but my hand, she just gets squeezed and dies. Poor ole cow,' he said with unexpected affection. 'Her'll just have to bide 'til Doctor gets here, that's all. He'll charge me half what the calf be worth,' he added. Long, contemplative seconds ticked by before he looked up, realising at last that he was not conversing with family members or two spirits of the moor. He asked, 'Be ye lost?'

'I do not believe we are,' said Holmes. 'Not if you're Harry Cleave.'

'That I am.' He put out a meaty hand that had all too obviously been but lightly sluiced since its last exploration of the cow's birth canal, and with only the briefest of hesitations, Holmes shook it. I left my own gloved hands firmly in my pockets, and instead smiled widely and nodded like a fool as introductions were made.

'Well,' said Cleave, 'no sense maundering, baint nothing I can do 'til Doctor comes. I sent the lil maid to vetch 'en,' he explained, 'when I seed how she lay. Let us go by the house and 'ave a cup.'

Paradise and ambrosia were the words he had uttered, and we crowded his heels across the muddy yard to the low stone farm-house.

It was warm inside, from a peat fire burning low and red in the wide stone fireplace. I removed my glasses and could see little, but my cold-shrivelled skin began tentatively to unfold, and my nose told me of a soup on the fire and fragrant herbs strewn underfoot. I patted my way to a bench near the fireplace and settled in for what I sincerely hoped was to be a long and leisurely visit.

The tea Cleave made for us was fresh and powerful and sweetened as a matter of course by our host; what was more, he had cleansed his hands with soap before making it. I removed a layer of clothing, resumed my warmed spectacles, and examined the room and the young man, wondering if both were typical of the moor.

Cleave was a quiet, self-contained figure, short but heavily muscled. His dark eyes shone with an intelligent interest, and humour lurked ready at their corners. His easy authority over the house and its furnishings spoke more of an owner than a hired man, and I thought the simple room, light and tidy, suited him well.

'So,' he said, settling himself at a scrubbed wooden table with his own teacup. 'You corned out auver th' moor for ta vine 'Arry Cleave, and naow you've vound 'n.'

I expected Holmes to follow his standard routine for such investigations, particularly useful in gossipy rural areas, which was to invent some piece of spectacular flimflam behind which he could hide his real purpose. I had even settled back in anticipation to watch the expert, but to my utter astonishment he instead chose to use the simple truth.

'I'm a friend of the Reverend Sabine Baring-Gould. He asked me to look into Josiah Gorton's death.'

At the first name, Cleave's humour bloomed full across his face in surprise and wholehearted approval. It dimmed somewhat at the second name, but he left that for the moment.

'The Squire, by Gar. How is he?'

'Old. Tired, and not very well.'

'Yair,' Cleave agreed sadly. 'That he must be, poor ole beggar. He were old when I 'as a child, and used to come across him digging his 'oles or writin' down zongs. Fey old fellow. I remember thinking once, he looked like God in Paradise, "walkin' in the garden at the end of the day." Proud and amused. So, he wants to knaw what happened to ole Josiah, mmm?'

'Yes,' said Holmes. 'Yes, he does.'

'And his legs won't carry him no more, is it? Pity, that. It's been a mort of years since he's been up the moor. Still, he'd be inter'sted, acourse. Wisht I could tell you what you want to knaw, but all I knaw is, Josiah was a-makin' 'is way out along Hew Down on the Sattiday night, we exchanged a word or two, and we both went our ways. I never saw nothin' like this "ghostly carridge" they be talkin' of. Nothin' 'tall.'

'What did Gorton say to you?'

"Tweren't nothin' much. Just "Evening" and a word on the weather, which were thundery and low and lookin' to spit down but wasn't yet, and I offered him the barn if he needed a roof, but he said no, and "Wish 'ee well" it was.'

'Did he say he had a place to stay? I shouldn't think there are many farms in that direction.'

"Fore dark he'd only have made it to Drake Hill, but he didnal, Drake hisself told me.'

'And after dark?'

''Tweren't no moon to speak of, and he wasn't carrying a lantern, but I s'pose I thought he was heading for one of his old mines. There's some still have buildings you could shelter in, if you wasn't too particular. That's right, that's what I figgered, because he said he would'n take my barn, he was lookin' to earn hisself a week's beer money.'

'His precise words?'

'Near 'nough. Zomething about buyin' me a pint when next he seed me. Any row, he liked 'is zecrets and his findings, did Josiah, so I leaved 'im to it.'

'Did he often buy you a drink?'

'Never in mortal memory.'

'Interesting.'

''E were a good'n, were Josiah. Kept hisself to hisself, 'side from zingin' all they ole zongs over 'is ale, but 'e 'ad 'is pride, and look as 'e might like a gipsy, 'e were as honest as the day be long. An' though he liked to keep to hisself, he were willin' to help out, in a pinch. The maid took ill one year just at the height of lambin' and ole Josiah nursed 'er for two days 'til she were hersel' again. A good man, that. He'll be missed.'

As a eulogy, one could do far worse.

We drank more tea, and Holmes questioned him further about the precise location and directions he and Gorton had taken. When a commotion sounded out in the yard and a girl of perhaps twelve burst in, Holmes allowed the farmer to return to his cow and the veterinarian, and before we could be pressed into surgical assistance to a bovine midwife, we took our leave.

A half hour brought us to the place where Cleave had seen Gorton, and another forty minutes to the Drake farm. It was down in a valley bottom, and we stood on the rise looking down at it. A more dismal site, or a more disreputable set of buildings, would have been hard to imagine. Even the trickle of smoke from the lopsided chimney seemed dirtier than usual.

To my surprise, Holmes turned his back on the farm and began to survey the ground that fell away from our hillock on all sides.

'Aren't we going down there?' I asked him.

'Gould thought it unnecessary. Unless Drake himself did away with Gorton, he would have no reason to lie about not seeing him, and according to Gould, Drake hasn't the wits to build a wall, much less arrange for a clever murder. And you'll have to admit, a man who can't bother to keep his chimney clean and is willing to live in the undoubtedly foul atmosphere that exists inside that house down there is hardly likely to go to the inconvenience of hauling a body to the other side of the moor. He'd be more inclined just to toss it down a nearby hole. Come.'

I stared at his back as he descended the hill away from the Drake farm. '*Gould* thought – Holmes!' I protested. 'When did you start accepting the conclusions of a total amateur instead of seeing for yourself?'

He turned and gave me an unreadable look. 'When I found an amateur who knew his ground better than I knew London. I told you, Russell, he was my local informant.'

It sounded to me as if the good Reverend Sabine was something more than that, but I could not begin to guess what.

We wandered back and forth across the landscape like a pair of tin seekers, climbing down to examine every low-lying place and stream-bed, stubbing our toes, twisting our ankles, and breaking our fingernails on the stones, catching our clothing on the gorse bushes, and developing cricks in our necks from the hunch-shouldered position adopted in the vain attempt to keep the rain from our collars. The wind began to rise, which dispersed the lower clouds but chilled me more than the rain had, and made it nearly impossible to avoid the increasingly near-horizontal drops. Dusk was gathering when I looked up from my regular occupation of scraping the sides of my muddy boots against a rock, and found Holmes gone. He had been there a minute before, so I knew he could not have gone far, but it was disconcerting to feel even for an instant that I was alone in that desolation. I called, but the wind snatched my words from my lips, then blinded me by driving the rain into my face. I made myself stop, and think.

After a minute I wiped the worst of the rain from my spectacles, and studied the land around me before making my way back to where I had last seen Holmes. Looking down into a deep, sharp-sided ravine with its complement of peat-brown water at the bottom, I saw his back disappearing around a bend. I called, but he did not hear me, so I was forced to follow him along the top of the ground; when he set off up a branch of the ravine I was obliged to scramble down into the depths as well.

I panted up to him some time later, and tried to catch my breath before I addressed him. 'We're not going to reach the inn before nightfall,' I observed casually. It was easier to talk out of the wind, and one could even find patches of rain-shadow against the sides of the ravine.

'No.'

'Nor are we sleeping in the Drake barn.'

'I fervently hope not.'

'You're looking for Gorton's shelter?' I ventured.

'Of course. Ah.' This last was at a scuff on a stone half grown over with turf, a scuff such as a rough-shod man might have made some months before. It might as easily have been made by a hundred other things, but there was little point in mentioning this to Holmes: He was off like a hound on a scent, and I could only follow in his wake and see where we might end up.

Where we ended up was a heap of rubble piled between a stream and one wall of the low ravine that the water had cut over the millennia. I could see nothing there but a heap of stones, albeit an orderly heap; however, Holmes walked up to it, walked around it, and vanished. I waited until he emerged, looking satisfied and standing back in order to study the adjoining walls of the little ravine.

'When Watson wrote up the Baskerville story,' he told me, 'he had me living on the moor in a prehistoric stone hut. Actual Neolithic dwellings, of course, have long been collapsed and cannibalised by farmers, until they are marked by little more than rough circles on the ground. A person might, conceivably, lie down flat beneath the height of the remaining walls, but as any roof they once had disintegrated a thousand years ago, there would be little benefit.

'What Watson meant, although it sounds less romantic, was one of these, a tin miner's hut – or in this case, to be precise, a blowing house, judging by the remnants of the furnace in that wall and the broken mould-stone that now forms the doorstep. Considerably more recent construction than the neolithic, as you can see.' During the course of this informative little lecture he had begun to climb up what my eyes were only now beginning to read as a man-made ruin rather than a natural rock-slide, and he now paused, balancing precariously on a pair of shaky stones, to reach with both arms into an indentation in the ravine wall. He tugged at something, which emerged as a much-dented bucket; hugging it to his chest, he leapt lightly down. 'Peat,' he said, and ducked again inside the pile of rock. This time I followed, into a room which was larger than appeared likely from outside, and had indeed once been a living space. 'You intend to pass the night here,' I said, not as a question, for Holmes was already laying a fire with the dry peat turves.

'If there are signs left of Gorton's disappearance, we shall see them in the morning,' he said placidly.

I stared into the thought of the long, hungry night ahead of me, and thought, Oh well; at least we shall be out of the rain, and reasonably warm.

I had, in fact, underestimated Holmes, or at any rate his preference for some degree of comfort. He pulled from his knapsack a second parcel of food, thick beef and mustard sandwiches and boiled eggs, and followed the meal with coffee brewed in a tin cup, which also served as the shared drinking vessel. We wrapped ourselves in our garments, and prepared to sleep. Holmes was soon asleep, his snores barely audible over the sound of the storm, but I was kept awake by the eerie sob and moan of the wind, like a lost child outside our stone hut, and the low gurgle of running water, sounding like a half-heard conversation; once I started awake from a doze with the absolute certainty that there were eyes watching me from the entrance. I was very grateful that night for the presence of Holmes, as sensible as a jolt of cold water even when he was sleeping, and eventually I grew accustomed to the peculiar noises, or they faded, and I slept.

In the morning we drank more peat-smoke-flavoured coffee, although there was nothing more solid to chew on than the grounds in the bottom of the cup. Holmes downed the first tin cup of coffee and ducked out of the hut as soon as it was light outside. I took my time manufacturing a cup of coffee for myself, since I could hear the rain continuing to drip off the stones and into the stream. What Holmes thought he could find out there, after weeks of rain, I could not imagine, and I had no intention of going to investigate any sooner than I had to. I brought the water to a boil, shook some ground coffee into the cup, stirred it with the stub of a pencil I had in my shirt pocket, and sat on my heels to drink it, straining it through my front teeth. Why was it, I reflected irritably, that Holmes' little adventures never took us to luxury hotels in the south of France, or to warm, sandy Caribbean beaches?

Holmes returned in three-quarters of an hour, looking smug. I poured the last of the grounds into the cup of water I had been keeping hot, stirred it, and handed it to him. He pulled off his gloves, cupped both hands around the cup, and drank cautiously.

'Had I known I should be called on to make Turkish coffee,' I said, 'I would have asked Mahmoud for lessons.' He grunted, and drank, and when the cup was empty he tapped out the grounds and filled it a last time to heat water for the ritual of shaving, sans mirror. He nicked himself twice.

'I take it you found nothing,' I said as I helped him daub the leaks.

'On the contrary, I made a very interesting discovery. Unfortunately, I cannot see what possible bearing it might have on the case.'

'What did you find?'

He reached into an inner pocket and drew out a small, stoppered bottle such as the chemist dispenses, dirty but dry.

'I found it in his "smuggler's hole", the traditional turf-covered cache the old miners used to hide their valuables. From the appearance of the stones he used to disguise the opening, I should say it has sat there undisturbed for more than a month but considerably less than a year.'

I took the phial and gently eased out the cork with my fingernails. There seemed to be a tiny quantity of fine gravel in the bottom the size of a generous pinch. I cupped my right hand and upended the bottle, then stared at the substance in my hand in disbelief.

'Can that possibly be – gold?'

CHAPTER FIVE

Among semi-barbarous tribes it is customary that the tribe
should have its place of assembly and consultation, and
this is marked round by either stones or
posts set up in the ground.
— A BOOK OF DARTMOOR

WITH THE HELP OF a torn-off corner of the map to make a funnel, we eased the gleaming specks back into their bottle. Holmes examined my palm closely, picked a couple of stray bits from their lodging place, and returned them to the bottle. Pushing the cork firmly into place, he slipped it into his pocket.

'It is an interesting substance for a tin miner to have in his possession, wouldn't you agree?' he asked.

'Particularly in that form. I would understand a gold ring he had found, or a coin from an ancient trove, but flakes? Surely there isn't gold on Dartmoor?'

'Not that I have ever heard. Perhaps I shall send this in for analysis, to see if chemical tests give us any indication of its provenance.'

'But gold is an element. There won't be any distinguishing features, will there?'

'It depends on how pure it is, if this soil is a recent addition or the ore in which the gold came to life. Impurities differ, if this is in its raw state.'

'There was nothing else in the cache?'

'A few knobs of tin and some tools. I left them there.'

'So,' I said with an air of moving on, 'where next?'

'North-west is where the farm-hand saw Lady Howard's coach; south-east is the place it was seen by Gould's courting couple. We'll start at the top and work down.'

Packing to leave our night's lodging was a matter of getting to our feet and buttoning on our waterproofs. We did so, and clambered up the slippery side of the ravine to the floor of the moor itself. There Holmes paused.

'One thing, Russell. Where we're going is a rather nasty piece of terrain. You must watch where you put your feet.'

'"The Great Grimpen Mire", Holmes?' I asked lightly, a reference to the sucking depths that had apparently taken the life of the villain Stapleton, after he failed to murder his cousin and legitimate heir to the Baskerville estate, Holmes' client Sir Henry.

'That's a bit farther south, but similar, yes. There are mires, bogs, and "feather-beds" or quaking bogs. With the first two, look for the tussocks of heavy grass or rushes around the edges, which offer a relatively firm footing, but if you see a stretch of bright green sphagnum moss, for God's sake stay away from it. The moss is a mat covering a pit of wet ooze; if one slips in under the mat, it would be a bit like laying a sodden feather-bed on top of a swimmer. Not a pleasant death.'

It was, I agreed, a gruesome picture. 'What does one do then?'

'Not much, except spread your arms to give the greatest possible surface to the ooze, and wait for help. Struggling is invariably fatal, as any number of Dartmoor ponies have found. With their typical dark humour, the natives call the mires "Dartmoor Stables".

'Other than the quaking bogs, the chief danger is from the elements. At night or when the mist comes down, depend on the compass or, lacking that, find a stream and follow it down. All water comes off the moor eventually, and reaches people.'

'Thank you, Holmes. And if I find myself going in circles, I'm to turn my coat inside out to keep the pixies from leading me astray.'

He bared his teeth at me in a grin. 'It couldn't hurt.'

Baring-Gould had marked with great precision the place on the map where the ghostly carriage had appeared, and an hour or so later Holmes and I stood more or less on the spot. It was difficult to be certain because the rain (to Holmes' great irritation) had immediately washed the ink from the surface of the map, leaving us with a small dark cloud instead of an X. Holmes began to walk slowly along the path, studying the spongy, short-cropped turf for the months-old marks of carriage wheels.

Quite hopeless, really, and after a couple of painstaking hours he finally admitted that there was little to distinguish the hoof and wheel of a carriage (both, presumably, iron-shod) from the naked hoof of any of a myriad of wandering Dartmoor ponies or the drag of a sledge or farm cart, at any rate not after a two-month interval.

Holmes straightened his spine slowly and stood for a while gazing up at the surrounding hills, several of which were crowned with the fantastical shapes of tors. The track we were on, unpaved and without gravel or metalling, was nonetheless flat and wide enough for a cart, and largely free of stones – which was enough to make it noteworthy – and of bracken, which made it visible against the brown hillside. It emerged from the side of one tor-capped hillock, wrapped around its side for a gently curving half mile or so, and then rose slightly to disappear at the foot of another tor, vaguely in the direction of Okehampton to the north-west.

'It does look like a road, Holmes. Or as if it had once been a road.'

'There are a surprising number of tracks across the moor, dating to the period when goods were moved by packhorse and the lanes of the countryside below were a morass of mud between the hedgerows all winter. Sailors used them, too, as a shortcut between putting in at a port on one coast and searching for the next job on the other.'

'Those lanes must have been truly horrendous if travel on the moor was seen as the easier alternative.'

'Indeed. I believe that this particular remnant is the continuation of Cut Lane, which intersects Drift Lane near Postbridge and joins with the ancient main track from the central portion of the moor to Lydford, Lych Way.'

'Cheerful name,' I commented. 'Lych' was the Old English word for corpse – hence the roofed-over lych gate outside most churches, for the temporary resting of the bier (and its bearers) on the way into the graveyard. I trusted that Holmes, a long-time student of linguistic oddities, would know this.

'Not by coincidence,' Holmes replied. 'The Lych Way was the traditional track by which corpses were carried to Lydford for burial.'

'Good heavens. Do you mean to say there are no churchyards on the entire moor?'

'Not until the year 1260, I believe it was, when the bishop granted the moor dwellers the option of taking their dead to Widdecombe instead.'

'Generous of him.'

'Interestingly enough, archaeologists find few burial remains other than burnt scraps of bone. I suppose that either the peat soil is so acidic that it dissolves even the heavy bones with time, or else when the turf alternately dries in the summers and becomes saturated in winter its contraction and expansion eventually pushes the bones up to the surface, where the wildlife finds them and hastens their dissolution. The two hypotheses would make for some interesting experiments,' he mused.

'Wouldn't they just? I tremble to think what the "cut" in Cut Lane refers to.'

'A passage dug into the hillside to make the transport of peat easier; nothing more sinister than that. This particular track wends its way along several peat diggings, although it is now in disuse because what peat is still taken off the moor goes by way of the train line just west of here. The track as it is would be quite sufficient to take a well-balanced carriage pulled by one or two horses – though not, perhaps, at any great speed.'

The thought of that ride made my teeth ache – or perhaps it was only that they were clenched hard against the cold. This local colour was all very interesting, but I thought it time to bring up one of the more essential matters at hand.

'Holmes, had you planned on taking a meal in the near future? How far is the nearest inn?'

'Oh, miles away,' he said absently. 'But there is sure to be a farmwife willing to sell us a bowl of soup. However, Russell, I must say I like not the looks of the weather.'

At first glance, the sky appeared just as it had since we first trudged up the hill out of Lydford, glowering and grey. Taking a more attentive look, however, it occurred to me that what I had taken as the commonplace annoyance of moisture condensing on my spectacles was in truth much more widespread and foreboding: wisps of mist were rising up out of the land and coalescing around us.

Muttering dire maledictions at himself, Holmes set off rapidly downhill at an angle away from the worst of it, and I hastened to keep up with him. The strategy worked for perhaps twenty minutes, after which the moor laid its soft grey hands around us and we stood blind.

'Holmes?' I called, determined not to panic.

'Damnation,' he said succinctly.

'I can't see, Holmes.'

'Of course you can't see, Russell,' he said peevishly. 'We're in a fog.' I was relieved, however, to hear his voice begin to come closer. I began to talk, as a sort of audial beacon to bring him in.

'I don't suppose you can do your blind man's trick of finding your way across the moor as you can across London?'

'Hardly,' he said, nice and near now. There was even a dim, dark shape from which the voice seemed to emanate. 'Do you have your compass?'

'And a map,' I said, shrugging off my knapsack to get out the latter. 'Perhaps if I brought it up to touch my nose, I might even read it. You know, Holmes, I wouldn't want you to think that I don't appreciate these connubial efforts of yours; you must work very hard to invent little projects we can share. However, must you always take things to such an extreme?'

I stood upright with the map in my hand and the knapsack securely on my foot, and it seemed to me that where the reassuring dark shape had been, there was only unrelieved grey. 'Holmes?' I asked nervously. There was only silence.

'Holmes!' I said sharply.

'Quiet, Russell,' said a voice from behind me. 'I am attempting to hear.'

Had I moved, or had he? And what could he be listening to? I strained for a sound, any sound, even the unearthly banshee noises of the night before, but all I heard was the vague and omnipresent trickling of water, and then the sound of footsteps: retreating footsteps.

'Where are you going, Holmes?' I demanded.

'Just up the rise here to listen. Don't lose the knapsack.'

I felt around for the pack, which indeed was no longer weighting down my boot, and when I found it I made haste to put it on.

I waited, fog-blind and abandoned, and amused myself by inventing spectres. Baring-Gould's church grims were not too likely out here, perhaps, given that we were far from either Lydford or the 'modern', i.e., thirteenth-century alternative churchyard at Widdecombe, but bahrghests seemed just the sort of creatures one might expect to occupy the shifting monochrome on all sides. What of the long-legged Old Stripe? And what was the other spectre Baring-Gould had mentioned? A jacky-twoad? Perhaps there would not be one of those – but if I were to hear anything remotely resembling the footsteps of a gigantic hound, I knew that I should run away shrieking, easy prey for the tricks of the pixies. Fog invariably makes a rich spawning-bed for wraiths and threats and the malevolent eyes of watching foes, but that Dartmoor fog, combined as it was with the very real dangers of mire and boulder and sharp-sided stream, was one of the most fertile sources of spooks and mind-goblins that I have known.

I could not have stood in my position for more than six or seven minutes, but that was quite enough for the internal quaking to reach a point far beyond that which the cold, wet air would explain. Theoretically, I suppose, we could have simply sat and out waited the fog; even on Dartmoor it must lift sometime. I knew, however, that it would not be possible to remain there for any length of time without being scarred by the experience, because I had no doubt now that Dartmoor was alive, as Baring-Gould and later Holmes himself had intimated, alive and aware and quite able to look after itself against possible invaders.

It was very hard work to keep quiet when I heard the approaching slop of Holmes' boots, but I forced myself to do so. However, I could not entirely control my voice when I answered his call of 'Russell?'

'Here, Holmes,' I quavered.

'I believe we will find a farm-house just over the next hill. I can hear a cow and some chickens.'

'I still can't see, Holmes.'

'Nor can I, Russell. Still, I suppose we'll manage. Give me your hand.'

Willingly, I did so, and followed him through the unseen landscape.

We might have made faster time on our hands and knees but our pride and the sodden state of the ground kept us from it. The cold breath of the moor pressed in on us like the tool of a deliberate and watchful living thing, trapping us, trying us, seeing if it could force us to break and run madly to our destruction. Had I not possessed Holmes' hand, the god Pan might have taken me, leading me astray to the trickling sound of his pipe.

Little more than a mile it was, but for almost an hour we stumbled through the gloom, visited occasionally by the sharp terror of a looming figure, which would turn out to be a standing stone, grey and lugubrious, or a fence post, indistinguishable from the monument. The final of these came after we had found a wall and were patting our way separately and at a greater speed. Abruptly out of the murk there emerged the stark outline of a soul in torment: a thin figure as tall as a man, stubby arms outstretched, head thrown back in a frozen shriek to the heavens. My heart gave a great thud inside my chest, and settled down to a fast thumping only when I realised that I was looking at a moorland cross. Holmes could hardly have missed my gasp, but he said nothing, only the welcome words a moment later, 'I believe this is the gate to the farmyard.'

Such proved to be the case, when we approached a tiny, heavily lichened stone building in a hollow of ground. We had even timed it well, because the farmer and his hired man were at the table for their noonday dinner. The farmwife was startled to see us approach her door, but she soon rallied, explaining that she was quite used to the odd informal guest, although it was rare to see a rambler outside of the summer months.

I found the delicacy of her unspoken question amusing, particularly as it was couched in a nearly unintelligible dialect and put to us in a tiny, multiple-purpose room already overcrowded with humanity, two dogs, and a basket of newly hatched chicks peeping beside the inglenook fireplace that functioned as kitchen range. Who was she to question the insanity of two outsiders spilling onto her doorstep from out of the fog?

Holmes took off his hat politely, and answered her as she moved around us to fetch two more plates and the necessary cutlery and mugs to go with them.

'We're not exactly here on a holiday stroll, madam. We heard that there was a sighting of Lady Howard's coach not far from here, and we were eager to hear more. You see,' he said, warming to his story and taking his place on the bench and a spoon in his hand, 'we collect odd tales such as that of Lady How—'

There was a sudden gurgling, clicking noise from the inglenook, emerging from what I had thought to be a pile of blankets draped across a chair to dry near the heat. I could make no sense of the sound but it silenced everyone in the room, including Holmes. The two men and the farmwife all turned to stare at Holmes, and I saw with astonishment the look of chagrin spreading across his face.

'What was that?' I demanded. 'I didn't hear.'

'He – or she, I beg your pardon,' he said to the tiny huddled figure, and started anew. 'To translate, the remark was made, and I quote, "By Gar, who is it but Znoop Zherlock?" "Snoop Sherlock" was, I ought to explain, the nickname given me by the moor dwellers during the Baskerville case. We have here one of the older residents, evidently, who remembers me.' He extricated his long legs from the bench and went over to the pile of blankets, extending his hand towards it. A small, gnarled paw appeared, followed by another burst of unintelligible speech – badly distorted, I diagnosed, by a complete lack of teeth, but still of such a heavy dialectical peculiarity as to constitute a separate language. I had thought Harry Cleave possessed an accent; I was mistaken. In fact, I shall not even attempt to transcribe the words as they were spoken, since an alphabet soup such as 'Yar! Me luwers, you mun vale leery, you cain't a' 'ated since bevower the foggy comed' makes for laborious, if picturesque, reading.

At first hearing, the speech was beyond me, although Holmes seemed to follow the sense of it readily enough. I merely applied myself to the hot, simple food that was put before me, and drank the cider in my mug. The talk washed over me, and as the pangs of cold and hunger subsided, I slowly began to make sense of what was being said.

The folk in this isolated farm-stead were indeed aware of Lady Howard's coach, and did not like it one bit. The first witness to the apparition, back in July, had actually been a friend of the young farm-hand's second cousin, and Holmes made haste to interrogate the farm-hand as to the whereabouts of his second cousin's friend, whose euphonious name was Johnny Trelawny. It appeared, however, that Trelawny had fled the moor, despite being known far and wide as a brave man, a man indeed formerly thought fearless, who had done his service on the Western Front and to whom the occasional brawl was not unknown. There was no consideration that the intense teasing he had received during the month he remained the sole witness to Lady Howard's coach might be a contributing factor to Trelawny's disinclination to stay on the moor, and when Holmes enquired as to the man's employment, and was told that Johnny had lost his job after assaulting his employer (a known wag who came up to his employee in the pub and presented him with a tiny newborn puppy, asking if Trelawny thought it had been fathered by Lady Howard's hound), it seemed to me that fear was not perhaps the chief contributing factor in the man's departure. When Holmes ventured to suggest this alternate explanation, it was considered, and rejected. No, moor dwellers in general were staying away from the north-western quarter of the moor, certainly at night. Johnny Trelawny would be no exception.

Holmes succeeded in drawing out roughly the date when Trelawny had seen this vision, establishing that it was probably the Tuesday or Wednesday before the full moon. However, when he tried to find where Trelawny had gone, the only point on which the family agreed was that the lad would not have gone back to his family home in Cornwall, due to a long-standing feud with an uncle. Exeter, the farm-hand thought. Portsmouth, the farmwife suggested, and then used the opportunity to begin her own tale of another lad who had got a girl in trouble and run off as far as London, but the girl's father had taken his savings out of the jar in the woodshed to buy himself a train ticket, and as he set off across the moor on a dark night . . .

Stories tumbled out as the cider jug went around and the relief of confession began to be felt. Voices crossed and were raised and crossed again, with the constant running commentary of the toothless figure in the corner making a rhythm like a waterfall for the rest to talk over. Holmes had no difficulty in steering the tales towards the occult and the unusual, and out of the welter of sounds I received clear images and phrases, chief among which was a regular repetition of the phrase, 'a coorius sarcumstance', pronounced each time with a shake of the head.

I had to agree, some of the circumstances they described were 'coorius' indeed; in fact, I should have said they were highly unlikely. The black dogs and the mysteriously dead sheep any student of the supernatural might have expected, along with the standard two-headed foals and the infertile clutches of eggs, but the eagle carrying off a grown ewe made me raise an eyebrow, and when the farmwife swore that a bolt of lightning had shaken the earth and knocked one of her best plates from its perch, I closed my ears and reached for the board of gorgeous yellow cheese to accompany what I decided had to be my final glass of 'zyder': England simply did not have earthquakes, not even in Dartmoor.

'Snoop Sherlock' valiantly listened to it all, trying hard to shape the conflicting narratives into hard fact of places and dates, contributing the odd remark and trying hard to deflect the inevitable spate of Baskerville reminiscences from the aged figure in the blankets. He finally brought the Babel to a close by the desperate measure of pulling out his watch and exclaiming theatrically over the passage of time, looking pointedly at the window and declaring that the fog seemed to have cleared, and finally standing up to leave (dealing his head a mighty crack on the low roof beam). We paid generously for the food, caught up our rucksacks, and made our escape, with the farmwife's thanks and the old woman's voice following us out of the door and across the weedy yard.

I quickly realised that having the fog clear on Dartmoor meant a transformation into rain. Uncomfortable, but infinitely better than the fog.

We took greater care to avoid total immersion in our next interviews, but we need not have worried. Of the courting couple who had later seen the coach and its dog, the girl refused to say anything, just burst into melodramatic tears and collapsed into the arms of a handsome young man. We were led to understand, moreover, that this young man was not the same beau with whom she had been the night of the apparition, and in the course of ascertaining the whereabouts of the former suitor (the one whom Baring-Gould had referred to as 'stolid and unimaginative') we nearly came to blows with the current gentleman.

The rejected suitor, Thomas Westaway, lived two miles off and was happy enough to interrupt his labours on a stone wall in exchange for some silver. Avoiding as best he could the touchy issue of Westaway's erstwhile ladylove, Holmes questioned him closely as to the precise location and times of the sighting.

The first query was settled by the lad pulling a piece of sacking cloth over his shoulders and leading us down the lane, over a stile (not a wooden contraption, merely lengths of stone protruding from the wall to form crude steps) and across a field. Built against the farther wall was a low shed, providing a sheltered feeding place for animals – and, no doubt, a sheltered private place for people. Baring-Gould's analysis of the situation was remarkably accurate, I thought.

On the other side of the wall was a flat track, similar in shape and wear to the track we had seen at the first site, either a part of the same road or a branch leading to it.

'This is where you saw the coach, is it?' Holmes asked, leaning against the wall and taking out his pipe and tobacco.

'Right here,' young Westaway agreed. 'Us heerd'y there, stood up and saw'n there, and seed 'er go by not forty feet off.'

'You saw a woman inside, then?' I asked.

'Didn't see no one. It were fair dark inside the box.'

'But you said—'

Holmes interrupted my protest. 'I believe you'll find that the pronoun refers to the coach itself, Russell, not its occupant. Devonshire speech uses a creative approach to the gender of its pronouns.'

'I seed her, I did, glowin' white with the bones of 'er vour 'usbands.'

'Of course,' said Holmes. 'You say the carriage followed the track up and around the hill?'

'Oh yes. A course, we baint 'zackly seed 'er go, bein' halfway to th' house and all.'

'Because of the dog?'

The lad had gone pale, and now swallowed hard. 'He were there, afore thicky gert stone there. He just standed and stared at us, and whined like he wanted to come over the wall at us, bevore the driver whistled him on. That's when we ran.'

'Were there any other noises, voices perhaps?'

'Just the harnesses clatterin' and thicky whistle. An' the growl.'

'Growl?'

'Sort of a hiss, or maybe a rattle.'

'From the dog?'

'I z'pose,' he said dubiously. 'He just sort a' corned with th' carriage.'

Holmes thought it over before deciding not to press further with the hissing, rattling growl.

'And the horses?'

'Dark, they was,' the lad said promptly.

'Could you see whether there was one, or two?'

'Didn't see they a'tall.'

'Then how did you know what colour they were?' Holmes asked with remarkable patience.

'Because I couldn't see they, is how I knew they was dark.' It made sense to me, although for some reason, Holmes seemed to think the lad's logic less than impeccable. 'Heered the harnesses a-jangling something mad, though, zo there may've been two, even more.'

'But you did see the dog. It was light enough?'

'The moon were up, I saw her fine.'

'What time did you two come up here?'

'Just past evening chores, us . . .' He saw his slip too late, and looked, away. 'The moon waddn' all that high, I reckon. It must've been still light, stays light late come August.'

'You came up here while it was still light, but the moon was up when you left,' Holmes said, completely ignoring his witness's attempt to save face.

'I z'pose. We come to talkin', you know?'

'I understand.'

The lad looked hard at Holmes, ready to climb on his dignity and ride away at the least sign of humour or criticism, but the expression on Holmes' face was merely blandly expectant.

'I z'pose it was three, four hours altogether,' he admitted. 'We corned up like I zaid, after evening chores, and it were vull dark when we got back. 'Cept for the moon, of course.'

'Where was the moon in the sky, when you looked over the wall and saw the dog?'

Our witness stood for a long moment, his face twisted in thought, before his hand went up to a point on the horizon. 'There, more or less. It were a day or two past vull, but very bright, and it was a remarkable clear night. We'd been talking about all the ztars,' he reminisced, and then ducked his head, blushing furiously.

We carefully did not see his discomfiture, but busied ourselves with climbing over the loosely laid stone wall to the track on the other side. There were no canine footprints to be seen; however, thirty yards up the hill we found a protruding boulder, one edge of which had been scraped to raw cleanness by a sharp edge. Holmes fingered it, and looked up at the farmer's lad.

'Has anyone been riding along here in the last months on a shod horse?'

'Why, no zur. Not that I know. A course, there's no telling what vurriners will get up to, in the summers.'

'True,' Holmes said, brushing off his hands. 'It would have been nice to know that we're dealing with an actual, iron-shod horse rather than a ghostly emanation. Spectral apparitions are the devil's own objects to lay hands upon. Still, I thank you for your time,' he said, before the lad could puzzle over his remark, and then he shook hands with the boy and gave him another coin. But before we parted, he gave the young man something else as well.

'Look, lad,' he said confidentially. 'I shouldn't worry too much about the girl. Best to find out now how undependable she is, instead of later, when there are children underfoot. No, you look around for a woman with brains and spirit. You'll never be bored.' He clapped the boy hard on the back and walked off; it would have been hard to say whether the lad or myself was the more nonplussed.

It was by now late afternoon, and although in the still-long days of August we might just have reached Lew Trenchard before darkness fell, we should certainly never do so on an already dim October's day. We made for the nearest inn, which Holmes said was in the hamlet of Two Bridges.

We passed a number of prehistoric settlements, now mere grass-grown foundations of the original circular huts, and picked our way over three streams. The fourth we followed downstream rather than cross, and entered into an extraordinarily weird area, a long strip of strewn boulders and stunted oaks that seemed to writhe in the half-light of the approaching evening.

'Odd to see trees again,' I commented, more to hear a voice than from any real need to communicate.

'A fey sort of place, isn't it? Wistman's Wood, it's called, which is either the corruption of a Celtic name meaning something along the lines of "rocky woods along the water" or else the corruption of a Saxon term for "foreigners", indicating it was a Celtic wood, which in turn may be supported by the name "Welshman's Wood" that some of the old people still use. You may take your choice of corruptions. Ah,' he said, as we emerged from the wood, 'nearly there.'

Along the river and past a farmyard, and indeed we were nearly there – but not before the most extraordinary thing we had seen all day passed in front of our eyes. Indeed, it nearly ran us down, as we stepped confidently out onto the black surface of an actual macadamised road, only to leap back aghast into the safety of the walls as a furious black mechanical monstrosity came roaring around the bend straight at us. After two days spent among sheep and standing stones, this reminder of the twentieth century came as a considerable shock.

Chapter Six

I may be mistaken, but it seems to me that cooking done over
a peat fire surpasses cooking at the best club in London. But
it may be that on the moor one relishes a meat in
a manner impossible elsewhere.

— A BOOK OF DARTMOOR

THE INN AT TWO Bridges, on the other hand, when finally we
navigated the dangers of the road and passed beneath the sign
of the Saracen's Head, was more akin to the sheep and the prehistoric
stone circles than it was to the motor car. The air was dense with the
fragrance of dinner and beer, pipe tobacco and long generations of
peat fires, and I immediately felt every cell in my body relax, secure
in the knowledge that my needs would be well cared for.

A smiling boy whisked our disreputable packs upstairs, a smiling
girl invited us to choose between a late service of afternoon tea and
an early service of dinner, or just a quiet glass of something while we
thought about it.

Greedily, I pounced on the offer of tea, asking only that it be
delayed briefly so I might go upstairs and make myself presentable.
Ten minutes later, I trotted back down and found Holmes (who
had somehow contrived to tidy himself with neither bath nor
possessions to hand) seated in a comfortable chair in front of a
glowing fire, one hand holding a cup of tea, the other the remnants

of a scone piled high with clotted cream and jam.

'I thought you didn't like cream and scones, Holmes,' I said mildly, wasting no time to claim the larger of the two remaining on the plate and setting to with cream and jam. Holmes poured me a cup of tea and put the milk jug where I could reach it.

'Very occasionally, after a cold and strenuous day, I welcome a scone with Devonshire cream.'

'Or two.'

'Or two,' he agreed. 'Are you satisfied to stop the night here? I could arrange for a motor to take us to Lew Trenchard, if you would prefer, as our set tasks on the moor are, for the moment, more or less complete. I ought to consult with Gould before we determine our next actions.' So saying, he stretched his legs out to the fire, rested his cup and saucer on the buttons of his waistcoat and half closed his eyes. Somehow, he did not look overanxious to hurry off.

'Is there any need to return tonight?'

'None. And on the contrary,' he said, lowering his voice, 'the public bar might make for an informative evening.'

'Grilling the locals while they're in their cups. Have you no shame?'

The corner of his mouth twitched and he allowed his eyes to shut. I ate my scones and poured out the last of the tea, refused the offered refill of both solid and liquid, and sat staring contentedly into the fire. When my cup was empty, I sighed, and glanced over at the relaxed figure in the next chair.

'Holmes, if that cup isn't empty, you're about to have an unfortunate stain.'

It was not empty, but he drained it, replaced the cup on the tray, and we adjourned to the stronger refreshment and heartier companionship of the public bar.

* * *

The companionship we found went some distance beyond hearty, nearing raucous, and I slept late the following morning in the cloud-soft bed. I woke eventually, and lay staring through one eye at the teacup on the table beside the bed. I could smell the tea, could nearly taste the clean, acrid heat of it scouring the fur off my tongue, but I did not care much for the movement required in transporting cup

'God,' I said, and then: 'Do I remember dancing last night?'

'Briefly,' said Holmes from somewhere across the room.

'God,' I said again, and carefully pulled the bedclothes back up around my head.

We did not make an early start that morning. I am not certain it was even still morning when we left the Saracen's Head behind. I half wished I could leave my own head there, too.

'But I only drank cider, Holmes,' I protested, when a mile of fresh air lay between us and the inn.

'Powerful stuff, Devonshire zyder.' I had thought him untouched by our night of carousing with the natives, but on closer examination I decided that he, too, was moving with a degree more care and deliberation than was normal.

'Did we extract any information from the local inhabitants, though?'

'You don't remember?'

'Holmes.'

'One of the lads told me an interesting tale about his wife's granny, who was alone in her house one night when the rest of the family had not yet returned from a wedding in Lydford, who heard a dog scratching at the door. She is, the boy admitted, very deaf, but her own dog raised such a noise trying to get out of the door it attracted her attention.'

'Now there's a piece of hard evidence,' I said. Sarcasm is a ready companion to a sore head.

'When did you learn to play the tin whistle?' Holmes asked innocently. 'This is a talent you've kept well hidden from me.'

'Oh Lord, I didn't play the tin whistle, did I? Yes, I suppose I did. I was going to surprise you with it someday; I thought it might prove a useful skill the next time we found ourselves disguised as gipsies or something.'

'You did surprise me, and it did come in useful.'

'Did it? I'm glad. How?'

'Do you recall the old smith-turned-motor-mechanic, Jacob Drew? With the full white beard and the red braces?'

'Er, vaguely.' I remembered him not in the least, but I thought I would not admit it.

'He took quite a fancy to you, and came over to tell me while I was trying to tune that wretched excuse for a fiddle that we were not like all the summer trippers, and proceeded to recount some of their madder antics. Such as the pair of Londoners who stopped the night atop Gibbet Hill back in July and came down swearing they'd seen Lady Howard's coach of bones travelling across the moor.'

'You don't say. Well, having met Dartmoor in all its forms, I can well believe in Lady Howard's coach, and in any number of black and ghostly huntsmen and their dogs as well. Where is the delightfully named Gibbet Hill?'

'The other side of Mary Tavy from here. We have to go near it in any case; I thought we might take a look.'

'Sounds a charming place. Are we required to pass the night on its summit?'

'I think not.'

'Good.'

The rest of that trek across Dartmoor was uneventful, other than finding me wet, cold, hungry, and plagued with a headache. I also discovered what a *kistvaen* is by the simple process of falling into one (a burial hole ill-covered by a cracked and unbalanced slab of stone), and we met a herd of immensely shaggy, long-horned highland cattle, looking very much like prehistoric creatures recently risen from some weed-grown swamp. They did not much like the looks of us, either, and as a group took exception to our presence; fortunately, there was a wall nearby. Unfortunately, there was a small mire on the other side of the wall. When we came to Mary Tavy, it was with difficulty that we persuaded an innkeeper to allow us in, and then we were banished to the kitchen for our luncheon.

By afternoon, the clouds were high enough that Holmes thought it worthwhile to look and see what the two mad Londoners might have witnessed, so we trudged up the slippery sides of Gibbet Hill. This was not, as I had both assumed and hoped, so named because of some fancied resemblance of a rock formation, but because there had been an actual gibbet on the top of this prominent hill, employed on highwaymen captured on the busy road below, their bodies left high as an admonishment to their colleagues. It was an appropriately cheerless sort of place, gouged about with the remains of mines around its base and topped now not by a gibbet, but by a water-filled quarry, green with scum.

The view, however, was not without interest, and did indeed stretch for miles – or would have, given a clearer day. Holmes squatted down with the map, now in its final stages of returning to the state of pulp but still legible in the rectangles between the fold lines. He found a flat rock and aligned the map to the view in front of us, then began to tick off the landmarks: Brat, Doe, and Ger Tors, which I could see; Great Links and Fur Tors, which Holmes claimed he could see; all the sweep of the moor, emerging green and russet from the mist.

Placing his two index fingers on the map, one at each sighting of the ghostly coach, he compared the map and the land in front of us, his head bobbing up and down, up and down, until I began to feel a return of my earlier queasiness and went off to contemplate the waterlogged quarry.

I returned when I heard Holmes rising and trying to fold the map into a manageable size.

'Anything?'

'Not conclusive. We don't even know which way the coach was going when they saw it. We must try to find those two.'

'Two stray Londoners on holiday in the middle of summer?' I exclaimed. 'How do you propose to do that?'

'They may have spent one night shivering up here, but you can be certain they'd not repeat the experience. They will have made for the nearest kitchen and hot bath, and once there, they will have signed the guest register.'

Holmes had a tremendous knack for sounding certain of himself, usually on the flimsiest of evidence. I took a deep breath and let it slowly out, and was just opening my mouth to agree to this scouring of all nearby inns, public houses, farm-houses, and cottages when Holmes interrupted me.

'However, that is not for tonight, and probably not the most efficient use of resources to do it ourselves. Gould can muster a troop of Irregulars for us, men who know the ground.'

Immensely relieved, I swung my heavy knapsack back onto my shoulders, tightened my slack bootlaces to protect my toes against the downhill journey, and light-heartedly followed my husband down from Gibbet Hill.

CHAPTER SEVEN

Towards evening I was startled to see a most extraordinary object
approach me – a man in a draggled, dingy, and disconsolate
condition, hardly able to crawl along.
– A BOOK OF DARTMOOR

D ARKNESS OVERTOOK US ON the road back towards Lew
Trenchard. As I stumbled in Holmes' wake, barely conscious
of the vegetation and the people and the rich odours of dung and
grass and rotting leaves, I reflected that I had been wet, bedraggled,
and exhausted before – generally in Holmes' company – and after
two years of marriage to the man I had come to accept this as a
common state of affairs. I should have been somewhat happier about
it if only he, too, might show the same results, but Holmes had
always possessed the extraordinary ability to avoid grime. Given two
puddles, identical on the surface, Holmes would invariably choose
the one with the shallow, neatly gravelled bottom, whereas I, just as
invariably, would put my foot into the other and be in muck past
the ankle. Or go over a wall fleeing from a herd of horned Scottish
cows and land respectively on green turf and churned-up mud.

So it was that we approached Lew House, with me limping
and slurping in my boots while beside me walked my partner and
husband, his only dishevelment after three days of moor-crawling
the day's light stubble on his jaw and a high-tide mark of mud

around the lower half of his otherwise clean boots. He looked as if he were returning from a gentle day's shooting; I seemed to have spent the day wrestling a herd of escaped pigs through a bog.

The smell of wood smoke grew stronger as we came up the drive to Lew House, and I could see lights pouring from the windows, making the cold mausoleum seem almost warm and beckoning. Considering the late hour, in fact, the house seemed fairly blazing with lights. Nice of Baring-Gould to make the effort, I thought, and was aware of a faint feeling of warmth towards the man. Only when we were actually within the porch and I heard the voices within did I realise my mistake and by then it was too late to bolt for the servants' entrance.

Again, our host himself opened the door. This time, at his back and peering curiously around the cleric's high shoulder, stood another man, a wide, swarthy face topped with thick, greying, heavily pomaded hair. The man's liquid brown eyes blinked at the sight of us, and shifted from their initial astonishment to a politely, if inadequately, concealed amusement.

'Miss Russell,' our host said, 'you look a bit the worse for wear. Shall I ask Mrs Elliott—'

'No thank you,' I said, stung into asperity by the amusement in his voice that matched that of the stranger's eyes. 'It is predominantly external.' I sat on the bench and tugged at my bootlaces, praying fervently that they would not knot on me. I was saved from this small but final humiliation when the ties slid loose, allowing me to prise the boots from my feet. The sodden condition of the stockings I should simply ignore, along with the rest of my state. Pretend you've just come from the hairdresser's, Russell, I commanded myself. Imagine you've arrived at the home of a poor relation whose misbehaviours you have come to chastise. Put your chin up and cut them off without a farthing.

When my coat and hat had been peeled away and joined the sodden gloves on the bench, I turned towards the door and put my chin up and my hand out.

'Good evening, Mr Baring-Gould. I trust you are keeping well?'

'What? Oh, yes. Yes, thank you.' He stepped back so I could enter the house, where after a moment, recalled to himself by my attitude and my heavily applied accent of immaculate breeding, he took another step backwards and motioned to the man who was now at his shoulder rather than behind it.

'Miss Russell, this is a friend and neighbour, Mr Richard Ketteridge. Richard, Miss Mary Russell. And her husband, Mr Sherlock Holmes.'

The warm hand of the stranger gripped my own frigid palm solidly. His hand was as broad and muscular as the rest of him, at one with his almost swarthy skin and the pale patches of old scars on his face but contrasting oddly with his exquisitely tailored evening suit. On his right hand he wore a wide band of a strikingly deep orange-coloured gold, set with a small diamond. His eyes were dark, his nose was broad, and the tip of the small finger on his left hand was missing. Greeting me, the laughter in his eyes did not fade; if anything it grew, even when he turned to my tidy husband and took his hand as well.

'Evening, good to meet you. I was glad to hear the Reverend has friends to stay; he ought to do it more often, 'specially with his family away. I was dining with friends down the road a piece, just stopped in to see how he was doing.'

The speech was as vigorous as the handshake had been. It was also delivered in a ringing American accent, much the same accent my California-born father had possessed, and which lay beneath my own English tones (half acquired, half inherited from my London-born mother).

Baring-Gould shut the door behind Holmes and ushered us into the warmth. The room's fire was blazing, logs heaped high beneath the carved fox and hounds and warming the backsides of two more strangers. One of them was small, slim, and not much older than I, dressed also in evening wear and possessed of sleek blond hair and a neat beard surrounding a drawn-in mouth and rather stern eyes. The man beside him wore a clerical collar, a remarkably hairy tweed jacket, and an air of sporty bonhomie, and I was surprised when Baring-Gould introduced him as his curate, Gilbert Arundell – it seemed an odd pairing. The fair young man, who seemed much quieter than Ketteridge and whose dinner jacket was of a slightly inferior cut, proved to be the American's secretary. His name was David Scheiman, and the few words he spoke were also in an American accent, although an America farther east than that of his employer, and with both English and Germanic traces down at its childhood roots. His palm was damp and his grip was brief, and he had to draw himself together to look Holmes in the face (a not uncommon reaction when even the most blameless of individuals first met Holmes, as if they dreaded that he was about to look into their souls and see their inner thoughts and what they did with their private lives).

Ketteridge went to the cupboard and offered us a drink. Holmes accepted, saying he would merely go up and put on a pair of shoes first, but I smiled and demurred politely, and took my leave with as much dignity as I could muster. As I left, the conversation around the fireplace resumed: It seemed to have something to do with cricket.

Holmes did not catch me up until I was in the bathroom with the hot tap full on.

'You will come back down?' he asked, although it sounded more like an order than a question.

'Holmes, I'd rather starve to death.'

He seemed honestly puzzled, whether because he had missed the amusement in the two men or because he could not see why I should object, I could not decide. He might even have been putting on an act of obtuseness for some reason, but I decided it did not matter, that in any case my reaction would be the same.

'Enjoy yourself, Holmes, while I enjoy my bath.' I pushed him out and closed the door.

A long, hot, drowsy time later I became aware of a sound outside the door. I raised my ears clear of the cooling water, and listened for a moment. 'Holmes?'

'Sorry, mum,' said a young female voice. 'Mrs Elliott thought you might like a bowl of soup. I'll just leave the cover on it to keep it hot, shall I?'

'That would be fine,' I said. 'Thank you. And thank Mrs Elliott for me, please.'

'Yes mum.' I heard the gentle rattle of a tray being put down, and then the door to the bedroom closed.

After a final sluice to rid myself of the last of the mud that had lodged itself in skin and hair and nails, I wrapped my hair in a towel and myself in a dressing gown, and went to investigate the tray. The soup was still warm, and immeasurably better than the nearly rancid, gruel-like mixture served us the first night. There were also freshly baked rolls, a large slab of crumbling orange cheddar, a slice of lemon tart, and an apple. I finished everything.

My hair was nearly dry by the time Holmes came upstairs. He had paused to change more than his muddy boots, and looked very appealing, tall and slim in his jet suit and snowy shirtfront. One thing led to another, as is the wont in a marriage, and we did not get around to speaking about Ketteridge until after the housemaid had fetched up the morning tea.

I settled myself up against the pillows while Holmes perched in his dressing gown on the seat beneath the mullioned windows.

'Tell me, Holmes, who is Richard Ketteridge and what is a Californian mulatto with the scars of frostbite on his face and fingers doing in Lew Trenchard, Devonshire?'

'Interesting chap, isn't he?' he said. 'Gould sees a great deal of him.' I squinted against the pallid morning light, moved my teacup from my stomach to the bedside table, found my glasses and put them on, raised myself to sit more vertically against the pillows, and looked at him.

'Would you care to elaborate?'

'No,' he said, studying the burning end of the cigarette he held between his fingers. 'No, I don't think that I would. I should prefer to have your unsullied reaction after you have met him properly. Which will be this evening,' he added. 'We are dining at his house.'

'Dining! Holmes, I don't have a gown suitable for evening.'

'Of course you don't.'

'You go. Have a nice time with the other gents over your cigars.'

'I told him we were not kitted up for formal dress, and he assured me black tie was not required. A simple frock. You did bring a frock.'

'And the shoes to go with it.' It was a very nice frock, too, and unless I tripped going out of the door and went sprawling, I should not be disgraced in wearing it. I acquiesced. I was more than a little curious about Mr Richard Ketteridge, even without Holmes' enigmatic refusal to discuss the man. A man with the scarred skin and abused hands of a labourer wearing the clothing of a West End dandy, who could demonstrate his intimate familiarity with the prickly squire of Lew Trenchard by acting as drinks host, was no simple character.

First, however, was the good Mrs Elliott's breakfast table. I took with me a pen and paper, and as we sat I sketched in the dates we had accumulated thus far:

Tuesday 25 or Wednesday 26 July – Johnny Trelawny sees coach, dog
Friday 27 July – London ramblers on Gibbet Hill see coach
Friday 24 August – courting couple sees coach, dog
Saturday 15 September – Josiah Gorton last seen in north-west quadrant
Monday 17 September – Gorton found in south-east

I passed the paper over to Holmes, who glanced at it, took my pen, and added,

Monday 20 August – plate falls off shelf
Sunday 26 August – Granny hears dog

'Holmes!' I said in some irritation. 'You needn't mock me.'

'I am not mocking your calendar, Russell,' he protested. 'I am merely contributing to it.'

He seemed sincere, but I couldn't think what a broken plate or a lonely granny who heard noises in the night might have to do with Lady Howard's coach. Rather than arguing, however, I let it stand.

'Does the list tell you anything?' he asked offhandedly, reaching for the coffee.

'The moon was full around the twenty-sixth of July and the twenty-seventh of August,' I said, 'and that could explain why the coach was visible then.'

'Or rather, why the coach was out then, so as to be visible.'

'Precisely. However, that does not explain the timing of Josiah Gorton's death, which was a full eight or ten days before September's full moon.'

'Nor does it explain the broken plate.'

I was already tired of the broken plate, and decided he was merely using it to annoy me. I was grateful when Mrs Elliott chose that moment to bring us our breakfasts.

99

After we had eaten, Holmes arranged with Mrs Elliott for a troop of rural Irregulars to quarter the Mary Tavy inns, public houses, hostelries, and farm-houses in search of two Londoners who had seen a ghostly carriage. He then spent the day closeted with Baring-Gould, going over our time on the moor. I, too, spent the day with the man, though not in his physical presence. I uncovered a cache of his books and settled in with a stack of them beside my chair.

It was a singular experience. Odd, in fact. I had to admit that the man was brilliant, although I drew the line at 'genius'. He held an opinion on everything – European cliff dwellings, Devonshire folk songs, comparative mythology, architecture, English saints, werewolfs, archaeology, philology, anthropology, theology – and seemed possessed of a vast impatience with those who disagreed with him. Inevitably, though, the breadth of his scope meant a lack of depth, which he may have got away with in his novels and the werewolf book, but which rendered, for example, the works on theology quite useless. Theology is, after all, my field of expertise, and the best I could say for Baring-Gould and his conclusions (for example, that Christianity was proven to be true by the simple fact that it worked) was that he showed himself to be an enthusiastic amateur who might have made some real contribution to the world of scholarship had he possessed a more focused sense of discipline.

However, there was a strong pulse of life in even the more abstruse tomes, a bounce and vigour one would not have predicted. His occasional references to Devon, and particularly Dartmoor, sang with life and humour, and if he was sometimes pompous and often paternalistic, the passion he felt for the land made up for it.

The novels were embarrassingly melodramatic, but intriguing. There seemed to me a deep vein of cruelty, almost brutality, running through his stories, a distinct lack of tenderness and compassion towards his characters, particularly those living in poverty, that seemed odd in a man dedicated to God's service, and moreover an interest in savage, almost pagan emotions that was surely unusual in an otherwise calm and responsible squire. I began to understand his fascination with the moor, and also to wonder about the man's blunt dismissal of his children on that first night, describing them merely as 'scattered'.

I was in the final throes of a furious potboiler called *Mahalah* when Holmes came into the room. He said something; I grunted in reply and turned the page, and after a minute another page.

Ten minutes later I had finished the book and sat back, feeling equal parts exasperation and the sense of romantic tragedy that Baring-Gould had been trying to evoke. I looked at Holmes, then looked at him more attentively.

'Why are you dressing, Holmes?'

He glanced up from his task of threading one gold cuff-link into his cuff. 'Dinner, Russell. At Richard Ketteridge's? I did inform you.'

'Oh Lord!' I threw myself at the wardrobe and snatched up my frock.

'How long do I have?'

'The car is already here. Five minutes will make us only fashionably late.'

I flung my clothes on the floor and dropped the frock over my head, succeeded in hoisting my silk stockings without putting a ladder into either of them, and turned to the mirror to subdue my hair into some kind of order.

'Is it still raining?' I asked.

'It is.'

'I must have an umbrella. Go and find me one. Please.'

As always happens when I am in a hurry, my hair went up lopsided and had to be taken down and arranged again. Still, in the end I was presentable. I caught up a thin woollen wrap and hurried downstairs.

Baring-Gould was passing through the hallway downstairs, and he wished me a pleasant evening without, I thought, actually seeing me. Holmes was in the porch, and as soon as he heard me coming he stepped out onto the drive and opened a huge, bright green umbrella over our heads, and escorted me the few feet to the sleek closed touring car that awaited us. A liveried chauffeur was one step ahead of him, holding the door. I climbed in, followed by Holmes. The chauffeur claimed the umbrella, closed it, and drew it after him into the front, and drove us away from Lew House.

CHAPTER EIGHT

With every wish to promote the well-being and emancipation
of the working classes, I should be sorry to see – what is
approaching – the extinction of the old squirearchy, or
rather being supplanted by the *nouveaux riches*.

— EARLY REMINISCENCES

As we began to thread our way through the narrow, deep-cut lanes that led upwards onto the moor itself, I became aware of something odd in the attitude of the man at my side. The light outside was fading, but it was still bright enough in the car for me to study him. He was slumped down into the comfortable seat, his arms crossed over his chest, and his face had a sour look on it that I had seen any number of times before.

'Holmes, what is it?'

'What is what, Russell?' he said irritably, not taking his eyes from the passing stone walls crowned with hedgerows. 'I do wish you would refrain from asking me questions that contain no grammatical antecedent.'

'An antecedent is unnecessary if both parties are aware of the topic under consideration, and you know full well what I'm talking about. Your physical language is positively shouting your displeasure, but since this evening's social event was not my idea, I cannot assume that you are resenting my coercion. You are peeved at something; what is it?'

'Am I not to be allowed the privacy of my own thoughts without being subjected to an analysis of my "physical language"?'

'Not if you insist on indulging in those thoughts around me, no. If you wanted privacy, Holmes, you should not have married me.'

Bridling, he removed his gaze from the limited view outside the car windows and glared at me for a long moment before his good sense reasserted itself. His arms unknotted themselves and dropped to his lap, and he looked, if anything, almost sheepish. He lowered his voice, although the glass between us and the driver was thick and the whine of the climbing engine loud.

'I discovered only this evening that Ketteridge's house is Baskerville Hall,' he said.

I saw immediately what he dreaded: not, as I had feared, the feeling of a case taking a disastrously wrong turn, but rather the sort of fulsome praise he loathed. Holmes was fond enough of applause for those of his actions that he himself considered deserving, but he abhorred the popular notoriety that Watson's narratives had spawned.

'Holmes, it's been, what? Twenty years since that story was published. Surely—'

'Ketteridge's secretary was reciting whole swaths of it last night to his master's amusement. And Gould was playing along, curse him.'

'We could turn back to Lew Trenchard,' I suggested. 'I could take ill, if you like.' One of the unexpected benefits of marriage, I had found, was that it gave a convenient scapegoat upon which public blame could be heaped.

'Generous of you to offer, Russell, but no. Tribulation is good for the soul, or so I hear. Although I admit that had I known last night, I might have avoided the invitation to dinner. Which may be why neither Ketteridge nor Gould happened to mention it.'

'Well, I shall reserve the option of a ladylike attack of the vapours if the reminiscences become too nauseating.'

'Thank you.'

'Think nothing of it. How did Ketteridge come to own Baskerville Hall? If he inherited, why didn't he take the name?'

'He bought the place – lock, stock, and family portraits. Two years ago, according to Gould, he was on the final stages of a world tour when he passed through England and happened to hear about it from an acquaintance in a weekend shooting party up in Scotland. It appealed to him, he came out to look at it, and he ended up buying it from the sole surviving Baskerville, the daughter of the Sir Henry I knew.'

'Sir Henry had no sons?'

'He had two. They were both killed during the war, one in the Somme, the other somewhere in the Mediterranean, probably lost to a German submarine boat. Sir Henry died before the war, his widow in the influenza epidemic of 1919. With death duties, the daughter, who was only twenty-two or -three and unmarried, hadn't enough left to maintain the hall. It's one of those great stone sinkholes, a gold-hungry mire sucking down pounds and pence without a trace. As you can see,' he said, extending one long finger to point at the view through the window ahead.

The land beneath our tyres had climbed through the wooded fringe along the outer slopes of the moor and out into the tiny fields and walled pastures that occupy the edges of the moor itself. It had continued to rise until the low and homely cottages had fallen away, leaving only the bleak, boulder-strewn expanse of the interior. Unexpectedly, a dip in the barren ground fell away and grew trees. I caught a brief glimpse of what looked like a pair of thin towers rising above the branches, and then we dropped down into the trees.

The lodge gates showed signs of recent attention, for although the edges of the pillars were smooth and shapeless with age, the stone glowed as if freshly scrubbed and the elaborate tracery of the iron gates gleamed with new black paint. The lodge itself was fairly new and very tidy and tenanted by someone sufficiently house-proud to have starched the white curtains into crispness. As we passed through the gates, I looked up at the amorphous stone objects that topped the flanking pillars. I thought they resembled enormous potatoes; Holmes said they were the boars' heads of the Baskervilles.

On the other side of the gate lay a long avenue of old trees that had dropped most of their leaves onto the drive. Nonetheless, the branches that met over our heads were thick enough to block the last rays of the evening's light, so that we seemed to be driving into a long tunnel, illuminated from below by the powerful headlamps of the motor car. There was a row of light standards, planted at the side of the drive at regular intervals, but they were unlit, visible only in our headlamps.

Then, twenty feet from the end of the tunnel, the front windscreen of the motor car flared into a blaze of light, blinding us as if a powerful searchlight had been shone directly into our faces. The driver slowed and put up one hand to shield his eyes, and we emerged cautiously from the avenue of trees. The drive passed through an expanse of lawn lined with flower beds, and I found myself looking up at a house shaggy with ivy, its central block surmounted by the two towers I had seen from the approach. Impressive from a distance, they now looked crowded together, thrown out of balance with the original house by the addition of two modern wings. One huge light fixture hung from the wall above the porch, drenching the lower part of the house in blue-white brilliance. The upper reaches, shielded by a reflector, receded into darkness but for the squares of a few mullioned windows that had lights behind their curtains.

'Well,' said Holmes to himself, 'I see Sir Henry got his thousand-candle-power Swan and Edison.'

'Two or three lesser bulbs might have got the job done less dramatically.'

'His purpose was to expel the gloom.'

'He did that,' I said, although I could not help noticing that where the light eventually trailed to a halt, the dark seemed even more solid than it had in the unlit avenue.

Richard Ketteridge had been standing at his open porch door when we emerged from the avenue of trees. He came out onto the drive to greet us, and now his hand was on my door, opening it. I arranged a gracious smile on my face and permitted him to hand me out of the motor car. Fortunately, I did not trip and fall at his feet, and as the rain had momentarily slowed to a sort of falling fog, I waved away the driver with the umbrella.

Ketteridge began to speak the moment my door cracked open, his ebullient Americanisms spilling over us as he bowed over my hand and shook that of Holmes, pulling us inside all the while.

'Well, I must say, this is an honour, an honour indeed. Little did I know when I bought this place that I'd one day be welcoming the man who saved it from a rascal, all those years ago. Of course,' he confided to me, 'it was one of the reasons I bought it in the first place, that ripping good story about the Hound. I felt like I was buying a piece of English history, and an exciting piece at that. Come in, come in,' he urged, for we had reached the door. 'You'll find a few changes in the old place,' he said to Holmes, and scurried forward to fling open the door into the hall itself, nearly bowling over the butler who stood on the other side.

'Sorry, Tuptree, didn't see you there. Come in, Mrs Holmes, Mr Holmes, warm yourselves by the fire. What can we get you to drink?'

I decided that the butler must have worked in Ketteridge's house for some time, since he was not only resigned to his employer's hasty willingness to do away with his services by opening doors for himself, but he did not even react to receiving an apology from his employer. Perhaps, I amended my diagnosis, he had merely worked for Americans before.

The fire was enthusiastic and well fed, set in a massive and ancient fireplace surrounded by several yards of padded fender. I perched my backside on the leather, enjoying the heat and the crackle of the flames while Holmes and our host exchanged some innocuous words of greeting. After a moment, Tuptree came up with our drinks on his polished tray, and I then removed myself to a deep armchair of maroon leather and sipped my sherry, examining my surroundings with interest.

Sir Henry's passion for light bulbs had been indulged in the interior of his hall as well, with the result that I now sat in the best-lit Elizabethan building outside of a film stage. It was startling, particularly as I had not seen an electric light since leaving Oxford. Every dent and chisel mark in the balusters of the upstairs gallery were readily visible; I could see a small mend in the carpeting on the staircase, and pick out a faint haze of dust on the upper frames of the pictures. It was incongruous and somewhat disturbing – surely those high, age-blackened rafters were never meant to be viewed in such raw detail, nor the cracks and folds in the high, narrow stained-glass window picked out with an intense clarity they would not have even in full sun. The intense illumination made the old oak panelling gleam and brought out all the details of the coats of arms mounted on the walls, but on the whole it was not a successful pairing, for despite the apartment's rich colours and sumptuous, almost cluttered appearance, the harshness of the light made the hall look stark and new, a not entirely successful copy of an old building.

I realised belatedly that the two men were looking at me attentively.

'I'm sorry?' I said.

'I just asked what you made of the place,' replied Ketteridge.

'Actually, I was wondering how on earth you power all these lights.'

'Generators and batteries,' he said promptly. 'Sir Henry put them in. Did it right, too – I can run every light in the place for six hours before the batteries start to run down. When they don't break down, that is – a man from London is supposed to be here to look into what's gone wrong with the row of lights in the avenue. They've been out for days.'

'The problems of the householder,' I murmured sympathetically.

He looked at me sideways, opened his mouth, changed his mind, and took a sip from his drink instead (not sherry, but by the look of it a lightly watered whisky) before turning back to Holmes.

'So what brings you to Dartmoor this time, Mr Holmes? Not another hound, I hope?'

'I am on holiday, Mr Ketteridge,' Holmes said blandly. 'Merely paying a visit to an old friend.' He, too, raised his glass, and smiled politely at the American.

'Baring-Gould, yes. Did you meet him during the Baskerville case? He was here then, wasn't he?'

'He was here, yes, but no, I had met him before that.'

Ketteridge wavered, and I could see him ruefully accept Holmes' broad hint that any further questioning along that particular route would be boorish. He chose another.

'I believe we have a mutual friend, Mr Holmes.'

'Oh?' He was very polite; he did not even raise an eyebrow.

'Lady Blythe-Patton. You did a little job for her a few years back. I met the colonel at my club, and they invited me out to their country place for a weekend. Fine people. She had much to say about you.'

Only an American, I reflected, could actually form a new acquaintanceship at a men's club. I kept my face without expression when Holmes turned to speak to me.

'I found a necklace that she had lost, Russell, many years ago when I was a hungry youth with the rent to pay.'

'Recovered it within an hour of entering the house, she says,' Ketteridge elaborated with a no-false-modesty sort of joviality.

'Behind the cushions of the settee,' Holmes replied, sounding bored. 'I don't suppose that within her panegyric she included the advice I gave her at the time?'

'Not that I recall, no,' Ketteridge said doubtfully.

'I told her that in the future she ought to remove her valuables to the safe before imbibing as heavily as she had been, and moreover, that increasing her expenditures on domestic staff might make it possible for the overworked housemaids to clean more thoroughly, turning out the cushions at regular intervals. The settee was really quite disgusting.'

Ketteridge thought this hilarious. I waited until his laughter was subsiding, and then I asked Holmes, 'Did she actually pay you after that?'

'Do you know,' he said, sounding surprised, 'I don't believe she did.'

Our little piece of burlesque succeeded in putting Ketteridge off track just long enough for me to nudge the train of conversation off in another direction.

'Tell me, Mr Ketteridge, what do you do to amuse yourself, here on the moor?'

His answer wound along the lines of outdoor enterprises and the pleasures of restoring a down-at-its-heels building to a state of glory, interspersed with regular away trips; however, listening between the lines, it sounded to me as if the charms of Dartmoor had begun to pall, and the thrill of owning the piece of English literary history that was Baskerville Hall was beginning to fail in its compensation for the setting. What he did for amusement on Dartmoor, it appeared, was get away from it, to London, Scotland, Paris, and even New York. He had bought the hall in a burst of enthusiasm, spent many months and a great number of dollars arranging it to his satisfaction, and now that the rich man's toy was shiny and nearing completion, clean air, fox hunts, and conversations with the Reverend Sabine Baring-Gould would not be enough to keep him.

Ketteridge seemed to become aware of how thin his answer had been, and rapidly turned the topic back to Holmes. 'And you, Mr Holmes, down there on the Sussex Downs; surely beekeeping doesn't occupy your every waking hour? I've noticed how few and far between Conan Doyle's stories have been lately – you must keep your hand in the investigation business, if nothing else than to give him something to write about.'

Holmes took a deep breath, let it out slowly, and placidly answered, 'Active investigation is a task for younger men, Mr Ketteridge. I spend my days writing.'

I busied myself with my empty glass, but before Ketteridge could give verbal expression to the scepticism on his face, movement at the far end of the room attracted his attention. The butler, Tuptree, stood at a doorway and informed us that our dinner was served. As we turned towards him, Holmes shot me an eloquent glance. I raised my eyebrows a fraction, and he shook his head minutely. It seemed that it was not yet time for me to succumb to the vapours, despite the fact that since we had entered his house, Ketteridge had not allowed more than half a dozen sentences to pass without pulling the conversation back to the Baskerville case. For some reason, Holmes did not wish to leave. However, I decided that enough had become enough.

I went through into the dining room, followed by Holmes. Once inside, I stepped to one side, paused while Holmes walked past me into the room, and then turned on my heel to come face to face with Ketteridge, who necessarily jerked to a halt. I drew myself up, put a hand out to his sleeve, and, looking at him eye to eye (actually, I was a fraction taller than he), I spoke in a slow, clear, ironclad voice.

'My husband does not really enjoy talking about his old cases, Mr Ketteridge. It makes him uncomfortable.'

Most men, and certainly forceful men like Ketteridge, tend to overlook women unless they be unattached and attractive. I usually allow this because I often find it either amusing or convenient to be invisible. Such had been the case with Ketteridge, between my self-effacement and his fascination with Holmes, but now he reared back on his heels in astonishment. I merely held his eyes for a moment longer, then smiled, let go of his arm, and left him to gather his wits and scurry around to seat us at the long, gleaming table that was set with four places and lit only by candlelight. The dim light was a great relief.

A distraction arrived in the form of Ketteridge's secretary, David Scheiman, adjusting his tie as he entered hurriedly and slipped into the fourth chair.

'Sorry I'm late,' he said. 'I got involved in my work and lost track of the time.'

'All you missed was a drink and some pleasant conversation, David,' his employer said. 'Both of which you can catch up with. Wine, Mrs Holmes?'

I am not certain why I did not correct his form of address to the surname I normally use, the one I was born with. Men do not change their names with marriage, and it had always struck me as odd that women were expected to do so. Perhaps I did not correct him because I did not wish to underscore the impression of unexpected strength I had just made on him, or perhaps it was for some other reason, but after a tiny hesitation, I merely nodded and allowed Tuptree to pour a dark red wine into my glass. Holmes did not remark on the incident, not even non-verbally, but I knew he had not missed it.

'What sort of work were you doing, Mr Scheiman, that so

occupied you?' I asked, more to set the conversational ball rolling than from any real interest. What I could see of him in the uncertain light confirmed that he was a pleasant if unprepossessing young man, fair-haired, prim, with a blond beard trimmed neatly low on his cheeks and a moustache that nearly obscured his thin lips. His hands, like those of his employer's, were large and callused, and the skin of his face was browned to an agreeable semblance of rude good health.

'Some old manuscripts,' he said unexpectedly. 'It's very interesting, the number of myths and legends that can be found about the moor. You wouldn't believe the diversity, even when the stories are basically the same. Take the myth of the black hound, for example—'

Holmes, across from me, winced perceptibly, but before he could slump into resignation, Ketteridge spoke up.

'Very interesting, I'm sure, David. Perhaps you could tell us a story after dinner.' Scheiman frowned in what appeared to be confusion, a sharp line appearing low on his forehead, but he did not press the matter. Ketteridge continued, 'You know of course, Mrs Holmes, that your host at Lew Trenchard is a great collector of stories, but perhaps he has not mentioned that he travelled to Iceland when he was a young man?'

'He hasn't said anything about it, no,' I replied, a literally true statement, although because of my day's reading I was aware of his voyage.

'A great traveller he was, like his father. Of course, he was practically born on the road, so I guess you could say it's in his blood. His father got itchy feet when the boy was about three or four, bundled his family up, popped them in a carriage, and took off for the Continent. That's how Baring-Gould grew up, moving from Germany to the south of France and back again, until he was about fifteen, when he finally spent some time here. What a way to spend your childhood, eh? No teachers, no rules, learning languages by speaking them and science when it interests you.'

It was much the same history that Baring-Gould himself had told us the first night, and now, having some idea of the man's life, I reflected that his parents' approach towards their son's education did explain something about Baring-Gould's flighty attitude towards research.

'Have you read his memoirs?' he asked us. I shook my head, having just taken a mouthful of food, and Holmes said simply that he had not. 'Very interesting book. Very interesting life. It's just the first volume, of course. The next will be out next year, and he's working on the third one now.'

'There's nothing about the Baskerville legend in the first volume,' Scheiman remarked.

'Of course not,' said Ketteridge, a touch repressively. 'It ends thirty years before that. Now tell me, Mr Holmes, you're something of an antiquarian. Do you think the Romans ever made it up onto Dartmoor?'

The conversation moved away from Holmes' professional life for a time while Ketteridge and Holmes discussed tin mining and Phoenician traders, moorland crosses, the conflict between the military and the visitor during the summer months, prison reform, and the possible meanings behind the avenues of standing stones (which personally I had decided were the result of near terminal boredom on the part of the natives, who would have found heaving large rocks into upright lines an exciting alternative to watching the fog blow about) while I sat and listened politely and Scheiman drank three glasses of wine.

Gradually the topic turned back towards Baring-Gould and his work, the problems the man had in maintaining a writing schedule with his failing health, and the progress of the third and final volume of his memoirs. At this point Scheiman again interjected a comment.

'I wonder if *The Hound of the Baskervilles* will be in that volume,' he said to Holmes. His speech was slightly slurred, and I thought that perhaps he had not missed his pre-dinner drinks, after all. Ketteridge shot him a hard glance.

'David, I think you've had enough wine,' he said. His voice was quiet but hard, almost threatening, and his secretary put down his glass in an instant and automatic response. Unfortunately, the edge of it caught the side of his dinner plate, a glancing blow but enough to jolt the glass out of his hand and send its contents shooting down the table straight at me. I jerked back, avoiding the worst of it, but not all.

Everyone but Holmes was on his feet, me dabbing at the front of my dress, Scheiman looking abruptly ill, and Ketteridge flushing with anger.

'David, I think you'd better leave.' Without a word, his secretary dropped his table napkin on his chair and obeyed. Ketteridge apologised; one of Tuptree's minions silently whisked away the place setting, I reassured him (I hoped not falsely) that no permanent damage had been done my frock, and we resumed our places and our meal.

Ketteridge picked up his fork and determinedly resumed the conversation where he had left off, regaling us with stories of our host in Lew House. We heard about the pet bat that used to perch on Baring-Gould's shoulder when he was a schoolmaster (the boys called it his familiar, and swore it whispered dark secrets in his ear), and the Icelandic pony he had rescued and brought home with him, about the long black bag he had taken to carrying as a travel case, draped over his shoulder and called by the pupils 'Gould's Black Slug'. Ketteridge had never met Baring-Gould's wife, Grace, who died in 1916, but had prised the story of their courtship out of Baring-Gould's half brother and one-time curate, Arthur Baring-Gould, and recounted for us the tale of how the thirty-year-old parish priest had seen a nearly illiterate, sixteen-year-old girl going home in her clogs from her work in the mill and known that she would be his wife. He sent her away to friends, who taught her a correct accent and how to make polite conversation, and when she was nineteen they had married: the tall, eccentric, middle-aged parson and the short, quiet, hard-working young girl with the gentle iron will and the generous heart and the unexpected dry sense of humour. It was an unlikely match of great affection and mutual dependence, and everyone agreed that he had not been the same since she had died.

To do him justice, I do not think that when Ketteridge began the story, he was aware that his two guests might take it as something more personal than a quaint and touching tale of another's marriage. His face gave away the moment when he did become aware that he was speaking to a man and a woman with an even more exaggerated disparity of age, if not of education, but he rallied and ploughed on as if unconscious of the potential discomfort his narrative might bring.

However, immediately that story ended, he went off on another tack entirely, and we were soon hearing about the Baring-Gould archaeological excavations on the moor and the reports of the Devonshire Association.

Sweet course and cheese disposed of, we returned to the central hall, bidding farewell to the serried ranks of purchased ancestors staring down at us from the dark recesses of the minstrel's gallery at the far end of what was more accurately a banqueting hall than a dining room. Back in the hall, we found the brilliant lighting blessedly shut down, replaced by the gentling glow of a multitude of candles. It had been an excellent meal, the food unadorned, even homely, but beautifully cooked; now, the chairs in front of the fireplace where we sat to drink our coffee and the men their brandies were comfortable, and the conversation, Ketteridge having laid aside his curiosity about Holmes' past cases, was amiable. All in all, a much nicer evening than I had anticipated.

Even the hall seemed more appealing. Without the stark electric lights, the room reverted to its proper nature, a richly furnished chamber that had outlasted dynasties, outlasted too the family it had housed for five centuries.

It was, despite its opulence, remarkably comfortable and easy on the eyes and the spirit. I had assumed that Ketteridge bought the furnishings along with the portraits, but looking at them again, I began to wonder. The pieces were all either very old indeed or too new to have been installed during the Baskerville reign, and surely a house put together by a woman could not have been so unremittingly solid, dark, and male. Even the many decorative touches were masculine, the carpets and statues, pillows, wall tapestries, and paintings all large, intense in colour, and lush in texture, the overall effect so rich one could almost taste it. Studying the room in mild curiosity, trying to analyse how this came about, I noticed the subtle use of geometry, from the square of the chairs and settee before the fireplace to the triangle formed by the arrangement of three discrete centres that were placed with deceptive thoughtlessness, across the expanse of floor.

It was a collection of deep red, blue, and black needlework pillows on the sofa opposite the fireplace that nudged me into realising what the room reminded me of: Moroccan architecture and decorative arts, the elaborate arabesques built around the most basic geometry, as if the strength of a Norman church were to be combined with the delicacy of a piece of lacework. It was very unlikely, given the setting of a building from the Elizabethan era risen from foundations two hundred years older, but the hall that had at first seemed cluttered and overly furnished with colour and pattern, now in the dimmer light of the many thick candles assumed the persona of an Oriental palace. I smiled: Our dusky host had made for himself a Moorish retreat in the midst of Dartmoor.

Holmes took a sip from his glass, and then beat his host to the questions. 'Tell us, Mr Ketteridge, just how a Californian who struck it rich in the goldfields comes to settle in remotest Dartmoor?'

'I see my friend has been talking about me,' he said with a smile.

'Gould has said nothing about your past,' said Holmes.

Ketteridge raised his eyebrows and looked slightly wary – the standard response when Holmes pulled personal history out of what appeared to be thin air.

'You guessed—' Ketteridge instantly corrected himself with a conspiratorial smile. 'You deduced that? Perhaps I won't ask what you based it on.' His smile was a bit strained, and he took a swallow from his glass before continuing.

'It was Alaska,' he began. 'Not the Californian fields, which were either worked out or under claim long before I was born. I was living in Portland in July of 1897, thirty-one years old and making a not very good living as a small shopkeeper, when on the sixteenth of the month rumours began to spread like wildfire that a ship had put in to San Fracisco with fifty-thousand dollars of gold in a single suitcase. The next day this old rust-bucket the *Portland* put into Seattle harbour with nearly two tons of gold – two tons! More than a million dollars of gold, right there in one ship. Two hours after the news hit Portland, my dry-goods store was up for sale, cheap. I unloaded it in less than a week, bought my provisions, and lit out for the north.

'I never did find how many ships full of gold seekers had already left, but I was on one of the first dozen. Still, the river route freezes early, and I couldn't risk getting stuck, so cross-country it was, to Skagway and Dyea, across the Chilkoot Pass and north into the Yukon. Thought I'd make it to the goldfields before winter set in, but between one thing and another, I met it full on. Jesus – oh, pardon me, Mrs Holmes. Lord, it was cold. I nearly died – you wouldn't believe the kind of cold there. Tears freeze your eyes shut and break your lashes right off, spit is frozen solid before it hits the ground, leather boots that get wet will crack right across if they're not kept greased. And oh yes, if you don't see a tiny hole in your glove, your finger's turned to ice before you notice the cold.'

Smiling, he held out his left hand and wiggled the stump of the little finger.

'Still, I was lucky. I didn't starve or freeze, or get washed away in a river half turned to ice or buried under an avalanche or eaten alive by mosquitoes or bears or wolfs or shot by an ornery claim-jumper or any of the thousand other ways to die. No, I made it, a little the worse for wear, it's true, but with adventure enough for a lifetime, and gold enough as well. Yes, I was lucky. When I got to the fields I found that there was still plenty of gold for a man possessed of stamina and a shovel. Within months of the discovery, the smallest creek and most remote hole were claimed.'

Richard Ketteridge was soon gone from the fields, with gold enough to buy his luxury for life.

'I married my childhood sweetheart, and buried her ten years later. Somehow it wasn't all so fine after she died, and so I sold up and began, to wander: the Japans, Sydney, Cape Town. I ended up here a couple of years ago, heard about it from a friend up in Scotland less than two weeks after I entered the country. Now if that isn't fate for you – it took my fancy and so I stayed. I like the air here. It reminds me of the best parts of Alaska, in the spring. Still, the winters are cold, and I'm beginning to feel the old itch again, more than the odd month in New York or Paris can scratch.'

His story had the worn and polished texture of a favourite

possession, taken out regularly to be handed around and admired, and I could easily imagine him sitting with his new friends in a Scottish hunting lodge after a day's rough shoot, trading stories of unlikely places and successful ventures.

'You plan to move, then?' Holmes asked.

'I think so.'

'Baring-Gould will miss you,' commented Holmes.

'I'll miss him. He's a crazy old coot, but he does tell some fine stories. I'll think of him when I'm sitting in the sun, in the south of France, maybe, or even Hong Kong for a real change. My secretary would like that, wouldn't you, David?'

I had not been aware of the secretary's presence behind me, so light were his footsteps and so heavy the carpeting. He came into the low glow around the fire, his shoulders hunched in embarrassment, and went to the coffee tray to pour himself a cup. He had been away less than two hours, but he sounded stone-cold sober now.

'I really must apologise,' he said to us. 'I have some sort of blood imbalance that makes me highly sensitive to the effects of alcohol. I shouldn't drink at all, really. I make such a fool of myself. I do beg your pardon if I seemed at all . . . forward.'

'My dear boy,' said Ketteridge, 'I'm sure you offended none of us. I was merely concerned, knowing your sensitivity, that you might make yourself ill.'

It had sounded more like anger than concern in his voice, back in the dining room, but I assumed that he was being generous in excusing the younger man's lapse. Employees did not normally indulge in public drunkenness, even in the relative informality of an American household, and Scheiman knew it: He sat in a chair apart from his employer and the guests, away from the fire.

'So, David. Do you have a story from Dartmoor for us?'

'I, er, they're not really all that interesting. That is to say, I find them interesting, but—'

'Mr Scheiman,' said Holmes in resignation. 'Perhaps you might tell my wife the story of the Baskerville curse.'

Scheiman looked startled, and glanced at his employer for instructions. Although Ketteridge had so firmly discouraged his secretary from inflicting these doggy reminiscences on us, he could hardly now insist that his guest be saved from them when it was Holmes himself asking. Ketteridge shrugged.

'As our guest suggests, David. Do tell the story of the black hound of Dartmoor.' And so Scheiman, looking uncomfortable, began his story.

'In doing some reading about the history of the area, I came across the story that the Baskerville curse was actually based on. Not the one as given in *The Hound of the Baskervilles*,' he said, with an apologetic glance at Holmes, 'but the true story. There lived in the seventeenth century a squire by the name of Richard Cavell or Cabell. He was a man of great passions, who had the fortune, or perhaps misfortune, to marry him a beautiful young wife.

'For the first year or two all was well, except that they had no children. Soon, however, he discovered that she was betraying him. He forbade her visitors and kept her at home, but it continued, and became ever more indiscriminate. He sent away every male household servant aside from the near-children and the truly elderly, he hedged her around with limits, but still his wife turned her back on him. His jealousy grew when he saw her flirting with a stable hand, he hit her and forbade her to ride. When he witnessed her in conversation with the farm manager, he punished her again and locked her in the house. He grew afraid that the women in the house would plot with their mistress to bring her lovers, and so he got rid of the old servants and hired new ones. He loved his wife and he hated her, and soon the only friend she was allowed was her dog.

'The day came when he again caught her in yet another transgression. He beat her nearly to death, threw her in her room, and took the key.

'By this time the woman feared for her life. She let herself down the wall of the house on the ivy and fled, on foot, for the house of her sister across the moor.

'She did not make it. He discovered her absence, mounted his horse, and rode her down and, in his passion of jealous rage, he killed her. But as he drew his knife from the body of his wife, the woman's only friend took its revenge. The dog went for him and tore out the throat of his mistress's murderer. The dog then disappeared, out into the desolation of the moor, where to this day he wanders, waiting either for his mistress, or for her husband.'

A short silence fell, silence other than the hiss and crackle of the low-burning fire, until Holmes stirred. 'Interesting,' he said in a bored voice, and pulled out his watch.

'Yes,' I said brightly. 'It is interesting. The—'

Holmes interrupted me loudly, no doubt fearing (with reason) my scathing response to the clean-up job the secretary had done on what was essentially a very dirty little story. 'My dear,' he said, all syrup and honey, 'I know you undoubtedly have a strong academic interest in the tale, but the hour is late.'

We faced off over the empty coffee service. Ketteridge dutifully cleared his throat, although he was no doubt conscious of how his social triumph of having Sherlock Holmes to dine in Baskerville Hall could only be capped by the marital battle he could feel brewing. I ignored him.

'As I was saying,' I continued, 'it is quite interesting. The squire's name might be related to the Latin for horse, *caballus*, or it might be a reference to a political intrigue or *cabal* in which the squire was involved, presumably as a Cavalier in the Civil War. But you know, the truly tantalising bit there is that his name is the same as that of King Arthur's beloved hound. The centre of Arthurian legend is somewhat to the north of here, I realise, but—'

Holmes interrupted again, with not a trace of the relief he must have felt at hearing only this nonsense. 'It could also indicate that Cabell was simply his name. It is time we were gone, Mr Ketteridge.'

Scheiman had been interested in what I was saying, but with the interruption I noticed that Ketteridge was looking at me oddly, so I subsided, and allowed the business of leave-taking to rise up around me.

In the car, Holmes sat back and said in a quiet voice to the back of the driver's head, 'You know of course the Latin words *cavillars* and *cave.*'

'Related to *calvi*, to sneer,' I said, also too quietly for the driver to overhear, 'and *cave:* beware.'

He smiled briefly, and we sat for the rest of the drive in amicable silence.

Chapter Nine

Some have speculated that the standing stones were intended for
astronomical observation, and for determining the solstices; but
such fancies may be dismissed . . . and as for stone gate sockets,
it is really marvellous that the antiquaries of the past did
not suppose they were basins for sacrificial lustration.
One really wonders in reading such nonsense as this
whether modern education is worth much.

— A BOOK OF DARTMOOR

IT WAS LONG AFTER midnight when the big car finished negotiating
the lanes and turned through the Lew House gates, but again all
the lights downstairs were burning. I could have used a relatively
early night, I thought with resignation; at least this time I was
dressed for an occasion.

'How on earth did I get the impression that Baring-Gould lived a
solitary life?' I asked. 'He seems to have an endless stream of visitors,
and at all hours.'

After allowing Ketteridge's chauffeur to open my door and
to retrieve the fur rug in which I had been wrapped, I thanked
him absently and followed Holmes into the house. There had
been no vehicle standing outside, and to my surprise, the
hall where I had first met Baring-Gould, and later been faced
with Ketteridge, Scheiman, and the curate Arundell, was now

deserted but for the cat asleep in front of the freshly fed fire.

'Hello?' Holmes called in a low voice. When no answer came he started for the stairs, then stopped abruptly. A figure was rising up from the high-backed chair that faced the fireplace, the figure of a bony, brown man in his late thirties with sparse hair, loosened collar, and rumpled tweed suit. He had obviously been asleep, and was now blinking at us in growing alarm. He reached quickly down and came up gripping the fire poker; still, he looked more ridiculous than threatening.

'Who are you?' he demanded in an uncertain voice. 'What do you want?'

'I might ask the same of you,' said Holmes, and calmly set about divesting himself of his outdoor garments. He dropped his hat and gloves onto a pie-crust table and began to unbutton his overcoat. 'Where is Mr Baring-Gould?'

'He's locked in his bedroom.' Holmes' long fingers paused for a moment at the implications in this statement. 'He said he was going to bed, and he just left, and I tried . . . They just . . .' He stopped, looking shamefaced but with his chin raised in an incongruously childish defiance. 'I said I'd just wait here; he has to come down sometime.'

Holmes' fingers slowly resumed their task. He pulled off his scarf and overcoat and tossed them across the back of a sofa, then walked across to close the inner doorway so our voices would not carry up the stairs. He then went over to the drinks cabinet, poured two glasses of brandy, walked over to where I was standing and handed me one, and finally took his drink over to the sofa, where he settled down, stretching his left arm casually along the cushioned back and propping his left ankle on his right knee.

'Correct me if I'm wrong,' he said after he had taken a swallow of brandy, 'but it sounds to me remarkably as if you pushed your way into

Mr Baring-Gould's presence, drove him to seek refuge in his bedroom, followed him despite, no doubt, the objections of his servants, attempted to force your way through a locked door, and then retreated down here to lay siege, drinking the old man's liquor and burning his firewood, secure in the knowledge that everyone under this roof is twice your age and incapable of enforcing their master's wishes.'

The man took a step forward and I thought for a moment that I was going to have to take action, since Holmes (another inhabitant nearly twice the man's age) was settled deep into the sofa. However, the fireplace poker in his hand seemed to have been forgotten, although I kept a close eye on it and mentally noted heavy objects within reach that I could grab up to pelt him with.

'No!' he protested furiously. 'I only want to talk to him. He has to be made to understand—'

'Please keep your voice down, young man,' Holmes interrupted sharply. 'And we might begin with your name.'

'Randolph Pethering,' he said more quietly. 'I'm a . . . I'm a lecturer. In Birmingham, at the teachers' training college. I must speak with Mr Baring-Gould about his anti-Druidical prejudice. He must withdraw the statements he has made, or at the very least speak up for my thesis. I can't get a publisher; they've all read his books and articles about the ruins on the moor, and they won't even listen to me. So I've drawn up a list of his mistakes, and if he doesn't help me by speaking to my publisher, so help me, I'll release it to the press. He'll be ruined. A laughing stock!'

His voice had climbed again during this all but incomprehensible tirade, but Holmes and I could only stare at him until he broke off wiping his brow and panting with emotion and the heat of the fire and no doubt the alcohol he had drunk.

Holmes balanced his glass on the arm of the sofa, steepled his fingers, touched them to his lips, and addressed the distraught figure.

'Mr Pethering, am I to understand that you regard yourself as an antiquarian?'

'I am an archaeological anthropologist, sir. A good deal more of a scientist than that old man upstairs.'

Holmes let it pass. 'And yet you are convinced of the presence of Druidical remains up on the moor?'

'Most certainly! The stone rows for their ceremonial processions and the sacred circles for religious rites; the sacrificial basins on the tops of the tors and the places of oracle; those exquisitely balanced logan stones they used for oracular readings; the Druidical meeting place of Wiseman's Wood near Two Bridges, rich with the sacred mistletoe; the great tolmen in the Teign below Scorhill circle; the stone idols – why, it's as plain as the nose on your face,' he exclaimed in a rush. 'And Baring-Gould and his ilk would have us believe that the circular temples are mere shepherds' huts, and that the runic markings on the—'

The rapidity of Holmes' movement surprised me, and it must have terrified Pethering, who nearly tumbled backwards into the fire as Holmes leapt to his feet, took three long steps forward, twisted the poker from the man's hand, and snatched him back from the fire. He then stood looming over him with a terrible scowl on his face.

'You are tedious, young man, and I see no reason to permit you to remain here and plague our breakfast table. Would you prefer to leave under your own power, or do we put you out?'

He left. Holmes latched the door. We then made our way around the entire perimeter of the building, checking every window and door, before going upstairs to bed. I had to agree with Holmes that there was no need to stand guard: Pethering was not the sort who would actually break a window to get back in.

The antiquarian Pethering was not at the breakfast table the following morning, Sunday. Neither was anyone else, for that matter, nor did the room show any sign that there had been an earlier setting. We eventually ran Mrs Elliott to earth out of doors, supervising the digging up of potatoes by an elderly gardener. The morning air was still and damp and smelt richly of loam, and I breathed it in with appreciation. Bells were ringing somewhere not too far off, that evocative clamour of an English Sunday. After a minute or two Mrs Elliott turned and saw us, and her face lit up.

'There you are, then, nice and early. I didn't know when you'd be wanting your breakfast, bein' up so late and all, but it's all ready, I'll have it in a moment.'

We tried to assure her that toast and tea would be adequate but she bustled us out of her kitchen and in a very short time presented us with enough food to keep a labourer happy. This was, it seemed, by way of a reward.

'I am so grateful to you, runnin' that rascal off the place. I thought Charley – Mr Dunstan – was goin' to fetch his whip, but Mr Baring-Gould settled it by up and goin' to bed. I half expected that I'd have to step across the man to take up the Rector's tea this morning, but then I heard you come in and him go out, and I went to sleep like a baby in sheer relief.'

'That's quite all right, Mrs Elliott. I only regret we were not back earlier; it might have saved some grief all around. Is he still in bed, then?'

Her dour countrywoman's face drew in and became pinched as with pain. 'There's days he doesn't get up,' she said. 'This looks to be one of them.'

'May I speak with him?'

'Oh surely, for a brief time. He doesn't sleep, he says, just thinks and prays. With his eyes shut,' she added. 'I'll take you up after you've had your breakfast.'

Her good temper had manifested itself in lovely soft curds of scrambled eggs, fresh toast, and three kinds of jam, and we soon put away our labourers' portions, sighing with satisfaction. Our introduction to the cuisine of Lew House the week before may have been dismal, but the meals since then had been of a very different order – not fancy, but good, solid English cooking. I commented on the change to Holmes.

'Yes,' he said. 'Mrs Elliott was away visiting her sister. The village woman left in charge did little but stretch the remnants of the previous meals, and no one seemed capable of adjustments to the central heating when it went off. Mrs Elliott arrived back the morning after you arrived; she was not pleased at the state of the household.' He sounded amused, and I could well imagine the proud housekeeper's reaction to the tough stewed rabbit we had been served. He drained his coffee cup and stood up. 'Shall we go and see Gould?'

'You go, Holmes.'

'Come along, Russell. You mustn't avoid your host simply because he is a rude old man. Besides which, he has quite taken to you.'

'I'd hate to see how he expresses real dislike, then.'

'He becomes very polite but rather inattentive,' he said, holding the door open for me. 'Precisely as you do, as a matter of fact.'

Gould was awake, but he lay on his pillows moving little more than his eyes. His voice was clear but low, and with very little breath behind it.

'Mrs Elliott tells me you've rid me of a household pest.'

'Does that sort of thing happen often?'

'Never. Only friends come here.'

'You should have sent for the village constable.'

'Pethering is harmless. I couldn't be bothered. Tell me what happened.'

Holmes pulled up a chair and told him, making a tale out of

it. I sat on the seat below the window, watching the two men. Baring-Gould's eyes, the only things alive in that tired, sallow face, flicked over to me when Holmes told him how I had moved closer to the collection of heavy objects as Pethering had raised his weapon, and they began to dance with appreciation as the story of the man's discomfiting progressed. Holmes embroidered it slightly, enjoying his audience, and at the end Baring-Gould closed his eyes and opened his mouth and began to shake softly in a rather alarming convulsion of silent laughter.

It was short-lived, and at the end of it he lay for a moment, and then drew a deep breath and let it out again.

'Poor man. Dear old William Crossing remarked somewhere that one of the great goals of the Druids seems to have been the puzzling of posterity. One could say they have been quite successful. Pethering hasn't shown up again?'

'Not yet.'

'When he does, tell him I'll write him some sort of a letter. He's a lunatic, but he has a wife and child to feed.'

'I'll tell him.'

'How was your dinner last night?'

'I was glad that you finally chose to warn me that we were going to be at Baskerville Hall, but we sorted it out eventually. Thanks to Russell, actually, who gave an astonishingly realistic performance of a young wife fiercely protective of her eminent husband's comfort and reputation. Ketteridge no doubt thinks her a fool.'

The sharp old eyes found me again across the room, and this time the twinkle in them was unmistakeable.

'That must have been quite an act,' he said.

'It was.'

Baring-Gould smiled gently to himself, and with that smile I had my first inkling of the nature of the hold this man had over Holmes.

'Russell and I will be away again tomorrow, but before we go, is there anything I can do for you?' Holmes asked him.

'Do you know,' Baring-Gould answered after a moment, 'if it isn't too much trouble, I should very much like some music.'

Without a word Holmes rose and left the room. I sat in the window and listened to the slow, laboured breathing of the man in the bed, and when Holmes came back in with his violin, I slipped out.

For two hours I sat, first in our rooms and then downstairs, trying to read Baring-Gould's words concerning the *Curious Myths of the Middle Ages* and then his *Legends of the Patriarchs and Prophets* while the violin played the same sort of wistful, simple music I had first heard on the muddy road from Coryton station. It filled every corner of the house, and finally I took the current book, his recently published *Early Reminiscences* (which I had unearthed in the study between a tattered issue of the *Transactions of the Devonshire Association* and a pamphlet by Baring-Gould entitled 'How to Save Fuel') and escaped with it out of doors. Even the stables were not free of the music, I found. It was not until I closed the heavy door of the Lew Trenchard Church that silence finally enfolded me.

I had passed the building several times, a simple stone square with a proud tower, nestled into the tree-grown hillside and surrounded by gravestones and crosses. This was the first time I had been inside it, though, and I left the book of memoirs in my pocket while I looked around. It was an unsophisticated little stone building that straddled the centuries, with suggestions of thirteenth-century foundations rebuilt two and three hundred years later. The windows were not large, but the gloom cast was peaceful, not oppressive, and there was light enough to see. The air smelt of beeswax candles and wet wool from the morning services, but oddly enough, the feeling I received was not one of completion, but of preparation and waiting.

The single most dominating presence in the church was the screen framing the chancel. It was a magnificent thing, thick with niches and canopies, cornices and tracery, heavily encrusted with paint and gilt – far too elaborate for the crude little church but undeniably bearing the imprint of Sabine Baring-Gould's hand. It was his idea of what a Tudor roodscreen should look like, and once I had recovered from its first startling appearance, I found myself liking it for its sheer vehement assertion that God's glory is to be found in a backwater parish on the skirts of Dartmoor.

There were other nice things in the church, somewhat overshadowed by the shiny new screen, and I spent some time admiring St Michael and his dragon on one bench-end, a jester dated 1524 on another, the triptych in the side chapel, the old brass chandelier, and the carvings on the pulpit, before eventually taking the book from my pocket and settling onto one of the better-lit benches with it. I did not think God would object to my reading in His house, particularly not the memoirs of the man who had created this unlikely chapel in the wilderness.

An hour or so later, the door from the porch opened and Holmes came in. He removed his hat and slapped the light rain off of it, and came around through the church to sit on the other end of my pew. He leant forward, propping his outstretched arms on the back of the seat ahead of him and holding the brim of the dangling hat with the fingers of both hands. The prayer-like attitude of his position was deeply incongruous.

I closed the book of memoirs and looked up at the screen with its scenes from the life of Jesus. After a minute I spoke. 'He's dying isn't he?'

'Yes.'

'Is that why you've come?'

'I would have come anyway, but yes, it makes the solution of the case that much more urgent.'

Other than the visual commotion around us, the church was utterly still. I thought I smelt incense as well as the beeswax, and I could picture Baring-Gould in his robes up in that pulpit, speaking a few well-chosen words that would have some of his parishioners squirming and others chuckling to themselves, and I felt a strong and unexpected bolt of sorrow to know that I would never witness that scene.

The case Holmes and I had just finished had begun with a debt to a dead woman. For several weeks over the summer I had lived with the fact that debts to the dead are heavier than those owed the living because there is no negotiation, no forgiveness, only the stark knowledge that failure can never be recompensed, that even success can only restore balance. That case was a hard one in a lot of ways, and I had only begun to think about the lessons it had driven into me when Holmes' telegram had drawn me away from Oxford. Holmes, too, was still in the recovery stage, judging by the fact that he was still puffing on the black cigarettes he had taken up again in the most frustrating days of the Ruskin case. It had been a depressing affair whose solution only landed us in greater complexity, and now here we were, faced with another client who might not live to see the end of his case.

If working for the dead was hard, working for the dying looked to be harder yet: The already dead had eternity, after all. Baring-Gould did not.

'How long?' I asked.

'Weeks. Perhaps months. He will be gone before summer.'

'I am sorry.' Precisely what Baring-Gould meant to Holmes I still did not know, but I could readily see that there was depth to their relationship, and history.

He did not refuse my sympathy, did not say anything about Baring-Gould's fullness of years. He just nodded.

After a while, we left the church. The flat ground surrounding the building was, inevitably, covered with gravestones new and ancient. One of the newer was at the foot of the church tower down a small slope, and I went over to look at it. As I had thought, the name on the stone was that of Grace Baring-Gould, the transplanted mill girl who had married the parson and ended up here, the squire's wife. On her stone were carved the words DIMIDIUM ANIMAE MEAE. 'Half my life', Baring-Gould had placed there. I had no doubt that he waited now to join her.

We turned and went up the road to the village of Lew Down, where we took lunch in the Blue Lion, then walked around to the public bar to ask if Randolph Pethering had been seen that day. The barman knew immediately who we were talking about.

'You've missed 'en, by abaut two hours. Gone aut auver th' moor.'

'Out onto the moor? Why?'

''Untin' 'ounds,' he declared. ''S' right, he's gone a-hunting the 'Ound of the Baskervilles.' He peered at our faces, waiting for a reaction, and laughed aloud at what he saw there. Then he explained. 'Mr Petherin's one of they story fellas, writes down any rummage people tell 'en. Ole Will'm Laddimer, 'e comes by while Mr Petherin's tuckin' into 'is eggs this morning, and 'e sits and 'e tells Mr Petherin' abaut the goin's-on up the moor. You heerd tell they been seein' Lady 'Oward's carriage, and them's seed the 'ound's footprints 'round abaut daid bodies?'

'We heard.'

Somewhat deflated, either by the loss of an opportunity to recount the story or because of Holmes' flat inflection, the barman went on. 'That's all, really. Mr Petherin' heerd the 'ound was seen near Watern Tor and went to looky. He'll be back tomorry most likely. A pity you've already beed aut along the tor – you could've meeted him there.'

As we carried our glasses to a table, I said to Holmes, 'I don't know why I imagined we might keep our business to ourselves here.'

'There's no privacy in a village; for that you need either a truly remote setting or a city. No, everyone in this end of Devon will know who we are and what we're about.'

'I did wonder why you made no attempt to conceal our identity upon the moor.'

'There's no point in even trying, not unless you're willing to sustain a complete disguise.'

I took a swallow of the dark beer in my glass and found it filled the mouth pleasingly, rich with yeast and hops. I took another, and put the glass on the table with respect.

'What next, Holmes?' I asked.

'For the next two or three days I think we need to divide forces. I will go north to finish quartering the ranges for Mycroft's accursed spies and get that task out of the way. You can take the south-west. We need to find out how that carriage gets up onto the moor, and there are a limited number of routes it can take.'

I reached out and turned the glass around on the table, and with an effort pushed down the cold apprehension that wanted to rise up at the idea of walking alone onto the face of Dartmoor. When my voice was completely trustworthy, I asked him, 'Why do you assume the carriage comes onto the moor? Isn't it more likely that it is kept on the moor and brought out when needed?'

'It is of course possible, but in fact there are very few houses up there where a carriage and a pair of horses could be hidden, whereas there are a hundred places around the edges of the moor with considerably greater privacy. The north-eastern edges particularly, which is why you on the south and west will be covering a greater amount of ground than I will.'

'Do we leave this afternoon?'

'In the morning. That will give you a chance to study your maps. And I think it might speed matters up if we arranged a horse for you. You'll be making a circuit of half the moor; you would be a week on foot.'

Although normally I prefer to walk rather than be tied to the needs of a horse, I did not argue. Anything that would cut short the number of days I was to spend up on that bleak place had my approval.

I spent the afternoon in Baring-Gould's study, alone but for the fire, one somnolent cat, and a visit from Mrs Elliott with a tea tray.

I was aware of movement in the house – footsteps in and out of the bedrooms overhead, kitchen noises from beyond the door, the arrival of a mud-caked cart that disgorged an old woman, wrapped in rugs and dignity – but I ignored them all.

Instead, I made a complete perusal of the shelves and their contents, climbing up on the back of a chair and hanging from my fingertips at the higher reaches like a rock climber. There was not a great number of books, considering that the man was supposed to be a scholar and had been in the same house for forty years, and the volumes on the upper reaches particularly were covered with a thick blanket of dust.

I did find quite a few books written by Baring-Gould. In fact, after the first dozen or so I only thumbed through them to get an idea of the topic, and then replaced most of them, not being particularly interested in *A Book of the Rhine from Cleve to Mainz*; *The Tragedy of the Caesars*; *A History of Sarawak Under Its Two White Rajahs*; *Iceland, Its Scenes and Sagas*; a biography of Nelson; or even *Post-Mediaeval Preachers*, although I did set aside monographs on 'The Lost and Hostile Gospels: An Essay on the Toledoth Jeschu, and the Petrine and Pauline Gospels of the First Three Centuries of Which Fragments Remain' and 'Village Conferences on the Creed', plus a few books with irresistible titles: *Freaks of Fanaticism and Other Strange Events*; *Devonshire Characters and Strange Events* (Baring-Gould seemed to like strange and curious events); *Virgin Saints and Martyrs*; and two novels, one called *Pabo, the Priest*, the other *Urith: A Tale of Dartmoor*, the latter of which I could at least justify by calling it local research.

At the very end of the afternoon, when the grey light of the day had long turned to black at the windows and the smells of dinner were coming in under the door, I found what I had originally had in mind when I had entered the study five hours before and forgotten in the pleasure of prospecting the shelves for nuggets: a manuscript copy of *Further Reminiscences*, the Baring-Gould memoir for the second thirty years of his life. The clean copy was probably now with his publisher, as the first volume had only just come out, and this version was sprinkled with cross-hatchings and corrections, but the small handwriting was surprisingly legible. I left it in place, as a loose sheaf of papers requires a sedentary reader, but I planned to return to it later. Of the third volume, 1894-1924, there seemed to be only thirty pages or so of manuscript in a manila folder inside the high writing desk, along with a pen with a worn nib, crusted with ink, and a dusty inkwell. I held the manuscript pages in my hand, wondering bleakly if he would ever finish the volume. It did not appear to have been worked on for some time.

The study door opened and Holmes walked in. 'Dinner in ten minutes, Russell. You ought to have memorised those maps by this time.'

The maps. I had not even looked at the things, although Holmes could not know that for certain, as they had been shifted around in the course of the afternoon's ransacking – I might, after all, have folded them up after having committed the pertinent sections to memory. I murmured something non-committal and began to search earnestly for a pencil. Holmes picked one up and held it out to me, not a whit deceived. I thanked him and stuck it in my shirt pocket, noticing as I did so the state of my nails.

'I think I ought to go and tidy up,' I said. A fair percentage of the several cubic feet of dust I had set free seemed to have settled on my person. I picked up the tall stack of books I had set aside for reading and tucked them underneath my arm.

'Don't forget these, Russell,' he said drily. I took the maps he was holding out, wedged them on top of the books, and made my way out of the crowded study and up the stairs.

After dinner we climbed the stairs to Baring-Gould's bedroom. We found him seated in a chair at the window, looking tired and ill and without strength. Looking what he in fact was: a man not far from his death.

Watching him, one could see the effort it cost him, but he succeeded in rallying his forces, his eyes coming to life, his mind focusing again on us and the problem he had given into our hands.

'We're off tomorrow, Gould, for two days,' Holmes told him. 'We need to find how Lady Howard's carriage is coming up onto the moor, and I have to take a closer look at the army ranges for Mycroft.'

A smile tugged at Baring-Gould's mouth. 'Don't let them blow you up, Holmes.'

'I shall endeavour to avoid becoming a target,' Holmes assured him.

'You don't mean they're actually firing up there?' I exclaimed.

'It is a firing range, Russell.'

'But—' I bit back the mouthful of protests and cautions, as there would be little point in voicing them. Besides which, I told myself, Holmes would never have reached his present age if he could not be trusted to dodge an artillery shell.

It was Gould who reassured me, or tried to. 'I shouldn't think they are practising this late in the season. They normally finish in September.'

'Before we go, Gould,' said Holmes, 'just take a look at the map for us and tell Russell if there are any points a person could take a carriage onto the moor that aren't obvious from the markings.'

'A ghostly carriage doesn't need a road, Holmes,' Baring-Gould said in a stern whisper. Holmes did not deign to answer, merely took a folded smaller-scale map from his pocket and shook it out, holding it up by the corners directly in front of Baring-Gould. The old man had only to pull down his spectacles from his forehead to study the map, but instead he smiled and waved Holmes away.

'No need for that; I can see it better with my eyes closed.' He did actually close his eyes, and Holmes laid the map over a table for those of us whose eyes were better than our knowledge of the moor. I took out a pencil.

'I think that, as the sightings have all been in the northern quarter, we need not bother with anything south of the Princetown Road. Is this reasonable?'

'For the present,' Holmes said, adding, 'We may have to expand the search later.'

'Very well. From the south, we begin at the point where the Princetown Road enters Tavistock.' I dutifully made a small circle on the map. 'From there up to Mary Tavy the gates are all on the east side of the Tavy, and will coincide with the lanes leading down to the river. Except,' he said, sitting forward and replacing his glasses onto his nose so he could take the pencil from me and circle an invisible fold in the contour lines, 'except for here, a lane that appears to skirt the field. Since the map was made, however, the farmer took down a section of the old wall, and now drives his cattle up onto the moor along here.' The edge of his fingernail traced a dip in the contour lines. 'Here is another place, but that should be obvious.' His eyes shifted sideways to take in my reaction. I nodded, and pointed to half a dozen other access points I could see. We both ignored the actual lanes and the labelled Moor Gates, looking only for the hidden places. 'Along here,' he said, 'there is an old miner's trail. And this here; it used to be a railway line for bringing peat off the moor. And of course this path here, marginally negotiable if the driver were very good and the horses strong.'

It did not take long for Baring-Gould's intimate knowledge of the moor to lay open the map to my eyes. I should begin by crossing the moor to the other side of Princetown, and from there work my way back to Lydford, while Holmes cut across the moor up to the north-eastern portion and worked his way counter-clockwise. We should either meet in the middle or, failing that, return here Wednesday night.

I took my leave of Baring-Gould with considerably greater warmth than I would have thought possible even a day or two earlier. Holmes played for him again that night, and although the music ended early, he did not return to our rooms until a very late hour.

CHAPTER TEN

I had almost written God-forsaken, but checked my pen, for God
forsakes no place, though He may tarry to bless.
— A BOOK OF DARTMOOR

I N THE MORNING I put together a bag – a simple enough procedure
that amounted to pushing everything I had brought with me except
my frock into the rucksack, borrowing a pair of sturdy riding boots,
and adding the book of Baring-Gould's memoirs and a map – and
walked down to the barn.

Here I was presented with a dilemma: Baring-Gould himself
had sent down an order that I be given the household's ageing
Dartmoor pony, a beast with a rough coat and a gloomy eye.
However, being a pony (even though not apparently interbred
with the Shetland) and I passing six feet in my boots and hat, the
picture I had of me on its back had a distinctly ludicrous air. I
wondered if perhaps Baring-Gould could be pulling some kind of
joke, and then dismissed the thought as unlikely.

'Surely there's another horse,' I protested to Charles Dunstan,
the household's equally ageing Dartmoor stable lad (whom I had
also seen working in the garden). 'What about this nice fellow here?'
The cob in the adjoining box was a good hand taller and, though
older even than the pony, appeared able and amiable.

'That's Red. He be th'orse what pulls the trap.'

'Can he be ridden?' To have a horse dedicated entirely to draught work was common enough on a big working farm, but unlikely here.

'Well, Mr Arundell rides'n all'y time, though he don't ride to the hunt. But, Winnie'd be better up the moor. More surefooted, like.'

'It ought to be, with six feet touching the ground. Oh, never mind, Mr Dunstan,' I said, waving away his puzzlement. 'Red will do fine.'

He was, fortunately, shod, and his saddle was soon on him, its stirrups lengthened to suit my legs and the roughness of the terrain. A leather saddlebag was found to hold my possessions and a small bag of oats, as well as a last-minute addition from Mrs Elliott's kitchen that took up as much room as all the other objects combined. I pulled my hat down over my ears and, before any further additions could be found, such as a bell tent or a butterfly net, I put my heels into Red's sides and rode away from Lew Trenchard in a light mist.

The horse was as solid and without frills as his name, capable of two gaits: a leisurely stroll and a spine-snapping trot. An experimental urge towards a canter met with a slowing of the trot and a laying back of the ears, a clear message that he was going as fast as he could, damn it, and if I didn't like it, I could just get down and run myself.

I decided that there was no great need for speed, and where we were going there was no safe expanse of unbroken turf on which to practise it anyway. I and the horse settled down to our respective tasks.

However, Red had another idiosyncrasy that I did not discover until it was far too late to do anything about it: He shied.

My first hint of it was when I found myself tumbling into a protective roll in midair and thumping down onto the hard surface of the road at his feet. All the speed he lacked in forward motion he saved up for this burst of lateral movement: Red leapt like a startled cat, straight up and ten feet to the side. He didn't then bolt, didn't kick, didn't play hard to get; he just flew to one side as if being yanked offstage by a giant hand, and then stood placidly, looking slightly puzzled as to why I had chosen to fling myself to the ground, and waited for me to catch the reins and remount.

Which I did, having first checked to make sure I was whole and then looked closely at his hoofs, legs, girth, and any place else I could think of for a possible reason for his extreme action. Finding none, we rode on cautiously, and when there was no repeat of this aberration, my grip gradually loosened and my attention returned to its wandering ways, and an hour or so later the same thing happened.

Why hadn't the accursed stable lad bothered to mention this small quirk? I wondered, picking myself up painfully from the rocks.

We did cover the remainder of the ten-odd miles to Tavistock without incident. I scraped the mud from my clothing, fed and watered myself and the horse at an inn, remounted, and turned upward onto the moor. The mist firmed up into a drizzle.

Perversely, Red seemed to enjoy hills, leaning into them at a faster pace than his usual amble. Climbing the steep hill up from Tavistock, for the first time since leaving Lew Trenchard I began to think this might not be such a bad idea after all.

The road wound up the side of a hill, climbing a thousand feet in a mile, all of it a narrow but well-used track. At one tight patch we were confronted by a lorry committed inexorably to its downward journey, and I was grateful that Red did not argue about the need to remove ourselves from its path with all speed. We cowered in a faint indentation in the wall, pressing against the dripping bushes, and I heard the vehicle scrape a quantity of paint from its opposite side before it was past, the driver calling a nonchalant thanks. The rest of the climb was made without incident, and the moor opened up before us.

I dismounted, to give Red a rest but also to allow myself a moment to study this strange place. Even with Holmes' assurance that I need only keep to the roads, I did not relish the thought of entering the moor by myself. I stood beside Red and thought about the clear sense of personality I had had forced on me in the fog, the idea that Dartmoor was alive. Are you going to allow me to pass? I asked it, only half mocking. Will you keep from throwing your rain and wind at me, pulling your mists up over my head, setting your haunts to plague me and your pixies to lead me astray? I don't much like you, I told the land before me, but I mean you no harm. There was no answer, other than the sound of Red cropping at the brief grass with a distinct lack of enthusiasm. After a bit, I got to my feet. Friend or foe, I had no choice but to enter.

The road stretched out across the flat, rock-studded ground, the same terrain I had seen north of here, interrupted only by a quarry gouged into a dip and curve of the road and by the prison, riding a rise some distance from the road near Princetown. A grim place like all its kind, it seemed to declare that there would be no coddling of felons here, that punishment, discomfort, and boredom were to be their lot. The motto over the gate, I had heard, read PARCERE SUBJECTIS, or 'To spare the Vanquished', and with Virgil I had to agree that it was marginally more humane to incarcerate one's enemy than it was to slaughter him. Built originally as a camp for prisoners in the Napoleonic War, Princetown Prison had seen the Black Hole and the cat-o'-nine tails, starvation diet and hard labour, and if recent years had seen a more enlightened regime, the image of life within those grey, circular walls remained one of brutality and deprivation, what Holmes had referred to as a place designed for the breaking of men's spirits. I suddenly realised that I had been sitting and looking at the prison for too long, and that I did not wish to have a guard sent down to ask my business. I put my heels to Red's side; for once he obliged.

He did not throw me again until we were nearly in Postbridge, when I was leaning inattentively in the saddle to look over a wall and found the wall coming rapidly up to meet me. Long years of martial training gave my body an automatic response to a fall, but hitting a padded gymnastic mat and flying into a pile of stones were different matters entirely.

I climbed back over the wall and grabbed the reins with more force than was either necessary or sensible. 'Damn you!' I shouted at him. 'A few bruises are one thing, but if you break my spectacles, how do you expect us to get home again?' I stormed around to mount, and had my left foot in the stirrup when a voice came from somewhere behind me.

'Does him usually hanswer you?'

I turned with my foot still in the irons, and nearly fell again. There was a face looking at me over the wall on the opposite side on the road, a person so wrapped up in scarves and hats as to make any sexual identification difficult, but I thought it a young woman rather than an unlined, beardless youth. I laughed, embarrassed more at my loss of temper than at having been caught talking to the animal.

'He hasn't answered me yet, but we only met a short time ago. It wouldn't surprise me too much if he did.'

'Him's Mr Arundell's 'oss, bainty?'

'Yes,' I said, surprised. Lew House was a fair distance from here.

'Thought so. They boft'n cheap 'cause 'e kept dumping the lady who had'n avore. Don't do it to menvolk, cooriusly enuv.'

A misogynist gelding. Dear God, what on earth was I doing here? 'You know Mr Arundell?'

'He rides down here sometimes when th' hunt's on, though he do like ter follow th' hounds on foot.'

'Having met Red, I couldn't blame him.'

'I knaw who ye be,' she said conversationally.

'Do you?'

'You're with Znoop Zherlock, baint you? I heerd tell you're 'is wife?'

I supposed the question on the end of her last statement was understandable, even without the oddity of our ages, as I was wearing the same sort of raiment as she was.

'That I am.'

'And you're here for the Squire, Mr Baring-Gould.'

'Here now,' I protested. 'What makes you think that?'

'Oh, me mum's cousin's close friends with the zister of Miz Endacott, who cleans for Miz Elliott three days a week.'

'What do they think I'm doing for Mr Baring-Gould?' I demanded; and walked across to look over the wall at this all-knowing gossip.

'Ye be axin' questions about old Josiah Gorton and the ghostly carridge.'

'Well, I'll be—' I stopped, stoppered my rising irritation, and asked more calmly, 'So, do you know anything about either?'

'I doan,' she admitted. 'But Eliz'beth Chase, along by Wheal Betsy, she be waitin' to see'y.'

'Wheal Betsy being . . . ?'

'Up from Mary Tavy.'

Which was nearly back to Lew Trenchard from here.

'What does she want to see me about?'

'An 'edge'og.'

I opened my mouth to continue this line of questioning, and then closed it, turned my back, and led the horse away. I would not be driven insane by the peculiarities gathered around me. I would not.

The rationale behind my expedition was fairly simple and really quite sensible, in its own way: The great inner sweep of the moor, in several remote spots of which a rather substantial ghostly carriage had been seen, was not, as Holmes had pointed out, a place overly endowed with facilities in which to store a coach and stable its horses. Granted, the moor was well populated with horses, but animals big enough and well enough trained to pull a carriage over rough ground by moonlight were hardly likely to blend in with the compact, wild inhabitants of the moor.

Around the edges of the moor, however, lived people, and people (as I had just demonstrated) noticed things and talked about them. The sound of harnessed horses at night, strange hoof prints in a lane, dogs barking at the moon, all would have attracted attention if they had come in from outside, passing through the circle of farms and villages. Therefore, a careful circuit of the moor's outer band of civilisation ought to tell us whether or not the carriage had passed through it.

On one level, the disproportionate use of our time hunting for something that might not exist was more than a touch ridiculous – what the detectives at Scotland Yard might have to say about our carriage hunt did not bear thinking. On the other hand, the search was typical of Holmes' approach to an investigation: One looked for an oddity, some little thing that stood out, and traced it to its source (praying that it was not a mere coincidence, a thing that was, unfortunately, far from unknown). This appearance of a mythic coach just at the time a moor man was killed was too much of a coincidence to be believed. Hence the hunt – or rather, our two hunts, one on each segment of the circumference.

Postbridge, unlike the earlier Two Bridges (which consisted of little more than the inn where Holmes and I had stayed the week before) was an actual settlement, boasting two churches and a telephone kiosk. I had a choice of inns there (if one used the term inn in its loosest sense), and I chose the place with the attempt at flowers near the entrance.

I was tired, and ached in a number of unfamiliar places. It was a long time since I had spent so many hours in the saddle, even without three violent collisions with the ground. I ate a meal that consisted mostly of flour in various forms (all of them inexplicably both tasteless and unpleasant to smell) and drank some thin, sour red wine that seemed to go with my mood, and then took myself to bed – without having questioned a single resident about traces of the coach. Holmes would positively quiver with disapproval when he discovered my neglect, I knew, but at that moment I could not have stirred myself into action had the threat of divorce been held over my head. I asked for a lamp to supplement the lonely candle on the bedside table, put on two pairs of woollen socks and a thick pullover, inserted myself between the clammy bedclothes, opened *Early Reminiscences* to read another chapter, and woke some hours later with the oily smell of the guttering lamp wick permeating the inside of my throat and nasal passages. I wound the wick down to extinguish it, pulled the covers over my aching head, and went back to sleep.

In the morning when I finally relinquished unconsciousness, the reason for the previous night's almost preternatural sense of smell as well as the odd disinclination to exert myself became obvious: I was working up to a cold.

Bleary, stuffy, aching, and thick-headed, I tottered down the stairs on legs that seemed less than securely connected to the rest of me.

Scalding tea helped, but not enough, and the thought of venturing into the heavy rain I could see pouring down the windows was more than I could face. When a gust of wind-driven rain came rolling over the countryside at me, I accepted that as an omen; I told my landlady that I should be spending the day in my bed, not to have the room tidied, and I should ring if I wanted anything. With that I retreated, and slept on and off for the remainder of the day.

Inevitably, I woke in the middle of the night. The inn was completely still, no creaks or groans, not even the perpetual background gurgle of rain through downpipes. The silence was so remarkable it pulled me up to wakefulness, then alertness. I became aware of other things: the stuffy air, the faint and offensive smell of stale onion from the half-eaten bowl of soup I had left to be cleared, which still sat on the table near the door. I got out of bed and went to open the window, but once at the glass I was held by the sight before me. I turned back to fetch my spectacles and the coverlet from the bed, and perched on the narrow window seat for my first sight of the moor without rain falling.

The crisp half-moon rode a black sky, dotted here and there with the wisps of a few very high clouds. Postbridge itself was in a little hollow near a river, but the back of this inn faced out over the moor, and the moor was a place transformed, a stark landscape of gentle moonlit hills punctuated by patches of black rock or hollows, quiescent and motionless and unreal.

After probably an hour of sitting huddled staring out at the view, I woke abruptly from a doze and caught myself leaning towards the open window. I stood up, pulling the warm bedclothes back around my neck, and cast another glance at the moor. Actually, I decided, the white moon against the black sky was very pretty, but the moor itself was just pale expanse with dark patches, with one tor tantalisingly silhouetted against the moon. Much nicer than the ceaseless rain, though. Perhaps the storm's passing meant that it would remain clear the following day.

Chapter Eleven

How noticeable in the progress of mankind in knowledge is
the fact that before the opening of a door hitherto shut,
another that has swung wide for generations should
be slammed and double bolted.

— EARLY REMINISCENCES

THE SKY WAS NOT exactly clear the next day, although it was not yet raining. Neither was my cold gone, though the fever had departed and my lungs were clean enough. I had no real excuse for indulging myself with another day in bed.

With my eye, however blearily, back on the job, I made my way methodically through the staff of the inn, asking my questions. To my growing consternation, every one of them knew who I was, why I was there, and had information saved up for me. Unfortunately, the information was all of the signs-and-portents variety, which might have proved interesting to a student of folklore but which led me no closer to the cold, dull realm of factual truth. I thanked each of my would-be informants, even the stable boy who gave me a thrice-watered-down version (or perhaps more accurately, thrice-added-to) of the fright a village girl had received from a neighbour's dog one night. I paid my account, and left.

Red seemed positively frisky after his day's rest. I wondered morosely how long he would wait before flinging me off, but his ears remained pricked, and we passed trees, standing stones, Scottish cows, and even a rabbit warren without incident. Perhaps it was the rain. Or being taken away from his warm stables, and we were now facing back towards home. Or a temporary brainstorm, Your Honour. Whatever it was, I found it a relief to remain seated and upright as the morning went by.

Aside from the horse's behaviour and the dry (if grey) skies, the day was one calculated to madden. Coughing and sneezing my way across the countryside, my level of energy too low to bother with imaginary demons beyond a vague wariness, I was greeted by each inhabitant with a dignified respect, as if I were the representative of a royal Personage. Heads were bared, work stopped, children lined up: even the bad curtsey, for God's sake.

They all tried very hard to give me something of value for my collection of strange events. Memories had very obviously been ransacked for anything out of the ordinary, anything at all: a pony missing, a neighbour's baby dead in its cradle, an uncle driven from his land, a cousin's friend disappearing. Under closer questioning, the baby had been sickly, the uncle old and ready to sell, and the girl who disappeared had come back a week later with a young new husband in tow. The pony was, admittedly, still gone; I promised to watch for it.

More than the frustration of fruitless questioning, it was the sense of ceremony that began to drive me mad, the feeling that the entire moor was bound together in a wordless conspiracy to honour the investigation. I did not know if it was Baring-Gould we were doing obeisance to or Holmes; all I knew for certain was, it wasn't me. The residents of the stone houses that huddled into the breast of the moor were invariably friendly, expectant, proud, and eager to help, and filled with the most arcane and useless pieces of information. Indeed, it seemed as if the most accurate knowledge they had was to do with me and my business, which I would just as well have left quiet.

Oh, there were plenty of coach sightings: twenty of them before the day was over, all of which faded to second- or third-hand reports, or coaches with headlamps swiftly floating along the macadamised roads, or coaches that were more probably the next-farm-but-one's cart.

Finally, when I was tired and aching and seething with frustration, and thought it could not get any worse, it was brought to my attention that I had a nickname. No: not even my own proper nickname, but a mere appendage to that of my husband. At two o'clock on Wednesday afternoon, the fifteen-year-old daughter of the house opened the door, gave me a beatific smile of welcome, and addressed me as Zherlock Mary.

Not even Snoop Mary, for God's sake.

I turned and left the farmyard, too demoralised even to ask my questions.

That farm was the last for a bit, the next one being about three-quarters of an hour away on the other side of a tor-capped hill. I was exhausted, my fever was creeping back up, my throat, head, and joints ached and my nose ran continuously. I felt ill and useless, I was certain that when I returned to Lew House I should find Holmes sitting with his feet up in front of the fire with the case neatly solved, and I was hit by a wave of homesickness for Oxford and books, my pen scratching peaceably in front of my own fire, a cup of lovely hot coffee steaming on the desk at hand's reach, the ideas marching cleanly out in logical procession, my own ideas that no one else could second-guess or circumvent or—

Red shied, and I hit the ground hard.

When I had come to a halt, I flopped over onto my back on the nice soft turf, gazing up into a sky that I had not realised was nearly clear of clouds, and I began calmly, easily, to weep.

It was not just the irritation and the illness that made me cry, although they certainly lowered my defences considerably. It was not even my fury at this damnable horse, which was powerful, but momentary. It was, I think, more than anything the emotional burden from the previous case spilling over, a burden of grief I had pushed away under the pressure of solving the murder, and then contrived to avoid by a change of scenery and more work when it ended.

So I lay flat on my back and cried like a child, in recognised grief for Dorothy Ruskin and fresh, raw grief for the dying Baring-Gould, in frustration at the ridiculous mockery of detective work I was forced to carry out and at my inability to anticipate the antics of my four-legged companion, in rage at the horse and at the sudden shock of pain; at everything and nothing, I cried.

Not for long, of course, because I soon could not breathe at all and I thought my head should explode if I did not stop. I gingerly raised myself upright, then got to my feet, and walked over to sit on a nearby boulder that a hundred years ago or so had fallen away from the tor that loomed over my head. I dried my face, blew my nose, rested my head in my hands until the pounding internal pressure had subsided – long enough for a rabbit to lose its fear and venture out of its burrow among the clitter. It ducked into hiding when I put my glasses on preparatory to standing and retrieving Red, but when I raised my head I thumped back down onto the boulder, more stunned than I had been by any of the falls.

For I saw: beauty. I saw before me an undulating sweep of green and russet hills crowned by the watchful tors and divided up by the meandering streams and the stone walls. A cloud moved in front of the pale autumnal sun, its dark shadow passing across the hills like a hand in front of a face, leaving the surface clean and refreshed.

Dartmoor lay stretched before me, quiet, ageless, green, brown, and open; not vast, but limitless; not open to conquest, but willing to befriend; calm, contemplative, watchful. It was, I saw in a flash of revelation, very like the Palestinian desert I had known and come to love four years before, a harsh and unfriendly place until one succumbed to its dictates and submitted to the lesser rhythms of life in a dry land.

Dartmoor was a wet desert, its harsh climate the other end of the spectrum from the hot, dry climate of Palestine, but with similar small, tight, ungenerous, and intense results. Fighting the strictures of a desert brought only exhaustion, ignoring its demands risked death, but an open acceptance of the perfection of the life to be lived therein – one might find unexpected riches there. And, perhaps, here.

The fitful sun went away eventually; and the moor stopped speaking to me, but when I got to my feet it was all different.

I was no longer a stranger here.

I climbed up the fat, weathered stones tumbling down from the tor and stood looking down at this miraculously transformed piece of countryside. At last I knew what we were doing here, why the death of an itinerant moor man should matter, why Baring-Gould had found his calling and the spiritual nourishment he required, breathing the air of Dartmoor.

When eventually I returned to Red and to my task I was chagrined to find that the change in my perspective did not have much effect on the frustration I felt in trying to question the moor dwellers, or on my physical state: It still felt like trying to carve blancmange, and I still ached and coughed and sneezed. It certainly had no gentling effect on Red, who managed to dump me off once more before we stopped for the evening.

It did, however, help me begin to understand the people I was dealing with, isolated individuals who were nonetheless bound tightly together by the land on which they dwelt. When I spoke to a woman feeding the chickens in her yard or a family squeezed together for a meal, I was speaking not just with solitary, hard-pressed people, but with members of the community that was Dartmoor.

And not a damn one of them had seen anything that sounded the least bit important.

Holmes and I had agreed to meet back at Lew House on Wednesday night. I could actually have made it back there, but it would have meant a job incomplete (even a futile job) and ten wasted miles to return in order to finish it. Instead, I rode down to Mary Tavy and placed a call from the post office there to the postmistress in Lew Down, asking her to have someone take a message to Baring-Gould saying that Mary Russell had been delayed and would not return until the following evening. I waited as the woman on the other end of the line wrote the message, and thanked her.

'Oh, that's quite all right, Mrs Holmes,' she said cheerfully. 'I'll have my boy run right down with it. However, I think Mr Holmes is still away as well. In London, you know.'

It was news to me, but I was not about to admit it. I rang off, shaking my head at a bush telegraph system that surpassed anything I had ever met in rural Sussex.

I found a room in a pleasant old inn in Mary Tavy (not, incidentally, the same inn where Holmes and I had lunched following our encounter with the Scottish cattle) and fell into bed for three or four hours when I first arrived. I woke hungry and went down for some dinner and what proved to be a very interesting evening with the locals – interesting not for the information received, which was nil, but for the insight.

It took me a little while to realise, in the course of conversing about local politics and the fiends in Whitehall, that there were two very separate groups of men in the pub: those who lived in the village, and the men who lived up on the moor. Slowly, through glances and silences and the sorts of tiny smiles that may as well be winks, I came to see that as far as the moor men were concerned, the villagers were a separate and, regrettably, slightly inferior race.

My first inkling of this attitude came when, to my surprise, I was not greeted by name, or even with the stance of familiarity that had been characteristic of the last few days. At first, I assumed with pleasure that I had found a roomful of natives who had not heard of me; then I began to notice the covert glances and secret smiles of the quieter, more roughly dressed members of the drinking community. One by one these half dozen men would catch my eye, touch his hat brim briefly or raise his glass in my direction, and turn back to his conversation.

It was a very peculiar and strangely warming sensation, being part of a secret society. Somehow, the fact that my fellow conspirators were impoverished, unwashed, and possibly illiterate farmers and shepherds was more amusing than anything else. Certainly they seemed to find it so, judging by the twinkle in a number of eyes.

Halfway through my second pint, one of the young men I had been talking with reached into a pocket and stretched out his arm to set something on the table beside my glass: a tin whistle. I looked at it, and then looked up into his weathered young face with the secret smile in the back of his eyes.

'I heerd tell you play'n,' he said.

I shook my head and moved the slim instrument back onto his side of the table.

'The noises I make with it couldn't be called playing, I'm afraid.'

'Baint what us hears.' He might as well have winked and nudged me in the ribs with his elbow, but I refused to blush at the memory of the evening in Two Bridges to which he was no doubt referring. He picked up his small flute, flipped it over and caught it, put it to his mouth, and started to play. When the first sprightly notes hit the smoke-filled air, the moor men glanced at one another, and then at the town dwellers, and one by one they cleared their throats and began to sing.

What I heard that night was a last vestige of the dying art of the

Dartmoor song men. They began with a cheerful tune and the story of a monstrously lazy young man whose father, a cutter of green broom, threatens to burn the house down around his son's ears if the lad doesn't go out and work. The young man hauls himself out to the woods, succeeds in cutting a respectable bundle of the broom, and on his way home is spotted by a wealthy widow. She is smitten, and instantly proposes marriage. He reluctantly agrees to sacrifice his career and leave off his labours for her sake, and the song ends with the sly observation:

'Now in market and fair, the folk all declare,
There's nothing like cutting down broom, green broom.'

The singers correctly read my broad grin as a request for more, and they launched into another song, this one about two star-crossed lovers, and then another about, of all things, a bell-ringing competition set to a gorgeous tune that wound the strong voices around one another like the ring of bells they evoked, ending precisely as a ring of bells would, with a low, final note, sustained and then hushed.

We sat in silence, united momentarily in beauty, but as I stirred to thank them, one of the villagers decided it was time to keep up their side. He opened his mouth, and as the words 'Tom Pearce, Tom Pearce, lend me your grey mare' rang out in the room, my heart cringed. Uncle Tom Cobbley rode off to Widdecombe Fair with his companions – accompanied, I was interested to note, solely by the Mary Tavy contingent. The moor men sat back, listening politely, but as soon as Tom and the rest had finally joined the old mare's ghostly, rattling bones, the whistle piped up again and set us on the road to another fair, one with considerably more risqué goings-on. (Two of the moor men glanced at me first before they joined in, reassuring themselves that I would be too innocent to grasp the underlying meaning of the references to locks, locksmiths, and the young lady's 'wares'.)

They sang for more than two hours, during which time they collected what must have been half the town, who stood watching from the doors and the nether reaches of the dim, ancient rooms. The village singers occasionally pushed a song in edgeways; when they did, the half dozen moor dwellers sat attentively waiting for them to finish, although I had the feeling that they knew the village songs, even if the villagers might not know those of the moor.

At long last, and sounding reluctant, the pub owner called for last orders. The young man who had begun the whole affair began carefully to clean his whistle on the tail of his shirt, but to my surprise instead of putting it away when he had finished, he held it out to me. To my greater surprise, I took it.

I thought for a moment, turning the simple instrument over in my hands, until I decided on a tune, a song I had learnt to play on the tin whistle's wooden brother a long, long time before, at my mother's knee. It was a sad, repetitive Jewish song that came from the heart; judging from the hush in the room, it went straight there, too.

I finished, having played blessedly free of mistakes, and gave my companion back his whistle. He took it without comment, but I thought, on the whole, that he approved.

'Time for one more,' he said, and raised his eyebrows to ask if I might have any suggestions.

'The song about Lady Howard's coach?' I asked tentatively. He repeated the little consultation ritual with which he had begun the evening's entertainment, glancing first at his fellows to assess their agreement and then at the villagers to make certain they were in their places. He then put the flute to his lips and began the restless, eerie tune that Baring-Gould had sung. Two of the villagers started to join in but one dropped out after a sharp glance from one of the moor singers, and the other stopped when he was kicked by a companion. The six members of my secret conspiracy were left singing, their voices harmonising easily in what was obviously a well-known song, one of them gently thumping the table in front of him to underscore the driving cadence. Unlike the other songs they had sung, however, this one was serious business. They seemed to be listening to the words as they sang, and stared in blank concentration at fire or glass, their only contact with one another, and with me, their intended audience, through throat and ear.

It was an odd song, and my first reaction was confirmed, that this was no bedside carol for a small child. I had to wonder how one particular small child, the imaginative eldest son of a land-holding family, felt about the verse that refers to Lady Howard drawing the squire into her coach.

The pub was still for a good ten seconds when they had finished. With a general sigh and murmur, the audience, including the village men who had themselves sung, expressed its appreciation and began to move away into the night.

The moor men, too, drained their glasses and got to their feet. With a nod of the head or a brief tug at the cap they each bade me their farewells. The pub was soon empty but for the girl collecting glasses on a tray; I went upstairs and left her to it.

CHAPTER TWELVE

The old woman was not regarded as a witch, but she was accredited
with a profound acquaintance with herbs and their virtues

— FURTHER REMINISCENCES

MY FIRST TASK FOR the new day was to hunt down the woman whose name I had been given (what seemed a remarkably long time before) by the girl speaking to me over the wall near Postbridge. Elizabeth Chase, the girl had said, near Wheal Betsy, wanted to see me about a hedgehog. It sounded unlikely enough to be true.

Wheal Betsy proved to be the still very solid brick engine house of a now-abandoned mine, formerly a rich source of lead and silver. It was also, to my amusement, directly at the foot of Gibbet Hill.

As I rode, I began to feel as if I had the spirit of a young Baring-Gould at my side. It was the invariable result of immersing myself in the man's words and his surroundings for the past week, but it was not a troubling presence. Indeed, I was finding him an amusing companion, this solitary youth with the passion for the moor and a mind as bright, energetic, and indiscriminate as a magpie.

A small shoeless child behind a gate leading to a muddy track pointed me towards the home of Elizabeth Chase. A man leading a horse, its off foreleg neatly bandaged but causing it to limp, confirmed it with a wag of his chin over his shoulder. Half a mile farther on, a woman hanging a heap of men's shirts out in the fitful sunlight directed me back on my steps, to a narrow lane that I had missed at the first pass. It was, unusually enough, a wooded lane, with actual overhead trees instead of the stunted, sparse shrubs that dominated this half of the moor. I followed it, on foot lest my hat be snatched off by branches, and came out at a scene from a children's story.

The cottage was ancient, tiny, orderly (but for the wayward curves of its walls and the thick lichen on its roof slates), and so clean the very stones seemed to gleam with polish. There seemed to be no one about – or at least no human. Six cats of varying colours and sizes lay distributed among a rough bench, a chopping block, and the rooftop, and three dogs (one of them missing a leg) wandered up to greet me. I could also see four breeds of chicken, a black swan with a crooked wing, two geese in a pen, a goat with a kid, and a shaggy Dartmoor pony with a bandage on its leg very like that on the leg of the draught horse I had seen being led down the lane – except that the pony's was on its near hind leg. I looked down at the grinning black-and-white face of the three-legged sheepdog, which also seemed to be lacking a number of its teeth, and said to it, 'Where's your mistress?'

As if it had understood me, it whirled around to look at the house, and when I did the same, I saw Elizabeth Chase in her doorway.

At first glance she seemed a normal size, until I realised that I should have to bend nearly double in order to walk through the doorway, yet she stood easily within its frame. I am accustomed to other women seeming small, but this one could not have been any larger than the average eight-year-old, and when my attention went back from her shape to her face, I knew that I had indeed entered a fairy tale. She was brown and wrinkled and stooped, and the tilt to her head, though undoubtedly a result of the hump in her spine, gave her an air of quizzical humour, as if she looked at the world with a sideways laugh. I was smiling when I introduced myself, and told her I had heard she was waiting to see me.

'Oh goodness yes, my dear,' she piped in an incredibly high, reedy little voice with a surprising lack of rural Devon in her accent. 'You must be dear Mr Holmes' wife, although I have to say you look more like a son in those clothes. Still, they're warm I'm sure on a cold day – although it's not so very cold this morning, now is it? I think I'll just finish making us a cup of tea and we can take it sitting right out here where we can look at God's good sunlight and pretend it's spring, instead of nearly winter again – goodness, how cold the winters get, my old bones just ache at the thought of another one, and it doesn't seem fair, the summers are getting so very short. Do you want to help me carry the tea things, then? That's very sweet of you, my beauty. No, no, this isn't for you, little thing.' The last sentence was directed at a thin grey tabby kitten halfway through adolescence, who had been in hopeful attendance from the moment its mistress stepped back into her cottage and all the time she had worked. The old woman's high voice sounded like ceaseless birdsong – or like the tin whistle the young man had played the night before – as she made the tea, shuffling around the watchful cat to kettle and tea caddy and cupboard and back. I had the strong impression that she talked continuously whether she had an audience or not – or perhaps I should say whether or not she had a human audience.

I took the tray from her and followed her with some difficulty out the door and to the rough-hewn bench in the sun. She lifted the somnolent cats down to the ground and told me to put the tray onto the bench, as the table that normally stood in front of the seat had collapsed the week before when a visiting cow had decided to use it for a scratching post, and it was now down at the neighbour's for repair.

She poured the tea and sweetened her cup with what looked like treacle but she told me was honey, brought her by a friend on the other side of the moor in exchange for a cracked hoof she'd managed to repair.

'You do a lot of animal doctoring,' I commented.

'Yes dear, I'm the local witch.' I blinked, and she began to giggle, a sound so high-pitched it had the sleeping dogs twitching their ears. 'I'm not a witch of course, child, though surely there are many here who would tell you I am. Just an old woman who knows her herbs and has the time to spend babying hurt creatures.' She closed her eyes and sat for a while, basking like a turtle in the faint warmth of the autumnal sun. I drank my tea and enjoyed that same warmth on my back.

'Now tell me, dear,' she said after a while (startling me, as my mind had wandered far away to Holmes and London), 'which do you wish to hear about first? My hedgehog or Samuel's dog?'

'Dog?' I sat up sharply. 'What do you know about a dog?'

'Oh, it was the son of Daniel down the road who saw it, last summer.'

'Why didn't I hear about this?' I demanded suspiciously. With the entire moor seemingly living in one another's pockets, why had no one thought to mention an actual sighting of the Hound?

'Daniel is very good at keeping things to himself. His Samuel was embarrassed, so he promised to say nothing, and he didn't, except to me. Perhaps you'd like to hear about the Hound first, then. Make yourself comfortable, child. It's a long story.

'As I said, it was the son of Daniel down the road that saw the

Hound. A fine young lad is Samuel, in school now of course, but then he was home on his summer holiday, and a good help to his parents he is, too. It isn't easy for them to be without him, but I told Daniel that his son's mind was too good to waste, and with a little help from me he won a place at the school in Exeter.

'But you're not interested in the maunderings of an old schoolteacher, are you, dear? You want the Hound, and although I might not tell it you if night was drawing in, on a sunny morning, I shall give it you.

'Samuel is a blessing and a help to his parents, and it so happened that his mother's sister up near Bridestowe had a baby the end of July, and though it all went well, thanks be to God, a month later she still was needing a bit of help with the heavy things. So Samuel was sent up every few days to take some fresh-baked bread or a dish of some kind that his mother had made, and help his aunty with the chores, and then walk back the next day. It's only five miles or so, and perfectly safe for a strapping young boy who knows to look out for mists and mires. Not like the city, which can be dangerous even for a full-grown man.

'Well, towards the end of August Samuel stayed later than usual. He was coming to the end of his holiday and, good boy that he is, he wanted to leave his aunty with a big pile of firewood and then finish the repairs to her hen-house that he'd begun. Of course, his uncle could've done those, but you know how boys need to feel they're indispensable.

'Between the firewood and the chicken run, then, he didn't leave until after tea. His aunty wanted him to stop another night and walk back in the morning, but it was a soft, clear evening and the moon was near full, and the little cot she had for him to sleep in was really too short for his growing legs, and his father liked him back of a Sunday morning to go to church, and aside from all that, his mother's breakfasts were better than his aunty's. Too, I think, knowing Samuel, it was an adventure, to cross the moor at night all by himself, when he'd only ever done it with an adult.

'You see, this was before all the stories got around about the strange happenings on the moor, although it was after I found Tiggy, which I'll tell you about in a minute.

'Samuel waited until the moon was up in the sky and then he kissed his aunty goodbye and left. He'd got in the habit of following the roads as far as Watervale, just this side of Lydford, because he sometimes found one of the neighbours driving home and he could take a ride in the back of their wagon or cart. That night, though, he didn't, so he left the road on Black Down and set off up the moor track.

'It's a goodly climb up the side of the moor, so Samuel used to go until he'd crossed the Tavy and then have a bit of a rest before the last bit. Sometimes his aunty'd give him a little something to keep him from starvation in the two hours it took him to get home, and that's when he would eat it, sitting on a stone over the river, waiting for his feet to dry before pulling his stockings and boots back on.

'That night it was a fruit scone with some preserves inside – a little stale, but Samuel didn't mind. He unwrapped it, and was sitting there eating it and watching the stream in the moonlight when something made him look up.

'At that place, the moor rises sharply, so it's quite a climb – too much for an old thing like me, but ideal for a boy like Samuel, just getting his muscles and proud of them. So when he looked up, the moor was over him, and outlined against the moonlit sky he saw a figure of hellish terror. At first he thought it a pony, it was so big, but then he saw how its tail raised up, and then he saw the light coming from the middle of its great, dark head.

'It was a dog, my dear, a dog such as hasn't been seen since Mr Holmes settled the Baskerville problem, a dog to bring a young boy nightmares and keep him locked inside when the sun is down.

'He ran, did Samuel, leaving his boots, his satchel, and his scone there by the river.

'Daniel never even considered that it might be his son's idea of a clever joke – one look at the state of the lad's feet and a person could tell that.

'Daniel wanted to take up his shotgun and go right back out, even if it meant carrying Samuel on his back, but the thought of going out into the night scared that brave little boy rigid. The next morning Daniel talked him into putting on a pair of old bedroom slippers and going back to the place by the river. The boy's boots and stockings were on the rock, right where he'd left them, but the scone was gone and the stone where Samuel had dropped it was licked clean, and the satchel he used for carrying his mother's cooking up to Bridestowe they found some distance off, torn to shreds.

'And a dog's footprints. Plenty of those, oh my, yes. Now, would you like to have another cup of tea before you hear about my little hedgehog?' the old woman asked brightly.

'Just a moment,' I said, thinking furiously and trying hard to assimilate this abrupt development, the fleshing out of a hound of ghostly rumours into a thing of flesh and bone, interested in the consumption of sweet scones. 'This was towards the end of August, around the full moon, and on a Saturday night?'

'That's right, dear.'

Which put it the twenty-fifth of August, the day before the full moon and the day after the courting couple had seen the dog with the carriage.

'And neither of them said anything about it?'

'Daniel loves his son. The boy shakes whenever anyone brings it up, so Daniel thought it best not to tell anyone. I only found out because I asked him what was wrong with the boy.'

'How old is Samuel?'

'Twelve, dear. A good, responsible age. Now I'll tell you about my Tiggy, shall I?'

I rubbed my brow, feeling a bit stunned, but said weakly, 'Do, please.'

'I was crossing the moor one day, back in the middle of summer,' she began.

'Do you know the date?' I interrupted, although by that time I knew enough to expect the answer I received.

'No my love, I'm sorry, but I haven't much need any longer for numbers on a page. I can tell you,' she continued, forestalling the second part of the question, 'that it was in July, and near enough the full moon as makes no difference, and it was a Saturday too, because I went to church services with my friend in Widdecombe the next day.' Even if she had been a schoolteacher, her answer was typical of those I had become accustomed to receiving, and in the end more precise than the answer of a calendar-user to whom days were easily forgotten dates instead of skies and seasons. She was describing the twenty-eighth of July, three days after Johnny Trelawny, and one day after the ramblers from London, had each seen Lady Howard's coach. I set my cup down on the bench and prepared to listen closely.

'I often go across, the moor, you know. I have friends in Moreton-hampstead and Widdecombe, and there's roots and things growing on that side and not this. So on a nice day when I don't have too many animals needing my eye – my "patients", as Daniel calls them – I'll take a sandwich and a bottle of tea and pay a call on my friends.'

Both of the places she had named were a good fifteen or twenty miles across some fairly rough countryside. 'Do you do the trip in a day?' I asked in surprise. Having seen her totter about, I doubted that she could cover more than two miles in an hour, and that on even ground.

'Oh, I stop the night there, dear,' she reassured me. 'Sometimes two nights, and come back the third day. One of Daniel's children feeds the beasties.' As if that was all that might concern me. 'But as I was saying, I was on the moor one day last summer when I heard the saddest little cry, it'd make your heart break to hear it. It was such a tiny noise, I had a time finding what was making it, until finally I found the poor wee thing in the shade of a standing stone. It'd been trying to dig a hole in the ground to hide itself in, but it hadn't a chance, even if it had been whole and strong.' She seemed not far from tears at the pathos of the thing.

'A hedgehog,' I said.

'That it was, a young Tiggy, would fit into your hand. I thought for sure it would die, it was that sorely treated. I decided all I could do was make it comfortable and sing to it until it passed on. So I popped it into my coat pocket and sang while I walked, and I took it out when I got to Widdecombe, fully expecting to have to borrow a spade and bury it.

'Only, don't you know, the little face looked up at me, so trusting, I just knew it would pull through. We gave it some milk with a drop of brandy in it, set its little leg – the back one, on the left – and wrapped it with a splint made from a nice smooth corset stay cut down to size, and I pulled together the great tear in its back with a piece of silk embroidery floss – green, it was; quite striking – and put it into a little box with some cotton wool near the fire.

'And in the morning it wrinkled its little nose at me, asking clear as it could, "Where's my breakfast?"'

'Was it all right, then?' I asked. Not perhaps the most professional of investigative enquiries, and certainly not the question Holmes would have had at that point, but I did want to know.

'Not very good, you understand, but it lived. I did have to take off its little foot with a pair of sewing scissors, I'm afraid. It was too badly crushed to save, and the infection would have killed it.'

I winced at the picture of two ancient ladies bent over the kitchen table doing an amputation with a pair of scissors, and moved quickly onto the proper questions. 'What had caused its injuries, do you know?'

'Now that's just it, dear,' she said, sounding approving. 'It was something moving fast – a cartwheel, maybe, or a boot – that squashed the poor thing's leg, but a dog had at it, too.'

The hair on the back of my neck stirred. 'How do you know that?' I demanded.

'Which, the cart or the dog?'

'Both.'

'Well, dear, I know that whatever it was squashed Tiggy had to be moving quickly, because if poor little Tiggy'd had a minute's warning he'd have curled up tight and been flattened right across, not just one stray leg. And the dog I know because any wild creature would've had more sense, and once tearing at Tiggy that way he'd either have stayed to finish him off or taken him home to feed his babies.'

Unlikely as it seemed, this was a witness after Holmes' own heart, and I took my hat off to her. Literally.

'What pretty hair you have, my dear,' she exclaimed, and reached out to pat it lightly. 'I had a cousin once who had strawberry blond hair just like yours, and she was bright as her hair, too.'

I had to admit that I was not feeling particularly bright, and asked her if she had seen any hoof marks or cart tracks.

'I'm afraid I didn't, dear. The ground was dry, you know, and it takes something pretty heavy to make a dent.'

I found it hard to imagine the turf of the moor dry and hard, but I had to defer to her greater knowledge of the place. I then asked her about the precise location of the hedgehog's unfortunate accident.

I offered her my map, but she waved it away, saying that her eyes found such fine work a difficulty, so instead she described her route subjectively – the hills and flats, a tor gone by, a stream crossed, the morning sun in her eyes – and I eventually decided on a stone circle below a rise that seemed to coincide with her description. I folded up the map and replaced it in the breast pocket of my coat. She seemed not to have finished with me, however, and sat with her head, at an angle and an expectant look on her face. I thought perhaps she was waiting for my final judgement, which I did not think I could give her.

'I have to admit, I don't know enough about the habits of hedgehogs to say if I agree with your ideas,' I began. Her face instantly cleared and she began to nod in understanding.

'Then you won't know the real question here, and that is, "What was Tiggy doing there?"'

'I'm sorry, you'll have to explain that.'

'Tiggy doesn't live out on the moor, dear. Tiggy likes the woods and the soft places.'

'And there aren't any?'

'Not in two or three miles of where I found him.'

'What if some animal had carried it? Whatever gave it the bite, for example, or a big hawk?'

'Well, that's possible, I suppose, dear,' she said, sounding very dubious. 'But I was wondering if it wasn't more likely that Tiggy was accidentally taking a ride on whatever it was run him down.'

CHAPTER THIRTEEN

. . . The reader is tripping over uncertain ground, not knowing
what is to be accepted and what rejected.

— A BOOK OF DARTMOOR

WHEN I TOOK MY leave from Elizabeth Chase, the good witch of
Mary Tavy, my mind, to borrow a phrase from Baring-Gould's
memoirs, was in a ferment. It was still only midday, and Lew House
little more than two hours away; I decided to take a look at the place
where she had found the injured Tiggy.

I found it without difficulty – there are not so many stone circles
on the moor to make for a confusion – but I was not quite sure
what to make of it. The site was typical of its kind, upright hunks of
granite arranged in a rough circle on a piece of relatively flat ground
and surrounded by the moor's low turf, broken here and there
by stones and bracken. A double row of stones (one of Randolph
Pethering's 'Druid ceremonial passages') lay in the near distance,
and a moorland track (the Abbot's Way?) ran alongside.

As Elizabeth Chase had indicated, the most curious part of the
hedgehog affair was why the animal should have been out here in
the first place. The more I thought about it, the more I had to agree:
The little beasts are lovers of woods and the resultant soft leaf mould
under which to take cover, a far cry from this blasted heath, which

even a badger would have been hard put to carve into a home.

I pulled from Red's saddlebag the cheese and pickle sandwich and bottle of ale that I had asked for that morning at the Mary Tavy inn, and carried them over to a stone that had once, by the looks of the hollow in the ground at one end, been upright. I laid out my sandwich and opened the bottle with the bottle-opening blade of my pocket knife, and ate my lunch, enjoying the sun and my prehistoric surroundings, and most especially the delightful image of a hitch-hiking hedgehog.

An almost light-hearted air of holiday had set in. After all, I had more or less completed my assignment, with an unlikely but glittering gem to carry back to Lew Trenchard and a mere handful of houses between here and the edge of the moor at which to carry out the formalities of my enquiries. My sense of taste had returned, I could very nearly breathe the air, and the sun was actually shining. I stretched out with my head on one stone and my boots on another, and rested for ten minutes before gathering my luncheon debris and swinging back up into the saddle.

'Home, Red,' I said to him, and endured a few hundred yards of his trot before pulling him back to his usual amble.

This time when he shied, I was ready for him. Unfortunately.

Given a negative stimulus of sufficient strength, one can train even the most stubborn animal to avoid a given activity. Red had trained me quite effectively: No sooner did my mind begin to drift away into its own world than it snapped back to apprehensive attention. Twice, this was unnecessary. The third time my quick reversion to full awareness came at the precise moment that Red jumped. I clung like a burr, knowing that he would calm the moment his feet set down again on solid ground. However, this time, with me on his back, he did not; instead he panicked.

I had thought the gelding capable of two gaits and no speed. I was proved wrong, over the most lethal terrain imaginable, a vicious combination of jagged boulders and the soft, almost mucky turf they were set into. We pounded furiously through two hundred yards of this before his front foot went into a shallow rivulet, and he slewed over onto his side, feet kicking furiously. At the last possible moment I flung myself out of the saddle, but one flailing hoof caught me as I went and I hit the ground, not in a balanced roll, but as any untrained person would: hard. I probably would have broken an arm had I not landed on the sodden bank of the stream. Coughing and choking, I pushed myself out of the water and perched on the edge of the bank with my boots in the frigid stream until my head stopped whirling, and fished around for my fallen spectacles when I noticed their lack was one of the things contributing to my disorientation. Very luckily, they were not smashed, only bent and scratched. I threaded them back onto my ears and looked around for Red; when I saw him, my urge to commit murder was snatched away and my heart went into my throat. He was standing with his head down and one of his front legs raised off the ground.

I scrambled over to him and bent to examine the leg, finding to my great relief that it was not broken, although the knee was bleeding, tender, and swelling rapidly. The same could be said of various parts of my own anatomy: The arms and shoulders that had automatically protected my skull from the worst of the rocks would be a mass of bruises tomorrow, my forehead seemed to be bleeding, and I was not altogether certain about one of the ribs on my right side. Still, I was conscious and walking, and so, barely, was the horse.

I led him back to the stream, pushing and pulling until he was standing in it, and I began bathing his leg and my forehead in the cold water. After a while, the cold began to work. Both of us stopped bleeding and he relaxed his bad leg farther into the water until it was actually bearing a portion of his weight.

It would not, however, bear mine as well. While I waited for him to recover some degree of mobility, I stripped him of his burdens and changed my dangerously wet garments for the dry clothing in the bag. When I had packed them again, I retrieved the torn and sodden map from my pocket and sat with it on my knees.

I was, I decided reluctantly, too far from Lydford to lead the horse, and I was hesitant to leave an injured, elderly animal accustomed to shelter out here on its own. The healing hands of Elizabeth Chase were even farther away, perhaps four hours at a hobbling pace. I could return to the tiny, dirty farm I had stopped at between here and there. Or . . .

My eyes were pulled north on the map by a patch of tree markings, noteworthy in that expanse of rough grassland, and by its label: Baskerville Hall.

I had not intended to make another, unannounced, visit to Richard Ketteridge. The awareness of his curious establishment had been with me over the last days, of course, and when I had turned north the previous morning I had briefly toyed with the idea, before deciding that any further investigation of Baskerville Hall was best left to Holmes, who knew the ground.

Now, however, I was in a spot, and needed aid of the sort that Ketteridge could readily provide: food, warmth, shelter for the horse, and alternative transport. Of course, it would necessitate appearing before him a second time in a thoroughly soiled and dishevelled state, but pride could be swallowed – so long as it was washed down with a cup of hot tea. I folded the map back into its pocket and went to extricate the horse from its cold bath. Taking another look at the swollen leg, I decided that a firm wrap might make him more comfortable. One shirt did the job, tied into place with a pair of handkerchiefs, and I could then transfer the bags from the horse's back to my own.

Together we limped across the deserted landscape towards

Baskerville Hall. The afternoon light faded, but with the map and compass at hand I was in no danger of getting lost, and my boots were slowly drying out. Red's leg seemed to improve as we went on; I, on the other hand, began to discover bruises I hadn't known were there, and the bruised (I hoped only bruised) rib made it difficult to breathe at all deeply. The heavy bag seemed to cut into my left shoulder, the tug of the reins yanked the right shoulder into flames, and there seemed to be something amiss with the hip below the bad rib as well. God alone knew what I looked like.

The high wall surrounding Baskerville Hall dictated that the horse at any rate should have to enter by way of the road. It was a long way around, and thoroughly dark when I found the gate, which was shut tight. Nonetheless, banging and shouts roused not only the sharp pains in shoulder and ribs, but a resident of the lodge house as well.

My appearance did not seem to inspire confidence. His wife, looking out of the window at me, was either more sensible or more near-sighted and ordered him to ring up to the house on the telephone to ask if I might be permitted entrance.

Permission was given, but the gatekeeper evidently did not bother with explanations or details. When he, the horse, and I finally emerged from the (still unlit) avenue of trees into the harsh glare of the thousand-watt Swan and Edison, both Ketteridge and Scheiman were outside the door peering in some agitation down the drive to see what could have delayed me. When we appeared, the two Americans made exclamations of surprise and hurried to take the reins and my elbow. I winced and retrieved the elbow.

'Mrs Holmes, what on earth happened here?' Ketteridge demanded.

'I'm really quite all right, Mr Ketteridge, although I know I must look as if I'd been set upon by thieves. The horse fell coming across a litter of rocks.'

'Your head—'

'Just a cut, I didn't even pass out. I'm afraid the poor old boy is out of the running for a few days, though, and as you were not too far off I thought I might beg of you a stable for him and a ride for me to Lew House.'

The agitation returned briefly, before Ketteridge took command of the situation and himself. 'David, show Mrs Holmes to the upstairs bath next to the stairway, and ask Mrs McIverney to rustle up some spare clothes for her. Jansen, take the horse down to the stables and have Williams feed and water him and look to his leg. Mrs Holmes, when you've had a chance to tidy up I hope you'll join me for supper – I'm afraid the car isn't here at the moment, but it shouldn't be away too long. House guests, who went back to Exeter this afternoon. I'll have the driver run you down to Lew when we've eaten. All right?'

I could not very well argue with my benefactor, although I should almost have preferred to borrow a horse and return to Lew Trenchard on my own rather than cool my heels over an evening of stilted conversation in borrowed clothing. Still, the appeal of a deep, hot bath was undeniable, and Ketteridge did not seem in a mood to be contradicted. I surrendered the horse and my burden, and meekly followed the secretary into the house.

There remained, though, discomfort in the air, which seemed actually to increase as we penetrated the house. Scheiman called perfunctorily for Mrs McIverney, for a bath to be drawn, and for clothing to be brought, ignoring my (admittedly feeble) protestations that none of this was necessary with a great deal more brusqueness than I should have expected in a mere secretary.

His almost audible sigh of relief when the door to the bath was shutting behind me confirmed the feeling I had received, that my arrival had interrupted something of importance and I was being got out of the way while it was tidied offstage.

A normal uninvited guest would have assumed an attitude of conspicuous blithe ignorance and been careful to remain unseeing. Being no normal guest, I put on the air of innocence but tightened my scrutiny. Giving Scheiman and the maid two minutes to retreat, I opened the door quietly and put my head out into the hallway.

The maid rose hastily from her seat on a hard chair and greeted me expectantly.

'I, er . . . I'm going to need to wash my hair,' I improvised. 'Do you think you could warm some bath towels to help dry it?'

'Yes, mum. It's being done.' She was cheerful and helpful, and had quite obviously been told not to leave her post outside my door. I might as well have been locked in. I thanked her, and closed the door.

The window was small and high and closed. I balanced on a chair and tugged it open, but there was nothing to be seen or heard, only the feeling of cold air sucking out the room's warm steam. This small, spartan, slightly grubby bathroom, a bath of the sort one might set aside for the use of poor relations rather than the gracious rescue of an honoured acquaintance's wife, was on the north end of the east wing, away from the main guest rooms, overlooking nothing but fields and moorland, far from any sound of voices coming up the main stairs. Far, too, I realised, from the front drive, the coach house, and the stables.

Much as I should have liked to sink into oblivion in the long, hot depths of the bath, I knew I could not submit to my imprisonment without at least trying to confirm my suspicions. Leaving the chair in place and the window wide open, I stripped one of the laces from my boots, tied it around a face flannel, and dropped the flannel in the water, swishing it around vigorously to give the maid the picture of my getting into the bath. I then resumed my perch with the other end of the boot-lace wrapped around one toe. From time to time I pulled the flannel about, to evoke the sounds of languid bathing, all the while growing ever more stiff and uncomfortable with my head resting on the window sill, waiting for a sound that would probably never come.

In the end, though, some ten or fifteen minutes after my vigil began, I was granted not only a sound, but a visual confirmation as well. The engine noise of Ketteridge's big touring car purred softly over the rooftops, and then a brief flare of the headlamps illuminated the tops of some trees that were at the very edge of my field of vision. The motor faded, going down the drive and away from the house. I did not know what it meant, but it was with satisfaction that I pulled down the window, replaced the chair and the laces, and slipped silently into the cooling bath.

CHAPTER FOURTEEN

> On the road passers-by always salute and have a bit of a yarn, even
> though personally unacquainted, and to go by in the dark without
> a greeting is a serious default in good manners.
>
> — A BOOK OF THE WEST: DEVON

KETTERIDGE WAS ALL SMILES and affability when I joined him, the agitation gone and a celebratory mood in its place. In fact, a bottle of some very fine champagne was nestling in a bucket of ice, to be plucked out and opened as soon as I entered the hall. Ketteridge was alone, and a small table set with two places was standing discreetly to one side. I was not at all sure about the intimacy of this tête-à-tête, but the hall lights were blazing, sweeping away the memory of the quiet and somewhat mysterious reaches of the room in the other evening's after-dinner candlelight, and Ketteridge did not seem in the least seductive, or even vaguely flirtatious. He seemed only brimming with high spirits, and his sun-dark face, full hair, and white, even teeth, though undeniably handsome, did not appeal to me personally (which was, frankly, a great relief, following the memory of a couple of very disconcerting moments with a man in the Ruskin case).

'Mrs Holmes! Come, join me in a glass of this marvellous stuff.' He poured two glasses, gave me one, and held his own up before him to propose a toast. 'To change!' he declared dramatically.

I hesitated. 'I don't know if I ought to drink to that, Mr Ketteridge. Not all change is good.'

'To growth, then. To progress.'

Not entirely certain what it was I was drinking to, I nonetheless put the rim of the glass to my lips and sipped.

'Are we celebrating something, Mr Ketteridge?'

'Always, my dear Mrs Holmes. There's always something in life to celebrate. In this case, however, I think I may have found a buyer for Baskerville Hall.'

'I see. I did not realise your plans to move on were so far advanced.'

'They weren't before; now they are. Sometimes decisions have to be made on the fly, as it were. Strike while the iron is hot.'

Privately, I agreed that striking at cold iron was not the most productive of exercises; however, neither was the availability of hot iron generally as accidental a state as he seemed to be suggesting. I found it hard to believe that a buyer for Baskerville Hall had simply dropped, preheated as it were, out of the air.

'I'm very glad for you. Do I take the champagne to mean that you have reached a happy agreement?' I was not so gauche as to ask how much he was getting for the hall, but I had found industrialists, particularly successful American industrialists, less likely to take offence at a discussion of pounds, shillings, and pence than the other sorts of wealthy Englishmen were, and a gold baron was surely an industrialist of a sort.

'Happy enough,' he said. 'Yes, happy enough. And I think Baring-Gould and his friends will be satisfied. The buyer is an older man – just as well, it's not exactly a family kind of a place, is it? – and he wants a quiet place to write and study while his wife joins the local hunt. An American – the place seems to have a tradition for outsiders, doesn't it? But I think they'll fit in well.'

It was something of a surprise that Ketteridge would even consider the respective suitability of his buyers and their new neighbours, given the amount of money at stake, and I was touched by his thoughtfulness. Not, I reflected, that he would refuse to sell to a rapacious financier with a scheme to knock the house down and replace it with a set of holiday flats to hire out to city dwellers by the week, but he seemed genuinely happy that he had reached a right solution.

'When will the sale take place?' I asked. 'Will you be leaving soon?'

'It's not completely settled yet,' he hastened to say. 'Some questions to hammer out first. Early spring, most likely. By June.'

Baring-Gould would have the entertainment of this odd American whom he had befriended, then, until the end. I smiled a bit sadly and drank my wine.

Ketteridge divided the remainder of the bottle between our two glasses (most of it having gone into his) and then rang for Tuptree, who came in and arranged the small table and two chairs before the fire.

'I thought this would be more comfortable, Mrs Holmes. The dining hall is a little formal, and damn – darned cold for someone who's just been swimming on Dartmoor.'

'That's very thoughtful of you. Although I have to say the dining hall is a room with a great deal of character. I should like to see it more thoroughly, sometime.'

'I'd be happy to give you the tour tonight, if you wish.'

'I would like that very much,' I said, and sat back to enjoy my meal.

We were served as attentively as we would have been in the formal setting, and the meal was, as before, simple food cooked superbly. I commented on it.

'Is your cook English, Mr Ketteridge, or American?'

'French, would you believe it? It took me three years to convince him that his sauces made me bilious and that the plainer meat and vegetables are, the better they taste.'

'How on earth did you convince a French chef of the virtues of simplicity?' I asked, amused.

'I threatened him. Told him the next time he resigned, I'd actually accept it. I pay him more than he could get anywhere else, so he learnt to change.'

I laughed with him. 'How clever of you. I shall keep the technique in mind.'

'I don't imagine you'd have much use for it,' he said. I kept my face straight, but he instantly realised how ill-mannered such a remark was and tried to cover his lapse. 'That is to say, Reverend Gould was telling me the other evening how simply you and your husband live, down in Sussex.'

'It's very true,' I said, sounding ever-so-slightly regretful. It was only to be expected that Ketteridge would want to prise any Sherlock Holmes gossip he could out of Baring-Gould, but either Baring-Gould or Holmes himself had neglected to mention that our unadorned manner of living had everything to do with choice and nothing with necessity. I toyed for a moment with the idea of making Ketteridge a cash offer on Baskerville Hall, then put it away. Independent wealth did not go well with the picture Ketteridge had formed of the Holmes household, and I decided that, for the present, I should leave the picture undisturbed. Besides which, he might actually accept my offer, and then where would I be?

'Tell me, Mrs Holmes, does your husband still investigate cases, or is he well and truly retired?'

Ah, I thought, Baring-Gould was not indiscreet enough to tell him everything.

'Very occasionally, when something interests him enough. For the most part he writes and conducts his research. We live a quiet life.' That Ketteridge did not burst into wild laughter told me all I needed to know about his ignorance of Holmes' very active career. 'Why do you ask?'

'I thought perhaps while he was down here I might hire him to look into the mysterious sightings of the Hound of the Baskervilles.'

'Oh yes?' Interesting, I thought, that everyone should be confusing the Baskerville Hound with the one accompanying Lady Howard's coach. Considering Richard Ketteridge's enthusiasms it was not all that surprising that he should do so, but I could only think that Conan Doyle's influence extended out here, twisting reality until it resembled fiction. It would not be the first time Holmes had confronted himself in a fictional mirror.

'You have heard of them?' he asked.

'The sightings? Yes, Baring-Gould mentioned them the other day. Why, have you seen it?'

'No. But I imagine they will be causing some uproar among my neighbours out on the moor.'

'I should think so, considering the last time it was seen. Actually, I was wondering if the hound might not come here. As I remember, the Baskerville curse was the reason for its presence, but there's nothing to say whether it's Baskerville blood that attracts him, or merely ownership of the hall.'

I studied him in all innocence, and saw a look of astonishment cross his face, followed by a great roar of laughter.

'Oh my,' he sputtered. 'Mrs Holmes, I never thought of that. Maybe I'd better start wearing garlic or something.'

'A pistol seems to have been effective the last time,' I noted.

His laughter faded, but the humour remained in his eyes. 'But the last time it was an actual dog, painted with – phosphorus, wasn't it?'

'Yes,' I said. 'Of course you're right. How silly of me.'

'Have you ever worked with your husband, Mrs Holmes?'

'On a case?'

'Yes.'

I spread some butter on a piece of roll and ate it thoughtfully. 'We did collaborate on a case, once, involving a stolen ham.'

The absurdity of the thing delighted him, as I thought it might do, and he insisted I tell him about it. I did so, emphasising the ridiculous parts until the story verged on the burlesque – not, I admit, a difficult task. When we had put that story to bed and been served the next course, I played the polite guest and asked about his life.

'What about you, Mr Ketteridge? You must have had some fascinating adventures in Alaska.'

'It was quite a time.'

'What was your most exciting moment?'

'Exciting good or exciting terrifying?'

'Either. Both.'

'Exciting good was the first time I looked into my pan and saw gold.'

'On your claim?'

'Yes. Fifty feet of mud and rock and ice – when I first staked it the stream was frozen. I had to thaw out the ground with a fire before I could get at the mud. But there was gold in it. Amazing stuff, gold,' he mused, looking down at the ring on his finger and rubbing it thoughtfully. 'Soft and useless, but its sparkle gets right into a man's bones. "Gold fever" is a good name, because that's what it's like, burning you and eating you up.'

'And the exciting bad?'

'The sheer terror. Had a handful of those, like pieces of peppercorn scattered through a plate of tasteless stew. Most of the work in the fields was dull slog – you were uncomfortable all the time, awake or asleep, always hungry, never clean, never warm except in summer when the mosquitoes ate you alive, your feet and hands were always wet and bruised. Lord, the boredom. And then a charge you'd set wouldn't go off and you'd get the thrill of going up to it, knowing it might decide to explode in your face. Or a tunnel you'd poked into the hillside would start to collapse, between you and daylight. But the most exciting moment? Let's see. That would either be when the dog sled went over a ledge into Soda Creek, or the avalanche at the Scales.'

The last name tickled a vague memory. 'I've heard of the Scales. Wasn't that the name for a hill?'

'A hill,' he said with a pitying smile. 'A hell more like it if you'll pardon my French. Chilkoot Pass, four miles straight up. Seemed like it anyway, even in summer when you could go back and forth, but in the winter, twelve hundred steps cut into the ice, the last mile was like climbing a ladder. And you had a year's worth of supplies to shift to the top – the Mounties checked to make sure; they didn't want a countryside of starving men – so you couldn't just climb it once unless you could afford to pay the freight cable to take your load up for you. There you were, in a mile-long line of freezing, exhausted men so tight packed it was left, right, left, together all the way, your lungs aching and your head pounding in the altitude, and just when you think you can't lift your foot one more time, that you're going to drop in your tracks and die, you're at the top, falling into the snow with the crate on your back. And when you've got your breath back you take the ropes off that crate, sit on your shovel, and slide down the iced track to the bottom, where you put another crate on your shoulders and line up to start again. After twenty, twenty-five times you have your supplies at the top of the hill, and you're ready to start on your way to the fields. Lot of men stood in Sheep Camp at the bottom of the Scales, saw what they were up against, and their hearts just gave up on them. Sold their supplies for ten cents on the dollar and went home.'

'But you didn't.'

'Didn't have the sense to, no. It was winter, but the weather was still uncertain, and I'd only shifted half my load when the snow turned warm. Six, eight feet of wet snow in a couple of days. The Indians were smart – they cleared out back to town – but stubborn us.

'I knew it was going to get dangerous, so I started climbing early, still night in fact. I nearly made it, had my last load on my back and was halfway up when the cliffs gave way. The whole hill, a mile of snow and ice, just moved out from under our feet, a mile-long line of hundreds of men, their equipment, their dogs, everything just bundled up and swept down into Sheep Camp in a heap of snow. Seventy, eighty men died, my partner one of them. I was locked in, upside down, though I didn't know it – couldn't tell, it was dark and I couldn't move anything but my right hand. It was like being caught in set cement. My boot was sticking out, and that's what saved me, when they found it and dug me out.'

'Good . . . heavens,' I said weakly. I did not have to manufacture a response; the claustrophobic horror of his experience made me feel a bit light-headed.

Ketteridge put down the glass that he had been nursing all during his narrative and looked at me with concern. 'I'm so sorry, Mrs Holmes, have I upset you?'

'No no, just the idea of that sort of suffocation. It's pretty horrific.'

'At the time, you know, I wasn't even frightened. Angry at first, if you can credit it – the thought that I'd have to carry everything up all over again just made me furious. I know, funny that should be the first thing on my mind. And then I was worried about my partner, who'd been just behind me, and then I was uncomfortable, all squashed and cold. But then that passed, and I began to feel warm; my wrenched leg didn't even hurt. Running out of air, I suppose, but it wouldn't have been a bad way to die, you know. Compared to some.'

He smiled. 'Shall we take coffee in the library, Tuptree? The car ought to be back soon.'

This last was to me, and I folded my table napkin and stood up.

'May we walk through the dining hall?' I asked, gently reminding him of his promise.

'Certainly, if you like. The lighting in there isn't very good, I'm afraid. For some reason Baskerville never had that room wired for electricity. It's better during the day.'

Ketteridge took up a candelabra and lit the tapers with the cigar lighter he carried in his pocket, and we went through into the great dim banqueting hall. It was like walking into a cavern, empty and full of shadows – although in times past the entire manor had gathered here for meals, the family on its raised dais, the servants at long tables in the rest of the room. A minstrel's gallery looked down from the far end, silent and abandoned by all except the painted Baskervilles, a cheerless substitute indeed for the music the spot was intended to house. We strolled in near complete silence ourselves, down one side and up the end. He held the light up for me to see the portraits.

'The Baskervilles seem a varied lot,' I commented.

'The last owner took all the good ones with her,' he said ruefully. 'She did leave these tapestries, though,' he added, and carried the candles over to the interior wall to show me the dusty, faded figures that had once blazed with colour and movement. We examined them critically. 'They're prettier in the daylight,' he said, and I allowed him to escort me out of the room and down a long and infinitely more cheery corridor.

As a working library the room we entered left something to be desired, but as a masculine retreat that used books as a decorative backdrop for deep leather chairs and a square card table, it was more comfortable than the draughty reaches of the hall or dining room. Heavy draperies covered the windows and Tuptree, bearing a tray of coffee, followed us in the door.

'It's a pity you haven't been to the house in daylight, Mrs Holmes. It's quite a sight – these windows here look up onto the moor, and there are six tors sitting there, looking like you could reach out and touch them. On a clear day, that is. You must try to come back during the day – you and your husband, of course.'

'I'd like that, thank you. I was so enjoying my ride out on the moor today, I hadn't realised how late it had got. I do apologise for keeping you up.'

'This isn't late, Mrs Holmes, by no means, and I was charmed to have you drop in on me, for whatever reason. Were you just out for a ride then?'

I had offered him that ride in case he wondered what on earth the good Mrs Holmes might have been doing in his deserted stretch of countryside. Whatever he was hiding from me, whomever he had spirited out from under my nose, might be as simple as a socially unacceptable buyer for Baskerville Hall or as embarrassing as an improper visitor of the female persuasion. In any case he could hardly suspect me of arranging the mishap that had delivered Red and myself here in such a state. I merely thought to divert his curiosity before it took hold in his mind.

'Yes, and what a place for it! I rode down to look at the Fox Tor mires and Childe's Tomb, and Wistman's Wood, and then the stone row near Merrivale, and I was aiming for Fur Tor, to get around the river, you see, when Red spooked and fell.'

He seemed imperceptibly to relax, whether because of my list of sights or due to the breezy conversational style I had gradually come to assume, I could not tell.

'It is an interesting slice of landscape, isn't it?' he commenced.

'Oh yes. Sitting on a tor and eating a picnic lunch with a stone row on one side and a tin-mining works on the other is not an everyday sort of experience.'

'I think my favourite is Bowerman's Nose, not far from Hound Tor. Do you know it?'

'Over near Widdecombe? No, I haven't been there yet.'

'Looks like a great stone man, staring defiantly up into the sky.'

'But it actually has a nose, does it? I rode completely around Fox Tor looking for some resemblance to a fox. I couldn't find one.'

'A bit like the constellations, aren't they? You'd have to have a good imagination, or bad eyesight, to see what they're named after.'

'Actually,' I said, 'the tor where I took lunch today resembled nothing so much as what one finds in the road after a herd of cattle has passed by.'

The earthy humour was to Ketteridge's liking. When he stopped laughing he swung his cup dangerously in the direction of the curtains and said, 'There's a tor just out those windows that I think I'll rename Horse-Dropping Tor, in your honour, Mrs Holmes. Looks just like one we had over our house when I was young, only it's cold, wet, and grey instead of hot, dry, and red.' His face, which when relaxed had been less handsome but more likeable, abruptly tightened. He put his cup into its saucer with a sharp rattle and began to pat his pockets in the semaphore of the tobacco smoker. The distant past, it would seem, was out of bounds in a way that his youth in Alaska had not been.

'If I were you, I shouldn't mention to Baring-Gould that you are giving his tors impolite names.'

He instantly relaxed again and stopped his search for tobacco. 'You're right. He wouldn't take to it kindly.'

Baring-Gould was a safer topic of conversation. I permitted him to retreat into it, and we talked about the squire of Lew Trenchard for a while. I did not think Ketteridge fully realised the precarious state of the old man's health, but I was not about to be the one to tell him.

In the middle of a sentence, Ketteridge paused and said, 'I hear the car.' He resumed what he had been saying, and appeared quite content to sit in front of the fire and talk until midnight, but I decided that investigation or no, I had had enough. My rib and hip throbbed, my forehead and the bridge of my nose hurt sharply, and I was not in top condition anywhere, even mentally. I rose to my feet.

'Mr Ketteridge, I have taken up far too much of your time. I am very grateful for the rescue and your company, but I cannot keep you any longer.'

As it transpired, however, I was not finished with him yet. When my (neatly repacked) bags were brought, Tuptree was carrying a man's overcoat and hat as well. Ketteridge was motoring down to Lew with me, 'Just to make sure you arrive without problem,' as he put it. Expecting that we would be attacked by highwaymen, perhaps? Or that I might be molested by his driver? It seemed, though, that this being the first pleasant evening in some time, he wanted to take a drive.

This meant that he actually did the driving, with Scheiman in the back seat alongside my saddlebags. Ketteridge held my door for me, then got in behind the wheel.

He was not a bad driver, although a touch aggressive and more apt to haul at the wheel than slip in and out between obstacles as his driver had. We flew down the tree-lined avenue and accelerated out through the open gate in a spray of gravel, and were very soon pulling into the drive at Lew House.

Somewhat to my surprise, he did not accept my invitation to enter.

'Paperwork to do, I'm sure you understand. But you'll let me know if Mr Holmes is interested in investigating the Hound sightings, won't you? We can talk about rates at the time.'

Hah, I thought. The days when Sherlock Holmes worried about how much to charge for his services was long in the past.

'I shall speak to him about it,' I said politely.

He stood next to the car until I had gone into the porch, and then I heard the car door close. The car circled the fountain with the bronze goose-boy, and drove away.

CHAPTER FIFTEEN

Hard by is Clakeywell Pool, by some called Crazywell. It is an old
mine-work, now filled with water. It covers nearly an acre, and
the banks are in part a hundred feet high. According to popular
belief, at certain times at night a loud voice is heard calling
from the water in inarticulate tones, naming the
next person who is to die in the parish.

— A BOOK OF DARTMOOR

I PAUSED IN THE LEW House porch for a long moment after the
noise of the car had faded down the drive, pondering the curious
etiquette required for entering a house in which one has been a guest
in the very recent past, yet has been away for some days, and returns
solitary when previously one had been an adjunct to a husband. It
would have been simple had there been a butler, but I was not about
to rouse the master of the house to open the door for me. I reached
out to try the door handle and found it unlocked, but instead of
letting myself in, I dropped my bags and walked back into the drive
and past the fountain until I was in the rose garden, where I turned
to take a long look at the house.

It was a puzzle. This house, this square block rising up in front of
me against the night, was in a sense a fraud, an artificial product of
one man's enthusiasms. Stuck-together bits and pieces stolen from
other structures, held in place by nothing more substantial than the

vision of an infirm and lonely old man, its cool and formal facade nestled incongruously into a tree-lined fold of English river valley; a run-down, ill-heated, understaffed, echoing pile of a place studded with anomalies like the opulent gallery ceiling upstairs and the faded but still glorious ballroom – the place ought to have seemed ridiculous, out of place, and easily abandoned to the brambles and oaks. Instead it stood, confident and unapologetic, as self-contained and idiosyncratic as the man who had created it.

Baskerville Hall, on the other hand, was the real thing. A structure grown slowly over the centuries and dramatically situated, it was filled with beautiful, cared-for things, well heated, adequately staffed, more than adequately lit (one could even get used to the electric lights, I knew), and mastered by a man in his physical and mental prime. It should have been an oasis of warmth and colour, an assertion of life and humanity shining out in the stony wilderness of the moor.

Why then did the substantial Baskerville Hall linger in the mind as somehow ethereal, unreal, and slightly 'off'? Was it merely the foreign influence on the Hall over the last three owners: Ketteridge, the Canadian Sir Henry, and old Sir Charles before him with his influx of South African gold? Could it even be as recent a change as Ketteridge and his exotic sense of design?

If so, then why was it that Lew House, which had undergone changes considerably more radical than modern lighting and a few Moorish cushions, felt the more solid on its foundations? Why did Lew House, that toy of its over-imaginative squire, still settle into its Devonshire home as if it had grown up from the very stone beneath its feet? Why was it Lew, run down though it was, that impressed a visitor with the secure knowledge that this house would stand, would still be here and sheltering its inhabitants long after the owls and foxes had moved into the windswept ruins of Baskerville Hall?

I decided I did not know. I also decided that champagne was too conducive to fancies, and it was time I took to my bed.

It was not even ten o'clock, but the house was silent. I thought it more than likely that the lights had been left burning for my sake, so shut them down and locked the door. (As my room was in the front, if another visitor came it would only be I who was disturbed.)

I was thirsty, with the wine and coffee I had drunk, so I went through to the kitchen for a glass of water, and then climbed stiffly up the back stairway, feeling all the aches I had accumulated.

At the top of the stairs I noticed a shaft of light coming from a partially opened door down the corridor. I thought it was from Baring-Gould's room, and I paused, not wishing to disturb him, yet not willing to walk away in case the old man might have been taken ill. In the end I went quietly up the hallway and, tapping gently, allowed the door to drift open under my knuckles.

The squire of Lew Trenchard lay propped on his pillows, his hands folded together on top of the bedclothes. A faded red glasses-case lay on the table beside the bed, along with a worn white leather New Testament, looking oddly feminine, a lamp, a glass of water, and a small tray with at least ten bottles of pills and potions. The pocket of his striped pyjamas had torn and been carefully mended, I noticed, and this touch of everyday pathos made me suddenly aware of how shockingly vulnerable this fierce, daunting old man looked. I stepped backward to the door, but one eye glittered from a lowered lid.

'Is that you, Miss Russell? I cannot see you.'

I stepped forward into the light. 'Yes, Mr Baring-Gould. Is there anything I can get for you?'

He did not answer my question, if indeed he had heard it. His eye drifted shut and his breathing slowed. I eased back towards the door and to my astonishment I heard him say, 'I am relieved to see you home again safely. The storm the other night would have been ferocious on the open moor. I dreamt . . .' There was a pause, so long a pause that I began to think he had fallen asleep. 'I dreamt I was a child by the seashore. The trees, you know. The Scotch pines and the oaks above the house sound remarkably like the surf on the coast of Cornwall, when the wind is blowing through them.'

I waited, but that seemed to be all, so I wished him a good night and went to my room. There was no sign of Holmes, and one of his bags was missing, so I went quietly to bed, and to sleep.

At five o'clock in the morning I lay open-eyed, staring at the ceiling. The portions of my body that didn't ache gently hurt actively, with the occasional shooting pain from my ribs for variety.

This is ridiculous, I decided, and began the laborious process of oozing out from under the bedclothes. Surely I can make it down the stairs without waking Baring-Gould, and make myself a pot of tea without disturbing Mrs Elliott. I wrapped myself in Holmes' dressing gown, pushed my feet into his bedroom slippers, and tottered downstairs, considerably less spry than Elizabeth Chase.

I need not have bothered with silence: Baring-Gould was sitting before the drawing-room fire, a half-full cup of tea with the cold skin of age on it by his side. He held a book on his lap, a small green volume with gilt letters, mostly obscured by his hands but having something to do with Devon. He was not reading it, only holding it while he gazed into the fire. By the looks of the coals, he had been there for some hours.

'Good morning, Miss Russell,' he said without turning his head. 'Do come in.'

'Good morning. I thought I might have some tea. Would you like another cup yourself?'

'That would be most kind of you. Although truthfully I can scarcely be said to have had the first one.'

I removed the cup and returned with a tray holding pot, cups, and paraphernalia. I poured his cup, milked and sugared it to his instructions, and hesitated.

'Please do sit down, Miss Russell. Unless, of course, you have work to do.'

'No,' I said quickly, stung by the faint, so very faint, note of request in the proud voice. 'No, I am between projects at the moment.' Oh dear, that didn't sound very good. 'You know how it is, one thing finished and the next still coming together in the back of the mind.'

'I envy you. I never had the leisure to think in advance about the next, as you call it, project.' He raised his tea to his lips to give me time to absorb the gentle scorn. This was not going well.

'What are you reading?' I asked him.

'Nothing, actually. My eyes are too bad. I do like to hold a book from time to time, though. Rather like conducting a telephone conversation with an old friend: unsatisfactory, but better than nothing at all.'

'Would you . . . shall I read to you?'

'That is a kind offer, Miss Russell, but not perhaps at the moment.'

Each time he said my name, it sounded as though he had it in italics. This unorthodox form of address was obviously more than he could swallow. I relented.

'Please, Rector, call me Mary.'

'Very well, Mary. One of my daughters is named Mary, and she too has a lovely voice. No, I think that, rather than read to me from books in my library that I already know, I should prefer to hear about your own efforts. My friend Holmes tells me you are in the final stages of writing a book of your own. Tell me about it.'

'I have finished it, in fact. The first draft, that is – I sent it to the publisher just before I came down here. There will be a fair amount

196

of work before it's actually ready to publish, of course, but it is very nice to make it to the end of the first time through.'

'Hmm,' he said. 'I never was much of one for second drafts. It always seemed to me that if my publisher did not like it to begin with, no amount of tinkering would set it right. Best to start on something new.'

'So you would just scrap it?' I asked, astonished.

'Not invariably, but generally, yes. Who is your publisher?'

I told him, and he asked about the editor, and we talked about the mechanics of publishing for a few minutes. Then he asked, 'And the subject? You never did answer me.'

'*Sophia*,' I said. 'Wisdom.'

'*Hochmah*,' he said in rejoinder. 'You are Jewish, I think?'

'I am. My father was a member of the Anglican Communion but my mother was Jewish, which under rabbinic law makes me Jewish as well.'

'Have you seen our church here in Lew?'

'On Sunday. It's very lovely.'

'*Paravi lucenum Christo meo*,' he said. I have prepared a lamp for my Christ.

I ventured a tiny joke from the same Psalm: '"For the Lord has chosen Lew Down, he has desired it for his dwelling place."'

He smiled. '"This is my resting place forever, here I will dwell for I have desired it." Truly,' he mused, 'I have both desired and chosen. I had thought to have my daughter Margaret paint a picture in the church of the mother of God as Sophia, but we haven't got to it yet. It was my mother's name, Sophia.'

'That is a portrait of you with her upstairs, isn't it? She was very pretty.'

'Do you think so? Prettier than her anaemic-looking son, at any rate. The painter took against me, didn't like my asking so many questions about mixing paint and the techniques of perspective, so he made me look even more priggish than I think I actually did.'

'It's a sweet picture,' I protested.

He snorted. 'You ought to see the thing I just sat for. Makes me look like an old boat.'

'Is it here?'

'Oh no, hanging in London. What do you have to say about *Sophia*, then, Mary?'

So, at five in the morning in the echoing old house, we talked about theology. He was an interesting partner in conversation – as inquisitive as a child, but intractable and opinionated on the things he considered he knew; impatient with extraneous detail but insistent about the detail he thought important; utterly imperious yet innately gracious at the same time.

Curiously like another enthusiastic amateur I knew, in fact; two members of a dying breed.

When we had finished with that topic to his satisfaction, he turned to another. 'Tell me what you make of Dartmoor, Mary.'

To help myself think of an answer, I dribbled the last of the tea into my cup, milked it and sipped it and nearly choked on it – I had not noticed that we had been there long enough for the pot to stew cold and bitter. I hastily put down the cup.

'I don't know where to start. I did not care much for it at first.'

'You hated it.'

'I hated it, yes. You must admit, it's one of the least hospitable places in the country.'

'A good place to be alone with one's thoughts,' he said.

Perhaps with fourteen children in the house, I reflected, solitude in any form was beyond the price of rubies. 'After a couple of days up there, though, it came to me that the moor is in many ways like the desert. Did your travels ever take you to Palestine?'

'Alas, no. I should have liked to visit the Holy Land.'

'Yes, it is a powerful experience. And I think you would have felt at home there. The harshness of the desert shapes the people and keeps them materially poor, but it also gives an immensely strong sense of identity and belonging.'

The old man was smiling into the fire and nodding gently. I went on.

'In truth, I found the sense of community here . . . daunting.' I told him how, beginning with the girl near Postbridge pointing me towards Elizabeth Chase, everyone I met knew an irritating amount about me and my business. 'Except for the villagers. They didn't know me, and when the moor men were with the village dwellers, they seemed almost to treasure the secret of who I was.' I began to tell him about the night in the Mary Tavy inn.

As I progressed, he grew more and more animated, sitting upright in his chair, then leaning forward that he might see my face more clearly. He made me describe the songs and the singers in detail, and hummed the tunes that I might confirm which ones the singers had used. His eyes positively sparkled when I told him about the authoritative claim the moor men laid on Lady Howard's song. When he had milked every drop of information from me about the music (he even made me hum the tune I had played on the tin whistle) he sat back in his chair, tired but pleased.

'"Green Broom" I collected from John Woodrich, in Thrushtleton,' he said, 'and the tune your singers used for "Unquiet Grave" was a melody I noted down for another song. Magnificent music, that. You like it?'

'It's very . . . human,' I said after a minute.

'People now lack patience, have no taste for a song that is not finished in three minutes. Modern music puts me in mind of a man I knew in Cambridge who had a mechanism into which one could put musical notes. It would then combine them to render a so-called tune, although to my ear they more closely resembled random cacophonies. Whenever I have the misfortune to hear a modern piece of music, such as when my American daughter-in-law assaults the piano, I begin to suspect that his machine is being put to considerable use.'

I laughed politely, and then returned to a previous thought which still occupied me greatly.

'I thought it odd that although the moor dwellers seemed well acquainted with me and my mission, the villagers didn't know me, not even in Postbridge, which is a tiny place. And I don't believe anyone in Ketteridge's establishment recognised what I was doing there, either.'

'The moor men keep themselves to themselves, and Ketteridge employs foreigners.'

'Foreigners?' I asked doubtfully. Other than Scheiman and the hidden chef, they all had sounded British.

'French, American, Scots, and even Londoners, even a Welshman, but not from here.'

'I see. How odd. That explains how, even though he lives on the edges of the moor, he's apart from the moor life. Isolated from the Dartmoor . . . would it be too much of an exaggeration to call it an 'organism'?' I asked. He did not answer, only smiled to himself, his eyes closed now. Very soon, he was asleep in his chair. I fed the fire to keep him warm, and crept stiffly upstairs to see if I could coax a hot bath from the pipes.

Baring-Gould was awake again when I came down an hour later, drawn by the smells of yeast bread and coffee and much restored by the plentiful hot soak. Mrs Elliott swept in and out of the kitchen doors with hot plates and cups and dainties to tempt her old charge's failing palate. One of these was a small crystal bowl of wortleberry jam, a relative of the bilberry, but from a far richer branch of the family. I exclaimed my praise, and Baring-Gould told me about 'gatherin' hurts' on the moor, an annual holiday spree akin to that of London's East End inhabitants who spilt out from the city every year to pick hops in the clean sun of Kent. I did have a question whose urgency had been growing over the last two days, but I waited politely for him to finish before I asked it.

'Do you know where Holmes is?'

'He is in London, of course.'

'Does that mean someone came up with the names of the two people who saw the coach from the top of Gibbet Hill?'

'How stupid of me, I was forgetting that you weren't here. Yes, Mrs Elliott's nephew found the farm-house they stayed in, although as there was no guest register the finding of them won't be easy. Still, Holmes seemed to think he could do it,' he said complacently.

'Did he say when he expected to be back?'

'I thought to see him yesterday evening. I imagine he will be on today's train.'

'How long have you known Holmes?' I heard myself asking. I had not intended to ask it: If Holmes wanted me to know, he would tell me, and it was possibly impolitic to let Baring-Gould know how little Holmes had mentioned him.

'Forever,' he said. 'His forever, that is, not mine. I'm his godfather.'

I was completely staggered by this calm statement. By this time, of course, I knew something about Holmes' people (I was, after all, his wife) but somehow other than Mycroft they had never seemed very real or three-dimensional. It was like meeting Queen Victoria's wet nurse. One knew she must have had one, but her existence seemed rather unlikely.

'His godfather,' I repeated weakly.

'I haven't done a terribly good job of it, have I?' He seemed amused at his failure, not troubled. I could think of no suitable response, so I remained silent. 'Still, he seems to have turned out all right. Been a good husband to you, has he?' If I'd had trouble before finding an answer, now my mouth was hanging open. 'He loves you, of course; that helps. Foolishly, perhaps, but men love like that, in flames compared to the warm steady love of women. I hope—'

I never found out what his hopes were, praise be to God. The ruckus outside must have been approaching for some time without us hearing – Baring-Gould because his hearing was so poor and me because of the astonishment pounding in my ears. The first intimation of a problem came with a huge crash in the kitchen and voices raised enough for even my host to stop what he was about to say and turn to the door.

'I say, Mrs—' he started to call. With that the door burst open and what looked like half the population of Lew Down spilt into the room, all of them gabbling at once.

Baring-Gould rose majestically to his feet and glared at them all. 'Stop this at once,' he thundered. Instant silence resulted. 'Thomas, what is the meaning of this?'

The man automatically tugged off his cap, polite even in the extremity of his emotional upheaval. 'A body, Rector,' the man stammered.

'There's a dead man in the lake.'

Chapter Sixteen

The care for the tenants, the obligation of setting an example of
justice, integrity, kindliness, religious observance, has been
bred in him, and enforced by parental warning through
three centuries at the least, on his infant mind.
What is born in the bone comes out in the flesh.

— EARLY REMINISCENCES

IT WAS FORTUNATE THAT I was already dressed and wearing my shoes,
because a pair of bedroom slippers would surely have been torn to
shreds, or left behind, long before I reached the quarry lake. I was out of
my chair before Baring-Gould could articulate a response to the man's
statement, out of the front door without pausing to catch up a coat,
across the drive, through the meadow, and on the edge of the watery
chasm before anyone else had even emerged from the house on my trail.

I was not, however, before any others at the lake. Gathering a
great breath, I cupped my hands and shouted at the full strength of
my lungs, 'Stop where you are! Don't touch him!'

Even over the constant splash of the waterfall my unladylike bellow
bounced off the stone walls with sufficient force to startle the would-be
rescuers. One of them slipped and fell backwards from the rowboat into
the lake, which distracted the others long enough for me to race around
the lake's rim and plunge down the closer of the one-time quarry's two
access ramps, now a steep hillside heavily overgrown with fern and

bramble, and slippery with fallen leaves. I caught my breath at the water's edge and waited for the boat to reach the shore.

Two other men had been picking their way around the precipitous south wall of the lake, and now stood eyeing me disapprovingly.

'Please,' I called to them. 'You must leave him there until the police have seen him. I know it doesn't seem respectful of the dead. But it's necessary, believe me. And try to walk back in the same place you went over.'

I suppose that had it been summer, I might not have been so quick to think of the possibility of what the police blotters call foul play. On a long summer's night I could well imagine the lure this cool, slightly ominous spot might be for a group of young men on their way home from the pub. But in October, and with the awareness of wrong-doing on the moor, it was the first thing that came to mind, and I did not want heavy boots destroying any evidence we might unearth.

The five men gathered around me, one of them dripping wet, none of them showing much inclination to leave. I suggested mildly that the wet one might be better off dry, and thus rid myself of him and an escort, but the three remaining men, one of whom I had seen working around Lew House, planted themselves like trees and looked suspicious.

'Do you know who it is?' I asked them. They did not, only that it was a man, and he was not from around here, both of which facts I had already determined by a brief glance from the quarry rim. (That, and the sure knowledge that it was not Holmes. Not that for a moment I actually thought it was: My mad dash from the house was set off by professional concerns, not wifely imaginings. Truly.) The trousers on those reassuringly short legs had never belonged to a Devonshire workingman. 'Has anyone gone for the police and a doctor?'

'Don't need doctor for that'n, missus.'

'A doctor needs to declare him dead. It's a legal requirement. Did you send for them?'

'Mr Arundell went to fetch'n.' Baring-Gould's curate lived in the house overlooking the lake.

'Good. Now, we can't use the boat again in case there are fingerprints on it. Can we find another boat? I'd like to take a look at the body.'

They were shocked. 'You baint wantin' to be doing that, missus.'

'You're quite right, I don't particularly want to, but I think I ought to.'

'Thicky be Miz Holmes,' the familiar-looking man said to the other two in explanation, and that indeed seemed to explain and excuse all manner of misbehaviour, because they suddenly became cooperative, even eager.

'You feel free to use thicky boat, missus. Baint nobuddy else as used'n in weeks. He were dry as an ole bone.'

'Well, in that case, good. Now, if you, Mr . . . ?'

We paused for introductions: Andrew Budd was the young gardener, Albert Budd his older cousin, and Davey Pearce the third and eldest, an uncle of some sort. We shook hands gravely, and resumed.

'If Mr Andrew Budd would come and handle the boat for me, and you, Mr Budd the elder, would take up a position on the top of this ramp and stop anyone from coming down, perhaps, Mr Pearce, you could make your way around to the top of the other ramp and stop anyone from interfering on that side. And if you see any footprints, any hoof or tyre marks, any scuffs, give them wide berth. Yes? Good.'

It was bitter cold out on the slate-coloured water of the submerged quarry. A layer of mist clung low to the surface of the lake, causing my inadequate clothes to go clammy against my skin, while over our heads the half-bare trees rose up in watchful disapproval, the flares of intense yellow from their remaining leaves the only colours in this tight closed-in little universe. Budd rowed the short distance over to where the body floated, face down in the water. A hat, sodden but not yet completely waterlogged, had lodged against a submerged branch ten feet away, and as soon as I saw the thin hair floating like pond weed around the head, I knew who this had been.

My thoughts were echoed in an imperious shout that would have had me in the water beside the corpse had it not been for the strong arm of Andrew Budd.

'Who is it?' The call came from high above; and I turned carefully and saw, to my amazement, Baring-Gould with half a dozen others, perched on the rim looking down. There was a chair behind him, I saw; he had travelled here by the simple expedient of having himself carried, seat and all, in a makeshift litter.

'It's Randolph Pethering,' I called back, and began to shiver. Budd saw it, and began to take off his coat, but I waved him away. 'Keep it on, I'll just get it wet. Can you get us a bit closer, please?' We eased up until the prow was touching the antiquarian's sleeve. He was only resting among the floating twigs and leaves against the bank, not lying up on it, and looked to be settling down into the water. Having said we must wait for the police officials to supervise the removal of the body, I was hesitant to interfere, but at the same time I did not wish them to be forced to drag this pit for a sunken corpse, and after all, it was highly unlikely that the constables in charge of recovering the body would pay the slightest attention to the niceties of investigation, anyway. I took a deep breath, gritted my teeth against the reaction of my ribs, and reached down my right hand to take hold of the back of Pethering's jacket. Budd made an inarticulate protest.

'I have to do this,' I told him. 'He's about to sink in the water. Back us away from the bank a little, please.'

When the body was free from the rocks, I rolled him over, taking care not to add any scrapes or marks to those he might already possess, and taking care too not to let go of him lest he disappear into the depths. As I moved him, however, I noted that this did not actually seem an immediate likelihood, which was in itself interesting. Furthermore, his face when it came up to the surface was dark with livor mortis where the blood had slowly settled after death. Pethering had not died in the water, and he had not died in the last few hours.

One side of the thin, pale hair was clotted with a brown bloodstain, and the heels of his sturdy walking boots were heavily scuffed and thick with mud. However, while I was hanging over the edge of the skiff and the body was floating alongside, I could not learn a great deal more. It would have to wait for a methodical examination on dry land, preferably by someone else.

'Can you reach his hat?' I asked Budd, and as I waited for him to manoeuvre to where he could bring the sodden thing onboard, I studied my surroundings. The two steep, overgrown access ramps, on the west and the south-east walls; the stream that Baring-Gould had diverted to fill his father's quarry splashing in from the north, pushing this body down to the south wall along with the other debris; a sad little boathouse, once cheerful; autumnal trees drooping over the water and depositing their leaves; and a crowd now of at least twenty men, women, and children watching with interest this underdressed woman with a corpse on the other end of her arm.

The ramp I had come down, in the south wall, had shown no drag marks; but then again, its top was very near the drive to the curate's house. The western ramp, on the other hand, though actually closer to the house, was more sheltered, and I thought it likely he had been placed in the lake from that ramp. One man could not have tipped him over the edge without a great deal more damage to the body than there seemed to be. Two adults might have swung Pethering and thrown him over, and if so, the launching site would have been precisely where Baring-Gould and the others were standing. I sighed. Little point to objecting, I supposed, but still: 'Rector, could you have those people move around to the other side? There could be footprints right there.'

One of the women at his side leant over to repeat my message in his ear, and in seconds the assembly was tiptoeing away from the gathering place, lifting their skirts and eyeing the ground as if it were about to bite them. Baring-Gould resumed his chair and he, too, migrated around the rim, where he was joined by the pink-cheeked, helmeted forces of law and order in the person of the local police constable. The voice of legal authority came, inevitably:

'Here, what are you doing down there?'

I left Baring-Gould to explain and to assert his own, considerably more ancient form of authority over the upstart with his shiny buttons and his shallow roots in the last century. I huddled in the boat, holding on to Pethering's coat with my now-numb fingers (his collar would have been easier, but I recoiled from brushing his cold flesh any more than I had to) and watching the glowering, gesticulating constable, and I decided that there was no point in maintaining an exactness in the investigative process. I was satisfied that Pethering had not been placed where he was found, and as I could not let go of him until he was unable to sink or to float off, it was high time to hand him over to properly constituted authority. 'Thank you, Mr Budd. Back to the ramp, I think. Try not to hit him with your oar.'

It was clumsy work, and after I tried, and failed, to keep Pethering out of the oar's way, Budd turned the boat and sculled it backwards with short, choppy strokes. At the ramp I let the constable drag the body up onto the shore, leaving it half in the water. Now that he had possession of the thing, he looked down at it in growing consternation, and did not notice at first when I got back into the boat. When the corner of his eye caught the movement of Budd pushing off, he protested loudly, more loudly than strictly necessary.

I tried to reassure him. 'I'm not going anywhere, Constable. I'll be right back.' To Budd I said, 'Take me over to the other side, please. I'd like to have a look at it before half the parish tramps it down.'

The PC did not like this at all, and raised his voice to order us to return. I can't think he imagined we had anything to do with the death, but for a man more accustomed to drunken farm-hands and petty break-ins than dead bodies, and faced with a pair in a boat who delivered a body and now proposed to row away, all he could do was to grasp hard onto the essentials – and we were as essential a thing as he could find.

Seeing us making our way to the only other exit from this pit, he turned on his heels and churned up the hillside and around the rim. I saw him flitting behind the half-bare trees, and my heart sank at what those furious boots would do to any marks on the ramp.

Davey Pearce was still at the top of his ramp, holding back his crowd of two very small children and studying all the activity with great interest. 'Try to stop him from coming down the ramp,' I called to him without much hope, and indeed, when the constable appeared at Pearce's side, he did not look open to reason. He pushed Pearce to one side and started down towards us.

However, I had reckoned without Baring-Gould. His old voice rang out with the authority of six centuries of landholders, John Gold the Crusader ordering his troops into battle with the Saracen. 'Pearce, hold him there.'

And Pearce, who was old enough to have the traditional ways built into his very bones, reached out through the thin veneer of governmental authority and laid a meaty hand on the constable, and he held him there. He sat on him, actually, with the beatific smile of licensed insurrection on his face.

Before I could climb out of the boat, Budd tapped me on the arm and held out his wool coat. I looked at the heavy pullover he still wore, and took the coat.

The sloping hillside before me must have been hellish for hauling up slabs of stone but it was no great obstacle for a strong person carrying the inert body of a small man across his shoulders, which is what the killer had done until he slipped on some wet leaves about halfway down. After that, he had dragged Pethering, which accounted for the marks I had seen on the backs of the antiquarian's waterlogged boots. At the edge of the water he had fumbled and splashed and no doubt got himself wet from the knees down, working to push the body out into the lake, before climbing back up to the rim (each step slipping slightly as his wet shoes hit the damp leaves) and making his way off.

Before I went to investigate his destination, though, I returned to the place where he had fallen, studying it with great care from all angles until I could visualise the man's movements precisely.

He had been carrying Pethering over both shoulders, I decided, left hand steadying his load, right hand out as a balance. When his right heel hit a patch of wet leaves and skidded out from under him, he thumped down on his backside, with Pethering landing on the ground behind him. I could see clearly where the man's right foot had stretched out to leg's length, where his left heel had dug in, where his right hand plunged into the leaves behind him, and where the seat of his trousers landed hard. The length of Pethering stretched out at cross angles, heels to the man's right hand, head to his left. The man got to his feet (no doubt brushing at his clothing in disgust) and went around to Pethering's shoulders to drag him off downhill the rest of the way to the water.

It was all remarkably clear, one of the most elegant examples of spoor I had ever seen, and I was very pleased with myself until I stood up, brushing off my own hands, and saw my audience stretched around the rim of the lake. They had been standing, stone still and silent, as I examined the ground, so intent on a precise recreation of what had gone on here that I had duplicated the man's very movements, dipping into a fall, flinging a leg out to mimic the sliding foot, standing and brushing and hoisting and pulling – all of my movements small and controlled, mere shorthand, as it were, but nonetheless vastly entertaining. Even the constable beneath Davey Pearce lay silently staring at me. My face began to burn, and I gruffly shouldered my way past the people at the top to examine the path that ran there.

The man who had brought Pethering here, however, had vanished into the scuffed leaf mould. The path was too well used for a single passer-by to have left his mark, and he was not so obliging as to have deposited a thread from Pethering's coat or a tuft from his trousers legs on a passing branch, not that I could discover.

I finally gave it up and went back to the lake, where I found the doctor arrived, the body being loaded onto a stretcher, and the stony-faced, muddy-coated police constable under the control of an inspector.

The inspector, whose name was Fyfe, did not know what to make of me; I could see him decide that it was best to defer judgement until all the votes were in. Non-committally, he tugged his hat politely at Baring-Gould's introduction and merely said he'd be speaking to me later. As none of what I had found could influence the first flush of his investigation, I agreed, asking only that he please do his best to keep the curious off the western ramp.

'PC Bennett is taking care of that,' he said mildly. I refrained from looking across at the hapless constable, reduced to guard duty.

I was also, quite simply, not up to the prolonged explanation and argument that I was sure would ensue when a rural inspector of police encountered a female amateur detective's analysis of a crime. All of a sudden I was deathly tired and enormously cold, and Baring-Gould, loyally standing by, looked even worse.

'Inspector, I'll go back to the house now and finish my breakfast,' I heard my voice say. 'The rector ought to be in out of the cold, as well.' I did not listen to hear the inspector's yea or nay; I only waited until I saw Baring-Gould turning to his waiting sedan chair and two strongmen leaping forward to carry him back to the warmth.

I did not even make it across the meadow before the reaction hit me. In part it was sheer physical cold, but also, and I think chiefly, it was the psychic strain of dealing competently and in a professional manner in the face of a bloating corpse, and moreover one that I had known, however briefly, alive.

I was shuddering with cold when I got back to the house. An anxious housemaid stood at the door, ordered no doubt by Mrs Elliott to stay there but eager to know what was happening. Her questions died when she saw my face, and she helped me take off the borrowed coat. I was shivering so badly I could barely speak, but I succeeded in telling her that the coat was to be returned to Andrew Budd, and that I was going to bath.

I used the nail brush on the skin of my right hand until the hand looked raw, and I drained the bath and ran it full and even hotter. My skin went pink, then red, but I still trembled inside, until the maid appeared (looking a bit pink herself – Mrs Elliott's stern hand had resumed control downstairs, a dim part of my mind diagnosed) with a tea tray and a cup already poured – very little tea in it, but a great deal of hot milk, sugar, and whisky. I drank the foul mixture with gratitude, and the fluttering subsided.

I began to relax, and then to think, and eventually I succumbed to a brief gust of shaky, half-hysterical laughter: Who would have thought I could make such a fuss over an irritating insect like Pethering?

CHAPTER SEVENTEEN

As the drift tin was exhausted, and the slag of the earlier miners
was used up, it came to be necessary to run adits for tin,
and work the veins.

— A BOOK OF DARTMOOR

INSECT OR NOT, THE squashing of him left me distinctly queasy, on
and off during the day. Baring-Gould withdrew to his room, leaving
Inspector Fyfe little scope for questioning apart from me. When we had
been over it all so many times even he was thoroughly sick of it, he left.

A few minutes later the housemaid Rosemary slipped in and
placed a tray on the table beside the chair where I sat trying to
summon the energy to rise.

'Mrs Elliott thought you could maybe use a coffee,' she
murmured, and slipped out again.

Bully for Mrs Elliott, I thought, to offer as refreshment a change
from the endless cups of tea we had been swilling all day. A bracing
cup of coffee to celebrate the (however temporary) repelling of
constabulary boarders, and along with it, I was amused to find, a
selection of three kinds of freshly baked biscuits that explained the
odours that had wafted in from the door that connected the drawing
room to the kitchen. If Mrs Elliott chose to work off her upset by
indulging in an orgy of baking, it was fine with me.

I wandered nervously in and out of rooms until I found myself in Baring-Gould's study, where I retrieved the manuscript copy of *Further Reminiscences* from the heap of papers where I had left it. Being handwritten, I thought, the going would be slow, but distracting enough to take my mind off the events of the day. And so it proved – when, that is, I could keep my attention on the pages at all. Time and again I caught myself staring blindly into space, and wrenched my thoughts back onto Baring-Gould's writing. His early parishes did not seem to have been successes, and his marriage was touched upon so lightly that it would have been easy to miss it entirely. The manuscript was, in fact, the least revealing autobiography I had ever read, being much more concerned with the minutiae of European travel and the triumphs of antiquarian explorations than his relationship with his wife or the birth of his children. Belgian art, the history of Lew, a trip to Freiburg, lengthy letters to his friend and travelling companion Gatrill, ghost stories, love philtres, and thirty pages on the collecting of folk songs were occasionally interesting, often tedious. The only thing that caught my attention was a brief mention of gold, but when I reread the passage I saw that he was talking about Bodmin Moor, some distance to the west, and I read on as he described being first lost in the fog and then sucked up to his shoulders into a bog.

The long day dribbled to a close, punctuated only by a solitary dinner (I very nearly asked if I might join the others in the kitchen, but decided it would be too cruel) and an eventual adjournment upstairs – not to bed, which would have been futile, but to allow the servants to close up the house for the night.

Three times during the day I had my coat on and stood at the door, ready to set off up the hill to the village post-office telephone, and three times I took off my coat and went back to my book before the fire. If this case were to be given over to Scotland Yard, a word in Mycroft's ear would cause a memorandum to travel sideways, across two or three desks, until it finally reached the desk of a man who could pick up the telephone and arrange for one of the more sympathetic Yard men to be sent.

But what if that did happen, what if they even sent Holmes' old friend Lestrade himself? Would it make any difference if the official investigator was friendly or not? In fact, would it not actually be better if the Holmes partnership was disconnected from the police forces, allowing us to get on with our own investigation without undue interference?(Assuming, of course, that Holmes reappeared to take up his share of the burden. The man's penchant for disappearing at inconvenient moments was at times maddening.)

In the end, I stayed with my book, deciding that the pull of the telephone was only the urge to be doing something (anything!) and meekly removed myself upstairs at an appropriate hour.

By one o'clock in the morning, I had given up the attempt to read and sat watching my thoughts chase one another around by the low flicker of the fire. By two I had ceased feeding the coals and climbed under the bedclothes, but I did not even attempt to douse the light. I knew that the pathetic back of the dead man's head would be waiting for me in the dark, so I let my mind poke and prod at the restrictions that ignorance had laid, trying with a complete lack of success to put together a puzzle missing half its pieces.

At three o'clock a stealthy sound from downstairs jerked me up into instant alarm: heart pounding, mouth open, I strained for a repetition. It came, and I instantly swung my feet off the bed and was reaching for a heavy object when my brain succeeded in asserting itself against the adrenaline. It was unlikely that a burglar or would-be murderer would have a key to the front door.

Sure enough, in less than two minutes my bedroom door opened quietly but surely, and Holmes came in, wearing the dark suit of London with an inexplicable quantity of mud and grass clinging to the ankles. He closed the door, turned, and stopped dead.

'Good Lord, Russell, what have you been up to?'

I had almost forgotten the state of my face, but whatever he saw behind the bruises and contusions had him by my side in a few rapid steps.

'What?' he demanded. 'What is it?'

I did not give him his answer until some time later, but then, I did not need to. Holmes was always very satisfactory at determining, with a minimum of clues, what in a given situation was the required course of action.

There are times when verbal communication, vital as it may be in a partnership, is insufficient; this was one of those times. I clung to him, and even slept for a while towards morning before finally, reluctantly, stirring.

'Pethering is dead,' I told him. He jerked and I felt him looking at my forehead. 'No, there is no relationship to my injuries – I got those in a fall up on the moor.' I gave him a brief sketch of my trip across Dartmoor and a slightly more detailed description of my impromptu visit to Baskerville Hall, then went on to the previous day's sequence of events, starting with theology at dawn and ending with meaningless words on a page at midnight. Once, I might have been too ashamed to tell him about my exaggerated response to the death of a scarcely known nuisance, but we had been through too much together for my overreaction to cause more than a pang of embarrassment in the telling. Or perhaps I was just too tired to care.

'They will do an autopsy?' he asked.

'Fyfe said they would do.'

'And he's preserved the marks on the ramp?'

'They had a tarpaulin over it.'

'Better than nothing at all, I suppose. Plaster casts of the heel marks?'

'I doubt it.'

'I shall have to insist.'

I laughed shortly. 'I don't know how much influence you'll have down here. Certainly the name of Sherlock Holmes' wife is nothing to conjure with.'

'Ah, poor Russell, forced to ride along in her husband's turn-ups. It is a backward area, with no respect for women's brains. Never mind; we'll both have to resort to Gould's influence before we're through.'

'It is very impressive, that influence. He had a law-abiding dairyman assaulting a police constable, just for the asking.'

'I told you it was a backwoods. They probably still practise corn sacrifice. Tell me about Ketteridge.'

I told him everything I could remember about my hours in Baskerville Hall. He listened intently, asking no questions, and when I had finished he rose and, wrapping his dressing gown around him, went to stir the fire into life. Having done so, he took up his pipe and lit it, puffing thoughtfully down at the newly crackling flames.

'You handled it well,' he said unexpectedly.

'At least I didn't fall apart until I was alone.'

'That is all one may ask of oneself.'

'I suppose. I feel stupid.'

'Human,' he corrected me.

'God, who would be a human being?' I said, although I was beginning to feel somewhat better about the episode and its effect on me.

'I've often thought the same,' he commented drily, and then returned to business. 'You have no idea who Ketteridge might have been escorting so anxiously off the premises?'

'None.'

'No smell of perfume, for example, or of cigarettes? The night he was here, Ketteridge mentioned that he smokes only cigars, and his fingers did not give lie to it,'

'No perfume. Cigarettes, yes, but I think Scheiman smokes them.'

'I believe you are right. Do you know, that entire ménage interests me strangely. Tell me: When Ketteridge allowed you the brief tour of the banqueting hall, did you notice a portrait of a Cavalier in black velvet, lace collar, and a plumed hat?'

'No,' I said slowly. 'A variety of uniforms, one blue velvet jacket, and an assortment of wigs, but no Cavalier.'

'As I thought, the portrait of old Sir Hugo Baskerville, the scoundrel whose sins led to the Baskerville curse in the first place, has been taken down from the gallery. I should be very interested to know when.'

'And why?'

'When might tell us why.' Having delivered his epigram, he tossed the barely drawing pipe onto the mantelpiece and began to pull clothing from drawers and wardrobe.

'Holmes, tell me what you found in London.'

'Breakfast first, Russell; the morning is half gone and I, for one, have not eaten since lunchtime yesterday.'

I forbore to look pointedly at the first pale light at the window curtains, merely removed my recovering body from the bed and proceeded to clothe it. Holmes was not the only one who could follow nonverbal commands.

Before we left the bedroom, however, there was something I had to know. 'Holmes, why did you tell me you'd met Baring-Gould during the Baskerville case?'

'I did not. I merely said that I had used him during the case.'

'You deliberately misled me. Why didn't you want me to know he was your godfather?'

He paused in the act of brushing his hair and looked over at me, startled. 'Good heavens, he is, isn't he? I had completely forgotten.' He turned back to the mirror slowly. 'Extraordinary thought, is it not?'

With that, I had to agree.

* * *

Mrs Elliott was up and ready for us, although Baring-Gould was not. I had not expected he would be, after the rigours of the day before; I could only hope he had not suffered from the unwonted expenditure of his limited energies.

The chimney in the dining room was still not functioning satisfactorily, so we had been served in the drawing room with the painted Virtues looking down at us, and there we remained for our council. I had to wait until Holmes had tamped and lit and puffed at his pipe, a delaying nuisance that had not grown any easier to bear over the years. I swear he did it deliberately to irritate me.

'Holmes,' I growled after several long minutes, 'I am going to take up knitting, and make you sit and wait while I count the row of stitches.'

'Nonsense,' he said with a final dig and puff. 'You are quite capable of talking and counting at the same time. Am I to understand that you wish to hear the results of my sojourn?'

'Holmes, when I left you on Monday, you were going to northern Dartmoor and returning here two days later. It is now Saturday, and the only word I have had were second-hand rumours of a hasty trip to London. I've told you about Pethering's death and my visit to Baskerville Hall; I see no reason to go into my trip over the moor and my conversation about hedgehogs with the witch of Mary Tavy parish until you've given me something in return.'

'Ah, I see you've met Elizabeth Chase.'

Sometimes I wondered what it would be like to have a husband whom I might astonish.

'Holmes,' I said sternly.

'Oh very well. Yes, I went onto the moor, and no, I was not blown to bits; I was not even lightly shelled. I even missed the worst of the storm on the Tuesday. I asked farmwives, shepherds, three stonemasons, two thatchers, a goose girl, and the village idiot whether or not they had seen a ghostly carriage or a black dog, had heard anything peculiar, noticed anything out of the ordinary. All but the village idiot gave me nothing but nonsense, and he gave me nothing but a smile.

'The testing ground for Mycroft's secret weapon (which, by the way, is a sort of amphibious tank) is to the east of Yes Tor, down to Black-a-ven Brook. It's a pocket of ground difficult to overlook except from the army's own observation huts, but I did find a patch of hillside outside the artillery range with an adit showing signs of recent use.'

'An adit being a horizontal mine shaft,' I said tentatively, dredging up the word from somewhere in my recent reading. Holmes nodded. 'Not an active mine, I take it?'

'By no means. Its entrance was heavily overgrown and nearly obscured by a rock fall.'

'How did you find it?'

'I smelt it.'

'You smelt . . . ?'

'Coffee. Whoever spent time in there brewed coffee, and threw the grounds at the roots of the whortleberry bushes growing near the entrance.'

'Good heavens.'

'Extraordinary oversight, I agree,' he said, which was not quite what I was exclaiming about, but I let it pass. 'The rest of his debris he simply threw back into the shaft – eggshells, greasy paper, tins, apple cores – but the coffee dregs went out in front. Presumably he was in the habit of drinking it at his front door, as it were, and dashing out the thick remnants in the bottom of his cup where he stood. As you are aware, Russell, habit is the snare by which many a criminal is caught.'

'How recently was he there?'

'Two or three weeks, I should say. Not more. And to anticipate your question, the new tank was last tested seventeen days ago.'

'Suggestive,' I agreed. 'But that does not explain five days and a trip to London.'

'Patience,' counselled my husband, one of the least patient individuals I have ever met. 'I returned here late on Tuesday, spent a pleasant evening with Gould, and on Wednesday a lad arrived with the name of the people we were looking for.'

'The London hikers?'

'Not quite, although he had found the farm-house where they stayed. Unfortunately, being an informal hostelry, they do not keep records of their guests, and as the two Londoners had not made advance arrangements, there was little evidence as to whence they came. However, they were a memorable pair, even without the tale of the ghostly carriage they brought with them down the hill: young, the man perhaps twenty-eight, the woman a year or two younger, who impressed the farmwife as being a "proper lady", or in other words, wealthy. The man, on the other hand, had a heavier accent, and seemed much more shaken by the idea of seeing a ghostly carriage on the moor than his wife was. He also had a bad limp and one "special shoe", and at some point during the stay told the farmer that he was studying to become a doctor.'

The limp, the nerves, and the student's advanced age gave him away as a wounded soldier. I asked drily, 'You mean to say you didn't get his regiment?'

'But of course. Not from the farmer, although he did give me the name of the village where the future doctor was injured during Second Ypres, and the War Office could have told me his regiment and thence his identity. However, I thought it simpler to phone around the teaching hospitals and enquire after a young man missing part of his foot. I found him straight off, at Bart's.'

'So simple,' I murmured.

'Regrettably so. Do you have the maps?'

'Upstairs. What is left of them.' I trotted up and retrieved the pile, some of them pristine, hardly unfolded. Those for the north quarter had seen hard use, and I pulled open the still-damp sheets with care and laid them across the padded bench that sat in front of the fire. There happened to be an elderly cat upon it, but the animal did not seem to mind being covered up. No doubt, living in the Baring-Gould household, it had seen stranger usage.

He pored over the maps for a long time, then said, 'Do we have the one-inch-to-the-mile here?'

I dug through and found it. He laid it out, found Mary Tavy and the nearby Gibbet Hill, and then took out a pencil. Using the side of a folded map as a straight edge and pulling the map to one side to find a flat place, he began to draw a series of short lines, fanning out from Gibbet Hill and touching the tops of half a dozen peaks and tors to the north-east of the hill. These were, I understood, the tors and hilltops visible from the peak.

'It was dark, and their sense of direction was sadly wanting, but they were quite definite that whatever they saw was to the north-east, that it wrapped around a hill, going from right to left, and after a minute or two disappeared behind a tor – probably, they thought, Great Links or Dunna Goat.'

'And what exactly was it they saw?'

'A pair of lights, old-style lanterns rather than the new automobile headlamps, mounted on the upper front corners of a light-coloured square frame. They had with them a strong pair of field glasses.'

'As if two lanterns on a coach built of bones.'

'As you say.'

'How would you judge them as witnesses?'

He shrugged. 'Ramblers,' he said dismissively. 'The sort of young people who would read up on the more arcane myths and legends of an area and spend a week traipsing about, raising blisters and searching for Local Romance.'

'Holmes, that sounds perilously close to what I have been doing this last week.'

He looked startled. 'My dear Russell, I was certainly not drawing a comparison between your search for information and the self-indulgent—'

'Of course not, Holmes. Did they see a dog, or any person either inside or driving?'

'Not to be certain, no, although they had convinced themselves that they saw a large black shadow moving with the horse.'

'Of course they did. Was there anything else to be had in London?'

'There was, but I should like to delay until you've read something. Just remain there,' he said, getting to his feet. 'I won't be a moment.'

He went out and, judging by the sounds of another door opening almost immediately he left the drawing room, I knew he was in Baring-Gould's study. A certain amount of time passed, and several muffled thuds, before he returned with a slim book in his hand. He tossed it in my lap and picked up his pipe from the ashtray on the table.

'How long is it since you've read that?' he asked.

'That,' to my amazement, was Conan Doyle's account of *The Hound of the Baskervilles,* looking heavily read. 'At least three years. I'm not certain,' I replied.

'More than that, perhaps. I should like to consult with Gould for an hour or two; you have a look at that and see if anything within Baskerville Hall strikes you as it did me.'

'But Holmes—'

'When I return, Russell. It won't take you long, and you might even find it amusing. Though perhaps,' he added as he was going out the door, 'not for the reasons Conan Doyle intended.'

Chapter Eighteen

Take my advice. Henceforth possess your mind with an idea, when
about to preach. Drive it home. Do not hammer it till you have
struck off the head. A final tap and that will suffice.

— FURTHER REMINISCENCES

Actually, although i would have hesitated to admit it in
Holmes' hearing, I enjoyed Conan Doyle's stories. They were
not the cold, factual depictions of a case that Holmes preferred
(indeed, when some years later he found that Conan Doyle had
set a pair of stories in the first person, as if Holmes himself were
describing the action, Holmes threatened the man with everything
from physical violence to lawsuits if he dared attempt it again),
but taken as Romance, they were entertaining, and I have nothing
against the occasional dose of simple entertainment.

In any event, it was no great hardship to settle into my chair
with the book and renew my acquaintance with Dr Mortimer,
the antiquarian enthusiast who brings Holmes the curse of the
Baskervilles, and with the young Canadian Sir Henry Baskerville,
come to the moor to claim his title and his heritage. I met again
the ex-headmaster Stapleton and the woman introduced as his
sister, and the mysterious Barrymores, servants to old Sir Charles.
The moor across which I had so recently wandered came alive in all
its dour magnificence, and I was very glad this book had not been

among my reading the previous weekend, leaving me to ride out on the moor with the image of the hound freshly imprinted on my mind. I could well imagine the terror raised by hearing the rhythm of four huge running paws (or the 'thin, crisp, continuous patter from somewhere in the heart of that crawling bank' of fog that Dr Watson described), the hoarse panting from between those massive jaws even without the eerie glow of phosphorus on its coat to render it otherworldly:

> A hound it was, an enormous coal-black hound, but not such a hound as mortal eyes have ever seen. Fire burst from its open mouth, its eyes glowed with a smouldering glare, its muzzle and hackles and dewlap were outlined in flickering flame.

So engrossed was I that I completely missed the reference Holmes had wanted me to see. Only when the Hound was dead did I recall the point of the exercise, and thumbed back to the previous chapter that described the evening when Holmes first saw the interior of Baskerville Hall. The reference startled me, and I sat deep in thought for twenty minutes or so, contemplating the 'straight severe face' which was 'prim, hard, and stern, with a firm-set, thin-lipped mouth, and a coldly intolerant eye' until I heard the door behind me open.

I said over my shoulder, 'You think Scheiman may be a Baskerville? Stapleton's son, even?'

'Stapleton's body was never found,' Holmes pointed out unnecessarily as he resumed his chair on the other side of the fire. 'I was never happy with Scotland Yard's conclusion, and always felt it possible that he had prepared an escape route and slipped through it while we were occupied elsewhere, but he was never seen, and after two weeks, Scotland Yard was satisfied with his fate in the mire and took their watch from the ports.'

'I have to agree that the description of the Cavalier painting, wicked Sir Hugo himself with his prim lips and his flaxen hair, does fit Scheiman.'

'Scheiman is by no means so clear a case, else I should have noticed it when first I laid eyes on him. If Stapleton married in America – although legal marriage it could not have been, nor indeed would Sir Henry's have been to Beryl Stapleton, the supposed widow – the woman contributed a great deal more to her son's looks than did the father. Ears, eyes, cheekbones, and hands are all hers; only the mouth (which you will have noticed he takes care to conceal beneath a beard) and the stature are his father's.'

'You wondered when the portrait of Sir Hugo had gone: If the surviving Baskerville took it with her rather than sell it with the others to Ketteridge, for the dubious privilege of preserving a memento of the family history perhaps, then its absence is innocent, whereas if it was removed after the sale, by Ketteridge or Scheiman—'

'Then the why is obvious: that Scheiman's family resemblance might not be seen by visitors to the house.'

'Visitors such as Sherlock Holmes. I don't think I told you, by the way, that Ketteridge was interested in hiring you to investigate the hound sightings.'

That brought a laugh, as I had thought it might do, albeit a brief one.

'What brought the resemblance to your mind?' I asked. Surely he hadn't picked up *The Hound of the Baskervilles* to read on the train?

'A number of things. Scheiman's interest in the antiquities of the moor, the dim lighting of the dining hall, how he spent the least amount of time possible with us – with me, who had known Stapleton. But, I have to admit, the actual possibility was got through hindsight.

'As I told you, the Ketteridge establishment interests me. It interested me when first I saw the man helping himself to Gould's liquor cabinet. He does not fit in Dartmoor, and does not seem eccentric enough to justify the oddity of his presence here.

'So while I was in town, I initiated some enquiries about Ketteridge and his secretary. The responses to my telegrams will take days, even weeks, but I did come across one thing of interest: The two men were not together when they boarded the ship coming over here. Ketteridge began his journey in San Francisco, but Scheiman joined the ship in New York.'

'There could be an explanation for that.'

'There could be any number of explanations. However, Ketteridge told us he came over in the summer, yet his passage was in early March.'

I had to agree that although the oddity was hardly evidence of criminal activity, it did call for a closer examination of the two men.

'You've sent wires to New York and San Francisco?'

'And Portland and Alaska.'

'So you think Ketteridge is involved.'

'He may or may not be. Scheiman is definitely up to something.'

The generality of the word *something* was unlike Holmes; after a moment's thought, and particularly when he would not look at me, I knew why.

'You believe that Scheiman is after Mycroft's tank,' I said in disgust.

'It does not do to theorise in advance of one's facts,' he said primly.

I made a rude remark about his facts, and went on. 'If this is deteriorating into a spy hunt, Holmes, you don't need me. It's been a truly invigorating holiday from my books, but perhaps I may be allowed to take my leave.'

'Two murders now, Russell. I should have thought that sufficient to overcome your distaste for the War Office.'

I dropped my head back onto the chair and closed my eyes. 'You really need me, Holmes?'

'I could ask Watson.'

Dr Watson was only five years older than Holmes, but his heavy frame had aged as Holmes' wiry build and whip-hard constitution had not. I dismissed his half-hearted suggestion. 'A cold day on the moor would cripple him.' That Holmes might rely on police help or Mycroft's men was so improbable as to be unworthy of mention. 'I'll stay and see it through. Although I can't promise that I won't blow up that flipping tank myself at the end of it.'

'That's my Russell.' He smiled. I scowled.

'Will you go down to see Miss Baskerville yourself, to ask about the painting?' I asked him.

'I should like to know as well some of the particulars concerning the sale of the Hall. Yes, I shall go myself. Now, you have yet to tell me about Elizabeth Chase's hedgehogs.'

'One hedgehog, and it does not belong to her. It now resides in the garden of a friend of Miss Chase's in Widdecombe-in-the-Moor, where Miss Chase carried it to nurse it back to health after finding it on the twenty-eighth of July, its leg crushed by a fast-moving wheel and its back bitten by large teeth.'

'Aha!'

'Indeed. Moreover, she goes on to offer us one large and spectral dog with a glowing eye and a taste for scones.' To my great pleasure, this statement actually startled Holmes.

I told him about Elizabeth Chase's wounded hedgehog and about Samuel's encounter with the Hound, and after telling him I sat forward and pulled the map to me, marking with an X the spot between the stone row and the hut circles where she had heard the piteous cry of poor wee Tiggy and the place where Samuel had seen the dog. Holmes took the pencil and drew in the probable route of the coach as seen from Gibbet Hill, added a star shape to mark the adit in which he had found signs of life, and we studied the result: my X, his line, two Xs for the sightings of the coach in July, and a circle to show where Josiah Gorton had last been seen. All of them together formed a jagged line running diagonally across the face of the moor from Sourton Tor in the north-west to Cut Lane in the south-east, roughly six miles from one end to the other. The imaginary line's nearest point to Baskerville Hall was three miles, although the closest sighting, that of the courting couple, was more than four miles away.

I sat for a time in contemplation of the enigmatic line while Holmes slumped back into his chair, eyes closed and fingers steepled. When he spoke, his remark seemed at first oblique.

'I find I cannot get the phial of gold dust from my mind.'

'Did you give it over for analysis?'

'I looked at it myself in the laboratory. Small granules of pure gold – not ore – with a pinch of some high-acid humus and a scraping of deteriorated granitic sand.'

'Peat is highly acidic,' I suggested.

'Peat, yes, but there was a tiny flat fragment that looked as if it might have been a decomposed leaf of some tough plant such as holly or oak.'

'Wistman's Wood is oak.'

'So are a number of other places around the moor. I shall ring the laboratory later today, to see if their more time-consuming chemical analyses have given them any more than I found. In the meanwhile, I think I can just catch the train to Plymouth, although it may mean stopping there the night. Perhaps you could go and ask Mrs Elliott if Gould's old dog cart is available.'

'And if the pony can pull it.' Red was still in residence at Baskerville Hall.

Holmes went up to put his shaving kit and a change of linen into his bag, and I put the breakfast things back on the tray and took them into the kitchen. There I found Mrs Elliott, looking somewhat dishevelled.

'Oh bless you, my dear. I don't know what I'm going to do. Rosemary and Lettice have taken to their beds with sick headaches – from crying no doubt; they'd be better off working and keeping their minds off that silly man, but there you have it.'

'I'm sorry, Mrs Elliott. Is there anything I can do to help?' I asked hesitantly. 'Washing up or something?'

She looked shocked. 'That will not be necessary, mum. But thank you for the kind thought.' She would have to be in a sorry state indeed before she allowed a guest to plunge her ladylike hands into a pan full of dishes.

'Well, please let me know if there is something I can do. But I need to ask, can someone take Mr Holmes down to the station? He needs to catch the train to Plymouth.'

She looked up at the clock over the mantelpiece and hurriedly began to dry her hands. 'He'll need to step smart, then. I'll have Mr Dunstan hitch the pony to the cart.'

She ducked out through the door. I eyed the stack of unwashed dishes and left them alone, going up the back stairs to tell Holmes the cart would be ready. I found him just closing his bag, and reported on the time constrictions. He nodded and sat down to change his shoes.

'What do you wish me to do while you're away?' I asked. I was half tempted to throw together a bag and join him, for the sake of movement if nothing else.

'We need to know more about Pethering,' he said. One set of laces was looped and tied, and the other foot raised. 'I want you to—'

'Sorry, Holmes,' I said, raising one hand. 'Was that the door?' We listened, hearing nothing, and I went over to the window. There was a motor car in the drive, but the porch roof obscured my view of the door, so, feeling a bit like a fishwife, I opened the window and put my head out to call. 'Hello? Is someone there?'

After a moment a hatted, overcoated man came into view, backing slowly out from the porch and craning his head to see where the voice had come from.

'Inspector Fyfe!' I said. He found me and tipped his hat uncertainly. 'Do come inside and warm yourself; the door is not locked. We'll be right down.' I drew in my head and latched the window.

Holmes was already out of the room, and I did not catch him up until he was shaking hands with a still-hatted Inspector Fyfe in the hall. As I seemed to be playing hostess (or rather, in the temporary absence of Mrs Elliott and her disturbed assistants, housemaid), I took his coat and hat. Not knowing quite what to do with them, I laid them across the back of a chair and joined the two men at the fire.

Fyfe rubbed his hands together briskly in front of the smouldering fire, while Holmes squatted down to coax it back to life. 'What can we do for you, Inspector?' I asked.

'I have some questions to ask Mr Baring-Gould about the man Pethering.'

Holmes looked up. 'What do you imagine Gould would know about him?'

'Well, I hope he knows something, because we can't find a trace of where he comes from or who he is.'

Holmes' eyebrows went up. 'I understood that he was a Reader at one of the northern universities. York, I believe Gould said.'

'They've never heard of him. Nor do they have anyone on their staff who fits his description, an archaeologist or anthropologist or what-have-you, with a wife and young family.'

'You interest me, Inspector. Mrs Elliott,' he said, raising his voice, and indeed, when I turned to look, there she was in the door to the drawing room. 'Would you be so good as to tell Mr Dunstan that I won't be needing the cart? I shall have to take a later train. And I

231

believe the inspector could make good use of a hot drink.' He swept the maps off the bench in front of the fire, uncovering the blithely sleeping tabby, and sat down beside the animal, gesturing Fyfe towards a chair. 'Tell me what you do know about him, Inspector.'

Fyfe settled onto the edge of the nearest armchair. 'I'll be calling in Scotland Yard this afternoon,' he said, sounding resigned about it. 'We don't have the facilities here. Meantime, about all we know about Pethering, or whatever his name might be, is that he arrived at Coryton station on the Saturday afternoon, walked up to Lew Down to arrange a room at the inn, had some tea, and then came here to Lew House, where he stayed from 'round about six until you turned him out, which Miss – Mrs – which your wife says was a shade after midnight.

'He then returned to Lew Down and knocked up the innkeeper, who let him in. He came down from his room around ten o'clock Sunday morning, struck up a conversation with William Latimer, who stepped in to deliver a basket of eggs his wife had promised for Saturday but couldn't bring because one of their boys fell out of an apple tree and broke his arm, and she was away at the surgery getting it seen to. Latimer told Pethering about the sightings of the hound on the moor, Pethering got all excited and rushed upstairs to get his map. Latimer showed him where to look, and Pethering ran upstairs again, put on his heavy boots, and packed two bags – or one bag and a large rucksack. He left the bag with the innkeeper, and walked off down the high road in the direction of Okehampton.

'A farmer near Collaven saw him 'round about two o'clock making for the moor. That's the last anyone saw of the man alive.'

I retrieved the one-inch map from the floor and looked for Collaven. It lay at the foot of the moor, two miles north of Lydford and a mile from Sourton Tor, on the edge of the area so heavily marked by our pencilled lines and Xs.

'Where was he going?' Holmes asked.

'Latimer told him the hound had been seen near Watern Tor.'

His elbows on his knees, Holmes gazed into the fire, fingers steepled and resting on his lips. 'Why the hound?' he mused.

Before Fyfe could respond, the rattle of crockery heralded Mrs Elliott's approach. Holmes prodded the cat until it jumped down, tail twitching in disgust, allowing Mrs Elliott to put the tray on the bench. She had thoughtfully included a high pile of buttered toast and three plates, although Holmes and I had only recently eaten. Fyfe, however, ate nearly all of it, drinking three cups of coffee as well before he was through.

'What was that about the hound?' he asked, his voice rather muffled with toast.

'I was merely wondering, Inspector, why the hound should be making an appearance.'

Fyfe swallowed. 'I understood there'd been a number of sightings over the summer.'

'Those were of Lady Howard's coach, which does indeed come complete with dog, but that does not explain why the dog should also appear sans coach.'

Fyfe had suspended his toast in puzzlement. 'I took it the hound referred to the Hound of the Baskervilles story.'

'They are very different hounds, Inspector, separated by their time, their ghostly genesis, and their mission. It is as if Jacob were to have appeared in Isaac's tent to receive his blessing wearing Joseph's coat of many colours: not entirely impossible, one would suppose, but not terribly reasonable either.'

'Different stories,' I translated for the inspector, who was looking confused. 'Everyone seems to be mixing up the two different hounds.'

'The only question is,' said Holmes, 'whether or not the confusion is deliberate.'

'Hardly the only question, Holmes,' I objected mildly.

'No? You may be right. Tell me what the post-mortem found, Inspector.'

Fyfe hastily thrust the remainder of his wedge of toast into his mouth and reached into his pocket for a notebook. When the page was found and the toast was out of the way, he began to read. 'A slim but adequately nourished male approximately thirty-seven years old, five feet six inches tall, distinguishing features a birthmark on his right shoulder blade the size of a shilling and an old scar on his left knee. Minor dental work – the description is being sent out – and otherwise in good health until someone cracked his skull open with a length of pipe.' The last sentence had not depended on the notebook.

'Why pipe?' Holmes asked sharply. 'Did the pathologist find traces?'

'No, I just said pipe to indicate the size and hardness. Could have been a walking stick of some dashed hard wood, or the barrel of a rifle, if the killer didn't mind mistreating his gun that way. 'Course it'd make more sense than the other way around. I once had a gunshot that we thought was murder until we had the victim's handprint off the end of the barrel – a shotgun it was, and he'd swung it at another man, and when the stock hit the other man, the gun discharged and took off the head of the man holding it. But that's neither here nor there,' he said, recalling himself to the matter at hand. 'Some blunt instrument a little thicker than your thumb, most likely from behind by a right-handed man. Went at a slight angle, up to the front.' He drew a line just above his own hairline, clearing the ear and ending at his right temple. It could have been a blow delivered by a left-handed individual standing above the victim, if Pethering had been on his knees, for example, but Fyfe's simpler explanation was the more likely.

'When was death?'

'Very soon after he was hit – there was not much bleeding into the brain, and external blood loss the doctor estimated at less than a pint. Rigor had come and gone, putrefaction had begun in spite of the cold. Doctor said all in all he was probably killed late Tuesday or early Wednesday, but he'd only been in the water a few hours. Less than a day, certainly.'

'Stomach contents?' Holmes asked. Fyfe looked sideways at me and put the next piece of toast down onto the edge of his plate.

'Been a long time since he'd eaten, just traces of what the doctor thought might be egg and bread.'

Which helped not at all, as that combination might be eaten at anytime of the day, from breakfast to tea, particularly on a hike into the moor.

Holmes jumped to his feet and held out his hand to Inspector Fyfe, who, after a quick pass at his trouser knee, shook it.

'Thank you, Inspector. That is all very interesting. You have taken the fingerprints of the body?'

'Yes, we raised some good prints, in spite of the puffiness from the water. Nothing yet, but we've sent them to London.'

'Good. Let us know what else you find. We'll be in touch.'

Chapter Nineteen

In La Vendée we saw men with bare legs wading in the shallow
channels that intersect the low marshy fields. After a moment
of immersion out was flung one leg and then another,
to each of which clung several leeches . . .
The women do not go in after them; and they are more rubicund,
and indeed more lively. Leech-catching is not conducive to hilarity.
— EARLY REMINISCENCES

NEITHER FYFE NOR I was quite sure how Holmes had come
to assume apparent control of the investigation, but the
arrangement seemed to have at least tacit understanding on all sides.
Fyfe took his somewhat bemused leave, having been reassured that
Baring-Gould would be questioned when he woke as to his past
communication with the man he knew as Randolph Pethering, and
that information passed on to Fyfe.

Holmes closed the door behind Fyfe and leant back against it
for a moment as if trying to bar any further complications from
entering.

'That is a poser, is it not, Holmes?' I remarked.

He did not bother to answer, but pushed himself upright and
walked back into the hall, where he stood looking oddly indecisive.

'Have you missed the train?' I asked. He waved it away as
unimportant, then drew a crumpled packet of cigarettes from his

pocket, pulled one out, lit it, and stood smoking while I put the maps and the second breakfast tray of the day in order.

'Let us go look at the bag Pethering left with the innkeeper,' he said decisively. He threw the half-smoked cigarette onto the logs, and swept out the door.

It was a paltry offering that Pethering had left behind at the inn, comprising for the most part the 'good' clothes he would not have needed while clambering over the moor. Holmes set aside the carefully folded if slightly threadbare grey suit, a silk tie that had the flavour of an aunt's Christmas present, a white shirt that had been worn once since being laundered, and a pair of polished shoes with mends in both soles. We examined the rest: another shirt, both patched and in need of laundering, and a pair of thick socks, also dirty, a pen and a small block of lined paper, a yellow back novel with a sprung cover and water damage along its top edge (the product, I diagnosed, of a book dealer's pavement display, already cheap but rendered nearly unsaleable by an unanticipated shower of rain), and a copy of a book by Baring-Gould that I had not found in his study, although I had been looking for it: his guide to Devon.

I picked up the guidebook, checked the inside cover for a name and found the first sheet carefully torn out. Pethering concealing his own name, perhaps, or was this book stolen from a library? I turned to the index and found Dartmoor, thumbed through to the central section on the moor, and found that Pethering had been there before me. He had used a tentative hand and a pencil with hard lead, but had made up for his lack of assertiveness in sheer quantity, correcting Baring-Gould's spelling, changing the names of some locations, and writing comments, annotations, and disagreements that crowded the side margins and flipped over onto the top and bottom.

I held out a random page to Holmes, who was busy dismantling a patent pencil. 'Would you say this handwriting belongs to Pethering?'

He glanced at it and went back to the object in his hands. 'Without a doubt.'

'Do you think Fyfe would object to my borrowing it? Even without Pethering's comments, I had intended to read the book, only I couldn't find a copy in the study.'

'You may have noticed that the study is now largely inhabited by volumes no one has valued enough to carry off. Gould keeps this book in the drawer of his bedside table along with his New Testament and Book of Common Prayer. And no, I'm sure Fyfe would not notice it gone.'

'Baring-Gould keeps a guide to Devon in his bedside table?' I said. It seemed an odd place to find it, particularly as the man could scarcely see to read, even in a bright light.

'Sentimentality, I suppose.' Holmes gave up on the pencil and tossed it back in the bag. 'He can no longer get onto the moor, and can't even see it from the house, so he keeps his books easily to hand, along with one or two photographs and a sheaf of sketches.' His words and gesture were so matter-of-fact as to be dismissive, but the lines etched on his face were not so casual.

I was so struck by the poignancy of the image that I did not think about his words until we had left the inn and were going down the hill towards Lew House.

'You said he keeps his books beside his bed. What are the others?'

'Just *Devon* and his book on Dartmoor. Oh, and a few manuscript copies of some of the songs he collected.'

'I should very much like to look at the Dartmoor book.'

'He wouldn't mind, I'm sure. It's not particularly rare, just something he treasures.'

'Good. Now, how are we dividing up?'

'I shall follow Pethering's track up onto the moor, if you hunt down Miss Baskerville in Plymouth.'

I had known he would suggest this particular arrangement rather than its reverse – even towards me, Holmes was usually gallant about shouldering the less comfortable tasks. Of course, this meant he took possession of the more interesting leads as well, but in this case I would not argue for the privilege of walking back out onto the moor. I merely asked when the next train left Coryton. Holmes took his watch from an inside pocket and glanced at it.

'Mrs Elliott will have an ABC, but I believe you'll find going to Lydford will put you on a train in a bit under two hours.'

That would leave me time to change from my habitual trousers into the more appropriate all-purpose tweed skirt I had brought. Coming past the stables, I put my head inside and asked Mr Dunstan please to get the dog cart ready again. I smiled a sympathetic apology at his sigh of patient endurance, and trotted up to the house to pack the overnight bag I was sure to need.

Holmes came in as I was standing and surveying the room to see what I had forgotten. He held out a book.

'Gould says he hopes you find it of interest.'

'Thank you Holmes,' I said, and put it in the bag, first removing Pethering's copy of *A Book of the West: Devon*, whose tiny, pale annotations would, I knew, prove diabolical in the poor light and movement of the train. 'Did Baring-Gould have any idea where to find Pethering?'

'He filed the man's letters down in the study, although he is certain the address was only care of the university. I'll dig them out before I go, and send them to Fyfe.'

'Will you go tonight, or wait until the morning?'

'It will save me nearly two hours of daylight if I stop the night in Bridestowe or Sourton and set out at dawn. And unless I come across a problem, I ought to be back here Monday.'

The 'problem' he might stumble across could very well be related to the problem that had landed Pethering in the lake. Without looking at him, I asked, 'Are you taking a revolver with you?'

'Yes.'

I nodded, and fastened my bag shut.

'Good hunting,' he told me.

'And you, Holmes,' I answered, and to myself added, Just don't you become the prey.

It might have been faster to walk to Lydford, but I did arrive relatively unsullied by mud, and reached the station with ten minutes to spare. I walked up and down the platform in an attempt to keep warm, my breath steaming out as the sun sank low in the sky, taking with it any heat the day might have had. As usually happens, the clearing of the skies meant a sharp drop in temperature. There would be frost on the ground tonight, and tomorrow Holmes would find the moor a bitter place.

The train when it came was well populated, which was a blessing in disguise, for the carriages were old and draughty, and the only source of heat in my compartment was the three other passengers. We huddled in our overcoats (the others had the insight, or experience, to have brought travelling rugs) and watched the ice gather on the corners of the windows. It was far too cold to read, even if I had been able to turn the pages with gloved fingers. Instead, I wrapped my arms around to keep them and me warm, hunched my shoulders, and endured.

We stopped in every village that possessed more than six houses. It was black night when the train shuddered into Plymouth, although only eight o'clock. I stumbled towards a taxi and had the driver take me to whatever he judged to be the best hotel in town, where I took a room, a hot bath, and some dinner. It was too late to call on Miss Baskerville anyway, I told myself, and climbed into bed with *A Book of Dartmoor.*

Dartmoor was the essential Baring-Gould: quirky, dogmatic, wildly enthusiastic, and as scattered as a blast from a bird gun. We began with quaking bogs, stepping into which he compared to a leisurely investigation of the underside of a duvet, adding with heavy-handed whimsy that whether or not the man who conducts such an investigation 'will be able to give to the world benefit of his observations may be open to question.'

He then moved on to the beauties of furze, the glories of furze-blossom honey, tors, whortleberries, and tenements, Chinese orthography and customs, flint arrowheads and Christian saints, the rheumatic attack of Archbishop Lawrence, the peculiar phosphorescent characteristics of the moss *Schistostega osmundaca,* the Domesday book, dolmens, menhirs, and country roads. When he began to discuss the 'twaddle and rubbish' of the Druid-supporting archaeologists I roused slightly, thinking of poor, mysterious Pethering, but Baring-Gould's discussion of the wind atop Brentor soothed me, and by the time he hit Elizabethan tin works and mediaeval adits, my eyelids were descending.

And then the word *gold* caught my eye, and I was jerked out of my torpor:

> That gold was found in the granite rubble of the stream beds is likely
> [wrote Baring-Gould, adding] A model of a gold-washing apparatus
> was found on the moor a few years ago. It was made of zinc.

Full stop. That, it appeared, was all the Reverend Sabine Baring-Gould had to say about gold, although I read on attentively for another hundred pages while the author discussed such compelling topics as a forty-year-long lawsuit, the comparative vegetation of the east and west sides of the moor, the Welsh 'martyr maid' St Winefred, the sycamore versus the beech, and the benefits of Dartmoor air for young men with weak lungs; nary a word about gold, or even the machines with which to wash it, or why I might care that they were made of zinc.

In disgust I shut down the light and pulled the bedclothes up to my chin. Despite the length of the day and the almost complete lack of sleep the two previous nights, I did not drift off for a long time, but lay contemplating the image of Josiah Gorton's hidden phial with its pinch of gold granules.

CHAPTER TWENTY

But to return to family portraits. That, in spite of the influx of
fresh blood from all quarters, a certain family type remains,
one can hardly doubt in looking
through a genuine series of family pictures.

— OLD COUNTRY LIFE

THE FIRST THING I SAW in the formal drawing room of Miss
Baskerville's house the following afternoon was the portrait of
a Cavalier with fair ringlets and a stern, thin-lipped face, dressed in
black velvet and a lace collar, taking possession of his surroundings
from his place above the fire.

It had taken me some time to gain entrance to the room and
the Cavalier's presence, for although I had been at the door at what
I had thought a sufficiently early hour for a Sunday morning, the
mistress of the house had already left.

The housemaid could not tell me precisely where her lady had
gone, although she was happy to tell me that it was her habit of a
Sunday morning to call on any of a number of her father's old and
retired servants who lived in the area, enquiring as to their wants
and transporting them to their respective churches (or, in one case,
chapel). She would then arrive for the midday services at her own
church, before dismissing her driver to attend to the redistribution
of the old retainers to their homes, and walk home or, if the weather

was too foul, wait at the rectory until her motor car came to take her home.

I therefore had been obliged to take my place in the back of the Victorian monstrosity where she worshipped, which, even though I claimed a seat directly over a vent from the floor heating, was nonetheless intensely cold until about two-thirds of the way through the service, when the heat suddenly shot on and had us steaming and discreetly shedding garments.

During the sermon I reflected on something Mrs Elliott had mentioned in passing, that Mr Baring-Gould was one of those all-too-rare proponents of the ten-minute, single-topic sermon, to the extent that he would begin to clear his throat if an underling went to fifteen minutes, and rise briskly to his feet at twenty. This particular specimen of the clergy before me did not suffer from brevity of speech, although he compensated by displaying a considerable brevity of both wit and learning. The stout, sweating man beside me was kept from snores only by the sharpness of his wife's elbow.

The housemaid had given me a fair description of the lady I was seeking, and after the service had finally broken up I approached her outside on the pavement where she was pulling on her gloves and talking with friends. I waited until the friends had finished their business, a luncheon arrangement for the following week, and as they departed and she turned to go, I stepped to her side.

'Miss Baskerville, I believe?'

'Yes?' she asked.

'My name is Mary Russell. I'm a friend of the Reverend Sabine Baring-Gould, who asked me to look you up while I was in town.' Which was not strictly true, but the look of reserved politeness she gave me was clear evidence that, while she knew who he was, she was not about to be mentioning my small deception in any casual letter or future conversation.

Our gloves clasped briefly while I explained that her housemaid had told me how to find her, and asked if I might walk back with her.

'Certainly,' she said, not sounding at all certain.

'There are a few questions I need to ask you,' I said as we turned in the direction of her house, and began to explain the bare outlines of my (unnamed) husband's long-time friendship with Baring-Gould, the reverend gentleman's state of health, and the memoirs he was trying to assemble.

She was a small, neat woman, who listened with her head bent and whose steps began briskly, only to slow with her increasing involvement in the story. She did not seem over gifted with a subtlety of mind, becoming only more confused as we went, and although she appeared anxious to be of service to the squire of Lew Trenchard, that old friend of her father's, she did not know what she could do for me. On her doorstep, she turned to me and said just that.

'Might I come in for a short time?' I suggested.

'Of course. Perhaps you will take luncheon with me?'

I assured her it was not necessary; she assured me it was no inconvenience; she gave instructions to the housemaid who had taken our things that two places were to be set at the table; and she then ushered me into the drawing room.

Aside from the painting of Sir Hugo, the room was light and feminine, with walls of cream and apricot and flowered-fabric chairs and draperies. It was not to my personal taste, but it was, I could easily see, tastefully if conventionally done.

'Would you like a glass of sherry, Miss Russell? I don't drink, myself, but . . .'

A hot rum toddy might have served to drive away the chill of the walk, but as that was not offered, and considering my hostess' abstinence, I declined. The hot tea we were brought instead was a help, although, not having spent the morning fasting, as she apparently had, I had not much use for the bland biscuits that accompanied it.

I waited while she performed her duties over the teapot, studying her and trying to choose the best approach to take. I had quickly decided that, while this woman was no foe, and could not possibly be siding with Scheiman or Ketteridge in whatever it was they were up to, at the same time she would not make much of an ally. Sympathetic she might be, particularly towards her former neighbours, but she was completely lacking in anything resembling imagination: One need only look at the portrait of Sir Hugo, glaring down across the chintz and fringes like an accountant with a highly unsavoury private life, to know the woman bereft of perception.

I had to admit that the resemblance between Sir Hugo and Scheiman was faint, and that I should almost certainly have seen nothing had Holmes not planted the idea in my mind. The thin mouth, yes, and the general shape of the eye, but Scheiman's face, though thin, lacked the hardness of this portrait, and the cold disapproval behind the painted eyes was something I had never seen in those of Ketteridge's secretary. It came to me suddenly that Sir Hugo's portraitist had been afraid of his subject; moreover, I thought the fear justified.

'Miss Russell?' Startled, I turned to the small blond woman in the demure grey dress. A tiny frown line furrowed her smooth brow and abruptly, my mind being no doubt receptive for such a thing, I could see the line furrowing David Scheiman's brow, the night Holmes and I had taken dinner in Baskerville Hall. Just as quickly, I dismissed the sureness that tried to accompany the revelation, reminding myself firmly that two frown lines did not a nefarious plot make. However, I also decided, taking the cup she was holding out to me, that I was not going to tell her as much as I might have had that line not appeared.

'That is a very interesting picture,' I said. 'It looks quite old.'

'The date on the back is 1647,' she said. 'It is a distant relative of mine, Sir Hugo Baskerville. He is said to have been a rather naughty fellow, although I can't say he looks it. I rather like the design of the lace on his collar.'

'Do you have many of the old family portraits?' I asked innocently. 'I mean to say, Mr Baring-Gould told me that yours is an old family, and I imagine there must have been quite a few pictures.'

'I did bring two or three with me when I sold the house to Mr Ketteridge.' She settled back into her chair for a nice, light latter-church sort of conversation with a new acquaintance. 'There was a Reynolds of my great-great-grandfather that was rather valuable, and a nice portrait of a lady in a blue dress that just matched the boudoir set – I couldn't part with her – and of course the Sargent portraits of my parents. I hadn't actually intended to bring Sir Hugo – he seemed to go with the Hall, somehow, and I thought it might be best not to bring too many reminders of past glories, as it were. But Mr Ketteridge insisted I take it. In fact, he came down from the Hall himself with it wrapped in a sheet, saying he couldn't bear for me to lose all of my family, and after all, Sir Hugo is a little bit famous. Do you know the story that Mr Conan Doyle called *The Hound of the Baskervilles*?'

I assured her that I was familiar with the tale and with Sir Hugo's place in it (although I might have used the word *infamous* instead), all the while aware of how very peculiar it was for Richard Ketteridge to have so generously parted with what, to a man lusting after the Baskerville story, had to be the single most compelling object in the collection.

'When did you move here?' I asked. Her pretty face clouded somewhat.

'A little more than two years ago. My father died before the war; my elder brother in 1916, my younger brother disappeared at sea in 1918, and my mother was so devastated after that, she had no energy to fight off the effects of the influenza. She died in the winter of 1919. I am the last Baskerville.'

'How very sad,' I said, meaning it.

'I tried to keep the house up, but it was hopeless. I was there more or less by myself, as it was so difficult to find capable men, and I know nothing about the running of an estate. After two years I had to admit defeat, and when Mr Ketteridge offered to buy it, at what my solicitor agreed was a very fair price, I sold it and moved here.'

We had made our way through the tea and the biscuits, and when the maid bobbed her way into the room and suggested that luncheon was ready, we adjourned to the next room.

'I hope you don't object to a light luncheon, Miss Russell,' she said. 'I know that most people like a substantial dinner after church, but I can never seem to face it, somehow.'

I told her I was quite content with sharing her standard fare, and prepared to make merry with the consommé and tinned asparagus in aspic.

'Do you miss the moor?' I asked after a while.

'Oh, I don't know. At first I thought I never would, it was so bright and cheerful and . . . lively here. But now, well, I sometimes think about when the furze would blossom, and the drifts when the ponies are driven down from the moor, and the dramatic smoke and fires when they swale the heather. I even miss those dreary tors that I used to find so gloomy, staring down at the Hall.'

I laughed. 'Gloomy it is, but oddly beautiful.' I could well imagine, for a conventional girl only a bit older than I, that the huge old building miles from anything that might be termed society might well be a burden to be shed rather than an inheritance to be

248

valued. I also remembered that her mother had not been born here, but had come obedient to her husband's criminous plans, later to be transferred to the protecting arm of Sir Henry and kept on the moor for the rest of her life.

I judged it time to return delicately to my main area of interest. 'How did Mr Ketteridge come to hear about the Hall? An advertisement?'

'Oh no, I couldn't have done that. No, I wasn't actually even thinking about selling, really. After all, the land has been in the family for six hundred years – that's hardly something to be broken lightly. Although I know there's a lot of that sort of thing happening now, with the war and the change in the tax laws. Still, I probably would have held out for awhile longer, but he came to me. He'd heard I was interested in letting it, but he wanted to buy it outright. He was passionate about it, seemed to know more than I did about its history, and just . . . loved it. I thought about it for a few weeks, during which time I had a huge bill for the coal and another for repairing some frozen pipes, and an estimate on wood-worm and roof work – it all came at once.

'And I thought, Why should I be burdened with six centuries of Baskervilles? The house was built at a time when there was a huge estate of rich agricultural land, which various ancestors had whittled off over the years, leaving me with no means of keeping the roof standing. To me it was a burden – becoming a prison. To Mr Ketteridge it was a prize. I sold it.'

I wondered how she would feel when news reached her that he had already tired of his prize. I was not about to be the one to tell her; rather, I looked at her with a degree of admiration, both for her sense of history's injustices and her self-respect. There was one question to be asked, though, particularly considering the attractive face and deferential manner that nature had wedded to her monetary inheritance.

'Have you ever considered marriage?'

She blushed, very prettily. 'I had thought not to be granted that happiness, Miss Russell. I was once engaged, during the war, but six months later my fiancé was killed in France. Afterwards, well, it isn't quite so simple, is it?' She let her voice drift off as she considered me, Miss Russell, a woman five or six years her junior who wore, incongruously, a gold band on the ring finger of the right hand, where it could either be taken for a wedding band in the style of certain European communities, or for a memento. I did not enlighten her, letting her think that perhaps I, too, was one of England's many spinsters. Whole, eligible men in those post-war years were a rare species.

'However,' she resumed, studying the spoon in her hand, 'recently I have . . . come to an agreement.'

I wished her congratulations and felicitations, and turned back to the all important question of time.

'As I mentioned, the Reverend Sabine Baring-Gould is writing his memoirs.'

'I believe I read something about a volume being published recently,' she said, sounding none too definite about it.

'Well, as you can imagine, he is becoming a bit hazy when it comes to remembering specific details, particularly when it comes to the more recent events. You know how forgetful old people become in that way,' I said, sending up a plea for forgiveness to the mentally acute if physically deteriorating old man in Lew Trenchard.

'I do,' she agreed, sounding more sure of herself. Her charitable work with the aged retainers caused my generalisation to strike a familiar note.

'One of the things that was vexing him the other day was trying to remember when he first met Mr Ketteridge, so to put his mind at rest I told him that I would try to find out, while I was in Plymouth. Would you happen to know?'

'I should have thought very soon after Mr Ketteridge bought the Hall. Thank you, Mary,' she said, which startled me for a moment until I saw she was speaking to the servant, who was clearing the plates preparatory to bringing the coffee.

'Do you know when—' I began to say, but she had only paused to recollect her dates.

'He first came to the Hall in April,' she said finally. 'Yes, it must have been early April, because the pipes burst in the first week of March and we were without water for three weeks altogether, and that's when I decided to see if I could find a tenant and move into town. He happened to arrive the day the plumbers were setting to work. I remember,' she said with a smile, 'because at first I thought he was one of them, and I was astonished that a plumber could make enough money to buy a car like that.'

Her joke and the laugh that followed were wasted on me, because I was alert, almost quivering, like a bird dog at the first scent of the warm, feathered object it was bred to seek.

'The first part of April,' I repeated. 'And you decided to sell it to him fairly soon after that?'

'Oh, perhaps not all that soon. Just before the summer equinox, I believe it was. The moor is at its loveliest then, and the nights so short – I walked up after dinner to the nearest tor and sat watching the sun set, and when I went back down it was nearly midnight and the decision had been made.'

And yet Ketteridge had told us he first heard about the Hall in Scotland shooting – something one did not do in the spring or midsummer. A coorius sarcumstance, indeed.

'So he first came to Baskerville Hall in April of 1921, and suggested that you sell to him, and you decided to do so two months later in June. Is that correct?'

'Yes,' she said, and then the frown line was back as it occurred to her that it was odd I should be interested.

'Mr Baring-Gould,' I hastily reminded her. 'He gets so upset

251

when he can't recall precise details.' That she did not object to this statement told me how little she knew him.

'Of course, the poor old man.'

'Ketteridge would then have taken possession in the autumn?'

'I believe we signed the final documents on the first day of September. He moved in just after that.'

'So he probably would have met Baring-Gould around that time, August or September,' I said, as if an important question had been decided.

'I suppose so. If it matters, why don't you ask Mr Ketteridge himself?'

'I hate to bother him, and I was coming to Plymouth anyway. Besides, Mr Baring-Gould wanted to see how you were doing in your new home. It was nice of Mr Ketteridge to bring you the painting of Sir Hugo so soon after you had moved in,' I added negligently. 'A sort of house-warming present, I suppose he considered it.'

'Yes,' she agreed, offering me more coffee, which I refused. 'He and David – Mr Scheiman – showed up at my door before the furniture was in place, to hang Sir Hugo for me.'

I froze in the very act of bracing myself to begin the leave-taking process, seized by an awful premonition.

'Mr Scheiman,' I repeated slowly. 'Tell me, do you see much of David Scheiman?'

The pretty blush returned, and I felt a thud of confirmation, the physical kick of an absolutely vital piece of information so nearly missed, as she said, 'Oh yes, he has been very attentive to my needs. He is the one,' she added, quite unnecessarily. 'We are to be married in the summer.'

CHAPTER TWENTY-ONE

I think it not improbable that both the Archbishop of York and
Claughton of Rochester had inserted my name into the Episcopal
'Black Book', for I had shown precious little deference to either.
But, so far from this injuring me, it has availed in
limiting my energies to my own parish.

— FURTHER REMINISCENCES

I HAD NO IDEA WHAT it might mean, that Ketteridge's secretary, a
man with the mouth of old Sir Hugo, had proposed marriage to
the only living child of Sir Henry Baskerville, but I did not need the
kick in my vital organs to tell me it meant something.

For the life of me, however, I could think of nothing else to
ask Miss Baskerville. I made polite noises, extracted from her an
amorphous invitation for a return visit, and, with a final glance at
the Cavalier over the fireplace, left her house. I went up the street
and turned the corner, and there I stood, gazing into a row of severely
pruned rose bushes, until the gentleman of the house came out and
asked me with matching severity whether or not he could help me.

I moved on obediently, allowing my feet to drift me back to the
hotel where I had stopped the previous night. There I retrieved my
small bag, and took a taxi to the train station, only to find that I had
several hours to wait before I could catch a train to Lydford.

I had nearly memorised portions of *Dartmoor* by the time I climbed up into the train, into a compartment even colder than had been the one on the way down. I made no attempt to read, but sat, my scarf and collar raised around my ears, my hands thrust up into my sleeves, staring at a button on the upholstered seat back across from me, thinking.

I felt certain that the various pieces of information we had assembled, if laid in the correct order, would make a pattern. As always, the extraneous data confused issues, and as always, it was not easy to know what was extraneous and what central. The best way of trying to find a pattern that I knew of was to hold all the data in mind, and remove one piece, and if that did not cause the remaining pieces to shift and click into place, replace it, and remove another.

And so, as the train chugged and slowed and paused at every village between Plymouth and Lydford, I sat and stared at the button, completely ignoring the glances, giggles, and growing consternation of the two young women sharing their compartment with a person who appeared to be in a trance, a young woman whose forehead revealed a half-healed gash with its fading yellow bruise whenever her hat shifted. I pawed over my pieces, holding them up to look at, removing each one in turn, trying to decide which contributed to the overall pattern and which was foreign to it.

Josiah Gorton stayed on the table, as did Lady Howard's coach. And Pethering? He remained, although the reason for his presence, both on the moor and ultimately in the lake, was not clear. But in the centre of the picture, did we find gold – actual, shiny gold? Or military tanks? Or something else entirely?

Up and down went the pieces, round and round went the questions, and all the while I was aware that time was beginning to enter into the equation, and I had none to waste.

It was dark when the train reached Lydford, and I was mildly surprised to find no sign of Charles Dunstan and the dog cart. I had told them I expected to return on an afternoon train, but perhaps he had got tired of waiting, or the pony had thrown a shoe, or some other demand had been made on his time. It was not raining, and the moon, three days from full, would soon be high enough in the sky to light my way. So, leaving a message with the station master as to my whereabouts, I walked down the road to an inn and took a large, hot meal.

Some time later, filled with beef and leek pie, I gathered my coat and hat around me and stepped into the road. It was very cold, the sky clear, and there was no waiting dog cart. A motor car went past, an ancient Ford rattletrap by the sound of it, and when my eyes had begun to adjust to the night, I slung my bag over my shoulder and followed in the direction of the Ford.

I knew where I was going, having tramped most of these lanes over the past two weeks, and although they looked very different in the pale, tree-blocked light from overhead, I knew I could not go too far wrong before coming either into the high road that ran from Launceston to Okehampton or the Coryton branch of the railway. I was well fed, adequately insulated as long as I kept moving, burdened only by the light bag and unthreatened by rain; all in all, it was the most pleasant Devonshire stroll I had yet undertaken.

I did not even miss my way (although I did follow the road, bad as it was, rather than cut through the fields on the rough path to Galford Farm). I crossed the Lew near the old dower house, saying hello to the dogs at the mill, who quieted and snuffled my by-now familiar hand, and came to Lew House through the woods at its back. I detoured at the last minute in order to enter by the porch, knowing that Mrs Elliott would think that the more proper behaviour for a guest; and threw open the door to the hall, bursting with fresh air and goodwill.

I was also bursting from the brisk exercise coupled with the soup and Devonshire ale I had drunk, so I hurried through the still house and up the stairs. It was early, but once there, the bed caught my eye. The room was cold and the bed looked soft, and within minutes I had burrowed into it and found warm sleep.

It was still cold in the morning, even colder, I thought, than the day before, and when I had dressed, I went outside to appreciate the morning. My walk was not a long one, but the brisk air and the smell of burning leaves drifting over from Lew Down filled me with well-being and gave me a good appetite for Mrs Elliott's breakfast. Baring-Gould had been in his bed since Friday, she told me, but his energy was returning and she thought he might come down in a day or two. Mr Holmes had got off to a late start on the Sunday, and was not expected back until the next day. And lastly, if I heard strange noises from the dining room, I was not to concern myself, because it would only be the sweep, working on the blocked chimney.

After breakfast I went up and found the annotated book on Devon that had been in Pethering's bag and brought it down with me to the warm hall to read. I pulled one of the armchairs up to the fire, threw some logs onto the red coals, kicked off my shoes, and drew my feet up under me in the chair. It was very pleasant, sitting in the solid, patient old house, in the wood-panelled room with the threadbare, sprung-bottomed furniture. The fire crackled to itself, the cat slept on the bench, the fox and hounds ran across the carved fireplace surround, and occasional voices came from the other end of the house. Sighing, deeply content, I began to read.

The book, too, was like settling in with an old friend in a new setting. We began with a desultory exploration of the ethnology of the inhabitants of Devon and Cornwall and their mixture of Celtic and Saxon blood, and moved on to glance at the Dumnonii, the Romans, and the Picts. The Roman invasion was given a few scattered lines, the introduction of the first lapdog two pages. Baring-Gould bemoaned the way the tender, graceful melodies of the Devonshire countryside were giving way before the organ and the music-hall ditty, and how the picturesque and sturdy native architecture was scorned by the pretentious London professional. Anecdote tumbled after anecdote, tied together by sweeping generalisations with clouds as their foundations and romantic visions of lost times that were breathtaking in their blithe neglect of facts. Druidic fantasies he dismissed out of hand, while at the same time offering the presence of large crystals in some Neolithic huts as proof that those huts had belonged to medicine men (who used the crystals for divining) and numerous small round pebbles in others as evidence of the Stone Age love of games.

I was enjoying myself so much, lost in the pull between respect for the man's boundless enthusiasm and indignation at his inability to take scholarship seriously, that I did not notice Mrs Elliott's approach until she touched my shoulder to get my attention. I looked up startled, to see her holding a yellow envelope in her hand.

'Terribly sorry, mum, but this just came for Mr Holmes, and the rector says would you like to take lunch with him, upstairs. Also, was you expecting Charley – Mr Dunstan – to meet you last night?'

'No, of course not,' I lied. 'It was a very tentative arrangement.'

'Good,' she said, sounding relieved. With everything else on her mind, she had simply failed to ask Dunstan to meet me. It was nice to know that even the iron woman was fallible.

I took the envelope and told her, 'I'd be happy to take lunch with Mr Baring-Gould.'

'Twenty minutes,' she said.

I tore open the thin paper, but it was only from the laboratory in London where Holmes had left the gold with its soil sample. Wordier than it needed to be and sprinkled with technical terms that either the sender had misspelt or the telegraphist had found troublesome, it for the most part confirmed what Holmes had already found: a pinch of the purest gold in a dessert-spoonful of humus and sand. It did not tell me what the mixture meant.

I allowed my eyes to rest on the lively carving above the

fireplace, the high-tailed hounds and goose-stealing fox that Baring-Gould had said belonged to the Elizabethan period. It occurred to me, to my amusement, that he was quite strictly correct: It did, by style and setting, belong there, even if it had come into actual existence in a century far removed from those of Elizabeth's reign. I dropped my book on the chair, stroked the sleeping cat and the carved fox with equal affection, and went upstairs to make myself look presentable for the nearly blind and infinitely sly old squire of Lew Trenchard.

'Mary,' he greeted me, in a stronger voice than I had expected. 'Come in, my dear, and keep me company as I eat the good Mrs Elliott's fare.' He was sitting nearly upright in the carved bed, propped against half a dozen pillows, and a wide, solid table with very short legs had been arranged over his lap and laid with a linen cloth, silver, and a crystal water glass. A smaller, considerably taller table had been laid for me and set facing him at the side of the bed. I began to take my place, and then paused, and stepped around to the head of the bed and briefly kissed his smooth, aged cheek before taking my seat.

He looked both flustered and pleased, but did not comment. 'How are you keeping, Mary?' he asked. 'And how did you find poor Miss Baskerville?'

'I am well, thank you, and Miss Baskerville seems a good deal happier in the bright lights of Plymouth than I believe she would have been in Baskerville Hall.'

'A great sadness, though, that she had to give up her family's home.'

'Sadness that her parents and brothers died, I agree, but I personally am not convinced of the need to yoke oneself for life to the service of a mere building.'

'I have spent my life making Lew House.'

'And you have created a place of great dignity and serenity, but I cannot see you demanding that your son and grandson enter penury in order to keep it standing.' I do not know why I was so certain of this. One might have thought the immense investment the house represented, not only in pounds sterling but in painstaking thought and emotional commitment, would have caused its creator to demand an equal passion on the part of his descendants, but somehow I did not think that to be true of him. And indeed, after a long moment, he nodded, reluctantly.

'True. But it is hard, living so long and seeing so many old families forced to abandon their heritage and move away from the roots planted by their forefathers. Although I will say that the idea of opening up the central hall and the picture gallery to charabancs of lemonade-swilling families is almost more abhorrent. I sometimes wonder if it wouldn't be better to return to the Viking way, and burn each man's riches with him when he is gone. You are laughing at me, Mary.'

'I'm not,' I protested, but seeing the lift of his eyebrow, I admitted, 'Well, perhaps a little. But in this case it would be a great pity; to put Lew House to the torch.'

'You like it, then?'

'Very much.'

'"The lot is fallen unto me in a fair ground; I have a goodly heritage",' he said with a small sigh that I took to be of satisfaction, and then Mrs Elliott and Rosemary came in with the meal.

As I had noticed before, for a man staring death in the face he had a healthy appetite, and ate the simple fare with gusto. He asked me if I had ever tasted mutton from a sheep raised on the herb-rich traditional pasturage of my own Sussex, and I could tell him that yes, one of my neighbours had a small and undisturbed field that had been saved from the plough during the grain-hungry years of the Napoleonic War. He expressed his envy, and proceeded to talk about food, of his lifelong lust for roast goose with sage-and-onion

259

stuffing, which his wife had indulged as often as she could, of the superiority of spit-roasted beef over the pale, half-steamed modern version, of the cheeses of France and the shock of tasting an egg from a hen fed cheaply on fish meal and the war-time blessing of living in a community that produced its own butter. It ended with a small story about the portion of his honeymoon spent in London, when he had subjected his poor young bride to a pantechnicon with its improving display of knowledge through a variety of semi-scientific machines and lectures, and the dry sandwiches they had eaten on that occasion. The sandwiches, he said with a note of reminiscence in his voice, had seemed to Grace more than appropriate to the setting.

Then, as if I might take advantage of this slight opening and insert a jemmy under the edge of his personal history, he said quickly, 'Tell me what you think about Richard Ketteridge.'

I knew instantly that I could not tell him what I feared concerning Ketteridge; Baring-Gould had brought us here to solve the mysterious happenings on his moor, but I prayed it could be done cleanly, without leaving a trail of mistrust, uncertainty, and tension along the way. Holmes might decide to the contrary, but as far as I was concerned, last Friday's discovery of the body in his lake was quite enough involvement for a sickly ninety-year-old man.

'He must have had an extraordinary time up in the Yukon,' I said instead. 'Has he told you about being buried in the avalanche?'

We talked about that for a while, and I told him about the improvements being made to Baskerville Hall (carefully omitting any reference to a future transfer of ownership) and the secretary's fascination for Hound stories. By that time he seemed to be tiring, so I helped Mrs Elliott lift the heavy little table from the bed and prepared to leave him.

At the door, however, his voice stopped me.

'Mary, I would not want you to think that I failed to notice that you did not actually answer my question about Richard Ketteridge.'

I looked back at him, dismayed, but I could see no anger in his face, only a mild and humorous regret. 'I am ill, true, but I am not easily misled.' He closed his eyes and allowed Mrs Elliott to tug and shift his pillow, and I left and went back down the stairs.

However, my peaceful immersion in the prose of Sabine Baring-Gould was not, it seemed, destined immediately to continue. I sat down with *Devon* and the bell rang, and although Rosemary reached the door before I could, the doctor who came in insisted on talking with me. It took ten minutes to convince him of my complete ignorance about any aspect of Baring-Gould's condition save his appetite and his ability to maintain a conversation. Perhaps the man just enjoyed talking with someone who had no physical complaints, I speculated, and returned to my book.

Five minutes later a disturbance in the kitchen first distracted me, then drew me. I stood tentatively inside the door to ask if I might be of help in quelling what had sounded like a minor revolution but on closer inspection appeared to be a family with five children under the age of eight. They all had running noses and hoarse coughs, and this seemed to be the focus of Mrs Elliott's wrath.

'You cannot stay here; Mr Baring-Gould needs his rest, and I can't be risking him taking on that affliction.' The husband of the family seemed resigned to an immediate departure, but the wife was sticking to her guns.

'The Squire, he told us, if we needed anything, to come, and we've come.'

'Keep your voice down,' hissed Mrs Elliott, to little effect. On one hip the woman had a thin baby with a disgusting nose and wearing an extraordinary hotchpotch of clothes; the other children were seated in a row on a kitchen bench eating bread and butter and watching the exchange with interest. The contest between the two women seemed destined to drag on to evening without resolution, until it was interrupted by the furious entrance of Andrew Budd, assistant gardener and my boatman from Friday.

'Who put the bloody cow in the garden?' he demanded loudly.

Mrs Elliott made haste to shush him, the husband responded by getting quickly to his feet, but his wife only claimed this for her own sorrows, having been evicted with five babies and a cow. Without taking his eyes from her, the husband began to sidle towards the door and, between one moment and the next, he clapped his hat to his head and faded out of it, followed by the still-irate Budd.

With that exit accomplished, the other door opened and the doctor entered; I began to feel as if I had walked into a pantomime production. The medical man, however, possessed an authority recognised by all, as well as the means of cutting through the Gordian knot. He hustled the children into their garments and clogs (the two who had them) and sent them out, pulled the wife out as well by the simple statement that he had a house they could use for a week until things were settled, and pushed her out of the kitchen door with the parting over-the-shoulder shot that he would return in two days to check on his patient, but that Mrs Elliott was doing everything perfectly.

In the silence that followed, Mrs Elliott gave herself a vigorous shake to settle her ruffled feathers back into place, snapped at Rosemary to scrub down the table at which the children had been sitting, threw the tea towel she held onto the sideboard, and began snatching up the plates from which her invaders had been eating. Before her eyes could fall on me, I made my exit, and went back to my book.

Peace returned to Lew Trenchard, and peace reigned uninterrupted over the cat, the fire, and me for a good twenty minutes, until I found myself reading a story about a gold fraud on Dartmoor, and the afternoon was no longer a peaceful thing.

CHAPTER TWENTY-TWO

Gold bydeth ever bright.
— GOULD FAMILY MOTTO

IT CAME IN A chapter on Okehampton, buried between a lengthy
discussion of a white-breasted bird credited with being a harbinger
of death and a song, given in the vernacular, about a young man who,
vexed because his sheep had run away, 'knacked' his old 'vayther' on
the head and was condemned to hang.

The gold story was given as follows:

Some years ago a great fraud was committed in the neighbourhood.
It was rumoured that gold was to be found in the gozen – the
refuse from the mines. All who had old mines on their land sent
up specimens to London, and received reports that there was a
specified amount of gold in what was forwarded. Some, to be sure
that there was no deception, went up with their specimens and saw
them ground, washed, and analysed, and the gold extracted. So
large orders were sent up for gozen-crushing machines. These came
down, were set to work, and no gold was then found. The maker
of the machines had introduced gold-dust into the water that was
used in the washing of the crushed stone.

Gold fraud.

All my nerves tingled. This was not precisely what I had been looking for to make the pieces fall into place – gozen laundering and the sale of a large number of machines did not go far enough – but by God I knew that something about the concept of gold fraud was the key. What, I did not know.

I devoured the rest of the book, but again, Baring-Gould had finished playing with that shiny idea and did not return to it, not within those covers. He did mention using the idea in a novel, but I doubted the usefulness of a fictional development of gozen laundering. I felt like throwing the volume across the room.

I did not. Instead, I dutifully went back and picked my way over Pethering's remarks, the myriad tiny scratchings of his own mania. He knew nothing about gold, nothing about the moor, nothing about scholarship at all, I soon decided. Nearly every remark reverted to Druidical evidence, and whenever Baring-Gould wrote a criticism of the doctrine, it set off a tirade so intense that Pethering had taken to writing between the lines of print to fit it all in.

Long before I reached the end of the book, my nerve broke, and I did end up throwing the book against the wall, upsetting the cat and bending the book's cover irreparably. I put on my coat and went for a long walk in the freezing air, and in the course of the walk I came to a reluctant decision: Despite the fragile state of his health, Baring-Gould should have to be asked about gold fraud.

I went to see Mrs Elliott when I returned, finding her as usual in the kitchen.

'I need to talk to Mr Baring-Gould, Mrs Elliott, just for a few minutes. Could you please let me know when he's awake?'

'I'll not have you upsetting him,' she declared, the unerring mother hen, obviously still feeling the effects of the invasion of snotty-nosed children.

'I didn't do so before,' I pointed out, 'and I shall try my best not to do so now, but it concerns what he brought us here to do. Ultimately, it is in his own interest.'

She seemed to find this argument specious, for which I could not blame her. It was clearly self-serving. However, grudgingly she allowed that when he had eaten his supper (which he would do upstairs and alone) she would ask if he could see me briefly. I thanked her, and told her I would be in his study.

There I worked, pulling books from the shelves, thumbing methodically through them looking for further tales of auric crime and finding nothing more than dust. Rosemary came to tell me my own dinner was ready, and I ate it with a book in front of me, scanning each page, unaware of its contents aside from a lack of the word gold. It was a tedious and no doubt pointless way of doing research, and it would take a very long time to go through the ninety or more books of his that I had not yet read, but it gave me something to do while I waited.

Unfortunately, the waiting was prolonged by Baring-Gould falling asleep over his supper. Mrs Elliott refused to wake him, telling me firmly that he was sure to awaken refreshed in two or three hours, or perhaps four, and he would surely speak to me then.

In an agony of frustration I returned to the endless shelves, feeling like Hercules faced with his task in the stables. Rosemary silently brought me coffee at nine, and again before she went to bed at eleven. Jittering, unkempt, and black-handed from the books, I waited.

At midnight I heard footsteps in the silent house. Mrs Elliott's tread sounded on the stairway outside the study door, and faded, going into the kitchen. When she came out, I was at the study door, waiting.

'Come, dear,' she said cheerfully, and then, 'Oh my, you do look a little the worse for wear. Never mind, two minutes with the rector and then you can have a nice wash and into bed.'

Grimly, I followed her up the stairs and to Baring-Gould's bedroom, and there I waited while she gave him his hot drink and medicine and plumped his pillows and chattered cheerfully until my hands tingled with wanting to pitch her out the window.

In the end it was Baring-Gould who broke the impasse. The light from the single candle was not strong enough for his old eyes to pick me out, but I must have moved, for he craned his head forward and squinted at where I stood.

'Who is that?' he asked sharply.

'It is I, sir,' I said, and stepped into the candle's glow.

'Mary, it's very late. Surely you're too young to begin this habit of broken nights.'

'She has a question to ask you, Rector,' put in Mrs Elliott, and to my relief took herself out of the door with the hot-water bottle.

'Come, then, Mary. Sit down where I can see you, and ask. It must be important, not to wait until the morning.' I sat down as indicated, on the bed beside him.

'I don't know how important it is, just vexatious, because I can't find any more information. In your book on Dartmoor you mention that gold may be found in the gravel streams of the moor.'

'Did I? How very irresponsible of me,' he said with a complete lack of either interest or concern.

'Has it ever been found?' I persisted.

'Never. Ridiculous thought. I did use it in the *Guavas* novel, for the romance of it, but I don't believe anyone has ever actually filled so much as a single goose-quill from the soil of the moor. The closest to gold I have ever seen in a lifetime of wandering Dartmoor is the moss *Schistostega osmundacea*, which gleams with sparks of gold when seen in a certain light.'

'I see. But, in your book on Devon, the first volume of *A Book of the West*, you describe a gold fraud, which involved washing gold into samples of the gozen from old tin mines in order to sell great numbers of the crushing machines.'

He got a faraway look on his face, which after several seconds relaxed into one of delight. 'I had forgotten about that. Oh yes. Very clever, that.' He chuckled. 'Of necessarily limited duration, however.'

'Most frauds are. But what I need to know is, are there any other references to gold on the moor in your books, either speculations as to its presence or descriptions of fraud?'

A long minute ticked past as the old man put his head down and thought. When he raised it, my heart fell.

'I cannot think of any. Why do you need to know?'

'Rector, I'd really prefer not to go into that just now.'

'Does it have to do with Richard Ketteridge?'

'It may,' I said reluctantly. To my surprise, he reached forward and patted my hand.

'Don't worry, Mary, I won't press you. I'll hear about it when the story is complete. Much better that way.'

'Er . . . if Ketteridge comes to visit, do you wish me to have Mrs Elliott say you are not receiving visitors?'

'Heavens no. I certainly possess enough duplicity for that degree of deception.'

I got up from the bed. 'Goodnight, sir.'

'Goodnight, Mary. I wish you luck.'

'Thank you.' I turned to go.

'There was,' he said thoughtfully, 'another sort of fraud.'

I stopped and waited.

'It involved tin, though,' he said.

I came back to his side and sat down again. 'What happened?'

'I don't recall the details. Something to do with blowing bits of tin into the hillside to make the area look rich in the metal. Salting, don't they call it? I wonder what it has to do with salt?'

I was rocked back on my heels by the galvanic shock of his words, shooting down my spine like a bolt of electricity that set all the pieces of my puzzle shuddering as they danced across the table and began to bond together in front of me.

Salting, don't they call it?

Gold flakes in a spoonful of leafy sand. Josiah Gorton, killed for wandering the moor on a stormy night, and Randolph Pethering after him, for the same reason. A remote cottage in which the thunder knocked a plate from the hutch. God, I had it. I had it.

'Thank you,' I said calmly. I paused on the way to the door. 'Do you remember which book you wrote about that in?'

'Which one? My dear, there were so many. It might have been in *Curiosities of Olden Times*, or perhaps *Dartmoor Idylls*, or even *Old Country Life*. Does it matter?'

'I shouldn't think so. Goodnight.'

Mrs Elliott was coming back in with the gurgling water bottle in her hand, and her appearance made me think of something else.

'Mrs Elliott, that family that was here today. Where were they from?'

'I don't know, and I don't care.'

'What family was that?' Baring-Gould demanded.

Mrs Elliott shot me a dark look. 'Samuel and Livy Taylor came by here, and the doctor is giving them a place for a few days until they can arrange transport to her brother's place in Dorset.'

Baring-Gould answered immediately, without pausing for thought. 'Their farm is near the West Okemont, just below Higher Bowden.'

And old Sally Harper and her husband had just moved from their farm a mile or two away. And what of the ancient woman wrapped in rugs, who had arrived here the other day? I would ask

Mrs Elliott later, I thought. 'Thank you again, and goodnight,' I said with finality, and went back down to Baring-Gould's study.

It took me until four o'clock to find the reference, but find it I did, in a book entitled *An Old English Home and Its Dependencies,* a portion of a chapter on mineral rights. It told the story of a fraud committed, as Baring-Gould had said, by blowing pieces of tin into soil to create the appearance of a rich source.

If tin, why not gold?

I fell into bed and slept for three hours, and then rose and dressed and went down to ask Rosemary for directions to the doctor's surgery. I had to reassure her mightily that I was not ill, that I did not require her granny's tincture or a hot brick for my feet, only directions to the surgery. Reluctantly, she gave them.

The frost was thick on the lawns and the fallen leaves, but although I walked quickly, the doctor was already away, attending a difficult birth up on the moor. The doctor's wife, who ran the surgery, saw my disappointment and offered to help. When I told her I was looking for the evicted Taylors, she said with some asperity that she knew precisely where they were, and whose victuals they were eating as well. She pointed me down the road.

'My own house, that is; my sister lived in it until she died in the spring, and if that woman allows her brood to damage my mother's furniture, I'll not be responsible for my actions.'

The household, however, was not as chaotic as I had expected. Taking the upset and the number of children into account, it was actually almost controlled. I did, nonetheless, ask Samuel Taylor to step outside for our conversation.

I asked him who owned the house from which he had been evicted. He scratched his head and set himself to the achievement of thought.

'Wall, it were the judge up by Ockington, but now that were the problem, baint it? Because he soldy, didn't he, just three months gone now, and sayed as soon as t'crops were in, we'd have to go.'

'I don't suppose you know who the buyer was?' I asked without much hope, but he surprised me.

'Mr Oscar Richfield, he said, in Lunnon. I dunno what a Lunnon man wants with me zmall farm, but it be 'is now, and I hope it brings he joy.'

He was not being bitter; he truly hoped his spot of river bottom, would bring pleasure to its next owner. I myself very much doubted that joy would enter into the equation.

On my way back through Lew Down I stopped to use the public telephone. Mycroft had not yet left his Pall Mall digs for the office where he laboured, and I spoke briefly with him, explaining nothing, asking him merely to have discreet enquiries made about a Mr Oscar Richfield and his ownership of a tiny farm on the edge of Dartmoor.

When I returned to Lew House, I sought out Mrs Elliott to enquire about the old woman who had arrived the other day while I was working in Baring-Gould's study, and had since disappeared.

'You mean dear little Mrs Pengelly? Poor thing, had to leave the cottage her husband built with his own two hands, and go to distant family far away in Exeter. Still, she now has a bit of a nest egg to show for it, and that'll make her last years more cosy.'

'Where did Mrs Pengelly come from?'

'Oh, she's Cornish, I'm sure.'

'I mean to say, where was the cottage her husband built for her up on the moor?'

'Where? Oh my dear, I can't remember just where it was, but I'm sure it was not too far from Black Tor. A nasty place, to tell the truth, cold and lonesome. I told her she'd be much happier in Exeter.'

'I'm sure you're right, Mrs Elliott. Thank you.'

Rather confused, the good housekeeper left me alone with my thoughts, which revolved around this fact: Of the three individuals and families who had passed through Lew House in the recent weeks, each had come from virtually the same place on the moor. The very place where Holmes had set out the other night to investigate.

I did not like the tenor of my thoughts, but at present there seemed little I could do but stare out the window and wait for him to return.

CHAPTER TWENTY-THREE

She had not been long asleep when she was awakened by such
a clatter at the door as if it was being broken down, and it was
thundering and lightning frightful. Nurse was greatly frightened,
but lay still, hoping the knocking would cease, but it only got
worse and worse. At last she rose and opened the window, when
she saw by the lightning flashing, which almost blinded her, a
little man sitting on a big horse, hammering at the door.

– 'A PIXY BIRTH' IN A BOOK OF THE WEST: DEVON

As THE LONG MORNING drew on I became increasingly
distracted, anxious to lay eyes on Holmes, unable to sit still
any longer. I finally took my coat and told Mrs Elliott I would be
back in time for dinner, and left Lew House.

I ended up not far up the high road to Okehampton, sitting in
the window of an inn, drinking coffee and pushing a pastry around
on the plate in front of me, staring blankly down the road, when I
saw Holmes heave into view on a distant rise in the road. I quickly
gathered up my things, left coins enough to cover the bill, and went
out to meet him.

He came towards me, striding with brisk concentration and an
enormous rucksack complete with tin cup swinging wildly from a
tie on the side: A less likely member of the rambling brotherhood it
would have been difficult to imagine.

We approached each other rapidly, halted on the macadam facing each other, opened our mouths, and spoke simultaneously.

'He's salting the stream-bed,' said Holmes.

'He's planting gold to run a fraud,' I said, adding for good measure, 'with dynamite.'

'Black powder,' he corrected me, and added, 'using thunder storms to conceal the sounds of the explosions.' He took my elbow to turn me back in the direction of Lew House. 'Excellent, Russell. How did you work it out?'

'It's all in Baring-Gould's books.'

'What?' He paused to look at me in astonishment.

'In pieces, but it's there, for eyes that are looking for it.'

'Scheiman's eyes.' He started forward again.

'He is the bookish one of the pair, to be sure. He is also engaged to be married to Violet Baskerville.'

This time Holmes came to a complete stop. He worked his shoulders to let the rucksack thud to the ground, then sat on it, taking out his pipe and eyeing me expectantly. I perched on a nearby stone.

'Miss Baskerville confirmed that Ketteridge was here in March of 1921, and purchased the Hall no later than June. And as soon as he had taken possession, he and Scheiman brought her the portrait of Sir Hugo, which now sits in her flowery drawing room looking truculent and very out of place.'

'So I should imagine,' he murmured around his pipe.

'How did you discover it?' I asked him.

'Shelling in the bed of the Okemont,' he said briefly, and having got his pipe going, he stood up again. I was about to protest, but decided that unless we were to risk patches of frostbite about our persons to match those of the gold baron, the story would best be told in the warmth of Lew House. I hopped down from my rock and reached for the rucksack, and in the process of heaving it onto my back, I was nearly sent staggering off the road into the ditch.

'What on earth is in this?' I exclaimed. 'Rocks?'

'A few rocks, yes. Also three books, a cook stove, and a very wet one-man canvas tent.'

'Pethering was camped out in the open during Tuesday's storm,' I deduced. I turned to face the right direction and leant forward to let the dead weight drive me along. 'He must have heard or seen them laying the charges that would drive the grains of gold into the gravel bed, and been foolish enough to allow himself to be seen.'

'It went beyond that. He had camped up in a protected area on the edge of Sourton Common, half a mile away, but I found signs of a struggle and blood that had seeped down between some stones, right near the river.'

'You think he was insane enough actually to go down and accost them, face to face?'

'Did he not seem the type?'

'I'm afraid you're right. God protect us from fanatics.'

Holmes dismissed Pethering. 'Were there any answers to my telegrams?'

'Just from the laboratory in London.' I told him what the report had said, adding, 'I'd have expected traces of the explosive.'

'Perhaps it was too small a sample,' he said. 'The lack of response to my other enquiries is irritating. I had hoped to find a warrant outstanding for Scheiman, at any rate. What can they be doing?'

His irritation faded briefly when we entered Lew House and found a telegraph envelope on the table just inside the door. He ripped it open and read it while I was struggling to ease the load from my shoulders without allowing it to crash violently onto the floorboards. I straightened slowly and circled my shoulders experimentally to see if the ache was going to get any worse.

'Is your shoulder bothering you, Russell?' Holmes asked, his back to me. The irritation was back in his voice; whatever the news, it was not what he had wanted.

'It's fine. What does the telegram say?'

He thrust it at me and went off in the direction of the kitchen, where I heard him talking with Mrs Elliott for a moment before he returned to take up his place before the fire.

'You must have warned them not to use names,' I noted curiously, reading the flimsy a second time.

'I mentioned it was a rural area and circumspection was wise.'

Circumspection in this case may have been unnecessary, for the telegram from New York merely stated:

FIRST PARTY UNKNOWN SECOND PARTY HEADMASTER RETIRED DUE
TO ILL HEALTH. SCHOOL SOLD 1921 NOW FAILING.

M BRIDGES

The necessarily terse style engendered by telegraphic communication, even compounded by Holmes' caution, could not explain the dearth of information provided by this little missive. 'I'd say this raises rather more questions than it answers, wouldn't you agree?'

My partner's face twisted briefly in a moue of annoyance. 'My usual informant in the police department must be away. Bridges is his inferior officer, in the fullest sense of the word. Still, it would indicate that Scheiman left New York voluntarily, rather than with the hounds of the department on his heels. Interesting that he should have chosen to run a school, as his father did. In this case, the school's failure to survive his departure could be an indication of his having pillaged the coffers a bit too effectively, or merely a sign of the man's immense charisma on which the entire enterprise rode.'

I did not think it necessary even to respond to this last scenario. Instead, I said, 'Tell me about Pethering.'

Mrs Elliott came in then with tea and a plate of toasted muffins, and when she had returned to her kitchen, Holmes told me how he had spent the last three days.

'In the end I did not leave here until nearly midday on Sunday,' he began, although I knew that, from Mrs Elliott. Well after midday in fact; Holmes had stayed with Baring-Gould all morning, had waited while the old man recited the morning services, and had in fact not left until after the noon meal. I did not tell him I knew this, and he did not explain.

'I took a room at the inn in Sourton that night. I did succeed in prising a cup of tea from them before I left in the morning, but I could not wait until the kitchen was awake. I haven't had a proper meal, now that I think of it, until noon today.' He paused to reach for a buttered muffin.

'As you will have seen from the map, it is a stiff climb up onto the moor, closer akin to rock climbing than walking. However, it was the way Pethering took, so I had no choice.

'I came out on Sourton Common just after dawn on Monday, a short distance above the old tramway to the peat works at the head of Rattle Brook. It did not take long to find the place where Pethering had made his first camp, almost as soon as he gained the moor – he didn't even bother to look for a sheltered place, no doubt because darkness overtook him. I set off from there in the direction of Watern Tor, almost due east and four miles by the map, but nearly twice that on foot, what with the hills and the streams and the congregation of marshes that intrude in that place.

'There was no knowing for certain Pethering's exact route, but I came across signs of his passing. For a man who reveres antiquities he was very casual about what rubbish he strewed across the countryside.

'His second night he camped near Watern Tor, and judging by the number of tins I found at his campsite, he remained in that vicinity from teatime Monday until midday Tuesday, no doubt searching for giant canine footprints in the boggy areas, where I found a number of his own boot marks. He might have remained longer but for the storm, which began to blow in at about two o'clock in the afternoon.

'He may have thought he could get off the moor before it hit; certainly he would not have wished to remain where he had settled down, which was a very exposed and uncomfortable place. He packed up his rucksack in some haste, leaving behind one tent peg and a couple of unopened tins of food, and launched due west, aiming, I believe, for the ravine of the West Okemont, which his map would have told him would be windy, but less vulnerable than where he was.

'The storm caught him just after he'd crossed the river, three hard miles short of Sourton. He found a low place in the hill leading down to the river, got his tent more or less up, and crawled inside.

'It must have been a wild night for him, with nothing to eat but cold beans spooned from the tin, the roof of his tent blowing about and leaking in a number of places – his sleeping roll, which I abandoned, weighed as much as all the other things combined.

'And then, at some time during the evening, just after the height of the storm when the soil was at its most sodden, something made him leave the tent and venture down to the river, slopping through the wet ground more than half a mile to a place where the river is bordered by a narrow strip of primeval oak forest similar to Wistman's Wood.'

'Black Tor Copse,' I said, having read my guidebook and my map.

He nodded. 'There it was he met his death, in a stretch of rough but open terrain. Pieces of his broken hand torch lay between the rocks, and the blood that seeped down had been only lightly diluted by rain.'

'The storm blew through by midnight in Postbridge.'

'And slightly earlier to the north. He lay there for an hour or more, and after the rain had ended and begun to seep off the surface of the peat, his body was carried a mile or so down the river and hidden in an abandoned mine. His assailants then went back for the tent and his possessions, dragging and carrying them a lesser distance to the adit that I came across on my last tour of the area.'

'Ah. Too fastidious to share the watching place with a corpse,' I suggested.

'It would also indicate that they are not finished with the adit, whether they are proposing to use it for storing things or for watching from, or simply as a shelter out of the rain.'

'And yet you removed the rucksack.'

'It had been thrown far to the back in the collapsing portion of the shaft used for their rubbish tip, with the sleeping roll thrown on top. I thought it unlikely they would brave the unsavoury elements to retrieve it, so I simply rearranged the sleeping roll to look as it had before, and took the other possessions out from under it.'

I decided against closer enquiry concerning the type of rubbish in the tip; I also vowed to have my overcoat cleaned at the earliest opportunity.

'I found the adit first, and after I left there I continued downriver, where I found the signs of what I first took to be shelling from the range just north of there, as if the guns had overshot their mark. It had been roughly concealed, by spade work and a redistribution of leaves, and I imagine that in another month, with the last leaf-fall, it will be invisible.

'A short distance farther on, however, in a piece of broken ground that was once a tin works, I was interested to find the ground more freshly disturbed, with signs of digging still clear to be seen. On closer examination, I found pipes.'

'Pipes?' I said, as there flashed before me the bizarre image of a collection of meerschaums and briars planted stem-first into a hill.

'Empty steel piping, two inches in diameter and approximately two feet long. There were twenty of them altogether, arranged about four feet apart from one another, sunk into the ground and covered carefully with a cap to keep the inside clear of debris.'

'Not filled with pieces of gold and a charge of black powder?'

'Not yet.' His eyes gleamed briefly. 'I believe that the technique is to prepare the hole by drilling or shovelling down into soft ground and inserting a length of hollow pipe. One then takes a similar length of a smaller diameter of thin-walled, soft pipe which has had a good number of holes drilled or punched into it and then been loosely packed with the charge and the gold, probably an ounce or so mixed into a spadeful of river sand. The smaller of the pipes is then dropped – gently – into the larger, after which the outer pipe is withdrawn, and the wires on the detonators fastened onto a master wire running to the detonator plunger.'

'And, boom. Clean up the pipes and wires, and you have gold flakes in your stream-bed.'

'Farther down the river,' he continued, 'I found the mine where Pethering's body had lain. I left the rucksack beneath some rocks nearby, and walked down the footpath until I came to a farm.

'And do you know, the residents of the farm thought on the whole that perhaps they had heard a motor car, just after dark, on Thursday night.'

For a long moment I could not think why he was looking at me so intently. I began to reconstruct Thursday in my mind, and when I did I felt as if someone had hit me very low in the stomach.

'Just after dark? Oh Holmes, no. You don't mean . . . You can't mean . . .'

'Approximately how long was Scheiman gone with the motor car when you were at Baskerville Hall?'

'Perhaps three hours,' I answered reluctantly.

'Say fourteen miles from Baskerville Hall to the farm, a mile in and down to retrieve the body, fourteen miles back. Three hours sounds right.'

I put my hand over my mouth in revulsion. If Holmes was right, the car in which Ketteridge had driven me back to Lew House had also contained the two-day-old body of Randolph Pethering. Ketteridge must have known. He had to know.

'Did Ketteridge know?' I asked.

'So it would seem, unless you think Scheiman motored back home with his employer, and then immediately turned around and retraced his steps to bring the body here.'

'No. And I can't see Scheiman quite so cold-blooded, not to turn a hair at his innocent employer's getting behind the wheel with a corpse in the boot of the car.' I shuddered at the reminder that I had been in that car, had sat making inconsequential remarks about the beauty of the evening, while just behind me lay the folded-up remains of the man whose coat I would be hanging onto the following morning.

I pushed it away from me. 'Why not leave him in the mine? Why bring him here?'

'Look at the map, Russell. Even though the actual sightings cut across the diagonal from north-east to central west, I think we can safely say that their entire purpose has been to keep people away from the north-western segment of the moor. When they have been forced to create points of interest, such as where Josiah Gorton was left and the hound sighted, or Pethering's body found, each of those points has been away from the north-western quadrant. It would have been a risk to leave a body in a mine so near the area they wanted people to avoid – bodies have a way of getting themselves found, after all, particularly when they lie less than a mile from farms with their sharp-nosed dogs. And it would be arduous in the extreme to dig a large enough hole in the sodden peat to bury someone, and carrying him across the moor, to Watern Tor perhaps, would also involve the risk of discovery. Josiah Gorton they transported clear to the other side of the moor, but for some reason – grown cocky perhaps, or short of time, or merely the difference between disposing of a wandering tin seeker who had no family and a young and educated outsider whose death could be expected to attract a degree of attention – they decided to remove Pethering from the moor altogether. Your arrival that day at Baskerville Hall may have given them the idea, or they might have settled on it in any case.'

I thought about it for a long minute, dissatisfied, but there was no more to be done with the question at the moment. 'Have you been upon the moor all this time, then?'

'More or less. After interviewing the farmer I determined that there was, indeed, a place where a motor car had pulled off the road two or three days before. Dunlops,' he said, before I could ask. 'Relatively new, such as Ketteridge's motor runs on.'

'Thank God for that. I was beginning to think he was as ghostly as Lady Howard.'

'Though it's not much use as proof in a court of law.'

'True.'

'I then went to visit the army garrison near Okehampton.'

'Good heavens.'

'I had to be sure that what appeared to be shelling was in fact not.'

'Of course.'

'Major-General Nicholas Wyke-Murchington gave me a cup of tea.'

'How nice.'

'Not terribly. It was nine o'clock this morning and I could have done with strong coffee and a full breakfast.'

'Where did you stop the night yesterday?'

'In the farmer's barn.'

I had half expected him to say, in the abandoned mine. At least the barn would have been dry and, with any luck, warm.

'So you had a nice tea with the major-general.'

'And, with Mycroft's cachet in hand, he showed me his tank.'

'A singular honour.'

'Any self-respecting spy would have died laughing at the sight of it, although I can well believe it would not have sunk into the mire of Passchendaele. It distinctly resembles a duck perched atop a half-inflated balloon, and it moves – trundles is perhaps the word – at the pace of an arthritic old woman.'

'A truly revolutionary design.'

'He also gave me another piece of information that I think you will not mock so freely.'

'A radical model submarine boat with wings?'

'No, the schedule for firing.'

'But, didn't Baring-Gould say they only used the ranges in the summer?'

'Except when they wish to practise in foul-weather conditions!'

'I'd have thought the summer months here would suffice, but pray continue.'

'Night manoeuvres are planned, in moonlight, on Thursday night. The day after tomorrow. And the schedule has been posted on the moor notice boards.'

'Now, why should – wait,' I said, beginning to see what he was suggesting. 'We're past the usual season when one might reasonably count on the occasional thunderstorm, and yet Scheiman and

Ketteridge have been making preparations for another blast.'

'The occasional natural thunderstorm, certainly, but would not an artificial storm suffice to conceal their activities, with the thunder of guns instead of that from the sky? A man standing in the entrance-way to the old adit could easily see when the soldiers were away from the immediate area, but could also see the flash from the firing that would conceal the blast of the black powder.'

Another thought came to me. 'And the moon is nearly full as well. By God, one way or another, we may be able to catch them at it.'

Holmes smiled slowly, but merely said, 'I should be interested to see the references you found in Gould's books.'

We moved upstairs to our room, where I showed him the places and left him, stretched out shoeless on the bed with one book in his hands and one on either side of him on the counterpane. When I put my head in an hour later, he was asleep. I went quietly away.

Chapter Twenty-Four

Where the one-inch fails recourse must be had to the six-inch map.
— A BOOK OF THE WEST: DEVON

WEDNESDAY MORNING THE FROST had departed and the sky was dull with cloud, but inside Lew House there was a feeling of sunshine and relief, because the squire of Lew Trenchard was on his feet again.

Holmes and I had a great deal to discuss and some complicated arrangements to make before the army's scheduled firing on Thursday night; however, the topic being mooted over the breakfast table was honey. The painted Virtues looked on in approval and Holmes seemed more than willing to indulge his old friend, so I could only throw up my hands and give myself over to the game.

'I gave you some of the metheglin the other night,' Baring-Gould was saying. 'Now have a taste of the honey it was made from.'

Holmes obediently thrust his teaspoon into the pot of thick stuff before him on the table, twirled the spoon to keep its burden intact, and put it into his mouth. Baring-Gould and I watched, and even Rosemary stopped in the act of taking the coffee-pot to be refilled and waited for the judgement.

'Remarkable,' said Holmes stickily. He reached for his coffee cup.

Baring-Gould nodded vigorously. 'Didn't I tell you? It is produced from furze blossoms, a most superb and aromatic variety.

Keeping bees on the moor is no easy thing, as you know, because of the perpetual wind, but there is a monk down at the Buckfast Abbey who has succeeded Brother Adam, his name is – a young man, but already the head beekeeper.' (Was head beekeeper so hard-fought a position, I wondered idly, that only a monk of high seniority would be likely to win it?) 'He has some very sound ideas about breeding – you ought to get down there and talk with him.'

'Yes,' said Holmes, 'I have corresponded with Brother Adam. He consulted me recently on the acarine problem. I suggested he look to Italy, which I believe is free from the disease.'

'You don't say. He's a German, of course, which hasn't made it easy for him the last few years, but he's an original – a true character. Perhaps a bit over-enthusiastic, I admit, but all the more appealing for it in this age when detachment rules and cool indifference is the standard of behaviour. Do you know,' he said, warming to his new topic, 'in the old times there were men and women who stood out; now there seems to be a plague of homogeneity, spread by the machinations of the press and the ease of railway travel. Why, I am sure you have heard of this crystal wireless set which seems certain to achieve popularity; I imagine that the resultant instant communication will complete what modern education and quick travel have begun, and we will soon see the death of regionalism and individuality. Haven't you found this, Holmes? The world is becoming filled with sameness, with men and women as like as marbles. Not a true eccentric in sight.' I looked at him carefully, waiting for the twinkle that would tell me he was making a jest, but he was frowning as he drizzled furze honey over his toast. I glanced over at Holmes, who was nodding in solemn agreement over the tragic loss of eccentricity in the modern world, and I had to get up and go to the kitchen for a moment to ask Mrs Elliott if we might have another few slices of brown bread toasted. When I returned,

Baring-Gould was telling a story, apparently concerning one of his late-lamented characters.

'—begging, dressed as a seaman who had been shipwrecked, or a farmer whose land was under water in Kent. He would watch the newspapers, you see, for word of the latest disaster, and take on whatever disguise that might call for. One day he might be a householder burnt out of his house, taking up a position on the pavement wearing little more than a charred blanket; the next day he would appear as an impoverished soldier. He had letters of verification from magistrates and noblemen – forged, of course. The gipsies eventually claimed him, and elected him King of the Beggars. You could learn from him, Holmes.' He chuckled at the idea.

'Still, Gould,' said Holmes, 'there have always been degrees of rogue. One may feel a grudging admiration for Bamfylde-Moore Carew because of his sheer effrontery, but then there are men like the Scamp.'

'Oh yes,' Baring-Gould said, allowing his knife and fork to come to a brief pause. 'The Scamp was indeed a bad lot.' He resumed his meal, and spoke in my direction. 'The Scamp is my family's name for one of the eighteenth-century Goulds, Captain Edward – his portrait is on the stairway. He nearly lost us this estate, and certainly lost a great deal else. He killed a man, one of his gambling partners, and at his trial was defended by one John Dunning, to whom he also owed a great deal of money. An eyewitness to the shooting testified that he saw Edward Gould by moonlight, but at the trial Dunning produced a calendar proving there had been no moon that night. Gould was acquitted, though by that time he was so in debt to Dunning that he had to make over nearly everything he owned to the man, which would have lost us Lew Trenchard had it not been under his mother's name. And the funny thing was, the calendar John Dunning produced? It was a fake.'

It did not seem terribly amusing to me, and even Baring-Gould merely shook his head at the iniquity. Holmes did not even seem to be listening. His attention was on the door to the kitchen, and when Rosemary came through it his eye was on her right hand and the yellow envelope she carried.

'Yes, Rosemary?' said Baring-Gould. 'What is it?'

'Telegram, sir, for Mr Holmes.'

Holmes had the point of his knife through it before the door had swung shut, and his eyes dashed back and forth over the lines before coming up to mine. He nodded, then folded the square away into an inner pocket and turned to Baring-Gould with a brief and genial explanation and a deft change of subject.

After breakfast Baring-Gould went off to write some letters and take a rest, and Holmes handed me the yellow envelope. The author of this telegram had taken Holmes' concern for circumspection to heart, and the wording of his message was cautious indeed:

PRIMARY SUBJECT KNOWN TO US REGARDING ACTIVITIES INVOLVING SALE OF REAL PROPERTIES FOLLOWING UNVERIFIABLE MISREPRESENTATION OF MINERALS CONTAINED THEREIN. SUGGEST FURTHER ENQUIRIES COLORADO NEVADA SOUTHERN CALIFORNIA. SECOND SUBJECT UNKNOWN HERE. APOLOGIES FOR EXPORT TAINTED GOODS. LETTER FOLLOWS. HARRISON

'Ketteridge is known for fraudulently selling land, claiming it had "minerals" – I assume gold – when it did not,' I interpreted the paper in my hand. 'Harrison is with the Alaska police?'

'The Mounties, actually. The Canadians were largely responsible for policing the Territories during the gold rush. I would say by the tone of his apology and the fact that he has been following Ketteridge's career, he knows the man to have been guilty of gold fraud but could not pin it on him.' He paused and looked up, gazing through me more than at me. 'What was it Ketteridge said about his childhood? He let slip some description about the land, when he was talking to you at Baskerville Hall.'

'Red stone,' I said. 'Something about the hills where he grew up having tors, only they were dry and red.'

The far-off look on his face told of a search of that prodigious memory of his, as full of jumble as a lumber room. After a few minutes he suddenly came across the bit of lumber he had been seeking, and his eyes gleamed with satisfaction.

'San Diego,' he said. 'Late 1860s, perhaps 1870.'

'Sorry?' I prompted when he said no more. His gaze focused.

'There was a gold rush in the red hills outside San Diego, California, in the late 1860s. It was an actual discovery, but as was the case with most such finds, it was soon overwhelmed by the influx of swindlers, claim jumpers, and speculators.'

'And Ketteridge's accent comes from the southern part of California. But he couldn't have had anything to do with that; he's barely your age.'

'Fifty-seven, unless he lied about being thirty-one when the Klondike rush began. No, he is too young, but he may have learnt the techniques as a child – at his father's knee, perhaps, or merely seeing the activities around him as he was growing up. I shall look forward to receiving Harrison's following letter, which may allow us to pin the man down with his crimes where the police forces of two other countries have failed.'

It was only then that the full picture of what we were facing, mad as it seemed, hit me: the very real possibility of a gold rush on Dartmoor. The mediaeval tin seekers with their prodding and digging and dark, shallow tunnels in the earth would be nothing to the catastrophe set off by the whisper of that spellbinding word, gold. It would be over in weeks, of course, as soon as the blasted hillsides gave forth nothing heavier than tin and the diverted streams washed away everything but flecks of base metals from the flumes, but the devastation wrought by tens of thousands of hobnailed boots and spades and sticks of dynamite, the ruin they would leave behind across the ravaged face of the moor – it did not bear thinking.

I shook my head, more to clear it than in denial. 'Surely we wouldn't see an actual gold rush here. It's . . . preposterous.'

'You think the English immune to gold fever?'

'We've got to stop it.'

'I wonder,' said Holmes contemplatively, and stopped.

'About the possibility of a gold rush?' I prodded.

'No, that is clearly possible. Rather, I was reflecting on the care with which they have set up the elaborate mechanism of rumours. The hound and the carriage may be both a diversion while they are salting the ground as well as an essential part of the plot itself. A deeper layer of deception, as it were, to encourage potential speculators to reason along the lines of, "A: The rich American gold baron has been buying up land on the quiet and trying to frighten people away; B: The gold baron is a clever and successful investor; therefore C: The value of the gold at Black Tor must be considerable, and we ought to buy in now, without hesitation." I should think it would also make for an interesting legal conundrum,' he commented, 'if one were to sell pieces of land without actually making fraudulent claims as to its content, relying only on rumours.'

'Surely it would have to be illegal,' I said, although I was not at all certain.

'Ultimately, yes, it would be declared fraud, but only after lengthy consideration. However, one would assume that his plans include a hasty departure from the scene the moment the cheques from the auction are deposited.'

'And the house,' I added suddenly. 'Ketteridge even has a buyer for the house.'

'That was a surprise,' said Holmes thoughtfully. 'I should have thought Scheiman's goal was as much the restoration of his side of the Baskerville family to its place in the Hall as it was mere money, but he is far too close to the centre of things to hope to claim ignorance.

'Still, we haven't time to dig into that now, not with the deadline of tomorrow night. I can only hope,' he said, scowling out the window at the dark sky, 'the weather is not so inclement as to force postponement of the army's manoeuvres.'

'They did wish for realistic battle conditions,' I said to encourage him, deliberately overlooking the fact that with any luck, we should be out in the downpour, with the additional spice of twenty charges of black powder threatening to go off around our feet.

With the large-scale maps of the area, six inches to the mile, we began our campaign. Pausing only for lunch and whenever Rosemary came to the drawing-room door with coffee, we laid our plans.

The assumption we were working on was that Ketteridge and Scheiman would be in Black Tor Copse when the firing of the artillery guns began at ten o'clock on Thursday night, using the flash and noise of the guns to provide cover for the salting operation they had prepared. Furthermore, because we were nearing the full moon, it was possible that they would also take advantage of the moonlight to cause another appearance of Lady Howard's coach. Holmes and I would be in Black Tor Copse, waiting for the two men, but to keep track of them properly we were going to need the assistance of a band of competent Irregulars. I began to make a list as Holmes talked.

'Two to watch Baskerville Hall itself, so we know how and when they set off. If Mrs Elliott can find a young man with a motorcycle, that would be ideal, but a bicycle would suffice. Not a pony – they are difficult to hide beneath a bush.' I wrote down *Bvilk Hall-2-cycle*. 'They will need to know precisely who we are looking for, and where the nearest telephone kiosk is, to put a call through to the inn in Sourton.'

By teatime we had the mechanism of our trap smoothly oiled and functioning – or at least the plan for it. When Ketteridge and Scheiman left Baskerville Hall on Thursday night, whether by road or over the moor, they would be seen. The witness would then go to the telephone kiosk, place a call to another member of our Devonshire Irregulars waiting at the Sourton inn, who would then bring us the message – or, if something interfered with the generous time allowance, there was even a convenient hill above Sourton Common, visible from where Holmes and I would be hidden, for a simple, brief signal from a lamp or torch, in case the imminent arrival of the two men made approaching the copse itself inadvisable.

It was a very pretty little mechanism, complex enough to be interesting but with safety nets in case of the unexpected. And, as even the best-designed machine is apt to fail, the absolutely essential part of the procedure – in this case, witnessing the crime and laying hands on the criminals – was dependent only on Holmes and myself. All the rest was a means of providing testimony in an airtight court case when the time came. For that reason I suggested that for the overall witness atop Gibbet Hill we draft Andrew Budd, for his calm self-assurance (other than when he was faced with a cow in his garden) that would ride well through the witness box.

Mrs Elliott would be called on to ensure that Budd and our other Irregulars were brought to Lew House the following morning so we might explain what we needed, but until then the best use of our time was to take a good dinner and make an early night of it.

Just before we sat down at the table, a pair of telegrams arrived. One of them was from Birmingham, and cleared up a minor facet of our mystery:

RANDOLPH PETHERING ALIAS RANDOLPH PARKER IS JOB APPLICANT NOT LECTURER AT YORK. CURRENTLY EMPLOYED COUNCIL SCHOOL BEDFORD

NOT TEACHERS COLLEGE BIRMINGHAM BUT POSSESSES LONG-TIME
MONOMANIA CONCERNING HIGH JOB POSSIBILITIES IF ONLY DRUID
BOOK PUBLISHED. CONSIDERED QUOTE HARMLESS LUNATIC END QUOTE.

The other telegram was from Holmes' brother in London:

PSEUDONYM CONCEALING LANDHOLDER GOLDSMITH ENTERPRISES
MAIN OFFICES LOS ANGELES MANY HOLDINGS VICINITY OKEHAMPTON
GOOD HUNTING.

MYCROFT

'Oscar Richfield is a false front hiding a Californian corporation
that is buying up that part of Dartmoor,' I translated.

'And behind the doors of the corporation, I have no doubt stands
Richard Ketteridge,' said Holmes. 'Is that goose I smell?'

Baring-Gould was present at dinner, looking less tired than
he had been. Again the two of them set off on a meandering
peregrination of topics and tales, but I was well used to it by now,
and rather enjoyed it.

We were nearly finished with the goose course when Holmes
abruptly broke off what he had been saying and froze, head up and
intently listening. His raised hand demanded silence, but after half a
minute during which I heard nothing, I asked tentatively, 'Holmes?'

In answer he whirled to his feet and tore the curtains back from
the window. Again we all waited; again he held us in silence.

Three minutes passed, four, before it came: the briefest flicker lit
up the heavy clouds.

No matter it was past the season; a thunderstorm was on its way
to Dartmoor.

Chapter Twenty-Five

All at once I uttered a cry of 'Help me!' and sank to my armpits. It
was instantaneous. I was in water, not on moss; and in sinking all I
could do was to catch at some particles of floating moss,
slime, half-rotten weed and water weed . . .
I felt as if I were striving against a gigantic octopus that was
endeavouring with boneless fleshy arms to drag me under water.
— FURTHER REMINISCENCES

You don't think—' I started to say. The entire day's long and
elaborate plans had all rested on the assumption that the two
Americans planned to use the following evening's artillery fire to cover
their noise, that they were unlikely to wait for a natural thunderstorm.
Probably, they would remain snug at home tonight. Still—

'We cannot take the chance,' he snapped. 'I will bring the dog
cart up; you fetch the waterproofs and put on your boots, find two
torches. And, Russell? My revolver is in the drawer. Bring it.'

Without another word he dashed out of the door, leaving me to
soothe the affronted Baring-Gould. I could only tell him that the
case was coming into its final stages, and we would explain it all very
soon; with any luck, tomorrow. As I left him, I heard him declare in
a querulous voice, 'He always was a headstrong boy.'

I diverted through the kitchen to ask Mrs Elliott to throw
together a packet of sandwiches, as it looked to be a long night,

and ran upstairs to pull every warm and watertight garment we possessed out of the drawers and wardrobes. Holmes' revolver, with its box of bullets, was in the drawer beside the bed. I loaded it and put it in my pocket.

Downstairs I found Rosemary in the kitchen wrapping a stack of sandwiches in greased paper. Mrs Elliott, by the sound of it, was in the dining room, the object of Baring-Gould's feeble anger, so I asked Rosemary, 'Is there a shotgun in the house?'

'In the pantry, mum,' she said promptly, pointing to a door on the other side of the room. It took me a moment to see it, lying flat on a high shelf. There were six cartridges as well, standing in a neat row, which I scooped up and dropped into another pocket. I checked to be sure the gun was not loaded, asked Rosemary for a length of oiled cloth, and gathered up everything, leaving the house through the kitchen door.

Down in the stables, I helped Holmes with the last of the buckles and walked the shaggy pony out into the drive. Holmes lit a lamp and hung it off the side – highly inadequate as a headlamp, but enough to warn other vehicles we might meet on the road. I flicked the reins as soon as he was beside me and we trotted up the road, pulled by the bewildered but willing pony.

Holmes began to pull on layers of the clothing I had brought. Within a mile the first drops of rain fell, and by the time we passed through Bridestowe the rain was heavy and the going slowed. The pony was indomitable, as might be expected of a Dartmoor native, and he had no problem distinguishing the way even when we left the high road for the lesser road and, later, the lesser road for the farm track.

At the farm, Holmes splashed across the yard to the well-lit farm-house while I began to loose the pony from its traces. Before I had finished, a pair of thick hands took over from me.

'I'll finish that, mum,' said the man. I left him to it, taking the shotgun from under the seat and tucking its oiled cloth securely around it, then handing Holmes his gun and the bag of provisions.

The rain pelted down, and we set off for the moor.

It was a hair-raising two miles, up the steep side of the moor wall and across the river to Black Tor Copse. I have never had very good night-time vision, even without the downpour that made my spectacles approximately as effective as my uncorrected vision. The flashes from the slowly approaching storm provided me with the only illumination we could afford, not knowing when and from where Ketteridge and Scheiman would come (the question of if was momentarily shelved; time alone would answer that).

When we had splashed and stumbled up the bed of the stream for what seemed hours, finally the stunted trees of the copse began to rise up around us. There was no path, just hillside, and I wondered how Holmes thought we were going to fight our way across to the other bank without giving the two men enough prior warning for them to flee halfway to Mary Tavy.

'It's clearer farther up, and there is a path of sorts,' Holmes said in answer to my question. 'We need to be here to see them but there should not be a problem with crossing over when the time comes.'

I had to take his word for it, because we seemed to be at the place he had in mind. A slab of rock had fallen from above and lodged against two large standing pillars, giving us a small shelter, open at the back but keeping off the rain. I loosened three layers of buttons and shirt-tail to wipe my lenses.

Holmes excavated similarly for his pipe and tobacco pouch and waited for the next lightning strike to light the match, with his back turned to the gorge and his shoulders hunched. He smoked with one hand cupped over the bowl, that no giveaway glow might be seen.

We settled in to wait.

The rain poured down and the gorge was sporadically illuminated by the stark blue lightning, and I sat and sometimes squatted and every so often stood upright, bent over double beneath the stone ceiling, in order to ease my legs. I tucked my hands under my arms and rubbed my gloves together briskly and wriggled my toes inside my damp boots, and we waited.

Time passed, the centre of the storm drew closer, and the rain fell, and still we waited. Holmes did not light a second match, sucking instead at his empty pipe, and the harsh light flashed with increasing regularity along the gushing river and the bank of rock across from us and the furiously blowing branches of the oak wood, followed at ever more brief intervals by the grumble and crack of thunder, and still the two men did not come.

'"Those dark hours in which the powers of evil are exalted",' I thought I heard Holmes murmur.

'An evil night,' I agreed.

'An evil place,' he said.

'Come now, Holmes,' I protested. 'Surely a place cannot be inherently evil.'

'Perhaps not. But I have noticed that the great bowl of Dartmoor seems to act as a kind of focusing device, exaggerating the impulses of the men who come within its sphere, for better or for worse. Gould might well have been a petty tyrant if left in his parish in Mersea, bullying his wife and driving his bishop to distraction. Here, however, the very air allowed him to expand, to become something larger than himself. Similarly Stapleton – I've wondered if he mightn't have continued as a minor crook had he not come here, where he filled out into a deft manipulator of local lore and a would-be murderer. And now these two.'

I did not answer. After a while I pulled the bag over and offered Holmes a sandwich. Rosemary had cut meat from the carcass of the goose for them, and laid them in the bread with a layer of rich herb stuffing. They were delicious, but still the storm beat at the stones around us, and still we waited, and still the men did not come.

The hands of my pocket watch crept around, and the powers of darkness moved over the face of the moor. Midnight came and midnight passed, and neither of us had moved or spoken for some time, when I began to feel a strange sensation in the air around me. Looking back, it was probably only the psychic eeriness of the night combined with the physical sensation brought by the electric charges of the storm, building and ebbing, but it began to feel almost as if there were another person in the rock shelter with us – or if not a person, then at least a Presence. It did not seem to me, as Holmes had suggested, an evil presence, nor even a terribly powerful one, but I thought it old, very old, and patient. It felt, I decided, as if the moor itself were holding watch with us. Holmes did not seem aware of anything other than discomfort and impatience, and I did not care to mention my fancies to him. I was, however, very grateful for his warm bulk beside me.

And then, just when I was on the edge of giving up on our expedition, the two men came, with a brief bobble of a hand torch from up-river. My paranormal phantasms burst with the sight, and the spirit of Dartmoor sank back into the stones. Holmes put his empty pipe into his pocket and leant forward. I unwrapped the shotgun far enough to slide two cartridges into it, then laid it back down by my feet.

Two lights appeared, tight beams that lit the feet of the men and, as they came closer, the tool bag each carried in his left hand. They crossed by in front of us, picking their way along the edge of the stream, and stopped perhaps forty feet away. The next burst of light from the sky revealed two heavily swathed figures, one taller than the other, both looking down at a stretch of rocky hillside. The shorter of the two dropped to one knee, and the light flickered out, and a great thump of thunder rumbled down the riverbed.

We were still waiting, but at least now we had something to watch other than the rocks. Ketteridge knelt down for two or three minutes at his bag, and although I could not see what he was doing there, he had to be preparing the equipment for wiring the charge. While he was there, the taller man, who had to be Scheiman, moved around the area, stopping every few feet to bend to his bag and do something on the ground. Once I saw the gleam of a shaft of metal.

'He's sliding the smaller pipes, which are perforated and loaded with gold-bearing sand and the charge of black powder, into the holes, and removing the larger ones from around them,' Holmes murmured.

It was quite clearly a thing Scheiman had done any number of times before. Despite the furious weather beating at his slick coat, his movements were quick and sure. He planted six of the charges, and Ketteridge was beginning to unfurl a spool of wire when Holmes touched my arm. 'We've seen enough. Come.'

I pulled my clothes back around me, tucked the gun under my right arm, and followed Holmes, patting my way along the wall with my freehand. The rain had let up a fraction, but it was still rather like walking into sea waves breaking against a rocky cliff, without the salt. However, I kept my feet and pushed my way through the copse, and in twenty yards or so we came upon the promised path, and could stumble along at a marginally faster rate. Each time lightning struck we stopped moving, and when our eyes had readjusted to the dark, we went on.

We crossed the river around the bend from where the men were working and continued up the cliff and onto the moor above. The ground here was as usual littered with stone, but it was not entirely stone, which made it not only easier to walk, but to walk quietly. Holmes took my arm and spoke into my ear.

'They will have a vehicle somewhere, or at least horses tethered in the adit. I will immobilise it or loose them, as the case may be, and join you at the height of the tor just above where they are working. I will be ten or fifteen minutes behind you.'

Giving me no chance to argue, he disappeared into the night. I turned, put my head down against the wind and rain, and followed the path of the river back to a place opposite where we had been waiting. The tor was easy enough to see, outlined against the clouds of the night, and I suddenly realised the storm was abating somewhat, that the faint illumination of the clouds had to come from the full moon behind them.

I could hear voices now, snatches of disconnected phrases that served to warn me that noise would no longer be obscured by the storm.

'—go live in the desert after this, someplace it never rains.' Scheiman's voice.

'—afford to—'

A long, indistinct muttering came from below while I picked my way around the tumble of loose stones on their centuries-long journey from the top of the tor to the bottom of the stream. I heard the phrase '—the Hall?' and then another fit of low speech and a laugh. When the wind stopped for an unexpected moment I heard Scheiman's voice, so clear it startled me.

'Where the hell's the last one of these?' he said. My foot came down wrongly on a stone, shifting sideways and making me fight to keep my balance. I nearly fell, I nearly dropped the shotgun down into the ravine, but in the end I did neither, and their voices continued uninterrupted. I took a deep breath and found myself a secure boulder to sit on. The whole hillside seemed even less stable than the other tors I had known; perhaps the stream was undermining it at a greater rate? Or could the series of blasts the hillside had been subjected to over the last three months have weakened the already brittle stone? I sat cautiously and kept my feet still.

During the next long quarter of an hour the two men discovered that either they had failed to construct twenty of the devices or else left one somewhere. After an instructive few minutes listening to the genial Ketteridge's viciously flaying tongue, I heard them decide that nineteen would have to do, although Scheiman would not sleep until he was absolutely positive that he had not left one lying about the shed in Baskerville Hall. They went back to their task; I went back to waiting.

I was not close enough to the edge of the cliff to see them both, although their lights flickered occasionally on the oak copse on the opposite bank and from time to time one or the other would walk briefly through one of the places I could see. Ketteridge now appeared with the spool of wire in one hand. He made a loop of it, laid the loop on the ground, and put two or three rocks on it to hold it in place. He then stood up and began walking upstream, letting the wire spool out behind him, and disappeared around the bend.

I wondered how far he would go, to set up the triggering device.

I wondered if Holmes would give the river wide berth on his return.

I wondered what I should do if Holmes did not reappear shortly.

I did not wonder for long, though; to my horror I heard shouts echoing from upstream, loud shouts of anger that could only mean one thing. I flung myself off my rock and ran silently around the rise of the tor, and there I saw Holmes, caught in the beam of Ketteridge's torch, his open hands outstretched.

'Stand there and don't move a muscle, Mr Holmes,' Ketteridge was saying. 'I'm a dead-eye shot.'

'Of that I have no doubt, Mr Ketteridge,' said Holmes. He stood and waited while the narrow beam came closer, and soon Ketteridge was in front of him, blinding Holmes with his torch.

'Hands on top of your head, Holmes,' he ordered, and did a thorough search of Holmes' pockets, ending up with Holmes' gun, folding knife, and torch. By this time another light was shining from the riverbed and Scheiman's panic-laden voice could be heard shouting enquiries.

'It's nothing, David,' Ketteridge shouted back over his shoulder. 'Just an intruder. You'd better finish laying those charges before this storm is completely gone. I'll blow it as soon as you're ready.' The other torch beam wavered and then disappeared, and I strained to hear what Ketteridge was saying to Holmes.

'Well, well, Mr Holmes. I was afraid of this.'

'That, I presume, is why you attempted to distract me with Pethering.'

'I'm sorry it didn't do the trick. I liked you, Mr Holmes, and I'd have been just as happy to do my business here and be away without meeting you again. Speaking of which, where is your wife?'

I started, and began to creep backwards towards the safety of my tor.

'Asleep in Lew House I should think,' Holmes told him.

'No assistants at all, then?'

'I fear not.'

Ketteridge kept the torch on Holmes' face for half a minute, then without warning dropped it down for a fast search of the hillside. I leapt back as soon as I saw it coming, and backed rapidly towards the rocks from which I had come. I heard Ketteridge say something to Holmes, and then the two of them started towards me.

I thought Ketteridge would play his torch over the side of the clitter that faced the river and be satisfied with that, so I circled around to the far side of the tor. It appeared, however, that he was prepared to be a good deal more thorough; his light was coming around to my right, and unless I fled away over Sourton Common, where a chance lightning strike would show me up like a spotlight, I had to keep the central mound of the tor between us. I continued circling, feeling the shaky ground under my feet and balancing with the damned gun in my hand and no light on my way. He was gaining on me quickly, the very edge of his beam lighting the top of a pile of rocks to my right before skipping away, but in moments he would have me. I dived for the pile, thinking to freeze into a rock-like lump beneath my coat, but to my astonishment I discovered that the solid mound of rock was split down the middle. I shoved my way into the concealing crack, and precipitated head first into a low, smooth, and remarkably dry depression among the stones. I was thoroughly hidden, within the very heart of the tor.

I squirmed around to look out of the entrance, and watched the light approach. It lit the entrance with a shocking burst of brightness, but the flare of reflection as the beam passed over my glasses must have appeared like any other reflection from off the watery slope. I shrank back and watched them pass, and after they were well past I slowly emerged, as wary as any rabbit venturing from its bury.

They started down the slope, Ketteridge far enough behind Holmes to keep his prisoner at a distance, but too close for me to chance the scattered shot from my own gun, even if, as I found when I came to the edge of the cliff, they had not been on a direct line of fire. I sat down on my heels to see what developed.

Scheiman stood watching them come down the steep hillside, gun in one hand and torch in the other. His tool bag lay empty on the ground, the twenty heavier two-inch pipes in an untidy pile next to it, the nineteen charges buried in their place. Ketteridge put his pistol in his pocket and walked over to his own bag, from which he took a ball of twine. Approaching Holmes, he said, 'My secretary is not quite as good a shot as I am, Mr Holmes, but he is certainly good enough for this distance. Don't try to move.'

He bent and tied Holmes' hands together behind his back, then hobbled his feet loosely, but securely. He tied it off, cut the end with his pocket knife, and stood away from Holmes.

'Be seated, Mr Holmes. We won't be very long. David, watch him closely.'

Holmes looked around and chose a mossy rock, shuffled over to it, and took his seat. Scheiman watched him intently, and moved over near him.

'Don't stand too close to him, David,' Ketteridge warned, and then went back to finishing the connexion of each of the nineteen charges to the master switch at the end of the spool of wire. Lightning flared briefly overhead, but the grumble that followed was distant, almost perfunctory. Holmes had not looked up at me once. I could not tell if he knew I was there, although he would be certain I was not too far away. There was no other place for me to be. There was also no means for me to reach Holmes, no way I could dispatch the two men without putting Holmes into mortal danger, either from their guns or from the widespread of shot from my own. I should have to wait, and hope he could provide me with an opening. Meanwhile, I knew, he would encourage Ketteridge to talk.

Holmes eased his shoulders and spoke in a clear voice to Ketteridge where he knelt over the pieces of wire. 'Am I right in assuming that you and Mr Scheiman here first met on the boat from New York? This plan of yours seems to have been assembled somewhat, shall we say, piecemeal?'

Ketteridge's sure hands did not react. 'We did, yes. It was a very monotonous journey, and when David came onboard in New York, what else was there to do but talk?' He reached down into a pocket and drew out a small pair of wire cutters, and snipped the join before wrapping it methodically. 'I had no plans for England. It didn't seem the sort of place for my particular kind of scheme, so I was just going to relax, see the countryside, and spend some of the money I'd made . . . elsewhere.' Satisfied with his handiwork, he dug into his bag for a bit of broken tile, propped it over the wires to keep the rain off, and then shifted over to the next pipe. 'We talked around things, if you know what I mean. It was funny, a meeting of minds, you might say. Nobody else in the world would've known what we were really talking about, but David and I knew.' He paused to look over his shoulder. 'I suppose you might've known, if you'd been listening in. No, we recognised each other like two Masons with a handshake, and sort of told each other about our scams, without saying much direct. Anyway, when the boat docked we said good-bye without thinking any more about it. I mean to say, he'd amused me with his talk about the school he'd run in upstate New York that went bust – oh, don't worry, David,' he said at his secretary's protest, 'Mr Holmes knows about it, I'm sure. And David knew something about my little tricks in the goldfields, buying up dud land and selling it off as claims to men hundreds of miles away. Neither of us told the other anything that might be called incriminating, but we were sort of showing off our cleverness, I suppose; to someone who'd appreciate it.

'So, there I was in London having the time of my life when who should appear at my hotel but David, looking all excited and with a great plan for the two of us.

'Turns out David is a Baskerville.' He swivelled again to look at Holmes, and I could see his teeth gleam as he turned back again. 'Thought you might know that one, too. One of the reasons he came over here was to take a look at the family house that his father, who wasn't exactly legitimate, you might say, was cheated out of. So, when David gets to Plymouth, what does he hear but that the big old place is in the hands of one solitary little girl, who wants to find herself a tenant and move into town.

'Well, being a tenant isn't exactly what David has in mind, although he doesn't really have enough of the ready stuff to buy the Hall outright. He sits and thinks it over for a couple of days, and then comes to look me up with a proposition: He and I run a swindle, whatever kind of swindle I want, we share the results, and he can then afford to move in and become the lord of the manor.'

'Hardly a peerage,' Holmes said drily.

Ketteridge gave a dismissive wave with the wire clippers. 'Well, I had to tell him that city jobs aren't exactly my strong point. Too many foreign ideas, and way too many, what do you call them, bobbies? But I invite him to dinner and he tells me about this place, and I begin to get a few ideas. A remote place like this, a man can have some room to set things up. So, we talk it over and we come to an agreement from the land-sale side of things, and he takes care of scaring people away from the piece of ground we're developing as well as giving me a hand with toting and hauling.'

'Which he did by adapting some vehicle or other to resemble Lady Howard's coach, and then bringing in some large, dark dog to add to the charade. Actually,' Holmes said, 'I was rather wondering why you didn't make more extensive use of the dog.'

Ketteridge laughed and shook his head over the wires. 'Have you ever worked with a dog, Mr Holmes? Maybe the one we managed to get hold of was just particularly badly trained, but it was a real nightmare. Oh, it looked the part all right, and David even fixed a cute little contraption on its head to give it a "glowing eye" – powered by a battery – but the whole point of having the dog was making it ghostly, and a hundred and twenty pounds of dog is anything but. Lock it in the stables and it howls and scratches the door down; turn it loose and it chases sheep and gets itself shot at; you have to feed it meat and then clean up after it so your ghostly dog isn't leaving great stinking piles across the countryside; and you never know, when you're off on a Lady Howard run, if the dog isn't going to take off. We did two trips out with the "coach" back in July, and two in August, and halfway through the second one the damned animal lit off at high speed for a nearby farm where I'd guess there was a bitch on heat. We were unbelievably lucky there, because the family was away, all except one deaf old granny, but my nerves couldn't take it, and I had David get rid of the animal. I have to hand it to David's father, to go about his own version of the scheme with just a big dog. Damned if I know how he did it.'

'And for this he planned to get the Hall and you would get – what?'

'Oh, I'd have the lion's share of the actual money – which only seemed fair since I was doing most, of the expert work – and as we planned it, I'd then sell him Baskerville Hall – all fixed up and pretty as we made it – just as the swindle started, for what would be on paper a goodly sum but in actual fact would be less than a dollar. I'd take the blame and the profits and skip the country, he'd be left with egg on his face, having not only been so stupid as to choose such a crook for a boss but to have fallen for his boss's land scheme as well. But then again he'd have all the linen in Baskerville Hall to wipe it off with. And,' he paused again, this time sitting back on his heels to grin across at his assistant, 'this clever devil even went and got himself engaged to that pasty-laced Baskerville woman. He was looking to have it all.'

'Until Pethering.'

Ketteridge uttered a monosyllabic curse, and went back to his work. 'Yeah, until that blasted shrimp stumbled into our set-up. Jesus, what a piece of luck. I mean, the old guy last month, that was one thing, but then he goes and cracks the nosey little mutt of a professor on the head.'

'What else could I have done?' Scheiman shouted. 'We couldn't let him go, and he sure wouldn't be paid off.'

'You're absolutely right, David,' Ketteridge said freely. It sounded like a familiar argument, one in which he was not terribly interested any longer. 'But it did put paid to you taking over the Hall. Having the neighbours whispering among themselves that you had more to do with that damn American's swindle than it looks like is one thing, but actual murder, now, that's something I find neighbours are slow to overlook. No, David, like I've told you, you're just going to have to take your share of the money and abandon the Hall to the mice. Find a nice lady in some warm climate and set up a school there.'

He stood up and dusted off his hands, and shone the torch over his work to check it: nineteen bits of broken tile, nineteen leads running to the main wire, all of them neat and dry and ready to go. And what was he planning to do with Holmes?

'You tidy up those pipes, David, and make sure I haven't left anything behind. I'll take Mr Holmes and meet you at the end of the wire. Up you go, Mr Holmes,' he said, taking out his gun. 'Just follow the wire.' He aimed the torch at Holmes' feet, and followed him away from the tin works.

With Holmes held to a hobbling pace, they would be some minutes reaching the plunger that would set off the charges. I abandoned my post above the river and circled the bend to get there before them, and by the fitful light from the moon and the occasional pale flare of the far-away lightning, I scrambled down to the river, dislodging stones and risking life and limbs in my haste.

The plunging device stood ready, waiting only for its connection to the wire and the lowering of its contact points. I hesitated only a moment before deciding that it did not actually matter if another tiny quantity of gold flakes found their way into the gozen of old tin mine, and it would make for an almighty distraction. I found my penknife and with my torch shaded by a handkerchief and held between my knees on the ground, I hastily stripped the ends of the wire, looped them around the points, and screwed down the contacts as quickly as I could. I then picked it up and, tugging to make sure the wire was not caught on anything, stumbled rapidly downriver to the obscuring bend in the cliff face. I could hear nothing above the noise of running water, but in less than a minute I saw the glow of the moving torch, and I got ready to act. I did not know where Scheiman was, although I assumed he would not be far behind his boss, but I could think of no better plan. I did, I admit, say a fervent prayer for protection in an act of madness.

The torch approached, and I could hear a voice: Holmes talking loudly, which I hoped meant he expected me to be waiting in the only logical place, where indeed I was. I heard the sound of scuffing feet, and Ketteridge speaking sharply, and then they were on top of me.

I hit the plunger and raised the shotgun more or less simultaneously, just as Holmes threw himself backwards against Ketteridge. The sound of the blast and the unexpected attack conspired against the accuracy of Ketteridge's gun, so that although his finger tightened spasmodically against the trigger, the shot went wide and the torch flew out of his hand an instant later, its beam whirling crazily into the air. Holmes tumbled off into the darkness near the river, and I let off one barrel of the shotgun for effect.

Disarmed and barraged, Ketteridge did not hesitate, but whirled and sprinted back in the direction from which he had come, towards the slowly erupting hillside. He vanished into the cloud of dust, but I was not about to follow until I had Holmes safely up and out of the water.

My lawfully wedded husband had come to rest just above the waterline, wedged painfully among the rocks and swearing mightily. I propped the gun against a boulder and fished out my pocket knife, cutting the bonds of his hands first and then his legs.

'Thank you, Russell,' he said when he was upright and had his breath back. 'Precisely where I had anticipated, with even more effect than I had hoped for. Where is Ketteridge?'

'Off up the hill, heading for the vehicle. Or was it horses?' I held out a hand and helped him extricate himself from the slick rocks.

'A peculiar contraption, a motor car with very wide, highly inflated tyres and a great deal of padding over the engine – practically silent on the moor and leaving no tracks. However, he will not go anywhere in it tonight. And Scheiman?'

'May have gone with him.'

'He was behind us.'

'Oh God. I hope I haven't killed him.' I looked in apprehension back at the cloud of dust, swirling mightily in the still shaft of light from the miraculously unbroken torch that Ketteridge had dropped. It was only then that I realised the rain had stopped. 'I did not imagine that the blast would be so big.'

'It should not have been. Perhaps the cliff was unstable. I shall have to leave you to deal with Scheiman. Can you do that?'

'Holmes, you can't go after Ketteridge without a weapon. At least wait until we've taken Scheiman's gun away from him.'

'Russell, I will not permit a second villain to escape me on this moor,' he said grimly. 'Follow when you can.' He caught up the torch from the ground and flung himself up the hill after Ketteridge.

I replaced the spent shell, and with great circumspection I went downstream to the site of the blast, expecting at any moment to be pounded upon by the murderous secretary. When I found him, though, he was quite incapable of pouncing, being unconscious and half buried under tons of rock from the collapsed hillside. I checked his pockets, removing the sturdy clasp knife I found in one of them, and then set about digging him out.

One ankle was broken, and the bone above it as well, and I knew he would be black from the waist down by the next day. If he lived that long. I dragged him away, tied his hands behind his back, then took off my waterproof and my woollen overcoat and tucked them securely around him. I would prefer that if this escapade cost Scheiman his life, it be at the hands of a judge, not mine.

I did not find his gun, which must either have fallen from his pocket or been flung from his grasp, but I knew that if I could not see it, he was not likely to find it either. I turned to follow Holmes and Ketteridge up onto the moor.

From high on the remains of my protective tor it was an easy thing to find the men, two beams of light moving across the darkling plain, perhaps half a mile apart and going west, it was difficult to tell how far off the closer of the torches was, but I thought not less than two miles. I started down the hill in their wake.

Following the river upstream, I reached a place where it was little more than a stream, and there I found Ketteridge's vehicle, the means Scheiman had devised to frighten the moor dwellers: Lady Howard's coach. I took a moment to look at it and found to my surprise that underneath the big square superstructure with the remains of phosphorescent paint daubed on the corners – the 'glowing bones' of the Lady's hapless husbands – lay the same powerful touring car that had carried us to and from Baskerville Hall, with the standard Dunlop tyres replaced by large, highly inflated tubes that would leave no tracks and also serve to underscore the ghostly silence of the thing. They had probably been inspired by the secret amphibious tank, I realised – Mycroft would be incensed – and, the horse that had appeared to be pulling it must have been ridden by one of the men, with loose harnesses jangling for effect. Abruptly, I remembered that I had no time to moon over the device; I tore my attention from it and headed back out onto the moor.

My distance from the two men meant I had continually to climb the heights to keep track of their progress, so that run as I might, I could not gain on them. Each time I climbed, there were still the two of them, although the distance between them slowly decreased, as Ketteridge had to choose his path while Holmes merely followed. In fact, I began to wonder if Holmes was not deliberately keeping his distance. I redoubled my efforts.

The wind had calmed considerably, but when I thought I heard a faint cracking noise from the vast space before me, I could not be certain. I shone my light desperately all around, found a rise, followed it, stood on my toes on a boulder, and saw a light, one single light. It was not moving.

I ran. Oblivious of streams and stones and the hellish waterlogged dips and gouges of an old peat works, I ran, up a rise and down the other side and splashed three steps into the bog that stretched out there before my interior alarm sounded. I backed out laboriously, the muck holding fast at my boots and calves and only letting go with a slow sucking noise. I staggered when my heels hit solid ground and I sat down hard, then got to my feet and searched the basin. Rushes, Holmes had said, look for footing among the rushes, and indeed, along the edges of the bog stood tussocks of thick grass in a rough semicircle. Following those proved heavy going, but I did not sink in past my lowest bootlaces, and I made the other side of the mire with no further harm. Up that hill I went, and there below me, perhaps a quarter of a mile away, lay the beam of a single torch, lying, by the looks of it, on the ground, motionless.

I nervously checked to be sure the shotgun was loaded and went forward stealthily until I could make out the dark figure sitting on the ground beside the light. My heart gave one great thud of relief, like a shout, and subsided.

'Holmes?' I said. 'I thought I heard a shot.'

He turned at my voice, and then looked back at the terrain before him. 'You did,' he said. 'He would not allow me to approach.'

'Approach?' I asked, and walked up to stand by his side. His boots were mere clots of black, viscous mud, as were his trouser legs past his knees.

I played my torch beyond him to see what he was staring at, and saw there at our feet a stretch of smooth, finely textured turf, looking as if someone had spread a large carpet of some pale green stuff across the floor of the moor. On the side nearest us the carpet appeared scuffed, and the torchlight picked out some gleaming black substance splashed across the centre of it that I realised must be mud. The rest of the surface was pristine. A quaking bog, Holmes had called it. A feather-bed, was Baring-Gould's jocular name: a bed beneath which Ketteridge now slept.

Holmes inclined his head at it. 'The moor took him,' he said, and scrubbed tiredly at his face with both hands. 'He got halfway across before he broke through. I tried to pull him out, but he held the gun on me until the last minute, until only his hand and his eyes were above the surface. He shot at me when I tried to . . . I did attempt to save him.'

I bent down to pick up his torch, and when I had put it in his hand I allowed my fingers to rest briefly on the back of his neck. 'You said it yourself, Holmes. The moor took him. Come, let us go home.'

CHAPTER TWENTY-SIX

In my advanced old age I really entertain more delight in the
beauties of Nature and of Art than I did in my youth. Appreciation
of what is good and true and comely grows with years, and this
growth, I feel sure, is no more to be quenched by death than is
the life of the caddis-worm when it breaks forth as the may fly.
I do not look back upon the past and say, 'All is dead!'
What I repeat in my heart, as I watch the buds unfold, and
the cuckoo-flowers quivering in the meadow, and I
inhale the scent of the pines in the forest, and
hear the spiral song of the lark is 'All is Promise.'
— FURTHER REMINISCENCES

WE DID GO HOME, to our own home on the Sussex Downs,
soon after that. First, however, we had one final task to
perform on the moor.

Three days after the police had dragged Richard Ketteridge's
body from the grip of the quaking bog, we borrowed the dead
man's touring car, stripped of its costume and restored to its
Dunlops, and drove it up to the door of Lew House. While the
bronze goose-herd looked on, we piled the passenger seat high
with pillows, loaded the boot with a picnic of cold roast goose
with sage and onion stuffing, mutton sandwiches, and honey wine,
and waited while the squire of Lew Trenchard took his place on

313

the cushions. We tucked the old man in with travelling rugs and placed a hot brick beneath his shoes, and with Holmes at his side and myself driving, we took the Reverend Sabine Baring-Gould up onto the moor for one last earthly look at that region he loved best in all the world.

EDITOR'S POSTSCRIPT

> As I write these words the last home is being decorated with
> heather and moss to receive the body of one whom I shall bury
> tomorrow, the last of my old parishioners, one of God's saints,
> who has lived a white and fragrant life, loving and serving
> God, bringing up a family in the same holy line of life, and
> closing her eyes in peace to pass into the Land of Promise,
> which here we cannot see, but in which we can believe,
> and to which we hope to attain.
>
> — FURTHER REMINISCENCES

CONSIDERING THE CIRCUMSTANCES, IT is a little surprising that more of the manuscripts written by Mary Russell do not involve well-known public names. It may be, of course, that famous people have tediously familiar problems, and by this point in his career, Sherlock Holmes could not be bothered with any cases but those that most appealed to him. A connoisseur often finds him- or herself drawn away from the commonplace, excellent as it may be, and into the more unexpected or eccentric reaches of the area of expertise; that description surely applies here.

Insofar as I can determine, the bones of Ms Russell's narrative would stand: The Reverend Sabine Baring-Gould was most emphatically a real person, a true and unexpected British eccentric: an academic romancer, a gullible sceptic, a man both cold and passionate. With more sides to his personality than the Kohinoor has facets, he went his brilliant and self-centred way, ruling his family and his Devonshire manor with an air of distracted authority, setting off whenever the fancy struck him out onto Dartmoor, up to London, or over to the Continent. His wife, Grace, must have been a saint of God – although to Baring-Gould's credit it would appear that he was aware of it.

The mind-boggling scope of his ninety prolific years (150 books, fifty of them fiction) exists for the most part in the dustier reaches of library storage vaults throughout the world, from *Werewolves and their Natural History* to the relatively well-known *Songs of the West.* For those interested in the life of this scion of a pair of illustrious stems, I would recommend, after his two volumes of memoirs (*Early Reminiscences* and *Further Reminiscences*, each of which covers thirty years of his life), either of two biographies: William Purcell's *Onward Christian Soldier*, or *Sabine Baring-Gould*, by Bickford Dickinson (who was Baring-Gould's grandson and himself rector of Lew Trenchard Church from 1961 to1967). Further, there is a Sabine Baring-Gould Appreciation Society (c/o the Hon. Sec. Dr Roger Bristow, Davidsland, Brendon Hill, Copplestone, Devon EX17 5NX, England) where, for the princely sum of six pounds sterling per annum, one will receive three newsletters and the fellowship of a number of Right-Thinking people. And if the reader wishes to add a dimension to his or her appreciation of Baring-Gould by becoming an auditor, an audiotape comprising a sparkling selection of the Devonshire folk songs collected by Baring-Gould, along with excerpts from his writings and memoirs, may be found through The Wren Trust, 1 St James Street, Okehampton, Devon, EX20 IDW, England.

As an additional curious note, when another of Sabine Baring-Gould's grandsons, the equally brilliant and multifaceted William Stuart Baring-Gould, came to write his famous biography of Mr

Sherlock Holmes (which he called *Sherlock Holmes of Baker Street: A Life of the World's First Consulting Detective*), he seems to have turned to his grandfather's *Early Reminiscences* as a source of raw material from which he might construct Holmes' early childhood (about which, admittedly, nothing whatsoever is actually known). W. S. Baring-Gould changed only the dates; the rest, from the father's injury that discharged him from the Indian Army and his subsequent passion for Continental travel that led to family life in a carriage, the boy's early archaeological passion and his sporadic education, and even the names of the ships on which the families Baring-Gould and Holmes sailed from England, bear 'a truly remarkable similarity'.

The reverend Sabine Baring-Gould died on January 2, 1924, twenty-six days short of his ninetieth birthday, bare weeks after the events described in this book. It pleases me to think that when he left his body, which lies beside Grace's at the foot of Lew Trenchard Church, he did so secure in the knowledge that his beloved moor was safe from the worst torments of the twentieth century. I like to think that he died happy. Most of all, I want to believe that, all rumour to the contrary notwithstanding, he breathed the air of his moor one last time before he died.

– Laurie R. King
Freedom, California
St Swithin's Day 1997

I'm going, I reckon, full mellow
To lay in the churchyard my head;
So say, God be with you, old fellow,
the last of the singers is dead.

WITH THANKS TO

Dr Merriol Baring-Gould Almond and the Reverend David Shacklock, for correcting as many of my missteps as I would allow.

The Reverend Geoffrey Ball, rector of Lew Trenchard Church
Mr Bill Crum, a mine of information.

Ms Kate De Groot, for bringing Brother Adam to my attention

Mr Dave German and the other helpful shepherds of Princetown's High Moorland Visitor Information Centre.

Mr James and Ms Sue Murray, whose conversion of Lew House into Lewtrenchard Manor Hotel has been done with the same grace and warmth they show their visitors (and to Holly and Duma, who together do a very effective nocturnal imitation of the Hound).

Ms Jo Pitesky, for the lost Russellism.

Mr David Scheiman (the real one), one of the good people.

Ms Mary Schnitzer, and to all of the readers.

They are not to be held responsible for any factual errors that may, either through misunderstanding or with malice afterthought, have stubbornly persisted into the final work. There are times, after all, when a writer must twist the truth in order to tell it.

NEXT IN THE MARY RUSSELL & SHERLOCK HOLMES SERIES . . .

O JERUSALEM

1918. Forced to flee England, Sherlock Holmes and his young apprentice Mary Russell enter British-occupied Palestine under the auspices of Holmes' enigmatic brother, Mycroft. Their arrival coincides with a rash of unsolved murders that has baffled the authorities, yet no one is too pleased at Holmes' insistence on reconstructing the most recent homicide in the desert where it occurred.

What they unexpectedly uncover will lead Russell and Holmes through an exotic gauntlet of labyrinthine bazaars, verminous hovels, cliff-hung monasteries – and into mortal danger. In the jewel-like city of Jerusalem, they will at last meet their adversary, whose lust for power could ignite a tinderbox of hostilities just waiting for a spark . . .